Th

Teanna
on the h
She extended her right arm, her fingers spread
wide. Incredibly, the boulder began to rise into the air . . . five feet . . . eight feet . . . twenty
feet. For a moment the clouds parted and a pair
of angry red eyes stared at Mathew from the
darkness. He took a step back in shock. Teanna
turned back toward the lake with the boulder
still suspended in the air. She took a deep
breath and snapped her hand closed into a fist.

The power generated by her ring surged
around Mathew. The boulder shot forward and
struck the center of the storm.

An answering bellow of rage rang off the
cavern walls . . . and a tail the thickness of a
tree trunk and covered in iridescent amber and
black scales suddenly lashed out of the
storm . . .

Also by
Mitchell Graham

T̲HE̲ F̲IFTH̲ R̲ING̲

THE
EMERALD CAVERN

Book Two of The Fifth Ring

MITCHELL GRAHAM

An Imprint of HarperCollinsPublishers

EOS
An Imprint of HarperCollins*Publishers*
10 East 53rd Street
New York, New York 10022-5299

Copyright © 2004 by Mitchell Graham
Cartography by Elizabeth M. Glover
ISBN: 0-06-050675-X
www.eosbooks.com

First Eos paperback printing: January 2004

Eos Trademark Reg. U.S. Pat. Off. and in Other Countries, Marca Registrada, Hecho en U.S.A.
HarperCollins® is a trademark of HarperCollins Publishers Inc.

Printed in the U.S.A.

10 9 8 7 6 5 4 3 2 1

To my mother, Frieda, for all her
love and support

ACKNOWLEDGMENTS

My heartfelt thanks and love to Jane Schlachter and Douglas Gross for their help in reviewing the manuscript, and suffering through months of having ideas bounced off them without complaint.

THE
EMERALD
CAVERN

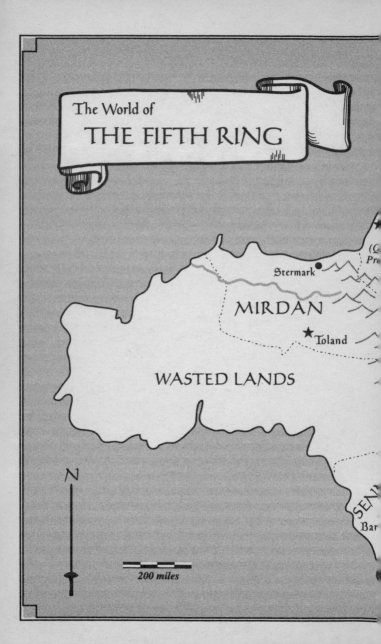

THE
EMERALD
CAVERN

PROLOGUE

Anderon, Elgaria 20 Alcandur 3173
From the diary of King Delain

I MET MATHEW LEWIN ONLY TWO TIMES. THE FIRST WAS
in the town of Tremont shortly before he destroyed the
Cincar and Nyngary fleets. The other was at the battle of
Ardon Field where he fought Karas Duren for the last
time. He is a strange young man, awkward, self-
conscious, and prone to bouts of seasickness, or so I was
told, yet capable of raising himself up when the situation
demanded it. Few could deny that it was by his hand that
our country was saved. The proof of what he and his ring
did was so much before our eyes that it would have been
obvious to a blind man. There would be no Elgaria today
were it not for him.

With my father dead, I have been on the throne now for
less than a year. In this time I have learned that rebuilding
a country is no small task, nor is it an easy thing to ac-
quire the nobles's support or the people's confidence. The
two are often at odds.

At my coronation I told all who were listening that Elgaria stood on the dawn of a new age. If we are to grow as
a people then we must not repeat the mistakes of the past.
We must become a nation of laws, just and fair to all. Law
is the very spine of our society. I believe this with all of
my heart. Simple words . . . but words which have come
back to haunt me.

Three months after we buried our dead at Ardon Field,
the king's constable, Jeram Quinn . . . my constable,

came to me, seeking a warrant for Mathew Lewin's arrest on the charge of murder.

Murder.

I could not believe my ears when he told me that young Lewin had strangled a man to death with his bare hands at a fencing tournament in his hometown nearly a year before. The man's name was Berke Ramsey, and the crime, if it was such, occurred after Ramsey killed Lewin's father.

It is unfortunate that Quinn made his request for the warrant in open audience with fifty barons, earls, and other nobles present. This left me with few options. Refuse to issue the warrant, and my high words about the law would be only that—words. Issue it, and destroy the one person who saved our country from certain doom. In the end it was the law that decided me, and that decision has left me sick to my heart.

The world is changing.

The letter I received from Gawl of Sennia says that the boy and priest are with him. He attempts to buy me additional time to consolidate my position so that I can issue a pardon without repercussions. He knows, as I do, that Mathew Lewin is the fulcrum on which the future of our world may rest. With Duren dead, Gawl would extend an olive branch to the nations of the East by dropping trade restrictions and opening his borders. He urges me to do the same. Would that it were so easy. Circles lie within circles, and one level is built upon another.

My heart tells me that we must move forward and embrace a new age or perish. To imprison Mathew Lewin could spell disaster not only for our country but for the whole of western civilization. This quiet dark-haired youth is the counterbalance that holds Teanna d'Elso in check. Though, I concede, it may be unfair of me to think this; to date, she has shown none of her mother's peculiarities. Both Mathew and the Nyngary princess each hold one of the five ancient rings of rose gold found by her uncle and long believed to have perished from the world. Two have been destroyed, one lies somewhere in Alor Satar, useless—until a perfect match can be found, which seems unlikely. No one knows if the lost three of the eight still exist.

Thought into matter.

The concept itself is so incredible that had I not been there and seen for myself, I would have refused to believe what had happened. Even now it is still hard, yet this is what the Ancients created.

Teanna is a twenty-year-old enigma whom I scarcely know. She is the niece of Karas Duren and the daughter of Marsa d'Elso, Duren's sister, both of whom were killed by Mathew Lewin. My first thought was that she would look to avenge those deaths. Nevertheless, it was *she* who halted Alor Satar's attack when they were on the verge of victory.

I am no closer now to learning her reasons than I was a year ago. The girl favors her mother physically, a tall, stately young woman of surpassing beauty and circumspect demeanor. Perhaps I was wrong. Perhaps this apple did not fall so close to the tree as we all believed.

Gawl's conference is but two weeks away and the decision is nearly upon me. If I travel to Sennia, I will be forced to deal with Jeram Quinn and bring the matter of Mathew's arrest to a head. If I stay here, the lack of my presence will be viewed as an indication that I do not support Gawl.

We are all balanced on the head of a pin. Set aside our mistrust of an old enemy, or embrace them now as friends and welcome a new age?

Circles within circles.

1

Sennia, Tenley Palace

"MURDER? FOR GOD'S SAKE, QUINN, THE BOY DIDN'T murder anybody."

"I didn't say *murder*, your majesty. I said a *homicide* was committed."

"Homicide? Murder? What's the difference?" the king asked. "Either way the other fellow's just as dead."

Jeram Quinn took a deep breath, which Mathew just barely heard through the open windows as he sat in the library on the next floor.

"There *is* a distinction," the constable replied. "Mathew is not charged with killing another by malice. The penalty for that under Elgarian law is death, just as it is under Sennian law, if I'm not mistaken."

"But the person he killed murdered his father. At least that's what they told me."

"That is true, your highness. I was there."

"Then, the boy was only defending himself," Gawl insisted.

Mathew put down the book he was reading, leaned back, and closed his eyes. It was not the first time in the last three weeks that the king and Jeram Quinn had engaged in this debate. If the past was any indicator, the volume of their voices would continue to increase over the next few minutes with neither yielding ground.

He had known in his heart the episode with Berke Ramsey was not finished, and he chided himself for being naive. Quinn was correct, he *had* killed Ramsey. Mathew neither regretted what had happened nor, in retrospect, would he have altered his conduct, even with the benefit of hindsight. If not for the intervention of Gawl Alon d'Atherny, who was the king of Sennia as well as his friend, he, Collin, Lara, and Father Thomas would be on their way to prison in Elgaria to await trial—his own for murder, or *homicide* as the constable put it; theirs for obstructing the king's justice.

On the day that Quinn had arrived at the Abbey of Barcora, Mathew met with him and they spoke together privately. The conversation was still vivid in his mind.

Neither the last six months nor the recent war with Alor Satar had changed Jeram Quinn very much, Mathew thought as they sat in the room together. The constable was still slender and dressed in dark blue, just as he was the day he rode out of Devondale with Father Thomas. *Perhaps the hair has a touch more silver in it.*

"You understand why I'm here?" asked Quinn.

"Yes, sir."

Quinn looked him up and down and shook his head slightly. "You've grown a bit since we last spoke, I suspect. You're wider throughout the shoulders."

Mathew remained silent.

"If the choice was mine alone, I would just as soon have avoided this trip," Quinn went on. "However, I took an oath. The law is not something that can be bent and molded to fit different situations . . . as much as I might wish otherwise."

"Your father and I served together in the army many years ago. Given the circumstances, I might have done exactly what you did. But that's not for me to decide now. I know you understand this. Unfortunately, the situation has now grown very much more complicated."

Mathew anticipated what was coming and interrupted Quinn before he could go on.

"I'm willing to return to Elgaria with you," he said, "on the condition that whatever charges I am to face involve me and *me* alone."

Quinn raised an eyebrow and leaned back in his chair.

"Mathew, I told you in Devondale and again only a moment ago, the situation changed considerably when Father Thomas and your friends chose to interfere. Obstructing the king's justice, not to mention pointing a loaded crossbow at one of his constables, is a crime in and of itself. To say nothing of turning my horses loose," the constable added under his breath.

Mathew nearly smiled at that. He was aware of what Lara had done to Jeram Quinn's horses before they left Devondale, but he kept his face neutral. The circumstances really left very little to smile about. "They were only trying to protect me."

"That much was obvious. However, this is now a matter for the prosecutor to deal with."

"But it's your decision about which charges are brought forward and which aren't."

"Technically that is true; however, the law leaves me little choice in the matter."

"Little choice . . . or no choice?" Mathew asked quietly.

Quinn's gray eyes narrowed, and there was a pause before he responded to the question.

"*Little* choice," he answered finally. "Regretfully, you are not in a position to bargain with me on the subject. There is nothing for you to do other than to return to Elgaria and stand trial."

Mathew stared at Quinn for a moment before he replied, "I can do quite a bit more than that."

There was a silence.

"Are you threatening me, *boy*?"

"No . . . , constable."

Much of Quinn's pleasant demeanor dropped away and he leaned forward in his seat.

"I was not at Ardon Field, though I've heard enough stories about you and your ring from people as far away as a hundred miles. I heard about walls of orange-and-blue flame colliding with each other. I heard about explosions, mountains crumbling, and the ground itself erupting. It was all quite impressive. The tales grew more and more fantastic with each person we met, but that is only to be expected. I ask you now, are any of these things true?"

"Yes," Mathew answered.

"The ring they spoke of . . . this is the same ring that Ramsey accused you of stealing?"

"Yes."

Quinn glanced down at the boy's hands and saw that he was not wearing a ring. His eyes strayed upward. There, on a leather cord around Mathew's neck, hung the odd rose-gold ring.

The constable cleared his throat. "As I said, it was all quite fantastic, but I'm a man who must deal with reality, as cold and hard as it may be. The matter is closed."

And with that the constable's hand slowly began to drift to the hilt of his sword.

"Don't."

Quinn's hand stopped. There was something in the voice, a subtle alteration of Mathew's countenance that caused him to pause. It had not been there a moment ago, he was quite positive about that.

A gangly-looking teenager with bright blue eyes returned his stare, unblinking. Something *was* different. The veneer of awkwardness he had come to expect from Mathew Lewin suddenly evaporated, replaced by something colder, and no longer lacking in confidence. By itself, that was disturbing enough, because he had observed nothing like it during the hearing in Devondale, months earlier.

Quinn considered whether to exercise the full weight

of his authority. Few men were able to hold up well under
his gaze, much less a boy composed largely of elbows
and knees. Out of curiosity he decided to wait and see
what Mathew would do next.

The constable leaned back in his chair and said nothing.

"I cannot let you hurt my friends, Jeram. I'll go quietly
with you, and without complaint, but I would like your
word that all charges against Collin, Lara, and Father
Thomas will be dropped."

"And what if I choose not to give it to you? I'm not in
the habit of—"

All four chairs along the wall behind the constable exploded in rapid succession, showering down in splinters
and bits of fabric.

Quinn leaped to his feet in astonishment. His men,
waiting just outside the door, burst into the room with
their swords drawn. Jeram Quinn raised his hand to indicate he was all right, then gestured them out again. The
deputies stared at the remains of the chairs, looked at
each other, then withdrew.

The constable turned back to Mathew.

Until that moment he had been more or less ready to
waive prosecution against Mathew's friends. Now he
found himself in a position in which he would appear to
be letting someone go who by all rights should be his
prisoner. If only a tenth part of what he had heard about
Mathew Lewin was true, then the boy could, and quite
possibly would, bring the palace down around their
heads.

"I might have expected more from Bran Lewin's son,"
Quinn said. "You make matters worse for everyone."

Mathew dropped his gaze and looked down at the
floor.

"I'm sorry, Jeram. I acted alone in what I did. You were
there. It's just that I don't want anyone else hurt on my
account. As I've said, I'll go quietly."

It's still there, thought Quinn. The same sense of guilt and responsibility he noted during their first meeting was still very much in evidence. He glanced at the ruined chairs and took a deep breath.

"Very well, young man. Your request is not entirely unreasonable. If I do agree to confine matters only to you, then I will expect your word that you will make no attempt to escape . . . and there will be no more . . . demonstrations with—"

"You have my word," he quickly replied. Mathew's hand slowly opened and the rose-gold ring swung free on the leather cord.

The constable searched Mathew's face for a moment, then got up, nodded to him, and left the room.

Shortly after, Mathew had informed Father Thomas, Lara, and Collin of his decision, a rider appeared at the gates of the abbey bearing an invitation for all of them to attend a dinner the king was hosting the following evening. The fact that the invitation specifically mentioned Jeram Quinn by name was not lost on Mathew. Although, how Gawl d'Atherny could have known of the constable's presence so quickly was a mystery. Nearly a week passed before he learned that the rider's opportune appearance was due almost entirely to Father Thomas. The moment the priest had heard of Jeram Quinn's arrival, he'd sent a message to Tenley Palace.

When Quinn arrived at the palace, Gawl promptly came out to greet him and was handed the warrant for Mathew's arrest. Quinn had procured it a month earlier in Anderon. The king examined the document and told him that he would be happy to cooperate. In the spirit of doing so, he then informed Quinn that he would dispatch an envoy to King Delain so as to clarify a question regarding the extradition treaty between their two countries. Gawl felt certain the matter would be cleared up quickly once the rider returned with an answer. Other than a brief look of annoyance that passed over Jeram Quinn's face, he took the matter in stride and merely bowed.

That was three weeks ago.

Since that time, both men had argued vehemently over a variety of matters, but principally over the question of Mathew's guilt, just as they were doing at the present moment. Predictably, the volume of their voices rose, just as Mathew knew it would. He gave up all hope of doing any more reading and closed the medical text he had been studying. The book was an old one about the diseases of the brain, written thousands of years ago. It had miraculously survived not only the ravages of time but the ravages of the Ancients' war. The palace library was small and stuffy and had a moldy smell to it, even though the double doors leading out to the balcony were open. Mathew pushed his chair back, and went outside for a walk.

Winter came earlier in the highlands of Sennia than it did in Elgaria. A sharp breeze blew down the corridors of the palace. There had already been one light snow in the past week. Mathew Lewin walked across the wide granite floors and out into the garden. A gravel path wound its way past various statues and benches. People often sat there and read, or simply looked at the art works on display. The first time Mathew had seen the garden, it was a mild surprise. He learned that Gawl really *was* a sculptor, as he had claimed in their first meeting. Moreover, he was the one who had created many of the fine pieces decorating the grounds.

Mathew stopped to look at a statue of an athlete hurling a spear, marveling at how anyone could have created such a beautiful thing. It was all the more impressive that a giant nearly seven feet tall had done so. Everything about the statue gave the impression of strength and coordination, from the biceps, to the thickness of the tendons and the strain of the muscles in its calves. It was as if a man had been frozen in time. The eyes of the statue were equally intense, staring off into the distance as if visualizing the spot where his spear would land after he hurled it. The body leaned slightly backward with the left arm extended forward in counterbalance. Mathew studied it a moment longer then moved on.

He rounded the corner of a low hedge and almost walked directly into Lara.

"Oh . . . I'm sorry," he said quickly, and stepped aside to let her by.

A pair of almond-shaped green eyes regarded him as she passed, but she said nothing in reply. The expression on her face was as cool as it had been for the last three weeks. She was still angry.

"Out walking?" he asked to her receding back.

Lara stopped and turned around.

"Mm-hmm."

"Still mad at me?"

Lara opened her mouth to say something, but closed it again.

Still mad, he decided.

"Would it help if I say I'm sorry again?"

"No."

"I am though."

Lara closed her eyes and opened them. After a moment the silence began to feel uncomfortable.

"Well, then, I'll just be . . ."

"I decided to take a peek at the statue Gawl's been doing of me," she said.

"Really? How does it look?" he asked, seizing the opening.

"Splendid," she answered. Her tone remained decidedly cool.

That afternoon Lara was wearing a fur-lined cape and a blue dress that clung to her figure. Lady Rowena, Gawl's companion, had taken her under her wing after their arrival and saw to it that she was provided with an adequate supply of dresses and other clothes.

"I'd love to see it," Mathew said.

For the last several months, Lara had been making the twenty-mile ride to Tenley Palace to pose for the sculpture. Other than dropping bits and pieces of information every now and then, she refused to tell Mathew what Gawl was working on. The only thing she would say was that Gawl was very talented. After seeing some of the examples of his friend's work, Mathew was inclined to agree.

"I really would . . ." he continued.

Mathew was doing his best to find the right expression while Lara made up her mind. Eventually, her face softened and she took a deep breath. But instead of walking back toward the studio, which was at the other end of the path, she sat down on one of the little stone benches and folded her hands in her lap. Mathew wasn't sure if that constituted an invitation or not, so he kept standing.

"I've been very angry at you," she said.

"I know."

"You had no right to agree to go back with Jeram Quinn before speaking with me."

"I know."

"And don't even *think* about telling me that you were trying to be noble, because I won't hear it."

"I know. It's just that I—"

"What am I supposed to do, wait for you while you spend the rest of your life in jail?"

"I'm not going to spend the rest of my life in jail," he said, patiently. "I've spoken to Father Thomas and he thinks that the worst it will be is two or three years . . . because of the circumstances."

"Two or three years!" she exclaimed, standing up. "That's horrible. It's all so upside down. I don't know what's wrong with Delain, allowing Quinn to come here. If it weren't for you he wouldn't even have a country. It's just ungrateful."

"I don't think he had a choice from what Jeram told me."

"Oh, it's Jeram now is it? I'm delighted to find you're

on familiar terms with the man who's come to arrest you. He's as ungrateful as the rest of them."

"Lara," Mathew said softly.

"If you hadn't killed Duren and his sister and those awful mercenaries there wouldn't even be an Elgaria now. And this is how they repay you?"

"Lara," Mathew said again.

He saw the tears beginning to brim in her eyes, stepped closer, and took her by the shoulders.

"It's not a matter of anyone being grateful. It's the law. We both know that. I'm not sorry for what I did, but I couldn't let Quinn charge you and the others with a crime. We can't spend the rest of our lives running."

"But Father Thomas spent six years in jail for killing a man," she sniffed.

Her words came as a shock to Mathew—he had never spoken of what the priest confided to him that night on the banks of the Roeselar. In a way he was glad the priest had decided to tell her what happened. Despite his brave talk, the fact that Father Thomas had gone to jail never left his mind.

"I don't think it was exactly the same thing," Mathew said, drawing her closer.

This time she didn't resist. The contact of their bodies together was electric—the fragrance of her hair, her fingertips on his face . . . They held each other without speaking for several minutes, and suddenly they were kissing. All of the anger, worry, and fear that had built up over the last few weeks melted into a desperate hunger and longing for each other. She kissed his face, his eyes, and his forehead. He kissed her neck and her ears. Again and again they found each other's lips, carried away by the void of their recent separation. A wall had risen up between them; it took a full six minutes to break it down.

"I'm sorry if I hurt you," he whispered, not certain if it was the right thing to say.

As it turned out, it was exactly the right thing to say.

She began kissing him all over again, then rested her head against his chest.

"What are we going to do?" she whispered.

"Go back and tell the truth."

"But what if they put you in jail?"

Mathew took a deep breath. "I don't relish the prospect, but I'll do what I have to."

She started to say something, but he put his finger over her lips. "Is Gawl's statue finished?" he asked, hoping to change the subject.

Lara pushed his hand away "Yes."

"I meant what I said before. I really would like to see it. You and he have been so secretive over the last few months. . . ."

She responded by giving him an unreadable smile, then turned and pointed to a large circular area of the garden that was under construction. It measured about fifty feet in diameter.

"That's where the new pond will be," she said.

"I see."

"The horses and statues will be in the middle, just like they were rising out of the water."

"Horses? I thought Gawl was doing a sculpture of your head."

He got that same enigmatic look. "Come," Lara said, taking his hand. "You have to promise not to say anything about it to anyone else. Gawl's very sensitive about his work."

They walked down the path toward a small, plain-looking stucco building with faded pink walls that served as Gawl's studio. When they got closer, Lara told Mathew to close his eyes and ran ahead to open a pair of double doors. Mathew dutifully complied. A second or two later he heard her returning and felt her take his hand.

"Now don't look until I say so, all right?" she said. The excitement in her voice was obvious as she led him forward.

Mathew laughed to himself. "Fine."

"Be careful there's a step here."

Mathew lifted his leg and stepped up onto a hard, smooth surface.

"You can open your eyes now," Lara whispered.

Mathew opened his eyes and blinked in surprise. There in front of him were two beautifully carved alabaster horses rearing up on their hind legs. The muscles in their necks and flanks stood out in exquisite detail. Their manes seemed to be flowing backward, blown by an invisible wind. Warm mid-afternoon sunshine streamed into the room through a section of the roof that had been removed and replaced with a skylight. The horses' heads were turned inward toward each other as they strained against their bridles. Mathew followed the line of their magnificent necks to their backs, and finally to the statues of two women who stood behind them, straining to hold the animals on tether.

For the second time in less than a minute he blinked in astonishment and his mouth fell open. Both women were completely naked. He looked closer. One of them bore a remarkable resemblance to Lady Rowena and the other looked like—*Lara!*

Mathew's mouth opened and closed but nothing came out. A casual passerby might have discerned sounds of a sort, but they could hardly be said to qualify as speech.

"Isn't it beautiful?" Lara asked. "It's going to be the centerpiece of the pond."

Mathew felt his face go scarlet. "Beautiful?" he repeated, looking at her. "But you're not wearing anything! I thought he was just doing a sculpture of your face."

Lara tilted her head to one side and looked at him. "He did do my face."

"But . . . but . . ." Mathew sputtered, "you're not wearing anything."

"I know," she said innocently.

"You know!" he exploded.

"Why, Mathew Lewin, I'm surprised at you. This is art. Don't you like the way I look?"

"What?"

"I said, don't you like—"

"Of course I like the way you look! But that's hardly the point . . . in the middle of the pond, you say?"

"Well . . . yes. That's what Gawl told us. In about a week he's going to have that banquet he's been talking about, and we'll unveil it then. There'll be dancing, and lords and ladies. It'll be so exciting."

"Have you lost your mind? I'm not going to allow you to be seen in public like . . . like . . ."

"Like what?" she asked.

"Like that!" he said pointing. "I absolutely forbid it."

Lara's eyes opened wide in surprise and she put her hand over her mouth. After a second or two it became apparent that she was doing her best to suppress a giggle.

She was almost successful.

"Pah!" Mathew said, throwing his hands up. He spun on his heel, stalked out of the studio, and began heading down the path.

Lara immediately ran after him and caught him by the arm.

"Where are you going?" she asked.

"To have a few choice words with his majesty, the king."

Lara put both her arms around his neck and looked up at him, her eyes wide.

"But I thought you would like my statue."

"Stop that," he said, removing her hands. "Liking has nothing to do with it. It's just not . . . it's not . . . proper."

He looked so stern and serious she had to bite her lip to keep from giggling again. She put her arms around his neck once more and kissed him lightly on the lips, then took his hand and gently led him back to the studio. Mathew reluctantly followed, still grumbling to himself.

When they got inside, Lara closed the door, bolted it, and walked back to stand next her statue.

"I think it's a very good likeness, don't you?"

Mathew nodded slowly. He found the he was staring at the statue's belly and breasts and it was only with an effort that he managed to pull his eyes away from the curve of the hips and long, shapely thighs back to Lara. She was wearing the same expression he had seen earlier. His jaw dropped once more when she reached behind and quickly undid the buttons at the back of her dress. She let it drop to the ground. A second later her slip followed.

"You haven't told me if you think it's a good likeness," she whispered.

There was a bed on the side of the studio where Gawl sometimes slept when he was working late there. In two quick strides, Mathew crossed the room and swept her up in his arms.

2

Tenley Palace, Two hours later

MATHEW OPENED HIS EYES AND SAT UP ON ONE ELBOW. Lara was standing by the window, looking out into the garden. He didn't even remember her getting up. She'd found a robe, and the light in the room, a warm, reddish quality, silhouetted her figure through the thin material. When she heard him stir, she turned around and smiled.

"Did you have a nice sleep?" she asked.

"Oh, yes. And you?" he replied, trying to keep his eyes on her face.

"Mm-hmm."

Unfortunately, he was only partly successful. Lara glanced down at the diaphanous material and quickly stepped away from the window, to his chagrin. She came to the bed and sat down next to him. They kissed again.

When they separated, Mathew leaned back against the pillows and said, "I'll talk to Father Thomas today."

"Father Thomas? What are you going to talk to him about?"

"Well, marriage . . . you know."

Lara sat upright. "Marriage?" she repeated.

"Well, of course. Don't you think now that we . . . uh . . . that we should get married?"

She took a deep breath and shook her head. "Mathew, we're both only nineteen," she said, pushing a rebellious lock of hair off his forehead.

"But your mother was eighteen when she got married. You said so yourself."

"That was another generation, silly. Things are different now. Just because we've made love, that's no reason to run out and get married. And it was very nice, by the way. Rowena says a man and woman need to really know each other before they make such a serious commitment."

Mathew realized that his mouth was open and closed it with a snap. He didn't know whether to be angry or offended. "Rowena? You've been talking to Rowena about us?"

"Just chitchat. You can't stand in one place and pose for hours without having some polite conversation, can you?"

"*Polite conversation?* You talked about making love and getting married with Gawl here?"

"Well . . . uh . . . he was here, but I don't think he was paying any attention. He gets so absorbed in his work, he's really oblivious to everything going on around him."

The last statement was too much for Mathew. He swung out of bed and pulled on his breeches and shirt. When he turned back to face Lara he noticed that she had stepped behind a screen to get dressed, which made about as much sense to him as everything they'd said over the last five minutes. If he lived to be a hundred, he would never understand women.

When she finished dressing, Lara came over and lightly kissed him on the cheek.

"It really *was* very nice you know," she said in his ear. "Wonderful, in fact."

He was certain there was a suitable reply, however he couldn't think of it at the moment, so he said, "I suppose we should get back before they come looking for us."

Lara slipped her arm through his and gave him a squeeze before they headed for the door.

They were barely outside before they spotted Collin

coming down the path toward them. When he saw them he raised his hand in greeting calling out, "Ho."

"Ho," Mathew replied.

Lara waved with her fingers.

"What have you two been up to?" Collin asked, shaking Mathew's hand.

"Oh . . . I've been showing Mathew—"

"Some of the sculptures in the garden," Mathew said, finishing the sentence for her. "Have you had a chance to see them yet?"

"Sure . . . a few."

"There are some really nice ones over here," Mathew said, taking Collin by the arm and guiding him to the side of the studio toward a lifelike statue of a deer and two small fawns.

Collin examined the sculpture for a moment, then shrugged.

"And there's a really amazing one of a blacksmith over there," Mathew said pointing. "I think it looks a little bit like Lucas Emson."

As they passed the window of the studio, again Collin glanced in and gradually came to a halt. He peered inside and a small frown creased his forehead. "Hey, that sort of looks like . . ."

He never got the chance to finish his sentence as Mathew all but yanked him along.

"Do you know, the feet and hands seem a little large on a lot of the statues that Gawl does, don't you think?" Mathew asked.

"I suppose so," Collin said, still looking over his shoulder. "I'm not all that much for art."

Lara listened to the exchange, sighed, and followed them.

"Say . . . you like sports, don't you?" asked Mathew. "There's an amazing statue of a man throwing a spear over there." He continued shepherding Collin along the path toward the spear-thrower, but then stopped abruptly. Something was wrong.

The first time he'd seen the statue its head was facing forward, in the same direction that the left arm was pointing. But now it was looking directly at him. Collin stopped also.

"Mat," Collin said, lowering his voice, "I don't mean anything by it, but back there in the studio . . . one of those statues looked like . . ."

Collin's words trailed away when he noticed the expression on Mathew's face change and turned to see what his friend was staring at. A second later, his own eyes grew as wide as saucers when the statue's arm moved. Then it slowly turned toward them.

"What the hell?" said Collin.

They both stopped so abruptly, Lara walked directly into them.

"What are you boys looking at?" she asked. When she saw what it was, she let out a gasp.

All three of them stood there, dumbfounded, as they watched the statue get down off the pedestal.

At the far end of the garden, the sound of stone grinding against stone caught their attention. The statue of a blacksmith had suddenly come to life. Like the first, it was slowly detaching itself from the marble stand. No one seemed able to move as both statues began walking toward them.

Instinctively Mathew reached for the leather cord around his throat that held his ring, only to find with a shock that it was missing. It was still in Gawl's studio. He had taken it off because it kept getting in the way while he and Lara were kissing. He muttered a curse under his breath and looked at the rest of the garden. There were lots of other statues, but only the two in front of them were moving.

Slowly, they all started backing away.

"Lara," Mathew said quietly, "I want you to get back to the studio. Lock the door. If you can, climb out one of the windows in the back and get help."

"Mathew—"

"Now."

Lara turned and ran.

"Spread out," Collin said, drawing his sword.

They moved away from each other. Mathew spared a quick glance over his shoulder to make certain that Lara was in the little building. The moment his attention shifted away, the first statue heaved its spear.

"Watch out!" Collin yelled.

Mathew barely had time to twist to the side as the spear came whistling past his head. More out of reflex than anything else, he drew his own sword but put it back in the scabbard again a moment later. *What good's a sword going to do against a piece of stone?*

Both statues plodded forward. Mathew's eyes opened wider as the statue of the blacksmith raised its hammer above its head. Step by step, they advanced. He could feel the heavy thud of the blacksmith's footfalls in the ground under his own feet.

"Damn. How do we fight these things?" Collin asked from his left.

"I don't know. There's got to be some way."

"How heavy do you think the top of that bench is?" Collin asked pointing.

Mathew glanced at it.

"More than a hundred pounds at least. What are you thinking?"

"If it's not attached, we could use it as a battering ram."

The spear-thrower was almost on them. When Collin and Mathew separated again, it stopped, fixed its attention on Mathew, and continued coming after him. Neither its face nor the eyes held any expression; both of its hands were reaching for him.

The first thing Mathew thought as he recovered from the shock of marble coming to life was that he had to get them away from Lara. The whole thing was insane; it couldn't be happening. Rapidly, his mind began to assess the situation. The statues were gradually forcing them backward, cutting off any chance of escape. There was a row of hedges lining either side of the path, which would make maneuvering a problem—assuming they could figure out a way to fight the things.

This is like a nightmare, he told himself.

From over the statue's shoulder, Mathew saw Collin break into a run and launch himself through the air, feet first. His friend struck the spear-thrower high on the shoulders and he bounced off, hit the ground, and rolled to his right. The blow was heavy enough to overbalance the statue and knock it forward. It began to fall like a toppled tree, still reaching for Mathew as it did.

Mathew dodged around the creature, avoiding a second grab that it made for him. Then the statue began to get up. He and Collin made a dash for the bench. Grunting with effort they pulled the stone top free and charged forward, striking the spear-thrower in its chest and knocking it over again. The impact sent splinters of marble flying in all directions. They also lost their grip and dropped it in the process. The statue of the blacksmith was no more than ten feet away from them. A sweeping blow from its stone hammer missed their heads by inches.

Collin spat out a curse.

Mathew opened his mouth to say something, but never got the chance because the spear-thrower was back on its feet again and coming for them once more.

"How the hell do we stop these things?" Collin asked, breathing heavily.

Mathew shook his head. *There has to be something,* he thought, as they backed away. Swords weren't going to have any effect on stone. Suddenly he remembered the workmen's tools by the pond.

"Did you see the construction area on the way here?" he asked.

Collin nodded but didn't take his attention away from the blacksmith who was closing on them. The spear-thrower was right behind him.

"There are some hammers and picks we could use. If we can lead these two into the center, we might be able to get them stuck," Mathew explained. "I think the ground is still soft."

"I get it," Collin replied. "I'll draw them left. As soon as I do, you make a break for it."

"Be careful."

The moment he and Collin separated, the statues focused on Mathew and proceeded after him, only this time they moved apart as well. Their eyeless faces appeared to be tracking every movement he made.

"Nice to know I'm so popular," Mathew quietly said to himself.

Out of his peripheral vision, he saw Lara step out of the studio. "Get back inside!" he yelled at her.

Collin drew his sword, stepped in under the black-smith's lumbering swing, and slashed at its leg. When the blade made contact, a large chip of marble flew into the air, but it had absolutely no effect whatsoever. Again and again Collin struck. On the sixth time he finally succeeded in getting the thing's attention. It responded by aiming a wide blow at his head, which he easily avoided. Collin stepped back and began waving his arms.

"Hey you . . . *you* . . . this way."

The creature obliged and began to follow him.

The moment Mathew saw his chance, he darted around the spear-thrower and raced for the pond.

With the advantage of mobility, Collin sidestepped the blacksmith and hacked at its leg twice more, putting all his weight behind the blows. His blade broke with a loud snap, and he found himself standing in the middle of the gravel path holding the hilt of his sword.

"Wonderful," he said.

Thus far, neither of them had had any trouble avoiding the lumbering creatures who were slow-moving and awkward, but the longer the fight went on, the smoother and quicker the statues' movements became.

"Better hurry, Mat," Collin called out over his shoulder, leaning away from another blow.

See the world. Sure. That's what I wanted to do, he thought. *At least in Devondale statues don't try to kill you.*

There were several shovels, a sledgehammer, and two pickaxes lying in a wheelbarrow, apparently left there by workmen from the day before. Mathew looked back over his shoulder to see where the spear-thrower was. He estimated forty yards. He hefted the sledgehammer a few times in his hand and decided it was too heavy. Like Collin, he also noticed the statues were beginning to move more quickly. It was only a matter of time before they became far more dangerous.

If this is a dream—please, God, let me wake up soon, he silently prayed.

The spear-thrower was no more than twenty feet from him. Mathew's fingers closed around the handle of a shovel and he waited. A series of wooden boards had been laid on muddy ground that led to the center of the pond. *If I can get it to follow me and into the mud . . .*

A second later, Collin came twisting and turning past the outstretched arms of both statues. Mathew stepped sideways and swung the shovel with all his might at the spear-thrower. The steel edge connected with the left side of the statue's face and bit a large piece of stone out of its cheekbone. Mathew winced as a shock ran down the handle into his hands, numbing them. He gripped the handle as hard as he could and swung again. This time a piece of the creature's lower jaw flew off, plopping into the mud. The effect was gruesome.

"Doesn't improve his looks any," Collin said. He picked up an axe and aimed a blow at the blacksmith, only this time the statue raised its arm and blocked him. The axe handle broke apart. Collin stared at the handle and then at the scowling bearded face. "Bad idea," he muttered.

A backhanded swipe hit Collin in the chest and lifted him off the ground. He landed on his rump fifteen feet into the pond. Mathew was unable to help and started backing up along the wooden boards, toward the pond's center. Both statues were coming for him again.

A pit filled with gravel had already been dug for the foundation of Gawl's sculpture. Foot by foot Mathew continued to move away, trying hard to maintain his balance on the narrow boards. The blacksmith and the spear-thrower came forward in single file.

Mathew could feel his heart pounding in his chest. He knew his timing would have to be just right. When he reached the gravel bed he waited until they were only a few feet away, then jumped sideways and began to run across the muddy surface back to the bank. To his surprise, he sank in up to his ankles. Expressionless, the blacksmith watched him for a moment then began to follow. The spear-thrower, however, stayed put and slowly raised its iron spear up to its shoulder. There was no doubt in Mathew's mind what was coming next. The left arm of the statue pointed directly at him and its right arm drew back into a throwing position.

Unexpectedly, a sharp cracking sound halted the statue in mid-motion. One of its marble ears flew off and landed on the ground. The statue glanced down, stared at it for a moment then turned around to face Lara, who was holding one of Gawl's mallets.

"Get back!" Mathew yelled, struggling to free himself.

Little by little, the blacksmith statue moved closer. Mathew desperately needed to put some distance between them. The blacksmith took one step followed by another, then like Mathew, it stopped completely. For a moment it simply stayed where it was. Slowly it raised one leg out of the mud only to have the other sink.

Another sound attracted Mathew's attention and he looked toward the bank of the pond just in time to see the spear-thrower's upper body shatter into a hundred pieces. Gawl was there behind it, holding a sledgehammer in one hand. The lower torso of the statue swayed back and forth in a macabre dance until Gawl kicked it over with one of his massive legs. Mathew's relief turned to pain as the blacksmith's fingers closed around his forearm. In vain he tried pulling away but its grip was impossibly strong. Gawl pounded down the wooden boards toward him, rushing to help. He was dimly aware there were other voices shouting, but he had no time to dwell on them. The blacksmith's free arm rose up, lifting the hammer high above its head. There was nothing Mathew could do to free himself.

Gawl knew that he would never reach Mathew in time and while still at a dead run, he bellowed, "Duck, Mat!" and heaved his hammer directly at the statue.

Mathew twisted his body to the side, though he was still pinioned by stone fingers. The blow that he expected to end his life never came. Instead, he found himself held by a headless body as Gawl's hammer found its mark. The statue's head toppled off its shoulders and thumped into the mud, staring up at him. Whatever spark of animation was present in the eyes, it slowly faded. The body fell over, dragging Mathew with it. Gawl retrieved his hammer, and with two more blows, he shattered the arms of the blacksmith, freeing him.

He backed away from the creature, his chest heaving. Gawl reached down and helped him to his feet.

"This is the first time I've seen your work," Collin said, trotting up the boards to join them. "I hope your other pieces are less lifelike."

"What happened here?" asked Gawl.

Mathew shook his head. So did Collin.

"I was just coming to get Mat when that thing and his friend got down off their pedestals and started walking toward us."

Gawl's expression turned into a scowl and he looked at Mathew, "I have no explanation for this," Mathew said. "I'm not even wearing my ring."

"Impossible," Gawl said. "Statues don't just simply get up and decide to go for a walk."

Mathew shook his head again, and started back for the bank with Gawl and Collin following before they could discuss it further.

Father Thomas and Jeram Quinn came running up.

"Mathew?" Father Thomas asked.

"I'm fine."

The priest looked at Collin, who nodded in reply, though he had a sizable bruise on his chest.

"What happened here?" Father Thomas asked, echoing Gawl's question.

"I don't know," Mathew said slowly. The full impact of what had just occurred was beginning to sink in.

Living statues? The whole idea was absurd but two blocks of marble had just tried to kill him.

"Can you tell us anything?" Father Thomas asked.

"No, Father. It's a complete mystery to me ... I swear."

Quinn surveyed the scene and said nothing. His face gave no clue as to what he was thinking. A number of people from the palace staff, having heard the commotion, came out to see what was happening. Gawl went over to talk with them and apparently said whatever was necessary to calm the situation. Most of them went back inside, but not before casting suspicious glances in Mathew's direction.

Their scrutiny made Mathew uncomfortable—such things always did. Over the last several months he had gotten more used to it, but had never quite been able to come to terms with the attention. Rumors of what had happened at Ardon Field during the final battle with Karas Duren seemed to be everywhere. It eventually reached the point when he ceased going into Barcora due to the buzz of conversations that would start even before he left a room. Fingers pointed and heads turned in his direction whenever he walked down the street, which made him ill at ease.

The more it went on, the more his discomfort increased. While he was at the abbey, the priests who studied there asked questions about the ring, trying to learn the extent of his abilities. Mostly, they wanted to know how his mind worked and what he was thinking of when he used it. A naturally loquacious and open individual, Mathew readily answered their questions, but quickly found that his tendency was to say too much rather than too little. One question always led to more questions, and ultimately he disciplined himself to say less in matters where the ring was concerned—almost like a man who would not trust himself to take a drink. His instincts told him that it was the best thing to do, and he relied on them heavily.

"Why didn't you use your ring?" Gawl asked as soon as the crowd had gone.

"I must have dropped it," Mathew answered. "I'm pretty sure I know where it is, but it wouldn't have made any difference because I gave Jeram my word not to use it."

Everyone there turned to look at the constable, who took a deep breath and blew it out through his lips. "Mathew, conceivably you misinterpreted our conversation. When I asked for your word, I intended only that you not use your ring to *escape*. If your life is in peril, you are certainly released from any such restrictions. I am here only to do my duty, not to see you or anyone else injured."

"That's all very well, Quinn," Gawl said. "I consider

myself a talented sculptor, but I have yet to bring any of my works to life. I'd like some answers. Things like this just don't happen."

"I agree, your majesty. But since no one here appears to have any answers, I suggest we adjourn and give the matter further thought. This situation will obviously have to be investigated. I offer my help, if you wish."

"Thank you," Gawl replied.

For a moment it appeared the king was going to say something else, but a look from Father Thomas forestalled him. He shook his head and turned to Mathew and Collin.

"A poor introduction to my garden, I'm afraid. If you'll excuse me, I think I'll take a walk around in case any of my other pieces have similar inclinations."

"I'm sorry about your statues," Mathew said, "but thank you."

"Think no more on it, young friend. I never liked that blacksmith anyway. He looked too much like an uncle of mine."

3

Sennia, Tenley Palace

MATHEW LOOKED UP TO SEE LARA HURRYING TOWARD his with a tall, stately woman.

Rowena, he said to himself.

Lara broke into a run and hugged him, then Collin.

"Thank God you're both all right," she said. "It was awful. What could have made—"

"Rowena," Mathew said, sketching an ungainly sort of bow to her.

Collin watched him then followed suit.

Rowena dispensed with formality and also hugged them as Lara had done. Gawl's companion was in her late thirties, but could have passed for a woman ten years younger. She was nearly as tall as Mathew with a mass of auburn hair, high cheekbones, and large brown eyes. The gown she was wearing was a darker blue than Lara's and was accented by a gold and diamond flower pin on her left shoulder. Rowena was a strikingly beautiful woman.

"Thank God neither of you were hurt," she said. "I want to hear everything that happened . . . after you've bathed, of course."

Collin frowned and sniffed his clothes. His reaction was enough to indicate that Rowena had a point. Both he and Mathew were covered in mud and muck from head to toe.

"Hmm," he said. "If you'll excuse me, I'll see you all at dinner," Collin said. He gave Mathew a squeeze on the shoulder and headed back toward the palace, leaving the three of them together.

Lara and Rowena both glanced down at their dresses, which were now stained with mud. Each of them let out a sigh and looked accusingly at Mathew, who blinked and took a half step backward.

"Sorry," he said.

"Come," Rowena said to Lara. "We'd better go in and change too."

Lara gave him a kiss on the cheek and the women followed Collin back to the palace.

Mathew stood there for a moment and watched them disappear around the corner of a hedge then headed back down the path toward Gawl's studio. The ring was exactly where he'd left it, on the small nightstand near the bed.

He slipped the leather cord over his head and looked around the studio. The room was dimly lit, but there was still enough light to see by. He had seen nude sculptures before, but never of anyone that he was personally acquainted with, let alone someone he had just made love to.

As he contemplated the statue, his mind wandered to more vivid recollections of Lara and the memory made him smile. Over the last few months she had changed, not in any profound way, but changed nevertheless. He wasn't sure how he felt about that. He got the distinct impression that his reaction to the sculpture had amused her, and being honest with himself, he had to admit that he did come off as somewhat pompous about it, which only annoyed him all the more.

They had come close to making love before, but had never quite taken the final step. Something always seemed to intervene. He stood there thinking about why it had finally happened and concluded that Lara had probably gotten tired of waiting for him to make the first move. He wanted to of course—quite a bit, actually, but doing so would have been difficult while they were living in the abbey. A person couldn't spit there without hitting a priest. Despite how enjoyable the experience was, it rankled him to know that she had talked about their relationship to Rowena.

What in the world was she thinking? he wondered. Some things needed to remain private. *It was just—*

"Lovely, don't you think?" came a deep voice from behind.

Mathew spun around. He hadn't heard Gawl come in.

"I'm sorry, I was just—"

"Quite all right, Mat," Gawl said, waving away the apology. "I really didn't think either of them could keep a secret this long. Did you find your ring?"

"Yes."

Gawl crossed the room, picked up a match from a small tin sitting on the corner of his workbench, and used it to light a lamp. When he finished, he flopped down in an oversized chair and stretched out his legs.

"It has been an education getting to know you, Master Lewin."

Mathew smiled and took a chair opposite him; neither spoke for a while. They simply sat there contemplating the huge marble sculpture and watching the light play off the muscles in the horses' necks and along their flanks. It looked as if they were in motion. Mathew studied Lara's face more closely trying to decide what her expression meant, but couldn't.

"It really is beautiful," he said after a while. "I wish I had the talent to create such things."

"Thank you," Gawl replied. "But something bothers you about it, yes?"

Mathew took a second before he answered. "Was it strictly necessary for them to pose in the nude?"

The question caused Gawl to laugh quietly to himself—"I'm sorry, it's been a long day. But to answer your question, no. It was actually Rowena's idea. Her view of things tends to be, shall we say . . . liberal."

"So I've noticed," Mathew replied, glumly. "It seems to be rubbing off on Lara."

"Is there a problem?" asked Gawl.

Once again Mathew didn't answer immediately. Instead, he stared out of the window for a space. "Yes," he finally said, turning back to Gawl.

The two of them regarded each other for several moments before Gawl got the message.

"I suppose I should have discussed it with you first, Mat. I apologize. Just out of curiosity, what did you say when you first saw it?"

"Not much," Mathew replied. "I think my mouth was opening and closing without anything coming out."

Gawl started chuckling again. He pushed himself up and walked over to the statue of a small boy in the corner. He lifted the head off, reached down, retrieved an ornate bottle and two glasses from inside the torso, then put the head back on and returned to his chair. He poured out two glasses of wine.

"Brandywine," he said. "It's as old as these mountains. Go slowly with it."

Mathew sniffed the contents of the glass and took a tentative sip. The liquid had a strong aroma that opened his eyes as it went down. The effect was warming and stimulating at the same time.

Gawl gave a curt nod of approval as he said, "Glad you like it."

"It's wonderful, but why hide it in there?" Mathew asked, inclining his head toward the statue.

"Rowena doesn't approve of drink. None of her people do. Their butt-pinched priests have got them all convinced that God gets personally offended whenever someone takes a drink of anything other than water."

"Seriously? I've never heard of such a thing."

"Um-hmm," Gawl answered, taking another sip.

"You and the priests seem to get along well enough," Mathew said.

Gawl downed the rest of his drink in one gulp, then poured himself another.

"We don't see eye to eye on many things, Mat, but it's an alliance we both need. When I took the throne, the country was on the verge of civil war. Rowena's father was regent at the time. Edward's a good man, but he was content to keep everything running just the way they had been for centuries . . . and a good portion of the clergy agreed with him. Sennia hadn't had a king for over three hundred years, and that pretty much gave them free run. Relinquishing power is never an easy thing. They still push as much as they can."

Mathew wasn't quite sure he understood all the ramifications of Gawl's last statement, and resolved to ask Father Thomas more about Sennian politics the next time they were alone.

"But you all work together now, don't you?"

Gawl shrugged.

"Running a country is infinitely more complex than I ever imagined. It's been eight years and I'm still learning every day. My chief goal has been to reduce the size of government and insure that my people prosper. Unfortunately, the cooperation of the church is pivotal in this because they can sway public opinion. A large faction would like Sennia to remain isolated from the rest of the world. Another group wants to open the trade routes and embrace our neighbors. The barons and dukes are divided on this point."

Mathew reached out and accepted another drink. "Which do you favor?"

"I say, love thy neighbor. We can't simply hide out here in our mountains and hope no one else notices. Sennia is a strong country, but she can't stand alone against Cincar, Vargoth, Alor Satar, and the rest."

"But we're not at war anymore," Mathew observed. In the flickering lamp light, he saw Gawl's teeth flash white. The smile didn't make his face look any gentler.

"There are more ways of fighting a war than with arrows and swords. A country can be strangled into submission economically. This is why the alliances I'm trying to forge must be carefully chosen. With Duren dead and his sons running things, there are new opportunities for trade with Alor Satar."

"Alor Satar?" Mathew said, shocked at the idea. Barely seven months earlier, the West had been at war with them.

"Nothing remains static," said Gawl.

Mathew decided then and there that the intricacies of politics were more formidable than he had imagined. He shook his head and looked back at the statues, then stared down into his drink.

"Now what bothers you, boy?" Gawl rumbled.

Mathew put his glass on the floor and looked at Gawl seriously. "Your reaction to what happened outside," he said, meeting the king's eyes.

Gawl nodded once, but didn't reply.

"You were surprised," Mathew went on, "but not *that* surprised. It's not everyday that statues get down off their pedestals and try to kill people."

Gawl regarded the slender young man in front of him. The blue eyes met his without blinking. He was aware the boy had a quick mind. That much was obvious in their first meeting, but he was perceptive as well. The king poured himself another drink and leaned forward in his chair.

"You're right, Mathew," he said, the quality of his voice suddenly different. "As I told you once before, I'm too old to start believing in fairy tales and goblins."

Before Gawl could go on, there was a light tap at the door. Without taking his eyes away from Mathew he called out, "Come in."

Father Thomas stepped into the room and closed the door. He was dressed in his usual black robes, as he had been since arriving at the abbey.

"Come in, Siward. Mat and I were just discussing the

unusual tendencies of my statues to go wandering around the palace grounds."

"Ah," said Father Thomas.

Mathew's brows came together—it was obvious Father Thomas's presence was not merely a coincidence.

Gawl got up, went over to a closet, and rummaged around in it. After a few seconds he produced another glass, then walked to the statue and poured a drink for Father Thomas who accepted the glass. The priest sat down in the last remaining chair in the room.

"I see you still haven't convinced Rowena to come around to your point of view."

"I'm making progress," Gawl conceded. "Actually, her objections run more to consuming hard liquor. She thinks that wine—in moderation, mind you—is acceptable for medicinal and religious purposes."

"Well . . . I *am* a priest," observed Father Thomas.

Gawl bowed to him from his chair and Father Thomas returned the bow.

"As I said . . . Mat and I were just talking about my statues."

"Is there anything you can add that might enlighten us, Mat?" Father Thomas asked.

Mathew looked at Gawl, then at Father Thomas. He shook his head slowly. The conversation had suddenly shifted and he was uncertain of his ground, so he retreated to his habitual wariness. "It might be a good idea if you both just say what's on your minds," he replied. He heard the words as they came out and was surprised with himself, at the directness of his speech. The hour was late and he was too tired for games.

Father Thomas's eyebrows went up and he leaned back in his chair, however it was Gawl who spoke first.

"Before we were interrupted, I was telling you that I'm too old to start believing in magic. Duren and his sister are dead, and *you* are the only one who possesses the ability to do what happened out there."

So they think I'm responsible for making the statues come to life? He didn't know whether to be angry or offended. Both men were watching him. "I'm not the only one," Mathew told them.

Gawl's eyes opened wider and he leaned forward, resting his elbows on his knees. Father Thomas said nothing.

"Duren had a niece," Mathew continued. "I mentioned her to Father Thomas when we were on the *Wave Dancer,* except I didn't know who she was at the time. Her name is Teanna and her mother was Marsa—"

"I know who she is," Gawl said.

"I remember the discussion," said Father Thomas. "But I thought you never saw her face."

"I didn't, but I know who she is now."

"How, my son? You've either been at the abbey or here at Tenley Palace since we arrived in Barcora. And I know you haven't worn your ring for quite some time."

Mathew looked out the window into the darkness of the garden. A silvery half-moon had risen, outlining some of the statues visible from where he was sitting.

Father Thomas and Gawl glanced at each other and waited. Eventually, Mathew turned back to them and began speaking again.

"Do you remember the battle at Ardon Field, Father?"

"Of course."

"Gawl and his people were attacking the enemy flank while I was fighting Duren. I was drained almost to the point of exhaustion and could barely stand, or even see for that matter. You and Colonel Targil were trying to break through their lines to get to me."

Mathew's words came out haltingly. He seemed to be struggling with the memories, like a man waking from a dream and trying to remember the details.

"Go on, Mathew," the priest said gently.

"Do you remember that I was gone by the time you got there."

"Yes," Father Thomas nodded. "We thought you had

been killed or had wandered off," Father Thomas said. "No one was able to find you. The whole area was devastated."

Mathew's eyes assumed a faraway look as he continued speaking. "I awoke to find myself lying on the grass of a town square. The problem was it wasn't real grass, and the town was thousands of miles beneath the earth's surface."

Father Thomas and Gawl exchanged glances once again.

"I know how it sounds, but I wasn't alone in the town. Teanna d'Elso was there as well."

"What?" Gawl said sharply.

"She was the one who whisked me off the battlefield and brought me there. We sat and talked with each other about a lot of things. At first I was afraid that she was going to kill me for what happened to her mother and her uncle. She could have, but she didn't. I wouldn't have been able to stop her if she had. It took me two full days to recover from my fight with Duren."

"You say she *brought* you there?" Gawl said. "How?"

"I don't know how she did it, Gawl," Mathew said, "but she possesses one of the rings. It was something the Ancients were able to do. That much I do know. I've tried to find out how during these past months, but my success has been limited. The fact is, Teanna can do a number of things that I can't."

"What was this place she brought you to, Mat? Where is it?" Gawl asked.

"It was a town the Ancients created. I've read about it in different books. The best I can tell is that it's about two thousand miles from here, somewhere in the northwest."

"Across the wasted lands?" Gawl said. "There's nothing out there."

"And you think Teanna d'Elso is responsible for what the statues did?" Father Thomas asked.

"No," Mathew replied, shaking his head. "There's someone else."

4

Sennia, Tenley Palace

THEY TALKED FOR NEARLY AN HOUR. GAWL AND FA-
ther Thomas were as shocked by his news as he was
when Gawl told him that Teanna d'Elso would be arriving at Tenley Palace within the week. The king's intentions were to begin normalizing relations between his
country and those of the Eastern Alliance. The message
he had received from Nyngary said that Teanna would attend the conference as her father's representative.
Mathew was equally shocked to learn that Bishop Willis
had approached Father Thomas shortly after their arrival
at the abbey and asked the priest to keep a close watch
on him.

It was an evening of revelations.

Their conversation would have gone on a great deal
longer had it not been for the appearance of Lady
Rowena, who had come to fetch the king to dinner. When
her footsteps sounded on the gravel path outside, Gawl
and Father Thomas looked at each other and said,
"Rowena" at the same time. Galvanized into action,
three fully-grown men managed to make a bottle of
brandywine and their glasses magically disappear, and
succeeded in returning to their seats in just under four
seconds. Rowena opened the door to find them engaged
in light conversation on the merits of traveling by ship as
opposed to horseback.

"Ah, come in, my dear. We were just talking," Gawl said, rising from his chair.

Mathew and Father Thomas followed suit, bowing to her.

Rowena came over and kissed Gawl on his cheek. Despite her height, he still had to bend to accommodate her. She had changed into a trim yellow dress, which accented her auburn hair well. A necklace of blue and white stones circled her throat.

"I thought this is where I would find you," she said, slipping her arm through Gawl's. "Alexander said dinner will be ready in a half hour. You know how he gets when you're late."

Mathew had met Alexander before. He was the Chief of Staff at Tenley Palace, a thin little man who seemed to be everywhere at once. Gawl had more or less inherited him from Edward Guy, the former Sennian regent, when he took the throne. Though Alexander could be punctilious in matters involving protocol, nearly everyone agreed that he *was* efficient.

Gawl nodded. "Quite so, my dear. Well, perhaps we ought to go." Then, tuning to Father Thomas, he said, "Siward, I asked you to remind me of the hour."

Father Thomas spread his hands and shrugged slightly.

"I swear, you men are worse than women when you start gabbing," said Rowena.

Mathew knew that his face had an annoying tendency to color when he was lying, so he decided to remain silent. A critical up-and-down glance from Rowena was sufficient to remind him that he was still covered in mud. It also provided an excellent reason to take his leave.

"If you'll pardon me, I'd better run along and clean up before we eat," he said. "Your servant, ma'am."

In response to his polite bow, Rowena smiled and stepped aside to let him pass. Her smile made him uncomfortable, and he hoped Lara had the good sense not to

talk about what happened between them earlier. The very
idea of discussing such an intimate thing was appalling.
He would have reflected further on this as he walked
along the path had it not been for the fact that he was
keeping one eye where he placed his feet and one eye on
the statues silhouetted in the moonlight.

5

The Great Southern Sea, South of Alor Satar

TEANNA D'ELSO LEANED AGAINST THE SHIP'S MAHOGANY rail and watched the harbor recede as they pulled farther from the land. She could still make out the shops along Umera's quayside. There were other ships at anchor in the harbor, their tall masts moving gently with the current.

Umera was the largest port city in Alor Satar and the winter residence of her cousin Eric, with whom she had been visiting when Gawl's invitation came. Surprisingly, the Sennian king was proposing that relations between Nyngary, Alor Satar, and his country be normalized, barely seven months after the war had ended.

Her cousin's first reaction was to toss the invitation in the fire, but Teanna was not of the same mind. Though barely past her twentieth birthday, the Nyngary princess was aware of the benefits that increased trade with the West might bring to her people. The fact that Gawl wanted to hold his conference in Barcora also intrigued her, since Mathew Lewin was in Barcora.

It took some effort to change Eric's mind. The prince of Alor Satar was fifteen years her senior and, like most men, the thought of revenge for the death of his father remained foremost in his mind. His older brother, Armand, the recently crowned king of Alor Satar, felt the same way. Teanna was more measured in her responses and public statements than either of them, something she had learned from her mother.

She had thought about Mathew Lewin many times over the last few months. Like her, he wore a rose-gold ring on the third finger of his right hand; and like her, he was the only other person in the world who could use it. It set them apart from others and made them unique—despite their differences. She had tried to tell him that once before, but it was too soon, and she was too impetuous at that time. Patience was another virtue she had lately acquired.

Mathew Lewin had intrigued her from the first moment their minds had made contact. He was modest, intelligent, and largely unaware of his own potential. Teanna was a great admirer of intellect in people. She was aware of how her looks affected most men, and it annoyed her that the suitors who came calling rarely got beyond what was on the surface. Of course, several had potential, but she quickly grew bored with their mundane conversations and clumsy romantic efforts. Her mind was the equal of anyone, and whomever she chose to spend her life with would have to function on her level as opposed to her coming down to his. Teanna had known that since she was a little girl. A princess deserved a partner, not a millstone.

As the ship rode over a swell, Teanna had to put out a hand to steady herself. The wind, now blowing sharply out of the southeast, pushed her long hair away from her shoulders. It was a cold wind, but Teanna didn't mind. She loved the sea, just as Mathew did, and the cold never bothered her the way it did many women. The prospect of crossing an ocean and visiting the Sennian Royal Court was exhilarating. Different people, different sights, even different sounds . . . it was all a whirl in her head.

And then there was Mathew. *What was to be done about Mathew?* she wondered.

If it were up to Eric and Armand, the question would have been settled some time ago by an assassin's knife, or a poisoned glass of wine. But Mathew Lewin was far too dangerous an opponent to approach directly. She learned as much from his battle with her mother and uncle. Despite their combined efforts, both had failed to kill him. It was something Teanna d'Elso had thought a lot about. In the end, she concluded that only a person capable of greatness could have survived such encounters. Such a man just *might* be worthy of her, under the right circumstances. It was difficult to say.

Teanna's musings were interrupted by a footfall, and she turned to see her cousin and his aide, Major Laurent, standing there. The major, a blunt-featured man just above middle height, bowed and discretely moved to the opposite side of the rail to give them privacy.

Eric Duren resembled his father, Karas, in many ways. He was tall, slender, with straight black hair and the same hooded eyes that seemed to run in his family. The languid pose he adopted in most situations masked a keen intellect and a highly perceptive mind. Of her two cousins, he was definitely the more dangerous.

"How can you stand this weather?" he asked, pulling his cloak tighter around his throat.

Teanna lifted her face to the wind and closed her eyes. "What's wrong with this weather, cousin?"

"Apart from being freezing, damp, and windy—nothing. On top of that, this pathetic boat rolls like an old wash basket."

"It's a ship, and it's not freezing. Why don't you go below if it's so unpleasant?" Teanna asked.

"Because it's infinitely more unpleasant down there. At least on deck there's someplace to throw up if I need to. I haven't done that in at least an hour."

"You won't throw up, Eric. The seas are fairly calm. They're not even running at three feet."

Her cousin gave her a sour look. "My stomach will be delighted to learn that," he said. "Did the captain tell you how long this trip will last?"

"Ten days, if the winds hold fair."

Eric Duren rolled his eyes and took a deep breath. "What are your father's feelings about Gawl's proposal?" he asked, changing the subject.

"Father needs more time to study the matter. That's why I'm going."

"More time? He's had two months. What's there to study?"

"That's just the way father is," Teanna said. "Mother was the one who made all the really important decisions. Frankly, he's a little lost without her."

Duren slowly nodded his head, and they continued talking with each other for quite a while about more mundane subjects such as the weather and family matters. Suddenly, her cousin shifted the subject again. "Have you given any thought about what will happen when you meet Mathew Lewin?"

Teanna paused before answering. "I suppose I'll say hello," she replied.

"Really?"

"We're going there under a flag of truce, Eric."

"So?"

Teanna blinked and stared at her cousin. "What do you expect me to do, lob a fireball at him as soon as we get off the ship?"

"Of course not. That would be vulgar. But I do expect a modicum of indignation out of Marsa d'Elso's daughter. He did kill your mother, you know."

"I know," Teanna answered, staring out over the water. "We weren't as close as you and your father were."

"My father wasn't close to anyone, but that's hardly the point. The family honor is at stake."

Teanna folded her arms across her chest and regarded her cousin. A moment later they both started laughing.

"Seriously," Duren said, "What is it you have in mind?"

The Nyngary princess shook her head. "I don't know. I'll guess, listen to what Gawl has to say about the trade agreements and deal with Mathew when the time comes."

One of Duren's eyebrows went up. "Oh?"

She made a dismissive gesture with her hand. "I'm not saying I'll *do* anything, Eric. I just want to see how we'll get on with each other."

" 'Get on'? What does that mean? Are you attracted to this fellow?"

"Maybe a little," Teanna said. She regretted the words as soon as they were out of her mouth.

"I see. We've never talked about it before, but I'm curious. Is that why you convinced Armand to call off the attack at Ardon Field?"

"I don't know . . . possibly," she said. "Mother wasn't able to defeat Mathew, and neither was your father. His strength is really quite unbelievable. I'll just have to see what happens when I get there."

Duren smiled and put his hand on her shoulder. "You're quite young yet, Teanna. There are plenty of eligible men in Nyngary, or Alor Satar for that matter. Why pursue a commoner?"

"I'm not *pursuing* anybody, but I will admit that he intrigues me. And as for being common, Mathew Lewin is the *least* common person in the world. Having royal blood has nothing to do with it. I just can't see spending my life with some brainless fop my father picks out. I need a partner . . . an equal."

"Ah, I think I understand . . ."

Teanna took in a long breath and let it out. "Father's a good man, Eric, but—"

"Quite," Duren said, holding up his hand. "Still . . . Lewin was raised in the West. He's a product of their culture, their values. Those people don't change. They're too intractable. You, should know that."

A silence followed.

"I'm not my mother."

"No . . . No, you're not," Duren replied. "I simply don't want you to make the same mistake she did."

Teanna looked at Eric Duren for several seconds. "I'll see you at dinner this evening," she told him.

The prince watched his cousin disappear down the companionway at the stern of the ship and glanced at his aide. The major tossed away the rope on which he was practicing knot tying and crossed over to him.

"Did it go well, your highness?" he asked.

Duren shrugged. "It wasn't the right time to discuss it with her. She's too preoccupied at the moment. I'm going to have the captain land us at Marigan so we can finish our business, then we can meet her in Barcora for the conference."

"There will be a conference, then?" asked the major.

Duren shrugged. "I suppose. We'll have to see how things play out, as Teanna says."

The major gave him a funny look. "She's a woman, highness, *and* she's your younger cousin. If you order her to destroy Lewin, she'll have to listen."

Eric Duren's smile was rueful. "Will she? It's hard enough telling a woman what to do under the best of circumstances, let alone the most powerful woman in the world, or perhaps you hadn't noticed that, Laurent. No . . . we'll just have to wait and see what develops."

6

Tenley Palace

THE WIDE CORRIDORS OF TENLEY PALACE ECHOED WITH Mathew's footsteps as he passed through the central rotunda. Shortly before Lord Guy had stepped down as regent, the church convinced him to commission an ornate fresco for the inside of the palace's huge dome. The scene depicted several angels and priests standing alongside a man wearing a crown, and although the man didn't look anything like Gawl, the message was clear enough. The church considered ruling Sennia a joint effort. Mathew glanced up at the painting and kept going.

Two guards were stationed on either side of a pair of intricately carved double doors which led to the entrance for the apartments. He waved to them and they both nodded back in acknowledgment. The one on the right, a heavyset, bearded fellow, held one of the doors open for him and said "better hurry" under his breath as Mathew passed.

He bounded up the steps two at a time to a large balcony with hallways on either end of it. He turned left and went toward his room, Rowena had decided to install Lara in an apartment on the other side. Collin's room was two doors down from his, and Father Thomas's was at the far end of the hall next to Jeram Quinn's. On his way, he noticed a ladder propped up against a wall and several buckets of paint under it in preparation for Rowena's redecorating. Earlier that evening, Gawl had forewarned him of the obstacles, complaining that it was the third time Rowena changed the palace.

He found a clean set of clothes laid out on the bed along with a note from Alexander informing him that dinner would be at eight o'clock sharp. The word "sharp" was underlined. Mathew quickly stripped off his things and dropped them in a pile on the floor.

One of the more pleasant surprises he had encountered when they arrived at Tenley Palace was running water and showers. Having grown up in Devondale, where all of the plumbing was outdoors, Mathew was delighted at the prospect of merely turning a faucet and producing a stream of hot water. He decided that whatever home he would eventually live in would have a shower. Lara, on the other hand, was partial to baths. On more than one occasion she reiterated her preference for owning a large copper tub with brass claw feet, like the one she had used in Elberton when they stayed at the Nobody's Inn.

The thought reminded him of Ceta Woodall as he turned on the water and stepped into the shower. He closed his eyes and allowed his mind to drift as the hot water cascaded down his head and back.

Father Thomas and Ceta Woodall had fallen in love with each other during their brief visit there. He smiled at the memory of the articulate Siward Thomas actually fumbling for words at the prospect of telling the lady innkeeper that he was a priest. Father Thomas was rarely at a loss for words. The same thought also made him feel guilty.

Instead of returning to Elberton as he had promised her, Father Thomas remained at the abbey with him for the last seven months. The priest's reasons for not leaving became clear only a short while ago when he told him of the church's concerns—all of which centered on him. Initially, Mathew's reaction was to be angry, but when he thought about it objectively, he understood why they felt the way they did. Much of the gratuitous advice the priests had given him about the corrupting influence of power now made sense in retrospect. Nevertheless, it annoyed him not to have connected the comments earlier. In spite of the fact that he had risked his life to kill Karas Duren, he was still an unknown entity to them. Whatever else they felt, the priests remained helpful by providing information and suggestions for his research. For months Mathew had poured over ancient volumes in their library, studying and learning. The longer he did the more a niggling suspicion began to play at the corners of his mind that the priests were holding something back, but he could never quite pinpoint what it was. A diary he had started reading, penned by one of the Ancients, disappeared from the library one day and could never be found again. It contained the recollections of a scientist that described how the rings had been made. No amount of searching was ever able to locate it. The same thing had happened with other books.

Mathew poked his head out of the shower and glanced at the small gold clock that sat on a shelf across the room. He still had fifteen minutes. He wrapped a towel around his waist and walked to the mirror. A fresh razor and shaving cream were set out for him, thanks again to Alexander, who seemed to think of everything.

The face that regarded him was a pleasant one, neither handsome nor ugly, in his opinion. His brown hair was slightly curly and came down just below his ears, consistent with the fashion of the times. Before he spread the shaving cream, Mathew felt the stubble on his chin. Over the last several months he had toyed with the idea of growing a beard or mustache, on the belief that it would make him look older and more dignified. But Lara's response of *"yuck"* when he raised the possibility, effectively put an end to it.

Mathew applied the shaving cream enjoying the sensuous feel of the razor scraping across his cheek. With five

minutes to go, he donned the gray breeches and black
shirt and headed for the door. The clothes were certainly
more elaborate than anything he would have chosen himself, but given his lack of familiarity with palaces and
their protocol, he deferred to Alexander's judgment.

When he reached the top of the stairs, he paused and
glanced across the balcony to where Lara's apartment
was located, in the hope that they might go down together, but the hallway was deserted. At the bottom of the
steps he turned to his right and proceeded along a corridor to the dining room. Tenley Palace was so large it had
taken him several days to get his bearings when he first
arrived.

By tradition, the king, his guests, and any visitors
staying at the palace all dined together in the informal
dining room. It was about half the size of the larger one
used for State occasions, and located directly across the
hall. Both could be reached directly from the kitchens
on the floor below.

A variety of tapestries and paintings hung along the
walls, depicting various religious and military scenes.
Mathew was only familiar with the scene at the very
end—a painting of the fabled Sennian Wedge, in a full
charge. The enemy stood waiting across a field, lances
ready, and swords drawn. The uniforms the Sennians
wore were archaic-looking and different from the way
Gawl's men now dressed, however the enemy soldiers
looked very much like the Vargothan mercenaries he had
encountered in Tyraine.

It figures, Mathew thought.

The room was already crowded with people by the
time he got there. Some people were standing and some
were talking quietly in small groups. Most of them were
strangers.

Three long tables had been set up in a U-shape at the
head of the room. Brightly colored banners decorated the
walls behind them. The ceiling was beamed with heavy

wood and to Mathew's right was a substantial-looking limestone fireplace with a mantel made of maroon and white marble. Logs smoldered on a grate, gently radiating warmth throughout the room.

A number of heads turned in his direction when he entered and the volume of conversations dropped. After the episode in the garden, he more or less expected that to happen, but he still felt his ears go warm. It took only a second or two to spot Collin, who was already seated at their table. Mathew headed toward him, nodding to Alexander as he passed. The Chief of Staff gave him a thin smile and inclined his head. The conversations returned to normal and the guests began drifting toward their seats. Apparently satisfied that everything was in order, Alexander nodded to a distinguished-looking gentleman dressed in black robes seated near the king.

Bishop Ferdinand Willis stood and raised his hands. Heads bowed in unison as he delivered the benediction. After giving thanks for the bounty they were about to receive, he asked the Lord to grant strength and wisdom to the king and to keep the people of Sennia safe from the corruption of the outside world.

Mathew listened to the sermon thinking the bishop's choice of words were strange. Apparently so did Gawl, who glanced up, raising one of his bushy eyebrows while managing to keep his head bowed along with everyone else. When the benediction was over, the food was brought out.

Steam was still rising from the bowl of soup a serving girl set down in front of Mathew, and the aroma reminded him just how hungry he was.

"Who are all these people?" he asked Collin under his breath.

"I didn't catch all of the names when I was introduced earlier, but that's Rowena's father, Lord Guy, to the left of the bishop. Her brother Jared is next to him. The man on Father Thomas's right is Father Kellner. We met him at the abbey. He's the one doing that archaeological stuff up in Argenton. Quinn, I guess you know already."

"Mm-hmm."

Mathew had met Aldrich Kellner, the church's chief archaeologist, a number of times during their stay at the abbey. He was one of the priests on the committee appointed by Bishop Willis who questioned him about the ring. Kellner was an intense individual with piercing dark eyes and long black hair that hung almost to his shoulders. Where the other priests, most of whom were also scientists, were content to ask questions and take note of his answers, he almost never was. The questions he posed reminded Mathew more of Jeram Quinn's cross-examination. It eventually got to the point where Father Thomas was forced to intercede and suggest to Kellner that he moderate his approach. To his credit, Kellner had apologized at once. Their relationship improved after that.

Mathew's reflections were interrupted by the arrival of the next course, which consisted of a variety of different fruits, a custom he had never gotten used to. In Elgaria and Devondale, where he was from, fruit was eaten at the end of the meal, for dessert. Sennians however, served it either at the beginning of the meal or after the first course. He glanced at Collin, who was cutting an apple in half and seemed sublimely unconcerned with what order the food was brought out in.

The meat course ultimately did appear, which in Mathew's view put them back on a proper schedule. In deference to Rowena and her family, no beer or other spirits were served at dinner.

Matthew was annoyed to find that Lara had been seated at the main table, on Rowena's right. He tried catching her eye several times throughout the meal, but was unable to do so. She appeared to be enjoying her talk with a broad-shouldered fellow next to her.

"Who's that next to Lara?" he asked.

"That's Jared Guy, Rowena's brother," Collin said, through a mouthful of food. "He's here for the Felcarin match tomorrow."

"Really? I thought he'd be taller the way everybody talks about him."

"He's amazing. Blake says he's the best striker to come along in twenty years. I tried to talk to him earlier, but I couldn't get close enough."

"Who's Blake?"

"Rodney Blake, the captain of Barcora's team. You met him. He's part of Gawl's bodyguard here at the palace."

"He's always so serious. I had no idea."

Mathew searched his memory for a moment before recalling Blake's face. He was a slender dark-haired individual with a quiet-spoken manner.

"Rodney's an excellent keeper. It's the same position Gawl played when he was on Barcora's team."

"I didn't know Gawl played Felcarin," said Mathew.

"Yep. That's where he and Father Thomas met."

Mathew put down his fork and looked at his friend. "You're just a fountain of information, aren't you?"

"If you'd take your head out of those books you've been reading, you could pick up a few things every now and then."

Collin glanced down at his goblet and made a face. "God, I hate this tea. When it's warm it tastes like sweat."

"It's cold," Mathew pointed out.

"Cold sweat," Collin said, morosely.

Mathew was about to reply when he heard Lara laugh at a joke that Jared had apparently just made. She chose that moment to look toward Mathew and flashed him a quick smile, then went back to her conversation.

Up to that point in his life, he had never considered himself either a jealous or possessive person. Lara should have been sitting with him. After all, hadn't they just made love only a few hours ago? Famous athlete or not,

he decided, Jared Guy didn't look all that impressive.
And he hoped Lara had more sense than to be awed by a
large pair of shoulders. Mathew sighed and returned to
his dessert . . . which consisted of a salad and cheese.

"What's the matter with you?" Collin asked.

The question interrupted Mathew's rearranging the
food on his plate for the third time.

"Huh? Oh . . . nothing."

When Collin didn't reply, Mathew glanced at his
friend, who raised his eyebrows and waited.

"What?" he asked.

"You've stabbed that cheese enough to kill it by now,"
said Collin.

Mathew put his knife down. "Have you noticed Lara
acting any . . . different recently?"

Before Collin could answer, a high crystal-chimed
laugh from Lara, accompanied by a toss of her hair,
caused them both to look up. She punctuated it by placing a hand on Jared's shoulder.

"A little," Collin replied.

"Wonderful."

"I think it's just a stage she's going through, Mat. Being around all these ladies and lords is enough to put anyone off their stride. I'm telling you, when this business
with Quinn is finished, I'll be glad to get out of this
place."

"I thought you wanted to see the world."

"This isn't my idea of the world," Collin told him.
"We've been at the abbey for the last seven months and
here for three weeks, now. I don't know. It's not so much
the place as the people. I don't mean Gawl . . . he's fine.
It's more the hangers-on and everyone trying to curry favors. Half the people here are just waiting for an opportunity to ask for something. The whole thing rubs me the
wrong way."

"How so?"

"Back home if you didn't like someone or they didn't

like you, it was pretty obvious—no beating around the bush. You know what I mean? But here, they smile in your face then talk about you behind your back. There are a lot of whispered conversations that stop a little too conveniently when a fellow walks in the room. They're welcome to it."

Mathew nodded slowly, digesting Collin's words. Across the room a raucous burst of laughter from Jared killed the reply he was about to make.

After dinner everyone adjourned to the sitting room for a musical recital by a string quartet. Mathew went along too, though only with reluctance. Because he was tone-deaf, such events were always tedious experiences. The only saving grace was that on this particular night a new musician, playing a large set of kettledrums accompanied the string quartet. Though he couldn't distinguish one note from another, Mathew's ear was highly sensitive to rhythm, so he concentrated on the drums and hoped the concert wouldn't last too long. For the sake of appearances, he did his best to look interested in what the musicians were playing, but his mind was very much elsewhere.

He was thinking about the rings again. The last eight his ancestors had created were special, different from all the rest that once existed in the world. Five were accounted for, and now, another was close by. He had no question about it. The feeling he received during the fleeting moment he had contact with the other's mind was unmistakable. What bothered him was why he had never felt anything from the holder before.

He was still mulling over the problem when he realized with a start that the music had ended and people were getting up. Some were leaving. He chose that moment to look up and saw Father Kellner watching him, but as soon as their eyes met, the priest turned away.

Lara was off to one side talking with Rowena. When

she saw Mathew stand, she excused herself and came over to join him.

"Wasn't that a lovely dinner?" she asked.

"Umm."

"I'm sorry we couldn't sit together, but Rowena wanted me to entertain her brother," she explained, taking his arm.

"It looked like you succeeded."

Mathew was sorry as soon as the words were out because they made him sound petty and jealous. But instead of being angry, Lara squeezed his arm. In fact, to his surprise, she made no comment at all, which only reinforced his belief that he would never understand women. He took a deep breath and kept on walking.

They found Collin in the hallway talking with Father Thomas, Gawl, Bishop Willis, and Father Kellner. All of them bowed slightly when they saw Lara approaching and she replied with a curtsy.

"Ah, there you are," Father Thomas said. "Did you enjoy the concert?"

"Oh, yes," Lara replied, "I thought it was wonderful, didn't you?"

Everyone seemed to be in general agreement that it was wonderful, so Mathew decided to simply smile.

"I trust you are all getting along well here at the palace?" Bishop Willis asked.

"Quite well, sir," Mathew replied. "We appreciate his majesty's hospitality."

The bishop was a man of middle height with snow white hair and a reddish complexion. Despite his age, his eyes were sharp and clear. Each of the two occasions they had met before were enough to convince him of the man's intelligence.

"I take it you'll be attending the match tomorrow?" the bishop asked. "One more victory and Barcora wins the championship for the third year in a row."

"Sure, I guess we'll be there," said Mathew.

When he thought about it he realized that he knew
even less about Felcarin than he did about Sennian politics. To make things worse he had no idea they were even
holding a match until Collin had mentioned it earlier. He
knew Felcarin was a popular game in Sennia and that it
was played by two teams of six players each on a large
field. The object was to get a ball about the size of a
small melon past the other team's keeper and score a
goal.

"Excellent," the bishop said. "Then we'll look forward to seeing you all there. We're hoping for a great
day tomorrow."

"Yes, indeed," Father Kellner added.

"If you'll excuse me," said Gawl, "I see Rowena waiting patiently. No point in pressing my luck. Will you and
Father Kellner both be staying the night, Eminence?"

"Yes, your majesty. Your hospitality is greatly appreci-
ated, as always," Bishop Willis said.

"I'll be staying as well, your highness," Father Kellner
told him. "But I'll be returning to Argenton tomorrow after the match."

"Just as well," Gawl said, lowering his voice. "If
Rowena catches you running around here with that red
clay on your boots, she'll kill you."

Father Kellner looked down at his boots and blushed
furiously. "Oh, dear heavens," he said. "I came directly
here from the dig and was in such a hurry, I forgot to
clean them. Please forgive me, your highness."

Gawl winked at him and put a friendly hand on the
priest's shoulders. "You can always tell when someone's
been to Argenton. It's the only place in the country where
the soil is that color."

Father Kellner started to apologize again, but Gawl
winked at him. "We'll keep it our secret."

Both the bishop and Gawl bade everyone goodnight
and took their leave. Father Kellner, cast a nervous glance
in Rowena's direction, then hurried off to find a groom to

clean his boots. This left Mathew, Collin, Lara and Father Thomas alone.

Father Thomas turned to them and said, "If you'll come and get me after breakfast tomorrow, we can all ride to the stadium together," then he said good night. They watched him until he disappeared around the corner.

"I hope this business with Quinn gets resolved soon," Lara said. "Father Thomas thinks we should know in about another two or three weeks."

"It'll be longer than that," Collin replied.

Mathew and Lara looked at him.

"He and I talked earlier," Collin explained.

"What do you mean?" asked Lara.

Collin glanced around the hallway before answering. "Look, Gawl never had any question about the extradition treaty," he said, dropping his voice. "He and Father Thomas cooked the whole thing up. Father Thomas says in about a week the passes will be blocked by snowfall, which will give Delain a few more months to consolidate his position. That way if he dismisses the charges against Mat, there won't be so much screaming."

Lara threw her arms around Collin's neck and hugged him.

"I love that man," she said. "If he didn't already belong to Ceta, I'd marry him myself."

Collin smiled and hugged her back.

Mathew was pleased by the news, though he knew it would only postpone the problem, not resolve it. Nevertheless, hearing it was a relief. All three of them turned and headed back toward the living quarters.

They had just begun climbing the staircase when Lara asked, "How do you gentlemen like your new rooms?"

"Huh?" Collin said. "I haven't changed my room."

Mathew was equally mystified by her comment.

"I meant the color, silly. That's what all the painting's been about these last two weeks. Mine's the most beautiful seafoam green. What color are yours?"

Both Mathew and Collin halted in midstep and looked at each other with blank expressions. Not getting a response from Collin, Lara turned to Mathew and waited while he frowned in concentration.

"Well . . . I'm sure there's a color," he said. "Uh . . . what did you say yours was, Collin?"

Collin shrugged helplessly and spread his hands.

Lara looked from one to the other and took a deep breath.

"Pathetic. You two are *just* pathetic."

They watched her walk the rest of the way up the stairs and turn right once she reached the balcony. She vanished down the hallway a moment later.

When Mathew got to his room, he and Collin both poked their heads in, looked around for a moment, then turned to each other and said "blue" at the same time.

7

Sennia, City of Barcora

THE FOLLOWING AFTERNOON MATHEW, COLLIN, AND Lara rode into the city along the cliff road. Like its Elgarian neighbor Tyraine, Barcora was also a port city and was situated on the eastern corner of the Sennian peninsula. Father Thomas had sent word for them to go on without him; he and Gawl would meet them later. The day turned out to be surprisingly mild for early winter, and with the sparkling sea stretching off to their right and the white sand beaches below, it was a very pleasant ride.

At breakfast that morning Mathew told Collin and Lara about his conversation with Gawl and Father Thomas. He also shared his feeling that another person was out there with one of the rings. Neither of them seemed particularly surprised by the revelation, given the incident with the statues. Collin was all for going out and finding whoever it was, but Lara maintained they had to exercise caution. Since Mathew had absolutely no idea who the person was, or where to begin looking, they were left with little choice in the matter. Lara went on to say that Father Thomas had asked to be notified immediately about anything unusual, no matter how insignificant they thought it might be.

"But see here," Collin said, "I don't understand why someone would want to kill you. We're not at war and you don't have any enemies . . . do you?"

"I didn't think so," Mathew answered.

"Maybe we should start asking around," Collin suggested. "At least that way we'd be doing something rather than sitting around on our butts and waiting for another statue to try and take our heads off."

"Who are we supposed to ask?" said Lara. "We can't very well start going about questioning people about whether they want to kill Mathew. That won't get us anywhere. Father Thomas is right. We have to stay alert and wait."

"Well I don't much care for being a target," Collin grumbled.

"Neither do I," Mathew said. "The problem is I don't understand why anyone would want to kill me."

"You have that effect on people," said Collin. "Maybe it was Quinn. He's got those beady little eyes that are always darting around."

"Quinn?"

"You know . . . kill you now so he doesn't have to worry about taking you back to Elgaria to stand trial."

"Oh, honestly," Lara said, annoyed. "Jeram Quinn didn't try to kill Mathew. Have you seen him wearing a ring?"

"Well . . . no, but that doesn't mean he couldn't have used it, then taken it off," Collin insisted.

Lara gave him a flat look.

"I don't think it was Quinn," Mathew said. "He's pretty direct about things, and we have an agreement with each other."

"What about Teanna d'Elso? She's got plenty of reasons and she's the only other person with a ring," said Collin.

"I already told you, it wasn't Teanna. I would have known if it was her."

"How?" asked Collin.

"When she pulled me off the battlefield and brought me to that strange town, we linked together momentarily. I'd be able to tell if she was involved."

At the mention of linking, Lara raised her eyebrows and looked at him.

"It happens when two people with rings do something together," Mathew told her.

His explanation didn't draw a response from Lara, other than a "hmph," which he heard under her breath. It was enough to convince him the subject needed to be changed, and he was more than grateful when Collin did it for him.

"This should be a fantastic match today," Collin said.

"Right," Mathew agreed.

To his surprise, Collin knew far more about Felcarin than either he or Lara ever imagined. For the rest of the ride his friend kept up a steady stream of conversation about which teams were in what places, and who the players were. Lara listened, or gave the appearance of listening, which was Mathew's impression of what she was doing.

"Of course Blake's a solid keeper," Collin said, "but he's got his work cut out for him today. Sedgwick has got two really solid wingmen. They're not in Jared's class, mind you, but they've already got more than two hundred points between them this season."

"Is that good?" asked Lara.

"Very. If our blockers can hold them off, we clinch the title. But like I said, it's not going to be easy. Sedgwick is no pushover."

Lara glanced at Mathew who shrugged. "I see," she said.

"By the way, that's a lovely horse you're riding," Collin said.

"Huh? Oh, Rodney Blake's letting me try him for a couple of days. He's the most amazing thing . . . the horse, I mean. He can practically turn on a coin. I worked out with the team a few days ago; Blake says I've got all the makings of a great blocker."

Collin leaned forward and patted the stallion on his

neck while Mathew tried to remember what a blocker did in Felcarin.

"Does he have a name?" Mathew asked, giving up.

"Cloud," Collin answered.

"What a pretty name," said Lara. "It's probably because of his coloring, don't you think?"

Collin stuck out his lower lip. "Maybe."

"They breed them for speed and agility," Mathew said, finally recalling a bit of information about the sport.

"Right," Collin said. "This fellow can really fly."

"Are you really going to play Felcarin?" Lara asked.

"I don't know," Collin said. "I've been thinking of giving it a try."

"There's the harbor," Mathew said, as they cleared the crest of the last hill.

Collin let out a low whistle and pulled Cloud up short. Mathew and Lara also stopped and looked out over the broad expanse of the city, with its long finger-shaped harbor shining like a blue diamond against the rugged coastline. Ships with brilliant white sails billowing in the wind glided silently across the water, some laden with goods to trade, others arriving to pick up their cargo.

Lara took a deep breath and remarked that she could almost taste the salt air. Mathew's face had that faraway look that was so familiar. She edged her horse closer to him, reached out, and squeezed his hand. It wasn't necessary to read his mind. She knew that he was thinking about Captain Donal and the crew of the *Wave Dancer*.

Oliver Donal was dead now, hanged . . . no, *murdered* by the Zargothan mercenaries toward the end of the war with Alor Satar. She could almost see the captain's face as it was in the painting that hung in his cabin, standing next to his wife and daughter. Mathew's pained expression was enough to tell her she had guessed correctly. She squeezed his hand again. It was a moment longer before he pulled his attention away from the ships in the harbor and smiled back at her.

Lara knew how much the recent war had affected him, and his tight-lipped silences didn't fool her at all. There had been times over the past few months when he started to talk about what had happened on the cliffs at Tremont, but something always seemed to stop him. Collin, who was also there, told her about the terrible storm that seemed to come out of nowhere, destroying the Nyngary and Cincar navies. They were less than an hour from the Elgarian coast. What Mathew did that day resulted in the deaths of over eleven thousand of the enemy along with Karas Duren's sister, Marsa d'Elso.

She knew that he wanted to talk about it, needed to talk about it, but was never quite able to manage. One night several months earlier when they were alone in her room, he had surprised her by asking if she thought Karas Duren was a monster.

"Yes," she had replied.

"Why?"

The question had come out of nowhere, but the answer was as plain as day. "Because he hated everybody and everything. He killed for the love of killing—thousands of people, Mathew, innocent people."

"So have I."

"Mathew."

"So have I," he repeated quietly, staring out the window.

"There's a difference, my love"—she'd put her arms around his waist and pressed herself against his back—"they were soldiers and we were at war. They were coming to destroy our country. If you hadn't stopped them, that's exactly what would have happened."

When Mathew opened his mouth to say something, Lara had cut him off before he could continue.

"If you're thinking about the mercenaries in the pass . . . I was there, remember? They were nothing but animals. They killed women and little children without a second thought. And for what? *Money.* That's all it was to them. Sometimes I still have nightmares about the bodies . . . that horrible endless line of people hanging along the cliffs. If I could have used your ring, I would have done exactly the same thing."

Mathew hadn't replied. He looked down at the ring of rose gold suspended on the leather cord around his neck and twirled it between his thumb and forefinger, then he kissed her goodnight and left. The exchange that night was as close as she had gotten to hearing him open up on the subject.

Shortly after they had arrived at the abbey, Mathew stopped wearing his ring. At first his decision had puzzled her. At the time she thought it was because he was self-conscious being the center of attention everywhere they went; questions and more questions seemed to follow him. He answered them on a daily basis, and it was only in the last few months that she came to realize that he'd taken the ring off because he was frightened. She'd thought about that a great deal. Mathew was afraid, so afraid of becoming Karas Duren, that he put the ring around his neck.

Oh, Mathew. As if you ever could. Lara sighed with a sideways glance at Mathew. It was a shock when she recently noticed he was wearing it again.

Soon they entered Barcora and stopped a passerby to ask where the Felcarin match was being held.

"It's in the stadium, about a fifteen minute walk from here," the man said. "Take this road until you get to a large church with two spires, then turn left and follow the crowds. You can't miss it. There's a stable where you can put up your horses, on the same street."

They thanked him and continued down the road past shops selling every sort of item from textiles to jewelry. Barcora was one of the thriving centers of commerce in the western world. Its streets, though paved with cobblestone and brick, were nearly as wide as the ones they had seen in Tyraine. Every few blocks they spotted a colorful banner on the side of a building or above a storefront window supporting one of the teams that would be playing that day. They followed the man's directions, located the stable, and negotiated a price to board their horses.

"A half crown!" Lara exclaimed. "That's robbery."

The stableman shrugged and said, "It's game day, mistress. You won't find a cheaper price for a mile around, except maybe down by the docks, and that would be quite a walk. Jenkins is charging the same thing as . . ."

The man's voice suddenly trailed off as he noticed Mathew standing there.

"Say, aren't you—"

"No," Mathew said quickly, sliding his hand behind his back. "I get that all the time."

The man looked closely at him for a moment and shook his head. "Sorry, young fella. Didn't mean to stare. Anyway, I'll take the lot for nine coppers. It's the best I can do."

"That'll be fine," Collin said, paying the man. "We'll see you after the game."

When they got outside, Mathew didn't offer any explanation, Lara turned to Mathew and as she thought he would. She already had a pretty good idea about why the man had reacted the way he did.

"We were in a tavern and people kept coming over wanting to shake Mat's hand," Collin explained. "We found out later that someone had put up a bunch of posters with his face on them. They even have a newspaper here that told about what happened at Ardon Field."

"I see," said Lara. She glanced at Mathew, who nodded in confirmation.

He had never quite gotten used to people pointing and whispering when he passed. A private person by nature, the notoriety made him uncomfortable, so he dealt with the situation by avoiding the city whenever possible.

There were times when he got the distinct impression people were looking at him as if they expected him to grow another head. He understood their curiosity and handled things the best way he could. It was particularly hard to accept that some people were actually afraid of him. Initially, he refused to acknowledge what was happening. Eventually the hurt turned to anger, then a grudging acceptance of the fact. It was a difficult thing for anyone to deal with, let alone a young man of nineteen years.

"That must be the church," Collin said, pointing to a large grayish building on their right at the end of the street.

"My goodness," said Lara, craning her neck to look up at a pair of elaborately carved spires. The church also had an enormous stained-glass window.

"I'll bet Gawl would like those," Collin said, pointing to a series of statues along the roof. "I don't think I've ever seen a church this big, except for the one at the abbey. It's huge."

Lara stared at the church for a minute, then sniffed and said, "I like our church in Devondale better. It's cozier."

Mathew was inclined to agree. As they walked toward the stadium and he saw a banner hanging across the church's door—GOD BLESS THE LIONS OF BARCORA.

A throng of people were all heading in the same direction just as the man had said, and it seemed a large number of them had chosen to wear purple and white that day. Mathew commented on this to Collin.

"Purple and white are the Lions' colors, Mat," Collin explained.

"Oh," Mathew replied, a little embarrassed at his lack of knowledge.

The closer they got to the stadium the more trouble they had making their way through the crowd, which seemed to have come to a complete halt. Outside the main entrance, a group of young women were clustered around a ruggedly handsome young man in his late twenties. He was signing autographs on sheets of paper, books, and even articles of clothing. With each autograph he smiled charmingly at the fortunate girl and gave her a kiss, which produced a series of giggles and blushes from the others; however none of them made any move to leave.

The moment Jared Guy caught sight of Lara, he excused himself and pushed his way over to her.

"Lara," he said, taking her hands, "I'm glad you made it. I was afraid you weren't going to come."

Jared was about to say something else when a discreet clearing of the throat by Collin caught his attention.

"Oh, hullo, Collin. Good of you to come, too. Say, you must be Mat Lewin. I've heard a lot about you."

Mathew smiled and shook Jared's hand. "Not as much as I've heard about you over the last hour," he replied, giving Collin a good-natured nudge in the ribs.

"I didn't know you were a fan of Felcarin. We should have a great match today," Jared said.

"Actually, this is my first game to. Collin's been telling us all about it . . . Lara and me, I mean."

"It turns out Collin's a pretty handy fellow," Jared told them. "He's been working out with our team. I think Blake's going to ask him to try out."

"Really?" Collin said, his eyes going wide.

"That's what I heard, but don't let on I said anything, will you? Blake would have my head on a plate. Where are you all sitting?"

"I don't know," Collin replied, frowning at his tickets. "This is my first time at the stadium. I got the tickets from Blake."

"Let's have a look."

Collin handed him the tickets. "Uh-oh," Jared said.

"What is it?" asked Lara.

"He put you on the Parbee side. That's all the way across the field."

"The what side?" Mathew asked.

"Parbees," Jared repeated, lowering his voice. "Wrong kind of crowd, if you know what I mean. Listen, I have an idea . . . just go through that gate there on the right. I'll fix it with the guard. You can sit behind our team—they're the best seats in the house," he added, winking at Lara. "By the way, are you coming to the party afterward?"

"I don't know anything about a party," she said.

"Oh, you have to come . . . all of you. It'll be at the King's Arms on Norwich Street. Anyone can tell you how to get there. Promise me you'll come," Jared said, taking her hands again.

"I suppose, if we wouldn't be imposing," Lara said.

"Not a chance." Jared smiled. "I've got to run now, so wish me luck. See you all later."

Mathew watched Jared trot away and disappear through the gate he had just pointed to. When he was out of sight, he turned to Collin and asked, "Parbees?"

Collin shrugged. "No idea."

Lara looked equally puzzled and shook her head.

"C'mon," said Collin, "We can ask Father Thomas about it later."

Mathew was in a bad mood by the time they got to the gate. He was angry with Jared for flirting with Lara and annoyed with her for letting him do it. For a few seconds he thought about saying something, but decided it would just make him sound petty. If Collin had noticed anything he didn't mention it. He was already talking excitedly about Felcarin again.

A woman at the gate took the tickets from Collin and directed them to a red-haired boy who was standing off to the side waiting for them, courtesy of Jared. The boy introduced himself as Jordan and said he would take them to their seats. This was fine with Mathew because he hadn't the slightest idea where to go and he was positive

Collin didn't either. Lara appeared to be unfazed by all the hustle and bustle, taking everything in stride.

Jordan led them down a wide corridor where people were buying food and drinks at a variety of different stands, many of which were also selling souvenirs. Mathew had never seen anything like it before. It looked more like a small marketplace than a stadium; the entire population of Devondale could easily have fit inside the building. As they walked along he noticed that Jordan kept glancing at him. He tried asking the boy a few questions about himself, but he only got one- or two-word answers in reply, so he gave up.

When they were finally seated, Jordan executed a little bow and fumbled around in his jacket for a moment. He fished out a note and handed it to Lara. She read it, smiled to herself, and put it in the pocket of her dress, which only succeeded in irritating Mathew further, since it was obvious that Jared had sent it. Jordan said goodbye to everyone and took his leave.

"Have you ever seen anything like this?" Collin asked.

Mathew and Lara could only shake their heads.

The stadium was the largest building Mathew had ever been in. He remembered his father telling him about the one in Anderon, but he had never gotten to see it on any of their trips. Gravenhage, the town just north of his home in Devondale, also had a stadium, but it was nothing compared to the one they were in.

Several rows away on their right, a roped-off area contained an odd cone-shaped contraption about six feet in length. It was bolted to the stadium floor by a single metal pole and had a curved tube running in one side of it and out the other.

"What in the world is that thing?" Lara asked.

"That's what the announcer uses to tell the crowd what's happening," Collin explained. "I don't remember what they call it, but there are eight of them all around the stands. That tube in the middle connects them together.

All the announcer has to do is to speak into the small end and his voice booms out all over the place—at least that's what Blake told me."

"I don't see why anyone needs an announcer to tell them what's happening when they could see it for themselves," Lara said.

"It makes the match more exciting . . . you'll see."

Mathew followed the tube around with his eyes and saw that the other eight contraptions were spaced equally throughout the stadium. *What'll they dream up next?*

They didn't have long to wait. Collin was in the process of explaining to Lara what she should look for during the game when a roar went up from the crowd. At the other end of the stadium, the teams were riding out onto the field. The first to emerge were the Sedgwick Hawks, dressed in scarlet and gray. A moment later Barcora's home team appeared and the noise grew deafening. The Lions were dressed in purple with white scarves.

"Oh, look, there's Jared," Lara said, waving.

"Umm," Mathew replied.

While the applause was still rolling around the stadium, Mathew noticed a heavy-looking man with a considerable paunch hurrying up the stairs. He was sweating profusely. When the man reached the announcer's box, he climbed over the rope, sat down, and wiped his face with a large handkerchief.

"'Bout time, Riddley," a man in a seat next to them called out.

Riddley waved back without turning around, then stood behind the large cone and began speaking into it.

"Good morning, ladies and gentlemen, and welcome to the final match of the season," his voice echoed throughout the stands. "It's a fine clear winter day here in Barcora, and it looks like we have a wonderful morning in store for us. The teams are already on the field so we should begin in about five minutes.

"If you will direct your attention to the scoreboards located on either end of the stadium you can see that Sedgwick is in first place with Barcora only twenty points behind. That means this match will determine our overall national champion.

"Let us all rise and join in the singing of our national anthem."

Mathew, Collin and Lara got up along with what looked like nearly thirty thousand other people. Down on the field a noise started, or at least it seemed that way to Mathew, who leaned forward to see what it was. It took a second for him to realize that what he was hearing was the sound of a band playing. Since he had no idea of the words to the Sennian national anthem, he folded his hands in front of him, and stood there quietly. As soon as the music finished the applause began all over again and people resumed their seats.

"Do you see those two large fellows at the end there?" Collin said to Lara.

"The ones carrying those pole things?"

"They're called batrocs. Those are Sedgwick's blockers, Kern and Mallory. Their job is to stop our wingmen from scoring. Jared's one, and Fred Lindstrom is the other. Rodney Blake's in goal for us."

"I see," said Lara. "Why are the sticks shaped that way?"

Mathew leaned a little closer to hear the explanation. The batrocs looked like Collin's quarterstaff, except they had a small pillowlike thing on one end and a curved basket on the other.

"Once a wingman gets the ball, the blockers can use the round end to knock it out of their hands. If the wingman's on a horse at the time, a blocker can even try to unseat him."

"But can't someone get hurt that way?"

"Sometimes," said Collin. "It's mostly bloody noses and loose teeth—that sort of thing. The referee, that's the fellow in the black shirt, is there to stop any real harm from being done."

"Hmm," Lara said, sitting back in her seat. Her tone was mixed with a good deal of skepticism.

Judging from the size of the blockers on Sedgwick's team and the poles they were carrying, Mathew wasn't quite as certain as Collin that the damage would be minor.

"All right, ladies and gentlemen, the teams are moving into position," the announcer said. "Our referee today will be Baron Victor Tolar, former captain of the Sennian National Team, and one of the all-time greats ever to play the game. Welcome back, Baron."

A lithe man in his early forties with salt and pepper hair and a crooked nose walked out onto the middle of the field and waved to the spectators, who clapped enthusiastically. When the applause began to die down, he signaled for both captains to approach. Mathew recognized one of them as Rodney Blake. His counterpart on the Sedgwick team was considerably shorter, and wore an intense expression on his face.

"That's Findlay, Sedgwick's keeper," said Collin. "He's supposed to be amazing."

Down on the field Blake and Findlay shook hands, then returned to their goals. Mathew quickly made a mental note that in addition to the six players on the field each team had another six men in reserve on the sidelines. Jared and Fred Lindstrom were in the middle positioned behind their two forwards, Jack Tate and Sandy Johnson.

The referee mounted his horse and rode to the sideline, then stood up in his stirrups and heaved the ball onto the field. A loud blast of his whistle started the game. Tate and Johnson dug their heels into their horses' flanks and charged for it. So did Sedgwick's forwards. Tate got there first, leaned down in his saddle, swept the ball up, then passed it backward to his teammate, who in turn tossed it to Fred Lindstrom behind him. Cheers and clapping broke out all over the stands as Lindstrom and Jared started up the field.

What happened next surprised Mathew.

Both of Sedgwick's forwards immediately converged on Lindstrom before he could get his pass away, but instead of trying to dislodge the ball from his hands, one of the forwards lowered his pole and hit the Barcoran player in the middle of the chest. The blow was so hard it dislodged the ball and nearly did the same for Lindstrom, who reeled in his saddle.

A gasp went up from the crowd as Lindstrom fought to right himself. Lara put her hand to her mouth in shock. Lindstrom succeeded in steadying himself, and gave chase. But he was too late.

Instead of passing the ball back to his wingmen, the Sedgwick player charged down the sidelines and cut sharply across the field toward the goal.

"Pick him up . . . pick him up!" Mathew heard Rodney Blake yelling.

Barcora's blockers tore after the forward, trying to intercept him. At twenty-five yards from the goal, he took his shot. By what miracle, Mathew would never know. Rodney Blake launched himself off his horse at the last possible moment and managed to deflect the ball, sending it wide of the goal. He hit the ground and rolled to his right

A tremendous cheer went up from the Barcoran fans.

"The first to reach five goals wins," Collin yelled over the noise to Lara, who was on her feet along with everyone else.

For the next thirty minutes the score shifted back and forth between the two teams. Eventually it stood at three to two in favor of Sedgwick when the mid-time break was called. The action was so furious and exciting, Mathew found himself enjoying it as much as anyone there. The speed and pace of the game were astonishing to him. It was easy to understand why Collin was so excited about the sport. He'd had a reckless streak in him ever since they were children.

When play resumed, Lindstrom took a pass from one of Barcora's forwards and set off down the field. This time the Sedgwick defenders, rather than going after him, fell back, keeping themselves between him and the goal. Jared shadowed his teammate all the way downfield. After they crossed the midfield line, Lindstrom angled his horse sharply to the right, then cut back at a full gallop to the left again. The Sedgwick players were unable to react in time. With a clear field, Lindstrom scored to the wide corner of the goal and evened the match.

It took a full two minutes before the audience calmed down enough for play to begin again. Not three minutes later, Barcora's other forward, Sandy Johnson, intercepted a poorly thrown pass and managed to score an easy goal.

With Barcora in the lead for the first time in the match, Sedgwick's captain asked for a time-out to huddle with his team. The Bacora players also dismounted and went to Blake. He dropped down on one knee and spoke to them rapidly, sketching a play on the ground. Across the field his counterpart was doing the same thing.

When the rest period expired, the referee blew his whistle and called for the teams at midfield. He was splattered with mud and looked almost as tired as some of the players.

Seconds after the game resumed, Sedgwick scored once again and the match stood even for the third time.

"We only have about three minutes left," said Collin. "If we're going to try the play we worked on in practice, we'll use Fred Lindstrom as a decoy and try and get the ball to Jared. It'll be our last chance."

"At least it will be a tie," said Lara.

"A tie won't do us any good," Collin answered, looking at the scoreboard. "If we tie, the championship will go to Sedgwick. We need to beat them outright."

Sedgwick's strategy soon became obvious, or at least it seemed so to Mathew, who was yelling as loudly as anyone in the stands by then. An errant pass by the Barcoran players turned possession of the ball over to the opposing team, but rather than attack, they contented themselves to merely pass it back and forth between their blockers and their wingmen in an effort to run out the clock. The tactic was effective, though definitely not popular with the crowd, who began to boo loudly.

"Well, ladies and gentlemen, it looks like Barcora's in trouble," said the announcer. "There's less than two minutes remaining and if they don't do something soon, they'll loose the championship on points."

"Put it in your hat Riddley," a man called out, several rows behind him.

The announcer kept talking, unfazed by the comment.

"It looks like Barcora's forwards may be making a move to try and force a turnover. Yes . . . that's exactly what they're doing!"

Mathew looked down at the field and saw that Sandy Johnson and Fred Lindstrom were closing rapidly on one of the Sedgwick forwards. Jared was trailing right behind them along with his teammate, Jack Tate. On the opposite side of the field, Barcora's blockers suddenly became attackers and charged Sedgwick's other forward.

"Amazing," the announcer shouted, "Blake's out of the goal. We have an all out assault here by Barcora. It's definitely a risky move. If Sedgwick can get off a shot, there won't be anyone left to defend."

With Johnson and Lindstrom almost on top of him, Sedgwick's forward tried to get off a desperation pass to his teammate, but he never got the chance. Lindstrom batted the ball out of the air and swept it back to Jared. Both of them immediately turned their horses and galloped up field past their opponents, making a dash straight for the goal. Sedgwick's blockers reacted at once. At thirty yards from the goal, Lindstrom went down when his horse collided with Sedgwick's middle blocker. The crowd gasped as Jared pulled up sharply on his reins, narrowly avoiding a collision.

Though Jared was a big man, his opponent literally dwarfed him. To make matters worse, he was directly between Jared and the goal and there was no way to get around him without going out of bounds. Everyone in the stands was on their feet, screaming at the top of their lungs. Suddenly the blocker swung his batroc at Jared's head rather than the ball. Jared pulled away, wincing in pain as it grazed the side of his check.

"Foul! That's a foul!" cried one of the men in the stands.

"What's the matter with you, Baron? Can't you see?" another man called out to the referee.

The blocker swung again, only this time Jared blocked it to the side and hooked the basket of his batroc around the larger man's neck, and pulling sharply to unhorse him. Mathew could almost hear the crack of bone when he hit the ground.

Jared wheeled his horse around and drove for the goal. The referee, Rodney Blake, and the players on both teams raced after him with the Barcorans doing their best to buy him enough time for his final shot. There were less than twenty seconds remaining. In front of the goal, there was a white semicircle painted on the ground that Jared couldn't pass without being disqualified. There, Sedgwick's keeper waited for him.

Out of the corner of his vision Mathew saw the referee raise the whistle to his lips. In another second the game would be over. When he reached the center of the circle, Jared pulled back sharply on his reins and the keeper went with him, trying to cut off any angle he might have for a shot. At the last possible moment, Jared stood upright in his stirrups and fired for the corner. Findlay stretched forward, straining with all his might to stop the ball that sailed past his fingers by inches and into the goal as the whistle blew.

"Barcora scores!" the announcer screamed.

Jared threw his arms into the air and was immediately mobbed by his teammates. Pandemonium broke out everywhere as people in the stands poured onto the field.

Mathew never saw if the referee actually awarded the final goal, because he and Lara and Collin were yelling and hugging each other along with the rest of the crowd.

"That was bloody brilliant," Collin shouted over the noise.

"Just amazing," Mathew agreed.

Lara was so excited she even hugged a total stranger next to her. Then she recovered her composure, took a moment to straighten her hair, and they all walked arm in arm down the stairs and out into the street.

8

Barcora, After the Match

BY THE TIME THEY MADE THEIR WAY THROUGH THE crowds and found the King's Arms, the victory celebration was already underway. People were singing and holding tankards of ale as they congregated in the street to toast one another. Once inside, the tavern looked full to the point of overflowing. They found a large, pleasant room with a fire slowly burning in a stone fireplace. All the furniture was made of polished dark wood, including the tables, booths and a long bar that ran the length of the establishment. No sooner had they entered than Father Kellner, smiling from ear to ear, came up to say hello.

"So glad you could come," he said, shaking each of their hands in turn. "Marvelous match . . . simply marvelous. I'm in the corner there with the bishop and a few friends, if you'd care to join us."

"Thank you, Father," Lara replied. "We'll try to stop by. We just came by to congratulate Jared and his teammates."

"Of course, my dear, of course. He's over there," the priest pointed. "By the way, is Siward Thomas coming? I missed him at the match today."

"We were supposed to meet him, but I guess he and Gawl were delayed," Collin told him.

"Certainly," said Father Kellner. "Do try to come by and say hello. I know there are a couple of people who'd like to meet you as well."

The last part of his comments were addressed to Mathew, who nodded in reply. The priest looked at him for a moment and returned to his table. Bishop Willis caught his eye, waved, and Mathew waved back. So did Collin and Lara.

"Do you know anybody here?" Mathew asked Collin.

"A couple of people," he replied, looking around the room. "I don't see Blake anywhere, but there's Jack Tate and Sandy Johnson—"

"Lara . . . hey, Lara," a voice called out.

Mathew looked up and saw Jared Guy making his way across the room to them. *Marvelous.*

"Great of you to come," Jared said, taking Lara's hand. "Oh, good to see you too, Lewin. You too, Collin. Did you enjoy yourselves?"

Mathew resisted the temptation to say, *"up until now."* Instead, what came out was, "It was wonderful—congratulations."

"Thanks. Oh, listen, Collin. Ned Castor is getting married and leaving the team this summer. I spoke to Rodney, and he says that if you're still around when the season starts again, there'll be a spot for you."

"No kidding?" said Collin.

"Nope," said Jared, clapping him on the shoulder. "We could use a good man like you. Rodney had to go back to the palace, but he'll probably talk to you about it tomorrow."

"Great," said Collin.

"It was so exciting," said Lara. "I've never seen anything like it. You were just brilliant."

"Well . . . a little lucky too," Jared replied, waving away the compliment. "C'mon, I want to introduce you to some of my friends."

Jared reached out to take Lara's hand again, but this time she deftly avoided it and slipped her arm through Mathew's.

A brief look that might have been annoyance flashed

across Jared's face, but was gone so quickly, Mathew wasn't certain if it was actually there.

"I meant all of you," Jared said, putting an arm around Mathew's shoulders. "Sorry if I wasn't clear. You're a bigger celebrity than I am. My friends have been dying to meet you."

"Oh, sure," Mathew replied.

When they got to the table, Jared's teammates pulled three more chairs up and made room for them, while he did the introductions. Fred Lindstrom joined them a few minutes later, his arm in a sling. It turned out that he had suffered a fractured collarbone during the game.

Mathew liked Johnson, Tate, and Lindstrom right away and even found himself warming up to Jared as the afternoon wore on. For the next half-hour the talk centered around the match, with Sandy Tate recounting some of the more spectacular moments for them. There seemed to be a general consensus that Rodney Blake deserved the majority of credit for their victory due to his planning and strategy. Twice during the conversation, Lara moved a little closer to Mathew and farther from where Jared was seated. Eventually she slipped her arm around his shoulders. The second time she moved, Mathew glanced at her, but her face gave no indication that anything was wrong.

"I understand that you're coming out for the team next season," Sandy Johnson said to Collin.

Collin shrugged. "It's not definite yet. It all depends on if we're still here. It might be nice to give it a try, though."

"You ought to do it," Lindstrom urged. "I watched you in practice. If you handle a batroc half as well as you do your quarterstaff, I wouldn't want to get into a confrontation with you on the field."

Collin chuckled and shook his head.

"How about you, Mat?" Jack Tate asked. "Any interest in Felcarin?"

"It's a great game," Mathew said. "I have to be honest,

that was the first match I've ever watched. Collin's been telling me how safe the sport is, but after seeing what they did to Fred, I think I'll stick with cards. He's much tougher than I am."

"Very true," Collin agreed.

"But see here, Mat, couldn't you just make everyone disappear if you wanted to?" Sandy Johnson asked.

A silence immediately fell over the table and Lindstrom elbowed his teammate in the ribs. Johnson gave him a sour look and turned back to Mathew.

"Look, there's no use going on about the whole thing. We've all been dying to ask you about it, but everyone's afraid you'd turn them into a toad or something."

Mathew started laughing in spite of himself. "It doesn't quite work like that."

"Well, what's the story, then?" Johnson persisted. "We've heard you blew old Duren up and half of the countryside with him."

"*And* brought a mountain down on the Zargothans—that's what my brother said. He was at Ardon Field," Lindstrom added.

"Wasn't there also something about him sinking the Cincar and Nyngary fleets?" Jared asked.

Mathew felt his chest tighten. The stories always seemed to grow in the retelling, and the memories were anything but pleasant, so far as he was concerned. Looking around at the eager faces, he could see that there was little choice in the matter. He glanced at Lara, who nodded her head slightly.

"I guess there's some truth in the things you heard," he said, "but a lot of it is exaggeration, too. It's as simple as that. To begin with, I can't fly around the room or shoot fire out of my arse, and none of it has anything to do with magic."

Mathew's comments produced general laughter.

"But what about all that stuff about explosions and mountains falling?" Lindstrom asked. "Tom—that's my brother—said there was a crater big enough to put the stadium into, and then some."

Mathew nodded. "He was right. There was an explosion, so that part is true. Duren sent a fireball at Prince Delain and his people; Lara was there too. I turned it back on him. That's how it happened."

"I don't understand," Jared said. "If it's not magic, how could you do something like that?"

"It's hard to explain, because I don't understand how it all works myself—at least not fully. What it comes down to is my ring lets me do certain things with my mind."

At the mention of the ring, Jack Tate snapped his fingers.

"That's it," he said to Lindstrom. "That's was what your brother was talking about. Can we see it, Mat?"

Mathew paused and glanced around the table. Collin responded by giving him one of those *so what?* looks. After a few seconds he took a deep breath and held his hand out.

"Is that it?" Johnson asked.

"Um-hmm."

"Strange color," said Jared.

"Can I touch it?" Fred Lindstrom asked.

"Sure," Mathew said, pulling the ring off his finger.

He handed it to Lindstrom who hefted it in the palm of his hand for a second or two. "It's heavier than it looks," he commented.

"That's the first thing my friend Akin Gibb said when he felt it," Mathew told him.

"So it lets you do things with your mind. Maybe you could fix Fred's shoulder," Sandy Johnson suggested.

Lindstrom promptly handed the ring back to Mathew and pushed his chair a little farther away. "Uh . . . no thanks. I'll let it heal normally, if you don't mind."

"It doesn't really work like that," Mathew explained.

"Fine with me," said Lindstrom. "You might want to use it to fix Johnson's nose."

"What's wrong with my nose?" Johnson asked, frowning.

"Nothing," Lara replied. "It's a very nice nose. It gives you character."

"Sandy doesn't need any more character," Jack Tate put in.

The conversation went on like that for quite a while, and Mathew found, to his surprise, that he was able to talk about the ring and what happened freely. He told them about how the Ancients had created it and how they linked it to the crystals, which amplified its power. Inevitably, someone raised the question of how he came to possess it. He told them about the fencing tournament in Devondale and Giles Naismith's death.

"So you're the only person in the world with the ring," Sandy Johnson said, shaking his head. "Amazing."

"Not really," Mathew replied. "Teanna d'Elso also has one . . . and there may be others around."

"Teanna d'Elso? Isn't she the Nyngary princess?" Jared asked.

"Right."

The talk eventually turned to other topics. Mathew learned that both Sandy Johnson and Fred Lindstom were in the army. Lindstrom was part of the palace regiment and Johnson had transferred from the southern army at Rodney Blake's request and was serving in Gawl's body-guard with him.

Eventually, Mathew excused himself and made his way to the bathroom at the back of the tavern. Two tankards of ale and an hour of drinking more or less made the trip a necessity. It occurred to him again that neither Father Thomas nor Gawl had shown up for the match, which was puzzling. He was still wondering about it when he felt someone take hold of his arm. Mathew turned to see two men standing there.

"You're him, ain't ya?" one of the men asked. He was the larger of the two.

"Excuse me?" Mathew said, disengaging his arm.

"You're him . . . Lewin, right?"

The smell of liquor reached Mathew. "I'm Mat Lewin. Have we met?"

"Told you he was," the man said, hitting his companion on the chest with the back of his hand. "We spotted you up in the stands."

"Oh, I see," said Mathew.

"You're the one that killed Duren, right?" the shorter one asked.

The last thing Mathew wanted at that moment was to retell the same story he'd just gone through. "I'm sorry. I'm with some friends just now. I've really got to be going."

His statement seemed to pass completely over their heads.

"I'm Jake Nealy," the big man said, holding out his hand. "And this is Duncan Carney."

Mathew shook hands, but had to lean backward to avoid their breath.

"Pleased to meet you both," he said, "but if you'll excuse me my friends—"

"Say . . . could you do us a little favor, Mat?" asked Nealy.

"A favor?"

"Duncan, here, he's a little down on his luck and we was wonderin' if you could like . . . uh, turn his dagger into gold."

"What?"

"You know, just blink or do whatever and turn the dagger gold."

Duncan pulled the dagger from his belt and held it out in both hands for Mathew to see.

"I'm sorry," Mathew said. "I don't think that's something I could do, besides—"

"Wouldn't take you a second," Jake persisted.

Duncan nodded in agreement and offered the dagger to Mathew again.

"I'm sorry. I really don't think I—"

"C'mon," said Jake, taking hold of Mathew's arm. "Wouldn't cost you nuthin' and you'd be helpin out a friend like."

"What goes on here?" a voice behind Mathew asked.

Mathew turned to see Father Kellner standing there.

"Oh, hello, Father," said Jake, dropping his eyes. "We was just asking young Mat here to do us a little favor."

"I think it would be best if you didn't bother him further and returned to your seats," the priest said.

"But Father . . ." groaned Duncan.

"Mathew and his friends are guests in our country, and the church would not be pleased if you offended him. Now off with you both."

Jake shrugged and mumbled something under his breath that Mathew didn't quite catch, then he and Duncan returned to their table. When they were gone, Father Kellner looked at Mathew and said, "I'm sorry about that, my son. It appears they've had a little too much to drink."

"It wasn't a problem, but thank you, Father. They didn't mean any harm."

"I'm sure they didn't." The priest smiled. "Perhaps a little too much celebration, I suspect. Barcorans tend to be good people on the whole. What was it they were asking of you?"

"They wanted me to change a dagger into gold."

Father Kellner turned down the corners of his mouth elaborately. "How creative. I must remember that in the future if I run short of funds. How have you been getting on, my son?"

"Well enough, Father."

"No injuries, I see."

"Oh . . . I suppose you heard about what happened the other day?"

"Yes, his Eminence told me. It's a blessing that no one was hurt. Do you have any idea why you were attacked?"

"Honestly, I don't," Mathew said. "It has something to

do with the rings. I'm positive about that. I've racked my brain and can't come up a thing."

"How strange," said the priest, shaking his head. "I'm sure the answer will reveal itself in time, but you must take care and remain vigilant. Do you think a trip to The Ruins would be useful to you? We are recovering some of the most amazing relics there and they might provide a clue if your ring is connected to what happened, as you say."

"It's an idea," Mathew agreed. "I'll talk to Collin about it."

"Wonderful. If you have the need to counsel, I am always available, my boy."

"Thank you, Father. That's very kind."

They chatted about the rings for a minute or two longer before the priest excused himself, cautioning Mathew once again to remain alert for any signs of trouble.

When he returned to the table Lara got up and said she was ready to leave. Collin got up as well. Mathew said his goodbyes to everyone and set off with them to find their horses.

They located the stable without any problem, thanks in large part to Lara having the clearest head of the three. Collin and Mathew, who had more to drink than she did, were both slightly tipsy but managed well enough, except Mathew did experience some difficulty negotiating the cobblestones. If Lara hadn't been holding his arm, he might have fallen. For some reason his last misstep seemed extremely funny to him. Lara drew a long-suffering breath and held on to him a little tighter. The next time it happened, he gave her an embarrassed smile, and acknowledged to himself that she had always been able to handle liquor better than he could. Collin's snickering earned him a sour look. Mathew did derive a small measure of satisfaction, however, when it took Collin three tries to mount his horse.

* * *

"That road will take you down to the harbor," Lara said wearily, stopping Mathew and Collin from taking the wrong turn at the edge of town.

"I knew that," Collin replied. "I just wanted to see if you were paying attention."

"I should let you both fall in. It might sober you up."

"We're sober," Mathew said, but an ill-timed hiccup spoiled the effect.

Lara rolled her eyes up and flicked the reins of her horse. "Just follow me boys."

A groom met them when they rode through the palace gates. By that time Mathew's head was a great deal clearer, even though it had started pounding a bit.

"Hey, there's Father Thomas," said Collin.

The priest saw them and came over to say hello.

"What happened to you today?" Collin asked.

"I'm sorry, my son. I was about to leave when I got a note that Paul Teller wanted me to come out to the abbey tomorrow. Then Gawl got delayed because Baron Chambertin and two of his sons decided to ride in and discuss their concerns over his new trade policy. One thing led to another. How was the match?"

"Unbelievable," Collin said. "Sorry you missed it."

"Who won?"

"Barcora did. Jared scored a last second goal."

"Ah," Father Thomas sighed, "that will make Gawl happy. He's been in a foul mood since the meeting. From the look on Chambertin's face when he left, I suspect neither of them found the discussions particularly satisfying."

"I'm glad I'm not king," said Collin, glancing up at Gawl's office window.

Father Thomas walked back with them into the rotunda. The candles were already lit, casting warm flickering glows of orange light on the floor. Alexander swept

by with a smile and nod, pausing only long enough to remind them that dinner would be at six o'clock.

"Would any of you care to ride out to the abbey with
me tomorrow?" Father Thomas asked.

"I promised Rowena I'd go with her to the market.
There are some things I need to get for the party next
week," said Lara.

"What things?" asked Mathew.

"Just girl things—makeup and such," she replied.
"Collin's coming with me."

"He needs makeup too," Mathew remarked to Father
Thomas, earning him a thump from Collin's shoulder.

"Honestly," Lara said, shaking her head. She kissed
each of them on the cheek and followed Alexander
down the corridor.

"See you at dinner," she called, over her shoulder.

When she was gone Mathew and Father Thomas
turned to Collin for an explanation.

"Jared's taking me to see a fellow who makes Felcarin
equipment. I told Lara I'd go along. The shop is supposed
to be close to the market."

"Looks like I've been abandoned, Father. I'll ride out
with you."

9

Tenley Palace

LARA HAD NO SOONER ROUNDED THE CORNER THAN SHE felt someone tap her on the shoulder. She turned to see Gawl standing there.

"Gawl," she said, putting a hand over her heart. "You nearly scared me to death."

Instead of answering, the king put a finger over his lips and said, "Shh." He glanced up and down the corridor to make sure no one was watching, then took her by the elbow and guided her into the small dining room.

"What are you doing? I don't—"

"Shh," he whispered again, gesturing with his hands for her to keep her voice down.

Lara's brows came together and she noticed that Gawl's eyes were alive with merriment. He was laughing quietly under his breath, barely containing himself. As soon as they were in the room, he carefully closed the doors.

"Where is he?" the king asked.

"Who?"

"Siward."

"Father Thomas?"

Gawl nodded. "Right."

"I just left him with Collin and Mathew. What in the world is going on?" Rowena was also in the room, seated at the table, looking like a cat who swallowed a canary. Lara turned back to Gawl. He responded by making a pirouetting motion with his hand. Confused, Lara turned around.

"Ceta!" she exclaimed, throwing her arms open.

Ceta Woodall stepped out of an alcove and ran to meet her friend. Both women hugged and began laughing along with Gawl and Rowena, who appeared to be extremely pleased with themselves.

"Oh, my God," said Lara. "What are you doing here?"

Ceta took moment to catch her breath. "You can blame Gawl. He wrote to me a few months ago and invited me to come for a visit. He said he was tired of Siward's moping around all the time and decided to take the matter into his own hands. Siward and I have been writing back and forth about when I should come. Every time we made plans something got in the way . . . my inn, fixing things up after the war, this business with Mathew . . . by the way how is Mathew? Anyway, you name it. Goodness, I'm babbling, aren't I? I sound like a silly schoolgirl."

Lara laughed and hugged her again. Ceta hadn't changed much in the last eight months. She was as trim and elegant as ever, though she was wearing her hair differently, Lara decided. The braid was missing and it looked like she had trimmed several inches off the bottom. It was now loose about her shoulders.

"He really missed you," Lara whispered in Ceta's ear.

The innkeeper's hazel eyes grew bright with tears but she quickly wiped them away.

"Did he really?" she asked, holding Lara's hands.

"Mm-hmm," said Lara, giving her a conspiratorial smile.

Gawl discretely cleared his throat behind them.

"Oh, I'm sorry," Lara said, putting her arm around Gawl's waist. "I take it you've already met his majesty and Lady Rowena Guy."

"We have," Rowena said, getting up from her chair. "Lara's told us so much about you I feel like we're old friends."

"I can't wait to see Siward's face," Gawl said. "God, it's fun to be king. If you'll excuse me, I'm going to relax a bit before dinner. This is going to be priceless. Are you coming, Row?"

"You run along, my dear," Rowena told him. "I want to make sure our guest gets comfortably settled in."

Gawl smiled and took his leave still laughing to himself as the door closed.

The women sat down and talked with each other for the next hour about what was happening in Elgaria and about the latest fashions. At one point during the conversation, Rowena disappeared and returned with a pot of tea and some cakes. From Lara's standpoint everything seemed to be going wonderfully well. Rowena and Ceta took to each other immediately, perhaps because they were close to the same age. Inevitably, the conversation got around to men.

Ceta was concerned about how Father Thomas would react to her sudden appearance, even though Lara assured her that he would be delighted. Ceta then explained to Rowena that she and Father Thomas had only known each other for about a week before circumstances forced them to part. Since then, their only contact had been through letters.

"I don't think you have anything to worry about," said Rowena. "You have a lovely face and wonderful figure. My guess is that Father Thomas will forget any other women he's had the moment he lays eyes on you."

Ceta blinked and sat back in her chair, the smile disappearing from her face. "I don't think Siward is like that," she said.

"Besides, Father Thomas is a priest," added Lara.

"He might be a priest, my dear," laughed Rowena, "but he's also a man."

"Siward and I have an understanding," Ceta told her.

"So do Gawl and I. So do my father and mother for that matter. It's just that men are men. I mean they're sweet and very useful to have around when you need them. It's just something you learn to accept. Nine times out of ten their flirtations are meaningless."

"Well, *I* don't have to accept it," said Ceta, putting her teacup down. "If I thought Siward wasn't loyal to me, I'd turn right around and head back to Elberton."

"Neither do I," Lara agreed. "If I caught Mathew fooling around with another girl I'd kill him, ring or no ring."

Rowena held up her hands in a placating gesture. "I'm sorry. I didn't mean to start an argument or to upset you. Forgive me. Sometimes my mouth starts moving before my brain knows it. I guess it's just that we're a bit more open about such things here in Sennia."

"Well, nobody was raised in a convent," said Ceta. "I trust Siward. If I didn't, I wouldn't be here."

"Of course," Rowena agreed.

"But you don't believe that, do you?" Ceta asked. "I can see it in your face."

"Let's just change the subject," Rowena suggested.

Unfortunately, her words had exactly the opposite effect. Instead of moving on to other things, the subject stayed exactly where it was—centering on the question of men's ability to be loyal, and Father Thomas's leanings in particular. It appeared that Ceta and Rowena were both women of strong opinions, and neither was willing to retreat from their position. The conversation grew more heated. Finally, in an effort to put an end to it, Lara said, "Look, we could talk about this until we're blue in the face, but there's no way we're ever going to know one way or the other, is there? I mean it's not like they're going to come up to you and say, 'By the way, dearest, I slept with another woman yesterday. You don't mind, do you?' "

A silence followed. Ceta and Rowena looked at each other and burst out laughing at the same time, something for which Lara was more than grateful.

"We do sound silly don't we?" said Ceta.

"Just a little," Rowena agreed. "But I do have to differ with you, Lara. There *is* a way."

Ceta and Lara looked at each other, puzzled.

"This is what I have in mind," Rowena told them.

A half hour later, Lara tapped on Ceta Woodall's door. "It's me, Ceta."

"Come in," a voice inside the room called out.

Lara opened the door an inch or two and saw her friend sitting on the bed, wrapped in a towel. She was staring at an elegant white gown that Rowena had sent to her. Next to it was a blond wig and a hat with a veil.

"I can't wear this," Ceta said, as soon as the door closed. "It's so tight it leaves *nothing* to the imagination."

Lara walked over to the bed, picked up the dress, and held it up to the light. The fabric was the finest silk she had ever seen, unfortunately it was so thin that the light shone through it. Her eyes grew a little wider and she swallowed. It might not have been completely sheer, but it wasn't far from it.

"I see what you mean," she said, putting the dress down.

"What am I going to do? I can't wear that thing. It looks more like a nightgown than a dress. All of mine are still packed, and they're so creased from travel, if I put one on I'll look like an unmade bed."

"I could loan you one of mine," Lara suggested. "We're about the same size. All we'd have to do is let the hem down an inch or two."

"I never should have made that bet," Ceta said, miserably. "If Siward finds out, he'll be furious or think I'm some kind of scheming shrew and don't trust him."

Lara tried to picture what Father Thomas would look like if he were furious and couldn't. She'd seen the priest concerned, pensive, loving, sympathetic, happy, and even a little angry every now and then, but he was such an even-tempered man, she just couldn't get the image to form in her mind and told Ceta that.

"This is marvelous," Ceta said. "After eight months, I cross an ocean to be with him and I'll be the first person ever to make him angry. Could I get any dumber?"

Lara sat on the bed and put her arm around Ceta's shoulders. "I know Father Thomas. He'll think it's a joke. That's just the way he is, I swear."

Ceta took a deep breath and looked at Lara.

"Maybe I should talk to Rowena about canceling the bet," Lara suggested. "It probably wasn't the best idea in the first place."

A long silence followed before Ceta finally replied. "I know Siward, too," she said. "And I'm not canceling anything. Now where's that dress of yours?"

It took some frantic last-minute sewing and pinning to get Lara's dress ready. To her surprise, Alexander personally answered Lara's request for a needle and thread and turned out to be a man of many talents. He picked up the dress, took one look at her basting, and politely suggested they allow him to finish the job. He also sent for a little stool and asked Ceta to stand on it while he got down on one knee and redid the pins. When he was satisfied that everything was hanging evenly, Ceta got down, stepped into the bathroom, and handed the dress back out to Lara. Alexander sat on the edge of the bed and began a running stitch, whistling softly to himself while Lara watched in frank admiration.

"I haven't done this in years," he said, not looking up, "but you never really lose the knack. My father was a tailor, you know."

"Did he teach you?" asked Lara.

"Yes. When I first came to the palace I was an assistant dressmaker to Rowena's mother, Elsbeth."

"Really? . . . How did you get to be the Chief of Staff, then?"

"Oh . . . one thing led to another. People came and went, as they always do. Old Pelsley was the Chief of Staff at the time, and he was away visiting his sister. His assistant, a fellow named Cooper, was a complete ninny who couldn't find his head with both hands. Lady Guy was hosting a party and simply beside herself because everything was in chaos. The desserts hadn't been made, the decorations were late in arriving, and two of the musicians were ill. I just happened to be in the right place at the right time."

"And you've been Chief of Staff ever since?" Lara said.

Alexander stopped sewing for a moment and glanced up at the ceiling while he thought about it. "Forty-two years next month, if I'm not mistaken."

"Forty-two years!" exclaimed Lara. "Did you hear that Ceta?"

"Yes," a voice called from the bathroom.

"There . . . all finished," said Alexander, handing Lara back the dress. He got up from the bed and brushed some lint off his pants.

"You're amazing," Lara said, admiring his work. "I can't sew a straight line. Ceta's even worse that I am."

"So I noticed." He smiled, not unkindly.

Lara knocked on the bathroom door and handed the dress in to Ceta, who emerged a minute later wearing it. "You're wonderful," she said, glancing down at Alexander's work. "This would have taken me two days."

Alexander gave her a slight bow in acknowledgment. "My pleasure, ladies. May I remind you that dinner will be in thirty minutes?"

They each thanked him again and he started to take his leave when he noticed the wig and hat sitting on the other side of the bed.

"Do you intend to wear these tonight, Mistress Woodall?"

Ceta took a deep breath and her shoulders slumped. "Yes."

Alexander raised one of his eyebrows, folded his hands in front of him, and waited.

"Ceta made a bet with Rowena," Lara explained. "She thinks Father Thomas will recognize her; Rowena thinks he won't. Rowena says that if he's like most men, he'll probably make a play for her before the night is over, or at least act like he's interested."

"It was a dumb idea," said Ceta, flopping down into a chair.

"Exceedingly," Alexander agreed.

"I don't know what I'm going to do. I've come all this way to see Siward, and I just know this is going to upset him. He won't find it the least bit funny."

"I see," Alexander said. "And this was Lady Rowena's idea?"

Ceta nodded.

"Rowena wanted her to wear this," Lara said, holding up the dress that Rowena had sent.

Alexander looked at it and frowned. "Hmm. She wasn't leaving much to chance, was she? It's most unfortunate."

"What is?" Ceta asked.

"It's unfortunate that Lady Rowena tends to judge others by her own standards. I've been married to my wife for thirty years and have never been disloyal to her. I suspect most people are the same way. There are always exceptions, of course, but from what I know of your Father Thomas, he seems like a good man. Gawl certainly thinks so, and that's no small recommendation. By the way, we'll be having a musical recital in the conservatory before going in to dinner. Enjoy the evening, ladies."

The evening was anything but enjoyable for Ceta Woodall. She was seated one row in front of and slightly to the right of Father Thomas and Bishop Willis. Throughout the performance she could feel the priest's eyes on her, and the glances that she was getting from the other men in the room didn't help matters any.

Prior to their going into the conservatory Rowena introduced Ceta to the other guests as Lady Portia Baines, an old friend who was visiting from Abbington province. Father Thomas bowed, kissed her hand, and said that he was pleased to meet her before he and the bishop moved on to speak with the other guests. The priest had only taken a few steps before he paused. He started to look back over his shoulder, but had to return his attention to the bishop, who was asking him a question.

Ceta saw it happen, and quickly glanced away. Veils were currently in fashion in Sennia and there were several ladies that evening wearing them. Hers was made of a delicate lace, effective enough to obscure her features. And in combination with the blond wig, she barely recognized herself the first time she looked in the mirror. It was a lovely and alluring combination, though at that particular moment Ceta very much wanted to be someplace else. Twice she thought about calling off the bet, and twice her own stubbornness prevented her from doing so. Rowena, who seemed to be enjoying herself immensely, stopped by to tell her that Gawl had been sworn to secrecy. He believed that they were playing a joke on his old friend. So Ceta Woodall gritted her teeth, made polite conversation with the other guests, and went on with the charade.

When the performance was about to begin Lara and Mathew took their seats on the other side of the aisle across from Ceta. Collin was seated next to them with a young lady who was clinging to his arm in a proprietary sort of way. Lara managed to catch Ceta's eye and gave her an encouraging smile. The innkeeper smiled back through her veil and was about to give her a little wave when she saw Lara's eyes suddenly go wide. Not being sure what was wrong, she frowned and looked more closely at her friend, who responded with an almost imperceptible gesture with her head.

Ceta glanced at one of the mirrors along the wall and caught her breath. Father Thomas had just changed seats and was now sitting more or less directly behind her. She felt her heart begin to race and had to take several deep breaths just to calm down, pretending that she was unaware of his presence. A second glance in the mirror confirmed that the priest was leaning to the side trying to get a better look at her face.

Fortunately, the music started and he sat back in his chair. Without being obvious, she tried to glean something from his expression, but couldn't because the stupid veil was in the way. What she did catch was the smug look on Rowena's face out of the corner of her eye.

Goddammit, Ceta whispered under her breath.

At that point she was ready to pull the veil off and confess everything. She wanted to do so, wanted to throw her arms around Siward's neck, but at that point it was a matter of honor. Now, at least, that was the way she thought of it. She'd given her word. Rowena was wrong and that was that.

"Who's that lady in front of Father Thomas?" Mathew asked, keeping his voice down.

"Don't stare," Lara hissed back at him.

"*Ouch*. You just dug your nails into my forearm."

"I'm sorry."

"I wasn't staring. She looks a little . . ."

Whatever the rest of Mathew's sentence was, it died on his lips, due in large part to the glare Lara directed at him. He pulled his head back a few inches, looked at her, and decided it was in his best interest to let the matter drop and concentrate on the musicians.

Across the way Ceta did the same thing.

The performance lasted a little more than three-quarters of an hour, which was forty minutes too long in Mathew's estimation. When it was over, Lara got up and made a beeline directly for the woman he had asked her about, all but dragging him with her. They got there a moment too late. Father Thomas stepped in front of them and asked *Lady Baines* if he could have the honor of escorting her into the dining room.

"Thank you, Father," Ceta replied, "but I think I'll excuse myself, if you don't mind. I seem to have come down with a slight headache. I'll just go upstairs and lie down for a while."

"I understand. Shall I get your husband?" Father Thomas asked, looking around the room."

"Oh . . . ah . . . no, I'm not married, Father, but thank you."

"Please . . . call me Siward. Perhaps you'll allow me to walk back with you, then. Which way is your room?"

Ceta threw a panicky glance in Lara's direction. For a second Mathew thought he saw Lara shake her head no, but it all happened so quickly he wasn't certain. He was about to pull her to one side and ask what was going on when Rowena and Gawl joined them.

"Ah, there you are, Portia," Rowena said, speaking to Ceta. "We'll be going into dinner now. Did you enjoy the performance?"

"Yes, very much, but—"

"I'm afraid your friend has come down with a headache," Father Thomas told them. "I was just asking Lady Baines if she would allow me to escort her back to her room."

Gawl started to say something but stopped when Rowena *accidentally* stepped on his foot, hard enough to make the king's eyes bulge.

"Of course," Rowena said, giving Ceta a concerned hug. "You just go right up and lie down. I'll have the kitchen send up some food. Our handsome Father Thomas can be your protector. Thank you so much, Father."

It was a good thing that Ceta was wearing a veil because it effectively hid the expression of pure hatred she shot at Rowena. When Father Thomas gallantly offered her his arm, she had no choice but to accept it. Then they both said good night and started off down the hallway.

"Was it a difficult journey from Abbington province?" Father Thomas asked, as they walked along the corridors.

"No, Father."

"*Siward,* please." He smiled at her.

"Siward."

"I'm really not familiar with that part of the country. I studied for the priesthood here, of course, but I'm originally from a small town in Elgaria."

"Really? Which one?" Ceta asked, already knowing the answer.

"Oh, I doubt you'd know it. It was just a little place on the banks of the Roeselar River. The town's name was Weyburn, but it was destroyed by Karas Duren during the Sibuyan War. It was a long time ago," he added softly.

A look that might have been pain at the memory of it flashed across the priest's face, but was gone a moment later. Ceta felt her heart go out to him. She wanted to say it was all right, and that she was there for him, but couldn't.

"Do you miss it very much?" she asked.

Father Thomas nodded. "Yes . . . from time to time. My father, mother, and sister all lived there. They had a little house on the outskirts of the town."

"Lived?"

"They're gone now. They were killed by the Orlocks."

"I'm so sorry," Ceta whispered, hating herself more with every step.

"Thank you. It's quite all right. As I say, it's been a very long time."

"Do you have any other family in Elgaria . . . , Siward?"

Father Thomas took a deep breath. "Not in the strict sense of the word. For the past thirteen years my church has been located in Devondale. Like Weyburn, it's also a small town and you get close to the people in your community. They're good people. You've probably met Mathew, Collin, and Lara; they're also from Devondale. Everybody tends to know everybody's business," he laughed, "so I guess it is something like a family, now that I think of it."

"No wife or children? I should have thought that an attractive man like you would have been snatched up a long time ago. You're a Levad, I understand. Don't their priests marry?"

"They do."

"I suppose you've just never found the right woman?"

"Actually, I thought I did . . . at one time."

Ceta nearly missed a step when she heard him say it, but she forced herself to keep walking. They turned to their right and crossed the rotunda, making their way toward the living quarters. A series of portraits hanging on the walls looked down on them.

"I see. What was the problem . . . if you don't mind my asking?"

"Well . . . if you'll pardon my indelicacy, her hips were too wide, and she had a big ugly wart at the end of her nose."

Ceta gasped and spun around to face him.

"She also had the most abominable sense of humor, and an annoying tendency to change the color of her hair. It was quite horrible really."

Her mouth was still open in shock when Father Thomas lifted her veil, looked into her eyes and whispered, "Ceta."

A second later his lips found hers and her shock turned to a longing so desperate it nearly hurt. To her surprise, the innkeeper from Elberton, who had crossed the sea to be with the man she loved found that tears were rolling down her cheeks. Father Thomas held her face in both hands and kissed them away. And when the blond wig fell to the ground she hardly took notice. It was still lying there when they finally separated. Ceta glanced down at it and, with one kick, sent it skidding across the marble floor. She slipped her arm through Father Thomas's, pulled him closer, then they turned and walked back to the dinner together.

Alexander was standing at the entrance to the dining room, giving some last minute instructions to one of the servants. He looked up when he saw the couple approaching and a tiny smile appeared at the corners of his mouth. He noticed the absence of the wig, though, ever the good servant, he kept his face neutral and characteristically folded his hands in front of him. Father Thomas saw him at the same time, disengaged his arm, and came directly over. The priest whispered something in his ear. Puzzled, Ceta watched the two men shake hands and was more puzzled still when Alexander turned to her and made a little bow with his head. The ghost of a smile was still on his face when he opened the dining room doors and announced:

"Sire . . . I have the honor to present Father Siward Thomas of Werth province, in Elgaria, and his bride to be, Mistress Ceta Woodall of Elberton."

Ceta's mouth opened in surprise as the room burst into applause and people came to their feet. Mathew and Collin nearly knocked over their chairs in their haste to get up and shake Father Thomas's hand. They changed their minds and hugged him instead. Gawl left his table, strode over, and lifted the priest off his feet in a bear hug, his face beaming with pleasure. Lara and Ceta embraced and even Rowena smiled happily at the good news. When she and Ceta were close enough to touch cheeks, unseen by any of the others in the room, save Alexander, who noted it and discreetly looked the other way, Rowena slipped two gold sovereigns into Ceta's palm and whispered, "I've never enjoyed losing a bet quite so much."

10

Sennia, Town of Bexley

THE NEXT MORNING MATHEW MET CETA AND FATHER Thomas at the stables. They all rode out through the main gate toward the cliff road. The night before, Lara had talked to Ceta about coming to the marketplace in Barcora, but the innkeeper politely declined, electing to ride to the abbey with her new fiancé. Though it might have been due to the winter weather, Mathew thought Ceta's complexion was still a little flushed.

Tenley Palace sat high on a ridge overlooking the city of Barcora, with its endless red tile roofs and harbor. Most of the trees covering the slopes were bare at this time of year. Four weeks earlier they'd been covered in vivid reds and golds. That morning the sky was a brilliant blue, with only a few high wispy clouds here and there. It was a view that Mathew loved, and however many times he saw it, it never failed to move him.

He stared out at the white sails gliding across a bay as startlingly blue as the sky above. It was the second-largest harbor in the western world. In the three weeks it took them to cross the Great Southern Sea on the *Wave Dancer*, Mathew had fallen in love with the ocean. Under Oliver Donal's tutelage he had learned how to navigate a vessel using the stars and a sextant to guide him. It was an accomplishment he still took great pride in, though he never once thought to speak of it to anyone else. Several times over the last few months the possibility of following a seagoing career had occurred to him, but like so many things in his life, he had put it aside. For the most part, the mystery surrounding the statues remained uppermost in his mind. A connection between that incident and the rings surely existed, but what it was he couldn't say.

The Ancients, who created the rings, had perished in a war of their own making—suddenly and cataclysmically. That much was common knowledge. They were his ancestors. The extent of their destruction was so complete, other than ruined cities, remnants of once massive roadways, and scattered artifacts, all that remained of them were stories that had been passed down from generation to generation.

Because of the paucity of records it had been impossible for Mathew to piece together exactly why the war began, or why it ended so suddenly. He found references in old volumes about the massive project the Ancients had undertaken, wanting to free themselves of manual labor forever, and assumed that was what formed the basis of the rings' powers. He also knew that virtually all men and women over the age of twenty once owned rose-gold rings. Each one was unique and crafted for only one person, or so the books said. It was through the rings the Ancients were able to access the crystals and the incredible machine complex that lay buried deep in the planet core.

A kaleidoscope of different images cascaded through his mind of the strange town Teanna had taken him to after the battle at Ardon Field. His brain was alive with activity, so much so he found it difficult keep steady in his saddle.

Karas Duren knew about the crystals and the machines, as did his beautiful niece, Teanna. According to Gawl, she was arriving in less than a week. The prospect made Mathew uncomfortable. How do you begin to carry on a conversation with someone whose mother and uncle you had killed?

But the fact was he *had* spoken with her—months before in an impossible town under the earth. Why his ancestors should have created such a thing was beyond him. Teanna told him there was power there—unimaginable power, and she wanted to share it with him. He had rejected her offer.

Power without knowledge.

Duren's words still echoed in his mind. Hardly a day passed when he didn't remember that dried-leather whisper. For months he'd searched dusty books written in the archaic old tongue, seeking answers. Though the records were admittedly sketchy, more than one source he had found made reference to the Ancients' desperate search to destroy the very rings they created. This made the least sense of all to him. Why would his ancestors try to destroy the very miracle they had spent so many years developing? Any why would they leave just eight?

His ring was certainly one of those eight. So was Teanna's. And now he had to contend with another person, a faceless enemy. He didn't know. One thing however was clear . . . statues didn't come to life on their own. He would have been a complete fool to think that someone or something wasn't directing them. The larger question was why?

Father Thomas exchanged a smile with Ceta, then looked at Mathew. It was obvious to both of them that the young man was preoccupied so they left him alone with his thoughts. The priest shook his head slightly. He was aware that Mathew had changed since they left Devondale, and more than physically. *The boy* now nearly six feet two, could look him squarely in the eyes; much of the painful shyness was gone, or at least moderated a great deal. But how much of this was due to maturity and recent events, he couldn't say. True, Mathew could be forceful and direct when the occasion warranted, yet Father Thomas could still see a bit of the young boy.

Jeram Quinn, he knew, was essentially a good man who saw his duty with a single-minded purpose. Despite what Mathew had done in stopping Karas Duren and the Orlocks, people had notoriously short memories, and Elgarian justice had none at all. He had spent six years in jail for killing a baron's son in a fight. Fair or not, it came back to him all the more vividly since his decision to take Mathew and flee Devondale.

Father Thomas did not envy the position Delain was in. The king had publicly announced his belief that the law and God stood above all things, and he was entirely too new to the throne to do anything other than stand on his word, regardless of how he felt personally. The letter which Jeram Quinn delivered to him privately confirmed this. Father Thomas had prayed for an answer to the dilemma. He had prayed for guidance, but the Lord had not yet chosen to reveal his plan.

Father Thomas, Ceta, and Mathew continued to ride along in silence, each occupied with their own thoughts. Eventually, the road turned west into the upper forest. At this time of year, travel in Sennia was not a problem. The snows had been light and the road was one which the Ancients themselves had built aeons ago. Portions of it were pitted and broken, the result of time and perverse weather conditions. Grass grew between small cracks in the surface of the road, around them the boughs of the trees were so close together they limited the amount of light filtering down to the forest floor.

It wasn't long before Mathew came out of his musings, looked up, and noticed his surroundings. They had been traveling for about twenty minutes and he had no memory of getting there. Father Thomas smiled at him.

"Did any answers present themselves to you, my son?" he asked, guessing Mathew's thoughts.

Mathew took a deep breath. "Not really, Father."

"Is there anything you would like to talk about?"

"No . . ."

"But something *is* bothering you, isn't it?"

Mathew glanced from the priest to Ceta and there was a pause before he answered.

"There are a lot of things bothering me. This business with Quinn, Lara, the statues . . . pick one."

"Perhaps it would be better if you picked one."

"Maybe this isn't a good time," Ceta tactfully suggested.

"No, it's all right," Mathew said.

Even in the low light Mathew could see Father Thomas's brown eyes watching him carefully.

"The other day I asked Collin if he thought Lara had been acting any different lately. He thought she was. I guess I do too. I thought she was flirting with Jared the other night and it wasn't the first time."

Ceta remained quiet and looked at Father Thomas, who nodded his head slowly. "It is possible that Rowena may not be the best influence on her," the priest said. "Lara is a sensible girl, but she is still very much a girl, despite her physical maturity. I think it is a good thing Ceta has arrived," he said, reaching over to squeeze her hand.

"What do you mean?" asked Mathew.

"Just this . . . like you, she was born and raised in Devondale, which is not exactly in the center of the civilized world. She is only lately away from her home, and for the last few months she has not had the company of other women to speak and socialize with. It's only natural, that lacking companions, or her mother, she has leaned toward Rowena to pattern her behavior after."

"I see . . . I think."

"Hopefully the association will be short-lived, because I tend to agree with you."

"You do?"

Father Thomas nodded. "I suppose you saw the sculpture the other night?" Mathew asked glumly.

Father Thomas cleared his throat. "As I said, her body

is very much that of a woman. Gawl should have spoken to you, or certainly with me, before asking her to pose."

"What are you both talking about?" Ceta asked.

Father Thomas took a moment to explain about the sculpture. Ceta didn't say much, but her eyebrows went up when she heard that Lara had posed nude.

"It was Rowena's suggestion," Mathew said. "I don't understand Ashots at all. I'm sorry, Ceta. They don't drink. They don't like red meat. But they've got no problem throwing off their clothes at a moment's notice. It doesn't make sense."

"Not all Ashots behave that way, Mathew," she told him. "In fact, most don't. For that matter, I don't. . . . She posed in the nude, you say?"

"Mm-hmm."

"Actually, it's only a small group who tend to follow such precepts," Father Thomas added. "Thankfully they're in a distinct minority."

"Most of them probably caught cold and died," Mathew muttered.

Father Thomas and Ceta began laughing. The priest reached over and slapped Mathew on the leg. In another moment they were all laughing.

The forest thinned out again as the road descended into a broad valley where the town of Bexley was located. The abbey was only a fifteen-minute ride beyond that.

"Perhaps we could stop for some breakfast," Father Thomas suggested. "It's still early and there used to be a good tavern in town. I went there often as a student."

Somehow the thought of Father Thomas being a student had never occurred to Mathew, or to Ceta, who cocked her head to one side and said, "I thought you were from Weyburn."

"I am. But when I studied for the priesthood, my friends and I came here to relax and listen to a little music now and then. The owner made the most unusual egg-toast. I haven't had it in years."

"Egg-toast?" they both said.

"Yes indeed. I recommend it highly."

A few minutes later they found themselves in front of a pleasant-looking country inn called the Drunken Duck. A small sign hung above the doorway depicting a duck sitting in a pond of water, who looked somewhat the worse for wear. The scene also showed a perplexed farmer standing at the edge of the pond with his hands on his hips. Mathew studied the sign for a second and shook his head before going inside. Ceta, who was an innkeeper herself, looked at the building with a critical eye and gave a nod of approval.

"Father, why is it all inns have painted signs on the front?" Mathew asked.

"Ah . . . well, you see in the old days not everyone could read. So innkeepers, being a resourceful lot," he said, kissing Ceta on the cheek, "devised a way of informing travelers of the type of business they had by using pictures, such as the one outside. The tradition has stayed with us through the years."

"What a name," said Mathew. They found an empty table near a window and seated themselves.

"The story of this place goes that the landlord came home one day to find his ducks lying dead by the side of the road. When he went to pick them up, he found they weren't dead at all—only drunk. Apparently the ducks found their way into a barrel of ale that he forgot to close; hence the name."

The image of several drunken ducks and their owner finding them in that condition caused Mathew to start chuckling to himself. He was still smiling when the owner of the tavern appeared.

The man was elderly and almost bald, save for a fringe of wispy gray hair just above his ears. He wore a black vest and a spotless white apron around his middle.

"Good morning, gentlemen . . . and lady. What can I get for you? Why, bless my soul, if it isn't Siward Thomas!"

The landlord's face broke into a broad smile and he threw his arms open. Father Thomas got up and hugged him.

"Let's have a look at you, boy," the man said, holding Father Thomas by the shoulders.

Boy? Mathew thought. He glanced at Ceta, who had an amused smile on her face.

"You look well, Robert," Father Thomas replied. "It's wonderful to see you after all these years. Mathew . . . Ceta, I would like you to meet Master Robert Barton, the proprietor of this fine establishment. Robert, this beautiful lady is my fiancée, Mistress Ceta Woodall of Elberton. Like you, she is also the proprietor of an inn."

"Always pleased to meet one of my colleagues," Robert said, offering his hand to her.

Ceta smiled back at him and shook his hand. "You have a lovely inn, Master Barton."

"Thank you," he replied, his face lighting up at the compliment.

"And this is Mathew Lewin, who comes from Devondale . . . my hometown."

"Well met, young man, though you travel in highly questionable company," he said with a nod in Father Thomas's direction.

"Questionable company?" Mathew repeated, shaking hands with the man.

"Indeed. Siward and his friend, Peter Baker . . . *Father* Baker now, I imagine, were two of the biggest mischievous makers in their class at the abbey. Always in trouble. I remember there was a time—"

"Yes, yes . . . no point telling tales out of school," Father Thomas interrupted.

Mathew and Ceta both looked at the priest, who pointedly did not return their glances.

"I'm glad to see you took the vows," Robert said, patting Father Thomas on the arm. "It's good to have you back, Siward. Will you be staying long?"

"Unfortunately not, my friend. I received a note from Paul Teller asking me to ride out to the abbey and meet with him. Mathew and Ceta have come along to protect me."

"I've heard there's been some trouble up there recently," Robert said, lowering his voice.

"What sort of trouble?" Father Thomas asked.

"I'm not sure. Everyone's been pretty close-mouthed about it, even the students."

"Robert's spy network is extensive," Father Thomas said, tapping the side of his nose. "I've been bragging to my friends about your famous egg-toast. Is it possible that you still make it?"

The innkeeper looked shocked at the suggestion and put his hands on his hips.

"Well, of course I do. Give us a moment. I'll send one of the girls out with drinks. What would you like?"

"Tea," Ceta replied.

"Juice for me," Mathew said.

"I'll take a mug of your brown ale," Father Thomas told him, with a quick glance in Ceta's direction.

She made a dismissive gesture with her hand and didn't comment.

"Done. Good to see you, boy," Robert called over his shoulder. "Your servant, ma'am . . . and yours, Master Lewin."

Father Thomas sat down and shook his head. "He hasn't changed in fifteen years."

"Boy?" Mathew laughed.

"It's the advantage of being eighty years old. He calls Bishop Willis and the abbot boy as well. Nobody's been able to change him. He is a good man, though."

Mathew sat back in his chair and started chuckling again.

A pretty serving girl appeared a moment or two later,

carrying their drinks. She had a round face and thick blond hair that looked like it could use a good combing. She curtsied and gave Mathew a friendly smile over her shoulder before vanishing back into the kitchen. While they were waiting for their food to arrive, Mathew looked around the room. It was empty save for the three of them. Nearby, the heat from a fireplace radiated outward and felt wonderful after the early morning chill. The common room was small and intimate. A tiny elevated stage stood to the right of the fireplace where, Mathew imagined, traveling minstrels would play their music or tell stories. And a tapestry with a now familiar hunting scene hung over the mantel along with the Sennian flag. Two comfortable-looking couches faced each other on either side of the hearth.

Ceta was glancing around as well. "Very nice," she said, putting her hand on Father Thomas's forearm.

They sat there sipping their drinks in silence for a time before the priest spoke. "Mathew, I would like to ask you a question, if you don't mind."

Mathew met the priest's eyes over the top of his mug.

"I'm aware you told Jeram Quinn that you would return with him to stand trial. We've discussed this already. I also know Collin spoke to you of Gawl's decision to buy Delain more time, so he could intercede without any major repercussions. What I would like to know, is what prompted you to tell Quinn you would go back with him?"

Mathew rolled the mug back and forth in his hands a few times and watched the contents swirl around.

"My father is dead . . . so is my mother. I have no uncles, aunts, cousins, or any relatives that I'm aware of. You, Lara, and Collin are the only family I have. Daniel too, I guess. I couldn't let what I did pull you all down, too. It was the best bargain I could make under the circumstances."

The priest started to speak, but Mathew cut him off and continued explaining.

"You told me once a long time ago that we're responsible only for our own decisions; that each person makes his or her choices as a free individual. I thought it out before I made mine, Father. I'm not sorry I did."

He spoke quietly, without embellishment.

Father Thomas raised his eyebrows and looked out the window while he continued to sip his drink. Ceta glanced at him, then at Mathew in turn. From the letters she and Father Thomas had exchanged over the last few months, she knew about what had happened in Devondale and why Mathew and the others left there. She was not familiar with the latest development, but felt certain that Siward would fill in the details for her later.

"I thought it was something like that," the priest said, letting out a breath. "I understand your reasons, but it would have been best if we had spoken first. Unfortunately, the die is now cast, so we'll just have to see what comes."

Before either of them could say anything further the food arrived, exceeding all expectations. Even Ceta, who normally ate very little for breakfast, remarked how good it was. The dish consisted of a large piece of bread that had been soaked in an egg and laced with cinnamon. It was cooked in a pan until it was a golden brown on the outside, yet the inside remained soft. Though one slice was all most people ever ate, Mathew surprised everyone by placing two more orders and devouring them just as quickly as he had the first one. The third time he did so it prompted Robert to come out of the kitchen for a closer look. The old innkeeper muttered something under his breath about growing boys and patted Mathew on the shoulder, then returned to his other duties. Father Thomas and Ceta exchanged amused looks, leaned back in their chairs, and watched in admiration as Mathew consumed the last piece on his plate.

"Had enough?" asked Father Thomas.

"Oh, yes," Mathew said, rolling his eyes. "In fact . . ."

His voice trailed away when he noticed that Father Thomas was watching three men who had just come into the tavern. One of them appeared to be a priest as well, but he was dressed in white robes with a gold chain belt around his stomach. The two men with him were large, rough-looking types. One of them had a full beard, and the other a pockmarked face, with a prominent scar across his cheek. Both were carrying short swords. The group made an odd combination, in Mathew's opinion.

A number of other patrons were also beginning to arrive. The white-robed priest glanced around the room and his eyes seemed to fix on Mathew for a moment before he took a table in the corner along with his companions.

"Is that man a priest?" Mathew asked.

"He's from Coribar. Their priests dress in white there rather than black."

"Isn't he a little far from home?" asked Ceta.

"The abbey is open to people of all denominations. Several times a year groups from across the continent come here to meet and exchange knowledge," Father Thomas explained. "Well," he said, pushing his chair away from the table, "would you like to see some of Bexley before we proceed?"

"Sure," Mathew said, getting to his feet. "I need to walk off this meal."

"You boys run along," Ceta told them. "I'd like to see if I can convince Robert to part with his recipe."

They all said goodbye and promised to meet in front of the inn in a half hour.

The town of Bexley was unlike like any Mathew had ever seen. The streets were made of the same type pavement as the ancient road they had just traveled. The central square was really more of a circle with all of the streets radiating out from it in different directions. When Mathew mentioned this to Father Thomas, the priest explained that Bexley was actually designed to look like a wagon wheel. Each of the streets represented spokes, with the little park they were standing in being the hub. A wide perimeter road circled the entire town, completing the picture of a wheel.

There were a variety of different shops located on the first and second floors of buildings around the square. Almost all of them were interconnected by a series of balconies, so that a person could pass from one to another without having to go down into the street again.

While Father Thomas and Mathew continued their stroll, Mathew noticed a number of people in different types of garb walking together in conversation and browsing the shop windows. Some of the styles were familiar to him and some weren't. After a while he decided Bexley had to be a popular spot with the clergy due to the number of priests he was seeing. Father Thomas pointed out people not from only Coribar, but Mirdan and Nyngary as well. At one point, Mathew saw three men dressed in turbans and short robes that reminded him of Darias Val, the Bajani general he had met several months earlier. The men bowed slightly when they passed and Father Thomas and Mathew returned their bows, which brought satisfied smiles to their faces.

One shop they visited contained different artifacts recently unearthed at the Argenton ruins. The store was small and unpretentious with an oversized eight-pane window in the front and the name William Baker, Ltd. stenciled across the top in gold letters. The trim was painted black.

"Good morning, gentlemen. Come in," a thin man standing behind a counter said when they entered. "I'm Bill Baker. Is there anything in particular you're looking for?"

"No, we're just browsing," Mathew replied, as he bent down to peer at a display case containing several silver frames. The case also had a variety of different coins, none of which were familiar to him. For the next few minutes he and Father Thomas wandered around looking at the different oddities there.

"You won't find better quality anywhere," the owner said to Mathew, who was examining a comb with rhinestones that he was thinking about getting for Lara. "I can let you have it at a good price."

"How much?"

"Well, let's see now," the man said, rubbing his jaw. "I could let it go for two crowns."

"Too rich for my blood," Mathew replied, shaking his head. It took some quick mental calculations on his part to convert the elgars they used in Elgaria to an equivalent amount in Sennian crowns.

"Are you looking for something for a lady friend of yours, young fellow?"

"Maybe," Mathew replied.

"I take it by your accent you're not from around here. Is this your first time visiting Bexley?"

"Right."

"How much for this hand mirror?" Father Thomas asked from across the room.

"That piece is in excellent condition. You can tell the quality just by looking at it. I can't say for certain, but the man who sold it to me said it was over two thousand years old. I'll sell it to you for five crowns."

"I thought I saw a similar one for a crown fifty across the street," Father Thomas told him.

The owner frowned and glanced out the window at a shop directly opposite them.

"Ted Walker's selling them for a crown fifty?"

Father Thomas turned up his hands slightly and smiled.

"Well . . . I'll tell you what, Father. Seeing as how you're a priest, and I do a lot of business with the priests from the abbey, I can let you have it for . . . two crowns."

"I'll give you a crown for it," Father Thomas replied. "It's got a small chip here."

"It's two thousand years old," the owner complained. "You have to expect *some* wear and tear. That shows it's authentic."

Bill Baker went on to explain to them the very reasonable and minimal profit he was making on the transaction. He also detailed the spiraling costs of his overhead as part of his argument. Ultimately, they concluded the bargain at a crown twenty-five. Mathew did almost as well, securing the comb he was looking at for a crown.

With their purchases in hand they bid goodbye to Master Baker and headed back toward the Drunken Duck.

A short distance away a group of children—four boys and two girls—were busy playing a game. Mathew and Father Thomas stopped to watch. For a moment it appeared to be tag, but then something one of the children said caught Mathew's ear. At first he wasn't certain he heard the words correctly so he moved closer, as did Father Thomas, whose brow had creased into a frown.

The largest boy was a slender lad with broad shoulders who couldn't have been more than eight or nine years old. He stood up on a bench, extended his arm at one of his companions and proclaimed, *"Death to Duren!"*

His victim, who appeared to be about the same age, had a face full of freckles with a shock of red hair to match. He clutched his throat in a properly theatrical fashion and slowly fell to the ground, made a few gurgling sounds, kicked his legs, then lay still.

Mathew and Father Thomas looked at each other.

Oblivious to their presence, the children continued the game, with the boy on the bench killing his enemies one by one, including the girls. Gradually, they noticed that there were two adults standing nearby. Either self-consciousness or prudence took over, and the children started to withdraw down an alley.

"Hello," said Mathew, stopping the girl nearest him and squatting down on his heels.

"Hello," she replied cautiously.

"What were you playing?"

"Just pretend."

"Looks like fun," said Father Thomas.

"Mm-hmm." The girl glanced up, and after noticing the way he was dressed, added a curtsy.

Two of the other boys who were watching from the alley returned to where she was.

"We're not doing anything wrong," the shorter one said.

"Of course you're not," Father Thomas replied, kneeling down next to Mathew. "My friend and I love games, and we were just wondering how yours was played."

"Harry was being Karas Duren and I killed him with my ring. I'm Mathew Lewin. Michael's King Gawl, and Jenny is Marsa d'Elso," the boy answered.

"I don't like being Marsa," complained Jenny. "I always get killed."

Mathew heard the words and couldn't believe his ears. His surprise was compounded further when he noticed that each of the children were wearing rose-gold rings on the fourth finger of their right hand.

"That's a neat ring you have on . . . uh . . ."

"Ben," the boy offered.

"Ben," Mathew echoed. "May I see it for a moment?"

Ben shrugged, pulled the ring off his finger, and handed it to Mathew. It was made of tin and tinted to resemble the color of his rose-gold ring. He kept his own hand behind his back while he did so.

"Thank you, Ben. I used to play pretend games when I was your age. Where did you get such an amazing ring?"

"We all have them," Harry said, "except for Michael. That's why he's King Gawl today."

"Oh, I see," Mathew said.

"You can get one at Rainey's over there," Jenny pointed. "He sells them."

"Thank you, my child," Father Thomas replied, straightening up.

"Yes, thank you," Mathew said, looking across the way to where Jenny was pointing.

"What's your name?" Harry asked.

"Mathew."

"Yeah, right," the boy answered, laughing. The other children also giggled at the joke and ran down the street to resume their game.

Father Thomas and Mathew glanced at each other again, and without another word they began walking toward the shop the girl had pointed out.

The closer they got, the greater the unsettled feeling in Mathew's stomach became. He and Father Thomas came to a halt and stood there staring in disbelief at a painting on prominent display in the window. It depicted Mathew standing on a hill doing battle with Karas Duren, who was in a castle at the end of a wide green plain. Beneath the castle, two armies were in the midst of a titanic battle. Blue lightning bolts, arcing from Mathew's fingertips, rushed to meet the orange flames shot from Duren's hands. Down on the field were two immense walls of fire that had just collided with one another. They rose upward hundreds of feet into the air.

A kaleidoscope of memories and emotions, suppressed for months, flooded back into Mathew's mind as he remembered the terrible battle he had fought with the king of Alor Satar. The painting was far from accurate, but whoever the artist was, he had done an extremely good job of capturing Duren's malevolent expression and his hooded eyes. It sent a chill down Mathew's spine.

To the right was another painting showing thousands of Orlocks storming the town of Tremont, with Mathew standing on the town's wall raining fire down on them. A different painting on the other side of the display showed Gawl, leading the Sennian Wedge in a full scale charge against the enemy.

At least they managed to get that right, Mathew thought indignantly.

There were other things in the window as well. Two halberds with signs hanging from them read AUTHENTIC ORLOCK WEAPONS. They were propped up on either side of the middle painting. Torn and tattered battle pendants from Vargoth and Bajan hung limply at the top of the display case.

Mathew blinked and thought for a second. *Vargoth and Bajan weren't even in the battle.*

Father Thomas shook his head and peered down at what had to be the most interesting of the objects there—two trays of rose-gold rings.

Before either of them could say anything, the door of the shop opened and a large man stepped outside. He had a full brown beard and wore a neatly pressed pinstriped shirt with black arm covers that came up to his elbows.

"Fine day, gentlemen. Gerald Rainey, at your service. Is there anything I can do for you?"

Mathew started to open his mouth, but before he could speak, Father Thomas said, "We were just admiring your collection, Master Rainey."

"Thank you, Father. It's quite something, isn't it?"

"I'll say," Mathew muttered.

"Are you interested in buying a ring as a souvenir, by any chance? They're excellent quality and I've got some good prices on them."

"Oh? Are they real?" Mathew asked.

The owner made a dismissive sound. "They're only imitations, lad. There's no rose-gold left in the world—except for Lewin's ring, of course. That's the only one."

"Really?" said Mathew.

"Absolutely. He told me so himself just the other day. He lives up at the abbey you know."

"Excuse me?" said Mathew, his eyes opening in astonishment

"Oh, yes," the owner continued. "He comes in frequently—chatty sort. You know the type?"

Gerald Rainey looked at Mathew a little closer and

frowned. "He actually favors you a little . . . except he's a good bit taller."

"Naturally," Father Thomas said, taking Mathew by the arm.

"Sure I can't interest you in a ring . . . or an authentic Orlock knife?"

"No. Thank you. We really must be on our way," said the priest.

"Well, sorry I couldn't help you with anything, Father. Listen, you want to be careful if you go into any of the other shops. There's a lot of fake stuff around town these days."

"I understand," Father Thomas replied, still pulling Mathew along with him. "The blessings of the church on you." Then, under his breath, he added, "You pompous ass."

For the second time that morning, Mathew blinked in surprise.

It took them less than five minutes to reach the Drunken Duck. Their horses were still tethered outside the tavern where they'd left them. Father Thomas was acutely conscious of Mathew's silence, as well as his change of mood. He stopped near the entrance to the tavern and looked at his young friend. Ceta was nowhere to be seen, and he assumed that she was probably inside. Strangely, instead of finding humor in the situation, the boy seemed to have become deeply saddened by what had happened.

"Mathew?"

Mathew didn't meet the priest's gaze for several seconds. He stared at the ground instead

"Mat?" Father Thomas prompted again.

Mathew looked up. "It's never going to be the same again, is it, Father?" he asked quietly.

Father Thomas took a deep breath and let it out.

"No, my son," he said, putting his hands on Mathew's shoulders. "I was not prepared for that either. It seems the story of what happened in Elgaria has spread quickly. I should have guessed."

"But, those paintings . . . and those things he said . . . none of them were true."

"People tend to create their own heroes, Mat. Sometimes the stories become larger than the truth. The important thing is to remember who you are . . . in here and in here," Father Thomas said, lightly touching Mathew over the heart and on his forehead. "Do you understand what I'm saying?"

"I guess so, Father. It's just that I'm not a hero. I just want—"

Mathew never got a chance to finish his sentence as two men coming out the front door of the tavern all but knocked him over.

"Here, watch where you're going, boy," one of them said. He had a pockmarked face.

Mathew recognized him immediately and he looked around for the Coribar priest who was with them earlier. He spotted the man off to one side, watching.

"I think you bumped into this young man," Father Thomas said, stepping in between the men and Mathew.

"Stay out of this, priest," his friend with the beard growled. "I saw what happened, and it was him who ran into us."

"I did no such thing," Mathew snapped.

"Are you calling me a liar, boy?" the man asked, his tone suddenly dangerous.

Father Thomas put his hand out to keep Mathew back, but he pushed it away.

"If that's what you're saying, then yes you're a liar. You bumped into me deliberately."

Both men separated. The man with the pockmarked face drew his sword and his companion pulled a dagger out of his belt. Mathew stepped back and began to reach for his own sword.

Everything that happened next was a blur. Without

warning the man with the sword lunged. Father Thomas slapped the blade aside with the palm of his hand and sidestepped the thrust. The weapon shot by him. Before the assailant could react, the priest hit him across the jaw, using his elbow rather than his fist, snapping the man's head sideways. In one smooth motion, Father Thomas swung his elbow back and caught him on the temple just behind his eye. There was a dull thud and the man went down like he was hit by an axe.

Seeing an opportunity his companion charged, the dagger raised above his head. Before Mathew could get to him, Father Thomas whipped off the white scarf he was wearing and caught the man's hand on the down-stroke. Using the other's momentum, the priest swung him forward into the side of the tavern. He hit the wall face-first and was unconscious before he reached the ground.

Father Thomas looked at him for a moment and straightened his clothes. He turned to Mathew, whose mouth was open, and said, "I suspect we should leave for the abbey now. I'll just step inside and fetch Ceta."

Mathew, who had seen the priest fight before, shook his head.

A few people were already beginning to file out of the building to see what the commotion was about. Ceta was among them, and from the look on her face she was any-thing but pleased by what had just happened. Father Thomas gave her a weak smile as he replaced the scarf around his neck.

"Siward, what happened here?" she asked, coming down the steps.

"Ah . . . it seems these men were trying to start a fight with Mathew and I just . . . uh—"

"Siward," she said, in a reproving tone. "I leave you alone for a few minutes and the first thing you do is get into a fight."

"They started it," he said, defensively.

Ceta placed her hands on her hips and arched an eye-brow at him. "You're a priest, for God's sake," she whispered. "What are people going to think?"

"They did, Ceta. Honest," Mathew told her.

Ceta took a deep breath and walked past them to her horse without commenting further. Mathew and Father Thomas looked at each other, then followed. As they rode out of town Mathew glanced over his shoulder at the two men on the ground. Neither had moved yet.

11

Sennia, Abbey of Barcora

THEIR RIDE ACROSS THE VALLEY WAS UNEVENTFUL. IN A short while the massive brown walls and tiled roofs of the Abbey of Barcora came into view. Situated on a hill overlooking the valley, the abbey was a sprawling complex that extended over several acres. It was made up of eight main buildings and five dormitories where both priests and students lived throughout the year. Inside was a cluster of four long one-story buildings, known as the commons. This was where meals were prepared and served to the almost fifteen hundred people normally in residence.

At the far end of the complex, a large domed structure was under construction. It could just be seen rising above the walls. Mathew was surprised to see how much progress had been made in the three weeks since they had left. The odd-looking building was to be the new observatory for astronomical studies, and it was almost entirely due to the invention his friend Daniel Warren had developed. When they first arrived, Collin had shown the farsighter to a priest named Father Gregory, who examined the metal tube with its polished glass lenses for a few minutes and immediately sent for two of his colleagues. A stir of excitement began to ripple through the abbey and it became a prominent topic of discussion at dinner for over a week. Construction on a much larger version of the farsighter began the following month and appeared to be in the final stages of completion. Mathew looked up at it and wondered if Daniel knew what he had started.

When they rode through the main gate the first thing that struck him was the presence of armed guards. Certainly, there hadn't been any when they left. In all the time he lived there, Mathew had never so much as seen anyone carrying a sword in the complex. Popular rumor had it that the main gate hadn't been locked in over eight hundred years.

Father Thomas noticed them as well.

One of the guards stepped into their path and raised his hand signaling for them to stop, which they did. Mathew and Father Thomas reined up their horses and dismounted, while Ceta stayed on hers. The guard, who Mathew thought was about the same age as he was, didn't have the look of a soldier, even though he was carrying a pike. His uniform was ill-fitting and appeared to be more ornamental than functional.

"I'm sorry, Father," the guard said. "Would you state your business here, please?"

Father Thomas raised his eyebrows. "My business? The last time I checked, I was a priest."

"I understand that, Father. I meant no disrespect, but there has been some trouble lately. These are the abbot's orders."

"What sort of trouble?"

"It would be best if you discuss that with the abbot, Father. It's not for me to say."

"Very well. I shall. My name is Siward Thomas and this is Mathew Lewin, of Devondale. The lady with us is Mistress Ceta Woodall. Paul Teller sent word to me at Tenley Palace to meet him—"

"Mathew Lewin?" the guard said, looking sharply at Mathew.

The mention of Mathew's name instantly got the attention of the second guard, who stepped away from the gate and came forward.

Mathew turned to Father Thomas, confused.

"You're Mathew Lewin?" the second man asked.

"Yes.

"Would you both come with me, please?"

At a signal from the second guard, two more sentries who were passing by hurried over to join them.

"What's this all about?" Father Thomas asked.

The other guards moved closer, but stopped in their tracks at a look from Father Thomas.

"Father, the abbot left orders that you were to be brought to him immediately when you returned," the second guard explained. "My name is Delmar Wynn and I'm in charge here. We mean no disrespect . . . to any of you."

In all the years Father Thomas had studied at the abbey, he could not recall *ever* having seen armed guards or a situation that warranted their necessity. He regarded the man evenly for a moment before making his decision.

"Very well, Delmar. Lead the way."

"After you, Father. It might be best if your companion waits here. The abbot said nothing about a woman."

Intelligent lad, Father Thomas thought. "Mistress Woodall will accompany us," the priest replied.

"As you wish."

Delmar began walking in the direction of the cathedral, but stopped when he noticed that Mathew hadn't moved from the spot he was standing in.

"You will need to come with us."

"I've had just about enough of this," Mathew snapped. "I've been gone for three weeks, come back, and get treated like a criminal?"

The two guards nearest to Mathew began to move closer to him. Without warning, a burly-looking man made a grab for his arm. The expression on his face and those around him turned to shock as he was lifted off the ground and hurled fifteen feet backward. His companion followed him a second later. Both landed on their backs, unhurt. The first guard scrambled to his feet, leveled his pike, and charged. Ceta screamed as Mathew drew his sword, stepped to his left, and parried.

"Stop!" a voice yelled from behind them. "Stop what you are doing this instant!"

Mathew heard footsteps approaching rapidly, but kept his eyes on the guard in front of him. The reaction to use his ring had been so automatic he never gave it a second thought.

"I said, stop! Put your weapons down at once. This is a house of God."

Out of the corner of his eye, Mathew saw the guards come to attention. The one holding the pike took a step back and lowered the point of his weapon. Mathew did the same and turned to face the newcomer.

Paul Teller, the abbot of Barcora, was a man just above middle height, with straight blond hair and a broad face, which made him look more like a boxer than a priest. A barrel chest, prominent jaw, and broad shoulders did nothing to take away from that impression. Mathew had met him several times during his stay at the abbey, though he knew very little about Teller—their contacts had been brief. That day, Paul Teller was not dressed like a priest. He looked more like one of the construction workers building the observatory. His brown pants were covered in dust and splashes of mud, and his shirt was stained with sweat despite the cool temperature.

"Master Lewin, unless you intend to use that sword, I suggest you put it away."

Mathew let out his breath and returned the sword to its scabbard.

"Thank you," the abbot said. "Good morning, Siward . . . Mathew. I apologize for your reception, though I'm glad you've returned." Then noticing Ceta on her horse, he added, "My apologies to you as well, mistress. I'm afraid I've not had the pleasure of your acquaintance yet."

Father Thomas introduced them. "What goes on here, Paul?"

The men shook hands and Ceta nodded. The abbot's grip was hard and calloused. It reminded Mathew of Oliver Donal, the *Wave Dancer*'s blunt captain.

"We can discuss all of this in my office—come."

Mathew still made no move to follow, nor did Ceta Woodall.

"We can talk about it right here," Mathew said. "I'd like to know why I'm being treated like a common cutpurse. I don't know what's changed, but I don't appreciate people pointing weapons in my direction."

The abbot stopped in mid-stride and turned around.

"Mathew," he said gravely, "I would consider it a personal favor if you and Siward would accompany me to my chambers. You are invited too, Mistress Woodall. There are things I do not wish to discuss in public. You have my word there will be no one else present except the four of us."

Ceta, who had not yet said anything, nodded and began to dismount. Father Thomas put a hand out to help her. Very much aware that the abbot and Mathew were still standing there looking at each other, Father Thomas feared trouble was about to erupt again. He was relieved when Mathew relented and said, "Let's go."

Paul Teller and the priest exchanged glances as Mathew walked past them, but neither chose to comment. Father Thomas gave Ceta his arm and escorted her toward the cathedral.

The abbot's chambers were located on the second floor of the administration building and had guards stationed outside the door. They came to attention when they saw the trio and the abbot approaching. Compared to other rooms he had seen during his stay at the abbey, Paul Teller's office was larger than Mathew expected it to be. A writing table stood in front of a granite fireplace. The walls and ceiling were covered in raised oak paneling. Three separate carpets covered a stone floor effectively dividing the room into distinct sections. The writing table occupied one, and a couch and chairs occupied another. The third was obviously reserved for reading, with two pairs of leather chairs facing each other near the fireplace. A lead-glass window took up nearly half of one wall, and a bookcase, filled to overflowing, ran along the opposite wall.

Paul Teller walked to his desk, but then changed his mind and went to the seating area instead, gesturing for the others to join him.

"I know you think our behavior is strange, but I assure you there are good reasons for it," said the abbot. "The day after you left for Tenley Palace, there was a murder here. Yesterday, a second one occurred."

Ceta gasped and Father Thomas said, "What? Who?"

"Edward Cole was the first; Rupert Walker was killed yesterday."

Father Thomas searched his mind for a moment, but was unable to place either man. He knew that Cole was the principal administrator of the library, reputed to be the largest in the western world. The other man was a complete blank.

Mathew was as shocked as his friends were. He was also keenly aware that Paul Teller was carefully observing his reaction to the news.

"Murdered," Father Thomas whispered, the full impact of the news beginning to settle on him. Ceta put a comforting hand on his knee and shook her head sadly.

"Murdered," Teller repeated.

Father Thomas sat back in his chair and asked, "How is this possible, Paul? Surely we would have heard something about it at the Palace."

The abbot paused before answering the question and appeared to be struggling to choose his words carefully.

"We did not want the news to leak out," Teller said. "Father Cole was found dead at the bottom of the stairs at the back of the library. Initially, we thought it was an accident. Rupert Walker was found hanging upside down from the topmost point of the ceiling in the cathedral yesterday."

"What? How in God's name is that possible?" Father Thomas said. "The ceiling has got to be over eighty feet high."

"Eighty-six feet to be exact," Paul Teller said, looking at Mathew. "It took us a full day to build a scaffold to get him down."

A picture of the cathedral's high vaulted ceilings and cavernous interior flashed into Mathew's mind, along with the gruesome image of the dead priest.

"How could anyone get up there in the first place?" Father Thomas asked.

"I have no idea. No one here does. The side of Edward Cole's skull was caved in. Rupert's skull was crushed in exactly the same manner."

The color drained out of Ceta's face.

"This is horrible," Father Thomas said. "How could such a thing happen?"

"That's precisely the question, isn't it? Rupert was seen eating dinner in the commons only hours before he was killed. If I hadn't seen it with my own eyes, I would never have believed it."

"Then I don't see how—"

"He's saying I did it. Isn't that right, abbot?" Mathew asked quietly.

Paul Teller looked squarely at Mathew. There wasn't a trace of humor or warmth in the man's face. Father Thomas was immediately on his feet.

"Paul!"

"*Sit down*, Father," the abbot said, never taking his eyes off Mathew. "This young man has just asked a question. He's entitled to an answer."

Father Thomas opened his mouth to speak, but Teller held up his hand, silencing the protest. "I didn't say you were responsible, Mathew."

"No . . . but that's what you think, isn't it?"

"Frankly, I'm not sure what to think. I would like to hear it from your own lips."

There was a pause before Mathew answered. "No, I didn't kill either Father Cole or Brother Walker."

"Brother Walker?" Teller asked.

"I met him when I was studying in the library."

"This is outrageous," Father Thomas said. "I've known Mathew since he was a child. I'd stake my life—"

"The abbot thinks that I'm the only one with the ability to have committed such an act," Mathew said. "Isn't that right?"

Instead of answering, Paul Teller raised an eyebrow and leaned back in his chair. The reaction he was getting was definitely not what he expected. In fact, there was almost no reaction at all. Given the magnitude of the news he had just delivered, the young man's self-control was astonishing. Anyone else would have been protesting their innocence at the top of their lungs. Teller was a keen judge of people, and could sense indignation coupled with curiosity, but that was about it. The chilling combination did more to increase his fears than to alleviate them. Still, Siward Thomas was adamant about the young man's character, and Siward was no one's fool.

"Rupert Walker's body didn't simply drift up to the top of the cathedral . . . unless the physical laws of nature have been temporarily suspended," said the abbot. "Have you any explanation how such a thing might have occurred?"

Mathew opened his mouth to speak, but then appeared to change his mind. He shook his head and sat back in his chair, closed his eyes.

Father Thomas and the abbot looked at each other. Ceta got up and started to go to Mathew, but stopped when Father Thomas held up his hand.

"What were Brother Walker's duties at the library?" Mathew asked.

Teller's eyes immediately narrowed. "Why do you ask?"

"Because of something I just remembered. He was always there when I was. He was always helpful . . . offering to get the books I needed. When I had questions, he answered them, except about one thing."

"I'm sorry, I don't know what you're—"

"*Yes* . . . you do," said Mathew. "It's possible I went crazy and killed both men. I certainly have the power to do it, using this."

Mathew held up his hand, showing him the rose-gold ring. Through the window, morning sunlight flooded into the room and reflected off its polished surface.

"The problem is that I haven't lost my mind, nor did I kill anybody."

"What is he talking about, Paul?" asked Father Thomas.

The abbot paused a long time before answering. "I can't tell you, Siward. It's something I'm sworn to secrecy about. This is a matter that will have to be decided by the council."

"The council? What does the council have to do with this? People have been murdered and you sit here playing games?"

"Hold your tongue and your accusations, Father. The choice is not mine. The order comes from the bishop himself."

"If you'll excuse me," Mathew said, "I'll be in the library. You can have one of the guards accompany me if you wish. I assume I'm free to go."

The abbot nodded once and gestured toward the door.

Mathew rose from the chair and looked at Teller for several seconds, then shook his head. The man clearly mistrusted him, and given the circumstances he would probably feel the same way.

"Perhaps you should tell him, Father," he said, before turning on his heel and walking out.

12

Sennia, At the Abbey

PAUL TELLER WAITED UNTIL AFTER THE DOOR CLOSED and turned to Father Thomas.

"Tell me what, Siward?"

Father Thomas took a deep breath, and with an effort, mastered the angry words forming on his lips. He recounted for the abbot Mathew's conversation with Gawl and himself two nights earlier. He told him about the statues coming to life, and the feeling Mathew had about a third person having one of the rings. The revelations had their intended effect and the color slowly drained out of Paul Teller's face. He sat back in his chair, tight-lipped as he considered what he had just heard.

"So many twists and turns," Teller muttered to himself. "It's hard to know where to begin."

"I'd like to know what Mathew meant when he said you were holding something back."

"Perhaps it would be better if your companion were to leave us," said Teller.

"She stays," Father Thomas flatly replied. "If Ceta leaves I'll do the same."

Paul Teller looked at both of them. "Mistress Woodall, will you give me your solemn word that anything you hear will remain confidential?"

"Certainly."

"Very well. To be perfectly candid, the boy is an unknown entity to us, Siward. He may well present the greatest danger since the cataclysm that nearly destroyed our world in the first place."

"Mathew? You can't be serious. Unless you've forgotten, he was the one who killed Karas Duren and destroyed the Orlock army, not to mention the Cincar and Nyngary fleets."

"I'm aware of all that," Paul Teller said. "What do you know of the ring he wears?"

"Only that it was created by our ancestors and that he can do quite a number of extraordinary things with it."

"Thought into matter—that's what the Ancients were able to achieve, Siward. They stood on the verge of the greatest accomplishment in human history, then destroyed themselves so utterly and completely, we have only remnants and stories of what they once were. In the end, their own science turned on them, tearing down their great cities and destroying the very wonders they created. You've seen the wreckage.

"We study those ruins, but they tell us little of the *causes* for their demise. The result of their folly was to throw us into a three-thousand-year-long dark age that we are just now emerging from.

"At one time, every adult man and woman throughout the civilized world had a ring of the kind Mathew wears. Did you know that? Each was made to work only with one person—its owner. It was based on the chemistry of their brain, but despite this miraculous achievement, suddenly and without any explanation, they began to destroy them. That's why there is no rose gold left in the world today. With all their powers, with all their great abilities, they were unable to control what they created."

"I don't understand," said Father Thomas.

Ceta looked equally puzzled.

"I know," Teller replied. He leaned forward and lowered his voice. "Deep beneath our world, almost at the core of the planet, there exists a machine so massive and complex it defies one's ability to imagine it. This machine worked with certain crystals that amplified the power of their thoughts to unimaginable levels. Combined with the rings, they were capable of translating a man or woman's thoughts into reality. Mathew's ring and Teanna d'Elso's are two of the last ones the Ancients created. Your revelation that another may exist comes as shock—more of a shock than you can know."

"But why destroy such a miracle?" Ceta Woodall asked.

"Why indeed? The war started slowly at first. There were a series of accidents and natural disasters. The countries of the East accused the West of secretly attacking them. The West denied it, of course, and mistrusted their old enemies in equal measure. Then the deaths began. Horrible deaths . . . things out of nightmares began occurring in both places. The scientists feverishly searched for answers, but without success. Then one morning in the early autumn, three thousand years ago, the Eastern Alliance struck without warning and the great war began. The weapons they used were conventional at first, but terrible in their power. Whole areas of the world were devastated beyond recognition, however those weapons were nothing compared to what the rings could accomplish. Had it not been—"

The abbot was interrupted by a light knock at his door.

"Come in."

The door opened and a small bespectacled man in his late sixties stood there blinking against the light. He couldn't have been more than five-foot-six and was dressed in a priest's robe.

"Come in, Marcus . . . come in. I don't believe you know Father Thomas or his friend. May I introduce Siward Thomas and Mistress Woodall of . . . uh . . ."

"Elberton," Ceta prompted.

"Yes, Elberton. Forgive me," Teller apologized. "This is Marcus Somerlin, our chief historian."

The old man shook hands with them and turned to Paul Teller, "He's in the cathedral."

Before Father Thomas could say anything, the abbot held up his hand and said, "I asked only to be kept informed of where Mathew is going and what he's doing. I assure you no harm will come to him."

Father Thomas appeared to relax slightly. "I don't know what game is being played here, Paul, but I don't like it at all."

"Fair enough," Teller replied, though there was no contrition in his voice. "Marcus, you may be better suited to finish this story than I am. Siward and I were just discussing what happened after the Ancients' war began."

The old man blinked again and rubbed a hand across his chin. He was in need of a shave and his hand had ink stains on it.

"Do you think it's wise to talk in front of an outsider?" Somerlin asked. "My apologies, mistress. I mean no offense."

"None taken," said Ceta.

"Mistress Woodall has given her word to keep our conversations private."

That seemed to satisfy the old man. "Very well . . . where did you leave off?" he asked.

"Just after the initial attack."

"I see," he said, glancing around the room. "Why don't you ever have anything to drink in here?"

The abbot rolled his eyes upward, pushed himself out of his chair, and went through a door into his private chambers. He returned a moment later with a bottle of red wine and four glasses. After Teller filled them, the historian stuck out his lower lip, examined the color for a moment, then took a sip.

"Very nice," he said. "Your taste is improving, Paul."

The abbot folded his arms across his chest and gave him a flat look.

"Dark thoughts," Somerlin said, staring into his glass. "In the end it was dark thoughts that nearly destroyed mankind."

Father Thomas wasn't sure he heard the man correctly and he glanced at Paul Teller, who nodded his head in agreement.

"Of course the Ancients knew of the problem when they began constructing the rings and they planned for it. Safeguards were developed to prevent one human being from harming another. If the crystals detected violent or evil thoughts coming from someone's brain, those thoughts were immediately isolated and the machines shut that person's ring down—forever. It was an effective deterrent. Our ancestors wanted to turn the world into a paradise, and they almost succeeded . . . except for one thing . . . dark thoughts."

"But, I thought you said—"

"That they built in safeguards," the historian added. "And so they did, but they miscalculated. They designed their great machines to stop all conscious attempts to harm others, but they forgot about what happens when the mind sleeps. What man or woman can know their own dreams?

"The Ancients didn't need to look any farther than their own mirrors to find out who was committing the terrible murders. They were occurring all over the world. Unfortunately, they realized the error too late. A desperate search was instituted to systematically destroy all of the rose-gold rings.

"Shortly after the war began, our scientists communicated their discovery to their counterparts in the East, but instead of calling off the attack, the East increased its efforts, seeking to carry their early advantage to a victory. Faced with the dismal possibility of their destruction, the Western Ruling Council—which was composed of eight members—ordered their scientists to remove the safeguards from their rings. *Only* theirs. It was a last-ditch effort to defend themselves. They believed that they could force a stalemate . . . but they were wrong. What they didn't know was that the rulers of the East had already done the same thing.

"The result was a devastation beyond anything you can imagine. Whole countries ceased to exist, and the very geography of the world was altered. Rivers changed their course, tidal waves rose up from the sea, and mountains crumbled in explosions so massive only deep canyons and valleys remained.

"Three thousand years later Karas Duren learned the same facts I've just told you about. Eight rings had been hidden away and were rumored to have survived the war. Duren began searching for them and enlisted the Orlocks to help him. Ultimately, he succeeded in locating five of the rings, though it was by the sheerest of accidents. As chance would have it, one of his own soldiers stole one and sold it to a merchant in the Galwin River District in your country. The man's name was—"

"Harol Longworth," Father Thomas said, finishing the sentence for him. "Who sold it to me as a prize for our fencing tournament. This is the same ring that Mathew now carries?"

The old historian and Paul Teller nodded their heads at the same time.

"All right," Father Thomas said, digesting what he had just heard. "This clears up a great many questions I've had. But why have you hidden the truth from Mathew?"

"Because he is an unknown entity to us, Siward," said Paul Teller. "Other than what you have related, we know almost nothing about this young man . . . and what we *do* know is not good. He killed one person in anger . . . which is hardly a recommendation. Granted the circumstances were extraordinary, but his response to them was *equally* extraordinary. Certainly, he is bright and resourceful, but our ancestors were also intelligent people . . . and they failed. He has the potential to do great good with his ring, just as he has the potential to become another Karas Duren."

"You can't be serious," Father Thomas exclaimed. "The man was a monster. He was totally insane."

"Father," Marcus said, "the Ancients had an expression. 'Power corrupts, but absolute power corrupts absolutely.' It is entirely possible Mathew knows this, at least intuitively. In fact, I suspect he does. Some time ago he stopped wearing the ring. They tell me he has started doing so again, which is troubling. I've met him twice, and he is a highly intelligent young fellow."

"I agree," the abbot said. "I'm also of the opinion it would be incredibly dangerous for us to simply let him go off unchecked."

"And what about this other person?" Father Thomas asked.

"Other person? What other person?" the historian's head came up, his gray eyes suddenly sharp and alert.

Father Thomas told him what transpired at Tenley Palace and about his subsequent discussions with Mathew. The old man sat there listening quietly, not saying a word. Several times during the conversation he and Paul Teller exchanged glances, but neither interrupted.

Another soft tap at the door caused Father Thomas to stop speaking.

A young guard stuck his head in the room and said, "He's gone to the library."

Paul Teller slapped his hands against his knees and got up out of his chair. "Let's go," he said.

All four left the room.

Mathew was aware that he was being watched from the time he left the abbot's office, but he was so angry about what Teller had said he didn't care. What he wanted was time to cool off and think. Two men had been killed, and shortly after that someone had tried to kill him, using the statues.

There were two guards stationed on either side of the main doors to the cathedral. Both of them saw Mathew coming but made no move to stop him when he walked in. As soon as he entered, he heard the sound of footsteps hurrying down the corridor and decided one of them was going to inform Paul Teller of his whereabouts.

He sat down on one of the benches and looked around.

He'd only been in the building a few times during his stay at the abbey and it was every bit as large as he remembered. The first time he, Lara, and Collin attended services there, Father Thomas told them it had taken more than eighty years to complete its construction. He also learned that the cathedral was over twelve hundred years old, an amazing accomplishment of architecture and craftsmanship.

Mathew thought once again of their little church in Devondale. It could have fit nicely inside the edifice . . . several times over. High above, a series of heavy stone beams that supporting the dome met at a point in the center. He looked up and gave a shudder at the thought of Rupert Walker's body hanging there. At the same time the logical part of his mind acknowledged the impossibility for someone to have murdered the priest and then found a way to get the body up there. It made about as much sense as stone statues coming to life.

The first time he had sensed the presence of the other ring holder he was totally shocked by it. He and Lara had been walking at the bottom of the hill behind the palace and he was using his ring to amuse her by making two peaches to float in the air and spin around each other. Suddenly, the image of another person popped into his head, but disappeared so quickly he couldn't tell if it was a man or a woman. Mathew's concentration broke and the peaches fell to the ground.

Lara had looked at them lying there. "Maybe you shouldn't give up on the idea of becoming a doctor just yet," she sighed. "I'm afraid you're just not cut out for a career in magic. In fact . . . what is it, Mathew?"

"I thought I saw . . ." he said slowly.

"What?"

"It's nothing. Probably just a memory," he had said, not wanting to alarm her.

"What sort of memory? You looked like you saw a ghost."

"It was nothing," he repeated absently. "I guess I was thinking about Duren. It happens every now and then."

She put her arms around his waist and gave him a hug, then stood on tiptoe and flicked her tongue at his earlobe.

"Wouldn't you rather be thinking of me?"

Mathew looked into her green eyes for a second while the specter in his vision receded farther and farther from his mind. He pulled Lara close and kissed her on the neck and she made a little sound. They kissed again. Eventually he forgot about the vision—until two marble statues tried to pulverize him.

Mathew squinted up into the shadows at the top of the dome, trying to sort things out. A noise at the rear of the cathedral caused him to turn when one of the guards poked his head in, then pretended not to be looking at him.

"Honestly," Mathew said, annoyed at the interruption. "I'm the only one in here. I promise I'll tell you if I decide to leave."

"Sorry," the guard called out. "Just doing my job."

Mathew waved to him and the man started to withdraw, but then stopped when Mathew called out, "I have a question."

The guard lifted his chin, indicating for him to go on.

"What's your name?"

"Warren Douglas," the man replied.

Mathew got up, walked over to him, and they shook hands.

"I'm Mat Lewin."

"I know."

"Did you know the two priests who were killed?" he asked.

"You said one question . . . that was two."

Mathew opened his mouth to protest, but closed it again when he realized Warren was teasing him. He chuckled and both men began to relax.

"You had me there."

"I know."

"You're not normally a guard are you?"

"No . . . not normally."

"I see. May I ask, what do you do when you're not carrying a pike and wearing a uniform?"

"I teach astronomy . . . which I might point out, is infinitely more interesting than standing here trying to look impressive with this ridiculous weapon."

Mathew laughed in spite of himself and tried to keep a straight face. "You're a priest, then?"

Warren inclined his head.

"I would like to ask you a question . . . actually a couple of questions about Father Cole and Brother Rupert."

"Go right ahead, Mathew. I've no instructions that prevent me from speaking with you. I'm only supposed to watch what you're doing."

"Oh . . . well, thanks."

"Not at all . . . what are your questions?"

"You did know both men, didn't you?"

"Yes."

"Do you have *any* idea why somebody would want to kill them?"

"Quite frankly, no. Both were quiet and inoffensive people. I am not aware either had any enemies, or common friends for that matter. Edward Cole was a mild mannered, pleasant man, and I can't recall Rupert ever having said a harsh word about anybody. Of course, over the last few months I had very little contact with them due to the construction of the observatory."

"There's got to be something," Mathew said, shaking his head. "These murders can't be coincidence."

"I agree. Priests get into disagreements like everyone else, but this is the first time I've ever heard of a situation ending in violence. The last time a murder was committed here was well over five hundred years ago. Generally, we tend to do more talking than hitting."

"I knew Brother Walker, too," Mathew told him. "He helped me find books in the library, but I never met Father Cole. What was he like?"

"As I say, Edward was a quiet, reserved man. He was a competent administrator."

"Administrator of what?" Mathew asked.

"Why, the library of course."

Mathew blinked and stared at the priest, then spun on his heel and took off at a trot down the corridor. He stopped after about fifty feet and called back to Father Douglas, "Oh . . . I'm sorry, Father, I'm heading to the library."

"So I gathered. I'll make certain to report it."

The abbey's library was nearly four stories high and was one of the eight main buildings in the complex. During the time he had lived there, the research he'd done on the origins of his ring was confined to the first two floors where row after row of the books were stored. From the signs located at the entrance to each staircase, Mathew knew the administrative offices were located on the fourth floor. He recalled Brother Walker once telling him that the top floors also had books, as well as maps and a variety of artifacts. He wasn't exactly sure what he wanted to see, but suddenly the top floor held a great deal of interest for him.

Maybe I'm clutching at straws. Two men dead . . . murdered, and both were priests who worked in the library.

Mathew emerged from the staircase on the third floor to find himself in the middle of a long corridor. Directly in front of him were two double doors behind which the books were kept. There were other doors along the corridor, too. If this floor was similar to the way the second had been laid out, each of the rooms would contain small specialized collections, devoted to one particular subject.

Before he had a chance to make up his mind he heard the sound of footsteps coming up the stairs behind him. Delmar, the guard they had met earlier, rounded the corner of the landing and came to an abrupt halt when he saw Mathew standing there.

"I'm just here to have a look around," Mathew told him. "You can come with me if you like."

"That won't be necessary," said Delmar. He recovered his composure and climbed the rest of the steps up to where Mathew was.

"I'm sorry about what happened before. I hope I didn't hurt you," Mathew said.

"It's all right. I should have explained what was going on to you. I'm a little new at this."

"Are you a priest too?"

"In training," Delmar answered. "I'm supposed to be—"

"Watching me. I know," Mathew said, finishing the sentence for him.

"Right."

"I understand. If I decide to grow another head, I'll make sure and tell you first."

Delmar smiled. "Everybody's just a little on edge with what happened. I don't like this anymore than you do. They told me most priests lead quiet, peaceful lives."

Mathew thought about Father Thomas for a second, but decided saying nothing would be best.

"Delmar, did you know Father Cole or Brother Walker?"

"No, I'm studying architecture. We're in the third quadrangle all the way at the other end of this place. I don't get down here very much."

"So why did they draft you for guard duty?" Mathew asked.

"Just lucky I guess. After Abbot Teller informed the

bishop about what happened, he ordered us to set up guards—the bishop I mean. And since I'm one of the more junior people . . ."

"But Father Douglas isn't junior? I assume he's the one who told you I was here."

Delmar nodded. "He did."

"He and Father Egan don't get along very well. Father Egan's the assistant abbot, in case you didn't know, and he's in charge of the guards."

Mathew was sorry he had brought the subject up. "I see . . . thank you. I just want to poke around a little. Do you want me to leave the doors open?"

"It might be a good idea," Delmar conceded. "What are you looking for?"

Mathew shrugged. "Something . . . anything. I just think it's a pretty large coincidence that both men who were killed also worked in the library. Don't you?"

"It sounds reasonable."

"Would you like to help?"

"With what?"

"Looking for clues," Mathew said. "After we're through, we can go up to the fourth floor."

"Uh-uh," Delmar said, shaking his head. "The fourth floor's off limits. You need the abbot's permission to go up there. That's okay. I'll stay here and guard you."

Mathew got only as far as the second room when Father Thomas, Ceta, Paul Teller and Marcus Somerlin all appeared in the doorway.

"May I ask what you're doing, Mathew?" asked Paul Teller.

"Until a little while ago, I didn't know Father Cole and Brother Walker *both* worked in the library. I was just curious if there might be something around that would be a clue as to why they were murdered."

"And have you found anything?"

"No. Just books," Mathew answered glumly. "I'd like

to see the fourth floor, but Delmar said I would need your permission."

The abbot turned to look at the young trainee who gave him a quick smile and then stared straight ahead.

"Delmar is quite correct. Unfortunately, I cannot give you my permission at this time. At least not until I speak with the bishop. I assume you all will be staying the night before you return to Tenley Palace. I'll arrange for rooms."

"What's so special about the fourth floor?" Mathew asked.

"We can discuss that in the morning," the abbot said. "Now if you'll excuse me, I have evening vespers. Perhaps we can talk further then. There are still several things I'd like to ask you."

At dinner, Mathew brought up the subject of the fourth floor again to Father Thomas, but the priest had no idea why Paul Teller had refused.

After the abbot had left them, Mathew, Father Thomas, Ceta, and Marcus Somerlin went through each of the libraries on the third floor one by one. In each case the results were the same—books and more books, but nothing the least bit unusual. The more Mathew thought about it the more he wanted to know why he wasn't being allowed up to the fourth floor if there was nothing to hide. Throughout the meal he kept expecting Father Thomas to tell him what he and the abbot had discussed, but his friend was unusually silent and seemed preoccupied. Eventually Mathew gave up, said good night, and went to bed.

His old room looked the same as the day he left it, functional and unpretentious with a single bed that was placed against the wall. There was a chest of drawers with an oval mirror hanging above it and a small desk in the corner. Out of curiosity he tried pulling out the second drawer in the chest—it still stuck in the same place. With a little effort he pulled it all the way out and saw, with some satisfaction, the initials ML, which he had carved several months ago. Mathew pushed the drawer closed and looked up at the mirror. A pair of bright blue eyes and a chin made slightly darker by almost a full day's growth of stubble regarded him. As he ran his hands over his chin the rose-gold ring glinted in the light. He pulled it off and dropped it into his palm.

He stared at the writing on the inside of the band, then placed back it on his finger. The familiar shiver flashed through his arm just as he knew it would and disappeared a moment later.

13

MATHEW LOOKED UP WHEN THERE WAS A LIGHT KNOCK at his door. He opened it to find Ceta Woodall standing there.

"Ceta?" he said, surprised to see her.

"May I come in, Mathew?"

"Sure," he said, stepping aside. "Is everything all right?"

"Actually, I was going to ask you the same question. Are *you* all right? You were pretty upset when you left the abbot's chambers."

Mathew rubbed the bridge of his nose with his fingers. "Wouldn't you be if people started thinking you were a murderer?"

"Yes . . . I would. I don't think you're a murderer, Mathew, and neither does Siward. These people are just scared, that's all. I wanted to stop by and see if I could do anything for you."

Mathew took a deep breath and plopped down in the chair. "There is something. I want to get into the library."

"But you were there earlier. We all were."

"Not on the fourth floor. The abbot wouldn't allow me up. I think they're hiding something. Something they don't want me to see. I didn't kill those men."

The lady innkeeper sat down on the bed and looked at him seriously. "If I thought you did, we wouldn't be talking right now. I've always trusted my instincts and I'd hate to think the man I'm going to marry is a poor judge of character. What are you looking for?"

"Honestly, I don't know," Mathew said, shaking his head. "It's just a feeling I have. I'd like to know why those two men were murdered."

"What is it you want me to do?" Ceta asked.

"I'm going to try to get in there tonight. My guess is they'll have someone posted to make sure I don't. Would you be willing to act as a lookout for me?"

Ceta took a deep breath. "Oh dear . . . Mathew, this wasn't exactly what I had in mind when I said I wanted to help."

"It's all right. I understand. I shouldn't have asked you. This isn't any of your affair."

Neither of them said anything for almost a full minute. During that time Ceta wrestled with her emotions. On one hand, she meant it when she said she wanted to help. On the other, she was a sensible, practical woman who had finally found the love of her life—a man she was going to marry. Getting involved in breaking into the church's private property was anything but sensible. She could just imagine what Siward's reaction would be when he found out. But there was no question in her mind about Mathew's innocence. Any fool could see that.

She looked at the solemn young man sitting in front of her and shook her head. Earlier that day Mathew had said that Siward, Lara, and Collin were his only family. It broke her heart.

Ever so gradually she felt the muscles in her face relax and a smile began to play at the corners of her mouth. *I wonder what that will make me after I marry Siward.*

The hallway was deserted. Except for the low hiss of gas lamps in the corridor, everything was quiet. Mathew took special care to muffle the sound of his footfalls in case he ran into someone, but at that hour of the night it was highly unlikely.

They made their way down the steps of the dormitory to the lobby and out into the night. The library was at the opposite end of the Charlton Quadrangle, two hundred yards away. Many years ago, all dirt paths crisscrossing the abbey complex had been paved over in brick. The lampposts were a recent addition, according to Father Thomas. Mathew checked to make sure the coast was clear, then signaled to Ceta.

A little farther ahead, a scrawny black cat rubbing its face against a bench stopped and looked directly at them. The cat cocked its head to one side and gave a tentative meow.

"Scat," Mathew whispered under his breath.

The cat meowed again and started walking toward them.

"Wonderful," Ceta muttered.

She looked at Mathew for a moment, then bent down, picked up a pebble, and tossed it in the cat's direction.

The cat stopped, its eyes suddenly alert.

Another pebble followed, slightly closer than the one before, which sent it scurrying toward the bushes where it promptly disappeared from sight.

There was a brief moment of concern about whether the door would be locked, but that proved to be baseless. Mathew turned the knob ever so softly and pushed against the door, opening it just a crack.

"All clear," he said.

They checked the corridor. It was as deserted as the quadrangle had been, so they headed for the stairs and went up. Mathew peered around the corner of the landing between the third and fourth floors and pulled his head back quickly—someone was sitting at the top of the stairs.

He mouthed the word "guard" and pointed.

Ceta allowed herself a brief glance as well. The man

was about fifty years old, and stretched out in a chair. He appeared to be dozing.

She tugged on his sleeve and pulled him close to her. "What are we going to do?" she whispered.

"I don't know. I've got to get past him somehow."

Ceta thought for a second and came up with the answer. The entire staircase from the first floor up was lined with portraits of men and a few women. They'd seen them on the way up, but neither had the slightest idea who they were. *Probably librarians*, she thought. "Hide on the third floor. I'm going to knock one of those paintings off the wall. When I do, the guard will come down to see what the noise is about. That should give you the chance you need."

"What about you?" Mathew whispered.

"I'll tell him I lost my way."

Mathew nodded and tiptoed back down the stairs.

Directly above Ceta's head the stern visage of a white-haired old man glowered down at her.

"Sorry," she said, and slowly began to push the frame upward

The painting hit the ground with such a loud crash it nearly caused the guard to fall over the back of his chair. He sprang forward, and charged down the staircase.

14

Sennia, The Abbey Library

MATHEW WAITED UNTIL THE MAN HAD TURNED THE COR-
ner, then took the steps two at a time. He opened the door
to the fourth-floor and stepped inside, gently closing it
behind him. The last thing he heard was Ceta apologizing
for her clumsiness, explaining that she had twisted her
ankle.

Now that he was there he wasn't sure what to look for.
Except for a sign that said RESTRICTED, the fourth floor
appeared very much the same as the other floors. Row after row of books lined the walls and the shelves. The
room also contained tables, chairs, and small carrels that
the priests could use for study, but nothing about the
place seemed in any way unusual. Perplexed, Mathew
stood there with his hands on his hips trying to figure out
what to do next. Then he spotted the four offices at the
rear of the room.

One of them bore a sign with the name RUPERT
WALKER on the door. The next two had names he wasn't
familiar with, but the last read EDWARD COLE with the
words SENIOR ADMINISTRATOR underneath.

Mathew walked to Rupert Walker's office and tried the
door handle. A flick of his hand opened the lock and he
went in. He waited until his eyes grew accustomed to the
dark and looked around. Fortunately a gas lamp right inside the entrance made the task a little easier. He spent
the next five minutes examing the bookshelves and pok-

ing through the drawers of Brother Walker's desk. Once
again everything seemed depressingly normal. Mathew
picked up a book from the side of the desk. It turned out
to be a journal listing the previous abbots of Barcora.
Each entry contained a brief biographical note, the years
the abbot held his post and his date of death. At the lower
left-hand corner of each entry was a letter with a number
next to it. Mathew frowned and stared at them; they made
no sense. He continued leafing through the book and noticed one of the pages had been torn out, but it was impossible to tell if it had been done recently. *That's
strange.*

He turned his attention to the desk, which was covered
with papers, as though Brother Walker had simply gone
to lunch and would return any moment, except he wasn't
going to . . . ever. One of the papers was an inventory of
the pieces Father Kellner's group had recovered in Argenton. The signature at the bottom was Aldrich Kellner's. Mathew glanced at the descriptions of pots, pans,
tools, and eating utensils. Each item was numbered.
About halfway down, several entries labeled TIME PAINT-
INGS caught his interest. He hadn't the faintest idea what
a time painting was. There were other things listed there,
but none of them appeared terribly important. Disappointed, he dropped the list back on the desk and slipped
out through the door again.

Father Cole's office was at least fifty feet away and almost completely dark, so Mathew decided he would have
to risk a light. He found a match in his pocket and struck
it against the wall. The room contained a lamp on the corner of Father Cole's desk. Once it was lit, Mathew turned
it as low as possible.

Except for being neater and more organized than the
office he had just come from, Father Cole's room was
quite unremarkable. It had a desk with two chairs in front
of it, several filing cabinets, and a locked bookcase.
Locked?

It was the first time he could remember seeing books locked up.

Why would anyone want to lock up books? He moved closer for a better look

Five separate shelves of books were visible behind a wrought-iron grating that was backed by a pane of glass. Mathew was about to open the lock when he glanced down and noticed the two red smudges on the floor. The image of blood immediately came to his mind.

No, the abbot said Father Cole was found dead behind the stables.

He looked at the marks again and decided that they were more orange than red, shook his head at his own silliness, and turned his attention back to the bookcase.

Mathew stared at the lock and a second later there was an audible click. He squatted down on his haunches and brought the lamp closer.

Now what's so important they have to lock you up?

Both the books and the shelves were both covered in a layer of dust, and it looked as though no one had opened the case in quite a while, *except* . . . One of them was missing. On the second shelf, the outline of where a book had stood was plainly visible in the dust. Mathew glanced at the rest of the shelf. Everything else was intact.

"Perhaps I can help you," a voice behind him said.

Mathew let out a yell of surprise and spun around.

Paul Teller was seated in a chair in the far corner of the room. Mathew returned his gaze, but didn't speak.

"Did you find what you were searching for, Mathew?" Teller asked.

"No. At least I don't think so. I was hoping to find—"

"Some clue as to why Edward Cole and Rupert Walker were murdered. I know."

"You know?"

"You didn't exactly make a secret of your intentions, Mathew. Warren Douglas and Delmar Walker both spoke with me. Neither of them thinks you had anything to do with the murders, by the way."

"And what about you?"

"Until late this afternoon, I wouldn't have known how to answer your question, but something Siward Thomas shared with me has changed all that. He told me—"

A soft rap at the door stopped the abbot. Father Thomas and Marcus Somerlin stepped into the room. The priest and Mathew made eye contact, but neither said anything.

"Siward, I was just relating our conversation to Mathew. Mathew, this is Marcus Somerlin, our chief historian."

Mathew and Somerlin acknowledged each other with nods.

"As I understand it, you believe someone other than you and Teanna d'Elso has possession of one of the eight rings. Is that correct?"

"Yes."

"Is there any chance it's Karas Duren or his sister?" Somerlin asked.

"I don't think so," Mathew replied. "In fact I'm positive it's not them. I know what their minds felt like."

"Why are you here, my son?" Father Thomas asked.

Mathew shrugged. "I don't know. I thought I could do something to help."

Father Thomas gave Mathew a quick smile.

"May I ask what you were looking for?" Paul Teller asked.

"I told you I'm not sure. I just thought it was odd for a bookcase to be locked. I also thought it was strange the two men who were killed both worked in the library."

Paul Teller and Marcus Somerlin exchanged glances and turned back to Mathew.

"Was your search of Brother Rupert's office any more profitable?" Somerlin asked.

"Not really," Mathew answered. "I guess this wasn't such a good idea after all. The only thing I saw was a book with a page missing, but I'm not sure if that means anything at all."

"Which book?" Somerlin asked, suddenly full of interest.

"It was a journal of some kind listing all the former abbots here. You weren't in there yet," Mathew said to Paul Teller.

"I'm very much relieved to hear it," he replied.

There was something about Marcus Somerlin's reaction when he mentioned the journal and the missing page that made him continue. Suddenly the empty spot in the bookcase took on a new significance.

"Did you know there's a book missing from this bookcase?"

Somerlin hesitated before answering. "What book are you referring to?"

Mathew shook his head. "I have no idea, but one of them is definitely missing."

"Show me," Somerlin said as he stepped closer.

Mathew waited until Father Thomas and Paul Teller also came closer, then he pointed to the empty spot.

"Excuse me for a moment," Somerlin said, "there's something I need to check."

"Do you mind if I ask a question?"

Somerlin, already halfway out of the office, paused and turned around.

"There were a series of numbers and letters at the bottom of the journal pages in Brother Walker's office. What do they mean?" Mathew asked.

Instead of answering, Somerlin said, "Give me a moment, please."

He disappeared through the door. Mathew, Father Thomas, and Paul Teller were in the process of making small talk when the old man burst into the room a short time later. He rushed up to Teller and began whispering in his ear.

Mathew couldn't hear what was being said, but he was positive he had hit on something. When Somerlin was finished he sat down heavily in his chair and looked at the abbot. A full minute passed before Paul Teller reached his decision.

"Mathew, I was going to wait until I heard from the Ecumenical Council before speaking with you. This decision should properly be theirs. Father Thomas already knows some of what I am about to tell you, but under the circumstances I think our waiting would do more harm than good.

"During your stay here, Rupert Walker was assigned to help you. He was also assigned to keep certain information from falling into your hands . . . at least until we were sure how you would deal with it."

Mathew opened his mouth to say something, but Paul Teller went on before he could speak.

"Allow me to finish and I'll be happy to answer your questions."

Mathew glanced at Father Thomas, who nodded, so he sat on the corner of the desk and waited for the abbot to go on.

Teller recounted to him basically the same story Father Thomas heard earlier. Mathew listened quietly, his face growing more somber as the revelations about the Ancients unfolded. It took the abbot several minutes to complete the tale.

"All right. I understand you weren't sure if I would start howling at the moon or take it into my head that I was equal to God. So why tell me now?" Mathew asked.

"Because of what you've just discovered."

"You mean the missing book and the torn page?"

Paul Teller let out a long breath. "Yes, I'm afraid so. At any rate we'll know in a few minutes."

The crease between Mathew's eyebrows deepened and he thought hard for a moment.

"Those letters and numbers on Brother Walker's book are some kind of code, aren't they?"

"They are. What I didn't tell you," Paul Teller said, turning to Father Thomas, "is for the past eight hundred years the church has been guarding a secret. More specifically, this abbey has guarded it. From generation to generation, each abbot has been charged with the responsibility of watching over one of the rings.

"Until Karas Duren made his discovery of the five rings, we thought the one here was the last of its kind."

"But you said the Ancients produced eight rings," said Father Thomas.

"That's true," Marcus Somerlin answered. "There had been no word about them for centuries; all the rings were lost and we thought destroyed. It appears we were wrong."

15

Sennia, In the Crypt

THE ABBOT, FATHER THOMAS, MATHEW, AND MARCUS Somerlin walked across the quadrangle past the dormitories to the cathedral. Two guards saw them coming and straightened their uniforms. Paul Teller greeted them and gave instructions that no one was to enter until they came out.

Once inside he led them up the center aisle to the altar. Memories of attending endless prayer services as a novice flooded back into Father Thomas's mind as he looked out over the rows of mahogany pews. Intricately crafted stained-glass windows ringed the perimeter of the cathedral, producing a myriad of colors that bathed the room in rainbows when sunlight flooded in. The floor, laid by hand over a thousand years ago, was mosaic tile with geometric designs that seemed to change in appearance if one stared at them long enough. Father Thomas smiled to himself at the number of times he had tried to count them during some of the less inspiring sermons that he sat through. His attention drifted upward to the vaulted ceiling high above him. Though he already knew the answer, he looked at the walls, to see if there was some way for a person to access the top of the cathedral without using a ladder. There wasn't.

"It took us more than a day for us to construct a scaffold high enough to reach him," the abbot said again.

Father Thomas had already reached the conclusion that

it would have been impossible for anyone to have scaled those walls, let alone do it while carrying a body. The fact that they suspected Mathew was ridiculous.

A clearing of the abbot's throat brought the priest out of his reverie. They were now standing directly in front of the altar. Teller glanced around the sanctuary, satisfied himself they were alone, then walked to the opposite end of the altar.

"Come," he said, beckoning to the others.

Teller went directly to the second of four high-backed oak chairs that were lined up along the wall and lifted one of its arms up. A wall panel next to the chair swung open a few inches with a click. In all his years at the abbey, Father Thomas had heard tales of secret panels and passage ways weaving throughout the building, but this was the first time he had actually seen one.

Beyond the panel lay a darkened hallway, and one by one they stepped through. The abbot searched for a match in the pocket of his pants, located it, and reached up to light a lamp hanging on the wall. The hallway was narrow, relatively short, and ended at a staircase. Teller motioned again and they followed him down the stairs. They emerged in large room located directly under the cathedral floor. They were in a crypt—the final resting place for the abbots of Barcora.

Wisps of smoke drifted up into the cool, dank air after Marcus Somerlin lit two more lamps. A number of thick marble columns that supported the floor above ran for well over two hundred feet in each direction. Father Thomas found himself standing in front of a sarcophagus. The lid showed an alabaster relief of the person resting within, and a date carved on the side said the occupant had died over four hundred years earlier. Gregory Jacolo's name, one of the old abbots, was only dimly familiar to Father Thomas.

There were other tombs, some more ornate and some quite plain. A few bore only the names of the deceased on the outside, while others had death masks or full body sculptures of the abbots resting with their arms across their chests, in permanent states of repose.

Father Thomas looked around the room, then at Paul Teller. He had already guessed why the abbot had brought them down there. In the dim light, he watched Teller walk over to one of the crypts and begin to feel around under its edge. A second later a small drawer popped open and he stared into it.

"Dear God," Teller said, "it's gone."

Marcus Somerlin pushed past Father Thomas and Mathew and stared in shock into the empty drawer.

16

Northern Sennia, Town of Argenton

IT WAS DARK IN THE CAVE AND THE TWO MEN WHO WERE making their way carefully along the narrow path needed torches to see properly. Outside, far below them in the northwestern part of Argenton, they could still hear the sounds of shovels and picks as workers unearthed more of the ancient city, buried for three millennia. The ruins were some of the most extensive ever found in Sennia and they offered archaeologists glimpses into metals, technology, and artifacts believed to have disappeared centuries before. Despite the impressive finds, everything paled in comparison to the recent discovery within the cave. Except for the two men, no one else knew of its existence.

After several hundred yards the path began to widen to a point where they could walk side by side. It also descended deeper into the mountain. Ahead of them they could see the strange green and amber lights moving over the rock walls.

Phosphorescence.

The men were able to stand upright in this part of the cave, no longer needing to stoop as the ceiling grew higher with each succeeding step. The entire journey was difficult and would last almost two hours. Aldrich Kellner, the church's young archaeologist, thoughtfully took the bishop's elbow and helped him down a small incline. The next section of the path was steeper than the previous ones, forcing them to descend sideways. Kellner, who had first discovered the cave, lead the older man and reached back offering his arm for support.

Normally finding a cave would not have elicited much excitement. The entire region was mountainous and honeycombed with caves. Six months earlier, while he was walking in Argenton's marketplace, Father Kellner had heard a local woman cautioning her children against playing on the hill or going into the cave. His curiosity peaked; he asked her why.

There were rumors the cave was haunted, explained the woman.

An educated man, Father Kellner laughed and assured her there were no such things as ghosts, though he agreed that a cave was not the best place for children to play. When he asked why she thought it was haunted, the woman told him that strange noises and lights were often seen coming from it. She also said there was no point in tempting providence, and she flatly refused to take him there. Instead she pointed to the hill near the edge of the town and told him that the entrance was located on the other side of a jagged outcropping of rock. Father Kellner squinted and tried to see what she was talking about, but when he turned back to ask another question, the woman had disappeared into the crowd.

His primary duties supervising the excavations kept him from looking for the cave for almost a week. During that time, work on the project continued. The section of Argenton they were working on had been abandoned centuries before due to flooding from the nearby river. Over the years the river had changed its course, and the town where the people lived was now located two miles to the east of the ruins themselves. As the days rolled by the crews unearthed the remains of a wide street. It caused an immediate stir throughout the camp and the surrounding province. Curiosity-seekers began to flock there. As a result, Lord Guy, who ruled the region at the time, had to post guards at the excavation because a number of artifacts that were recovered seemed to disappear without a trace. Interestingly, the street they found was at least fifty feet below the level of the abandoned part of the town. Apparently the new section had been built right over the old one. Continued digging soon revealed the foundation of a building. Another building was located shortly thereafter, then another, and eventually an entire network of streets, homes, and structures began to emerge. What were originally thought to be giant mounds of earth were painstakingly removed over a period of six years to reveal other buildings. Some were more than ten stories high. Excited by the discovery, Father Kellner sent word back to the abbey, along with a request for more men, which the church readily supplied. Argenton was proving to be a virtual treasure trove of relics. Each item they found was carefully removed from the rubble, cataloged, and returned to the abbey for study. The usual collection of brushes, combs, and coins were recovered, along with odd lidded boxes that opened up to reveal keyboards and screens. No one had the slightest idea what they were. None of the boxes functioned, but then one never knew what secrets they might ultimately reveal.

Six days after his conversation with the old woman, Father Kellner found himself walking in the hills above the town. He enjoyed the solitude because it gave him a chance to think without having to answer questions from those too lazy to think for themselves. He pulled his cloak tighter around him to keep out the chill. Snow flurries were becoming more frequent, and while the ground remained soft enough for his crews to continue working, he knew they would soon have to close down for the winter. Winters came early in northern Sennia, and they were almost always accompanied by heavy snowfall. Another four months would make little difference in the great scheme of things, he knew.

Aldrich Kellner was not only a practical man, but a pious one. He considered himself a priest first and an archaeologist second. Orphaned at the age of six, with no living relatives, the church had become both mother and father to him and the other priests his family. He learned church doctrine and scripture so well that he could quote them by heart. They were something he believed in deeply; something all men and women needed to follow if they wished to enter heaven. In his mind the holy word left little room for the niceties of interpretation, which modernists were so willing to adopt when the need suited them. Though raised among Levads, who tended to take a more flexible view of things, Aldrich Kellner proved an easy convert to fundamentalism. The hours he and Bishop Willis spent together discussing scripture convinced him of the man's devout nature as well as his wisdom. They both shared the view that the church had become misguided in recent years. That the College of Bishops had picked a commoner like Paul Teller to head the abbey was only further confirmation of how far they had strayed.

Many more thoughts filled Father Kellner's head as he walked. For three hundred years, the church had effectively led the people of Sennia along the true path by providing wise counsel and guidance to the regents of the country. For three hundred years there had been no king. Now they had Baegawl Alon d'Atherny, a seven-foot-tall giant, who had somehow managed to survive the Olyiad and assume the throne—to the dismay of church elders.

While the new king was properly respectful, it quickly became obvious that he listened more to his own counsel than to anyone else's. To make matters worse, he held both the love of the people and their support. The victory at Ardon Field only endeared him to them all the more.

Of course King Gawl observed the appropriate rites and rituals as any religious man should, but his relationship with the church had become increasingly strained over the last several months. His latest plan was to open the Sennian borders and drop all restrictions on foreign trade and immigration—unquestionably a disaster in the making. Why he was unable to see that such actions would expose his people to the influences and corruption of the outside world was a puzzle to Father Kellner. Clearly the man's judgment was impaired, a fact both he and Bishop Willis agreed on. Sennia had been protected for three centuries and they along with many of their brethren, saw little reason to change. When the miracle occurred, there could have been no greater confirmation for the bishop and young priest.

Father Kellner could still remember the first time he had seen the cave, as though it were only yesterday. The event was forever burned in his memory. It was late in the afternoon and the glow coming from the entrance had immediately caught his attention as he walked along. He paused to stare at the strange green lights ghosting across the rocks. While he did so his conversation with the old woman came back to him. This was her haunted place.

Father Kellner sighed. Country people were always attributing things they didn't understand to supernatural causes. Aldrich Kellner did not believe in ghosts. Not only was he a priest, he was a scientist, so he went into the cave to investigate.

It took only seconds and an experienced eye to banish the ghost theory in favor of a more viable one. *Phosphorescent rocks*, he smiled to himself. Not exactly an unheard of phenomenon.

The cave entrance was narrow and the roof was so low he was forced to bend, but it appeared to open up the farther back it went. Out of curiosity Kellner made his way toward the rear of the cave where the flickering lights were moving with a life of their own. A damp smell hung in the air, indicating there was water nearby. He searched around for the source, but in the changing light he could see nothing definite. Stalactites hung downward from the ceiling like fingers pointing, casting black shadows on the walls. To the right by a large boulder he spotted a rugged path that looked to go deeper into the mountain. It too became lost in the dark recesses of the cave. Father Kellner brushed the hair away from his eyes and took a few steps forward, straining to see better. A cool breeze filtering out of the opening touched his face. The dampness was definitely stronger there, and he concluded the water source was probably a large one to produce the moisture he was feeling. Unfortunately, he had neither lantern nor matches with him, and not knowing what lay ahead, it was entirely possible to step into a bottomless hole if he kept going.

Father Kellner decided to leave further exploration for another day and turned to leave. Despite his years of training, there was nothing in his experience that could have prepared him for what happened next. He had only taken two steps when a voice called out his name.

Aldrich Kellner. It was barely an audible whisper.

Father Kellner spun around in the direction the sound had come from.

"Who is that?" he called out. "Show yourself at once."

Only silence and the movement of wind answered him.

A minute passed while he remained frozen in the same spot, listening for any sound other than his own heart thumping. The priest was almost ready to conclude that his imagination had played a trick on him when the whisper came again.

Aldrich Kellner.

"Who are you? If this is a jest, I do not find it amusing."

Come to me, my son.

For the second time in less than two minutes, the priest drew his breath in sharply and took a step backward, flattening himself against the rock wall. He was certain he heard the words clearly this time, but they were in the language of the Ancients!

"Who calls me?"

Come to me, my son.

"Where are you? Are you hurt?"

Come, my child. Do not be afraid. I am with you.

"I don't understand. Tell me where you are. I'll come and help," the priest said into the darkness.

The way lies before you. Behold!

Suddenly the phosphorescent glow emanating from the rocks in front of him increased, illuminating the walls and highlighting the path. A hundred yards ahead the light began to slowly pulse.

Father Kellner swallowed, fought down the fear building in his chest, and began walking toward the light. For the next half hour the path continued to wind its way into the recesses of the mountain. Several times he passed through different rooms. Some were smaller than the first one he had entered and some larger. A few had openings that led off into the blackness, and he eventually concluded that he was in a labyrinth of some sort. The voice did not speak again, but the pulsing lights always stayed before him. At one point he entered a large room containing the most fantastic stalactites and stalagmites he'd ever seen, and he stared at them in wonder. Gradually, the surface of the floor changed from dirt to rock and then to smooth stone.

Father Kellner looked up at the roof of the cave, now nearly a hundred feet above him. He had no idea how deep under the mountain he had come, but from the amount of time he'd been walking, he knew that he was far below the surface. For a moment panic seized him. How would he find his way back? At the end of the room there were three separate doorways. Two were dark, but a green glow was coming from the one in the center. After a brief glance behind him to fix his direction, he went on.

The path grew narrow once again, causing him to turn sideways in order to squeeze past a massive twisting rock formation. Even as a boy, Aldrich Kellner had never liked confined spaces, and unbidden, his old childhood fears returned. Twice he stopped, wedged in tiny crevices, fighting to catch his breath. His feet seemed to be made of lead. Images of massive walls slowly closing and crushing him to death made him want to turn and scramble back the way he had come. Then he was through. He followed the path to a final room and found himself standing on the ledge of a cliff in an enormous cavern. Subtle mixtures of muted colors combined with more brilliant, sparkling ones played off the rock walls all around him. He stood there in awe, not only at the beauty of the natural wonders but at the two gigantic statues at the far end of the cavern. More than a hundred feet below a breeze from some subterranean source created ripples across a lake that looked nearly a mile across. Near the shore a yellow-white glow slowly undulated beneath the surface of the water.

To his right were a series of rough-hewn steps that had been cut into the face of the cliff. Father Kellner went down. A short while later he found himself standing on a sandy beach alongside the lake. The light was still there, but it was impossible tell what was causing it.

A minute passed . . . then another.

The priest's earlier fears slowly began to dissipate, replaced by curiosity, and a desire to learn who, or what, had brought him to this strange place. Few people other than clerics and scholars knew the ancient language, so he waited to see if the voice would speak again.

He didn't have long to wait.

The sound of water moving attracted his attention. The light in the center of the lake was drawing nearer to him. Father Kellner took a step back, then steadied himself. When the light was about fifty feet from the shore, the water around it began to boil. Tiny waves lapped up against the soles of his boots, but the priest didn't notice them, so intent was he on what was happening. The breeze he had felt on the ledge suddenly started blowing harder, pushing his long black hair off his shoulders. Father Kellner's mouth dropped open in shock as the figure of a woman rose from the churning waters.

She wore a long gown of pure white and floated above the surface of the lake, calmly watching him. Her face was the most beautiful he'd ever seen. A glowing nimbus of light surrounded her, causing him to shield his eyes.

"Aldrich Kellner," she said softly. Her voice had a soft musical quality to it, like striking pure glass chimes.

"Who are you?" he whispered.

A warm smile touched the woman's face and she inclined her head slightly. "Do you not know me, my son?"

Father Kellner blinked and stared more closely. It took a moment for the realization to dawn on him. His eyes went wide in shock and he gasped *"Alarice!"*

The woman closed her eyes and nodded her head once in affirmation.

Stunned into speechlessness, Father Kellner fell to his knees and clasped his hands together before her. He was in the presence of Alarice, patron saint of Sennia, and protector of its people. Images of her face in paintings and on frescoes in the cathedral came into his mind. An incredible marble statue of her carved by the great artisan Giotto stood in the novice's quadrangle at the abbey, but it paled in comparison to the vision floating before him.

"Dear Aldrich . . . do not be afraid. I have visited many before you, and none have ever come to harm."

Father Kellner slowly lifted his head as he held a shaking hand above his eyes.

"W-What do you want of me?" he stammered.

"Only to talk, my son. A great danger threatens our people. This is why I have called you here."

"A danger? What danger?" the priest asked.

"Baegawl d'Atherny leads our country down a road to disaster."

"The king? I don't understand. He is a headstrong man, yes, but I don't see—"

"Gawl is no longer guided by the wisdom of the church, Aldrich. He is now influenced by another. He seeks to open our country to all nations—East and West alike. For centuries our people have flourished, free of corruption, but if the king succeeds with what he intends to do, this will no longer be the case. Mirdanites, Elgarians, Felizians, Vargothans and others will come to Sennia. They will bring customs and practices to us that are an abomination in the sight of the Lord."

Alarice's eyes flashed as she spoke and the intensity of her voice reverberated off the cavern walls. Her words assailed the priest's ears, and touched his heart, awakening in him his deepest misgivings about the deterioration of morality. They struck a chord in his soul.

"I have thought this many times myself," he said to her. "But surely if we speak to the king and explain to him what will happen, he will listen."

"This was true in the past, but with each day he moves closer and closer to making Sennia an open nation. The Mirdanites consume herbs and imbibe potions that cause men to lose their ability to reason. The loyalty of a Felizian merchant is only to the money he makes and whatever advantage he can take from his dealings. Vargothans are little better, hiring out their swords to anyone who wishes to buy them. Elgaria is a ruined country seeking to rebuild itself at the expense of our nation. Need I go on?"

By the time Father Kellner emerged from the cave the moon was high, painting the landscape in a cold silver light. Small icicles hung from tree branches and it was snowing again.

The next day the priest returned to the cave, as he did the day after that and every day for the following week. He couldn't say how long he spent listening to Alarice, but the picture of doom that she was painting for the people of Sennia was ominous. In the end he found himself in full agreement with her. On the last day something Alarice said pricked his attention.

"You spoke of one who influences the king," he said. "Who is this person?"

Alarice may have smiled then, but the smile was somehow less warm than it was before. The waters around her began to boil in agitation and the light radiating off her body brightened, making Father Kellner squint.

"He is a young man, fair of face, and gentle in his speech. Do not be deceived by this, Aldrich. His name is Mathew Lewin, and even as we speak, he studies the ancient texts trying to find ways to increase his power."

The priest was shocked. Almost everyone in the country knew Mathew Lewin was the young man who had defeated Karas Duren and turned the battle at Ardon Field to victory. Kellner had met him a number of times at the abbey. *This simply can't be.* Alarice had to be mistaken. He was about to tell her so when he recalled several previous meetings with Mathew. For months the boy had been studying in the library, and had asked him about the Ancient's ability to do things with their mind. It was a subject that had never particularly interested Father Kellner, so he deferred it to the other scholars there. At the time he put it off to idle curiosity. The rumor regarding the Ancients' abilities was not an uncommon one.

Aldrich Kellner's heart skipped a beat as the connection became clear. There had been whispers about the boy, but he paid scant attention to them, so preoccupied was he with his work in Argenton. Suddenly it all began to make sense, though he was confused on one point. What possible influence could such a young man have over the king? He voiced these concerns to Alarice.

Once again her eyes flashed, but became gentle a moment later. "You above all people should know that evil can take many forms. Does it not say in the Holy Scriptures that the Devil has the power to assume a pleasing shape?"

"The Devil!" He made a sign against evil with his hand.

And so the talk went on. Deep within his heart, Father
Kellner felt the first stirrings of a desire to save his people
from this insidious influence. This was his calling, this
was the reason he had became a priest. He knew it then
with all of his heart. The bible was replete with stories of
angels visiting mortal men and providing them divine inspiration. And now the proof was floating before his very
eyes.

Each day Father Kellner made his way down into the
cavern to speak with Alarice. During these conversations
she confirmed what he had begun to suspect. God was
displeased with his people for disregarding the scriptures.
Gradually, a subtle change began to occur in the priest. A
stutter he had since childhood grew less and less until it
was barely noticeable at all. He knew that God was re-
warding him for his loyalty. However, after his fourth trip
the headaches started. At first they were so blinding he
could barely open his eyes. Fortunately, even they gradually subsided over time.

When he brought his revelations to the bishop, secretly
as Alarice had commanded, the elderly cleric was more
skeptical than impressed, but since he had given his word
to the priest, there was little he could do. He came to Argenton to see the miracle for himself. And see he did.

Just as she had done before, Alarice rose from the dark
waters of the lake. She told them that they had been chosen to lead their people back to the true path of the Lord.
Gawl had to be made to understand the error of his ways,
and by any means necessary, before it was too late.

Shortly before Bishop Willis's first meeting with Alarice,
Siward Thomas had come to him for help. He wanted
him to use his influence with King Delain to obtain a pardon for Mathew Lewin. Given the circumstances surrounding the crime, and in light of the fact that the boy
had almost certainly saved Elgaria from destruction, it
was not an unreasonable request. The bishop had heard

all the rumors and stories about the young man, as almost everyone in Sennia had by then, but Mathew's true purposes were not known to him at the time. On each subsequent trip, Alarice revealed more details about Lewin's plans.

She explained how in the first age the Ancient's own science turned against them, almost destroying the planet. The problem she told Father Keller and Bishop Wills was *pride*—they reached too high. The Ancients eventually came to think of themselves as gods. This, Alarice said, was the true reason for Mathew's study at the library. He wanted to learn how the ancestors accomplished such feats in order to avoid the disaster that had struck them down.

When Alarice casually mentioned the rose-gold ring as the source of his power, she was instantly aware of the change that came over the bishop's face. It took only some mild questioning on her part to get the old man to reveal that the church was in possession of another one of the eight rings. With this information in hand, Alarice outlined her plan to the priests. She told them that one ring used for good would be able to counter the evil forces arrayed against the people of Sennia. This was what brought them to their present meeting.

Both men looked up at the saint floating above the surface of the lake. She was dressed in a gown of dark purple, and if anything, she seemed even lovelier than the first time Ferdinand Willis had seen her, six months earlier. Just as she asked, they had brought the ring, hidden for so many years in the abbey's crypts. Now Father Kellner wore it on the third finger of his right hand. At first the young priest refused to have anything to do with it, calling it an instrument of evil, but after some gentle coaxing, he agreed to put it on. The first time he did, a headache struck him so violently it almost caused his knees to buckle, but fortunately it faded quickly until it was only a faint memory.

"Everything goes according to plan," the bishop told Alarice.

"Good, eminence . . . very good." But then she looked at Father Kellner. "Dear Aldrich, you seem troubled to me. Does something bother you?"

"Yes," he replied. "On our way here, his eminence told me of the murders that took place at the abbey. I knew both men."

"Terrible things indeed," Alarice said sadly. "There was nothing I could do to prevent it. Lewin's power grows stronger every day."

The bishop closed his eyes and murmured a prayer for the men's souls, but Father Kellner turned his head away.

Alarice's eyes narrowed and she looked at the priest closely.

"There is more you wish to tell me, my son," she said softly.

The priest faced her again. He appeared to be struggling. Twice he opened his mouth to speak and twice he changed his mind. The bishop and Alarice exchanged glances and waited. Finally, Kellner began to speak.

"When his eminence and I spoke with Father Cole about the ring, he flatly refused to help us. No matter what we said, he wouldn't listen. He even threatened to go to the abbot. That night, as you commanded, I entered his office and hid myself behind the drapery. I saw him remove the diary from the shelves, the same book we spoke of in our last meeting. It mentioned the ring, as his Eminence said, but not specifically where it was located, other than in the crypts.

"After that we spoke with Brother Walker in secret and told him of our meeting with you. I begged him to help us, but like Edward Cole he also refused.

"We found the grave registry book on our own, deciphered its code, and learned the ring's hiding place shortly after that."

Father Kellner paused and looked down at the rose-gold ring on his finger.

"Go on Father," the bishop prompted, placing a hand on his shoulder.

"Several nights ago I had a dream that Brother Walker and Father Cole discovered the theft. It was not the first time I had this dream. Each man confronted me and threatened to go to the abbot if the ring was not returned. Nothing I said could dissuade them and a struggle took place."

The priest paused because his voice was shaking, but he took a deep breath and controlled himself.

"I dreamt such horrible things. Things a man of God should never dream. And now both men are dead, exactly as I envisioned!"

Father Kellner covered his face with his hands and began to sob. The bishop looked at Alarice helplessly. Around her the nimbus of light changed from white to pink, then back again.

"And you believe you are responsible for these acts?" she asked.

"What other explanation can there be? You have taught me to use the ring . . . to do things with my mind. Now each of their deaths have come to pass exactly as I dreamed they would. When his eminence told me what happened at Tenley Palace with the statues . . . I knew."

"Statues?"

The bishop took two steps closer to Alarice and lowered his voice.

"My Lady, I was not at the palace when it happened so I did not see for myself, but a guard told me about it. Two of King Gawl's statues came to life and tried to kill Mathew Lewin. The king explained to everyone that it was a joke of some kind, but when I spoke to him, I could tell that he had been badly shaken. Everyone at the palace was."

A moment passed and Alarice nodded her head slowly.

"None of these things were your doing, Aldrich," she said at last. "Young Lewin is responsible for what has happened. He was attempting to deflect suspicion from himself."

"But, the dreams—"

"Do you remember what happened the second time you put the ring on?"

Aldrich Kellner thought for a moment, then turned his palms up indicating he did not.

"You told me you could sense Mathew Lewin's presence—that you could *feel* his mind. That was how you described it. For your protection, I taught you how to shield yourself. What you saw in your dream were *his* thoughts, not your own. I have looked into your heart, my son. You are incapable of such things."

"Praise the Lord," the bishop said.

Father Kellner put a hand over his mouth in shock. "They were his thoughts I sensed?"

"Did I not tell you how clever evil can be? We must be vigilant. If any more . . . *dreams* come to you, you must tell me at once."

"I will, my lady."

Alarice's smile was benign. "And what news from the palace?" she asked, turning to the bishop.

"In less than a week Gawl will hold his conference. Alor Satar, Nyngary, and Cincar will be there. Even King Seth of Vargoth has agreed to attend. Before I left, I was told that Prince James of Mirdan will also come, as will Delain of Elgaria. There has been no word from Bajan yet, because the passes are now blocked by snow."

"Then everything is in readiness?" she asked.

"All is prepared, my lady," he said. "But . . ."

"But?"

"Do you think there is any chance we can dissuade Gawl from his decision to open the borders? The people seem to love him and . . ."

"We must never give up hope, eminence."

Alarice looked down on the two priests and smiled.

17

Sennia, at Barcora's Stanley Market

THE MORNING THAT MATHEW, FATHER THOMAS, AND
Ceta had left for the abbey, Lara, Collin, Rowena and her
brother rode into Barcora. Like its sister city Tyraine, a
day's ride away on the other side of the mountains, it had
become one of the principal trading ports in the West.

For the last six months Lara had heard story after story
about the fabulous Barcoran markets, but she never had
the opportunity to visit them. So, when Rowena suggested they use the day for a shopping trip together, she
had jumped at the chance. Both women invited Ceta
Woodall to join them, but she opted to accompany Father
Thomas instead. Considering their long absence from
each other, it was certainly understandable.

Gawl's conference was six days away, and though
Rowena had been more than generous in supplying her
with an entire array of dresses and gowns, Lara was badly
in need of a pair of new shoes and makeup. Rowena, being fair-skinned, simply didn't have anything that
matched well with Lara's darker complexion and chest-
nut hair. Though the makeup was needed, it was not the
only reason Lara had agreed to Rowena's invitation.

For the past two weeks, her friend had been gently probing her with questions about Mathew and his ring, as well
as the nature of their relationship. At first Lara thought it
was because of the interest Jared was showing her.

Rowena's younger brother was ten years older than

Lara, and she'd sensed his attraction the first time they met. His advances at the tavern following the Felcarin match effectively eliminated any lingering doubts she had. Despite her lack of encouragement, Jared seemed undeterred. On several occasions when he escorted her to dinner, she had found it necessary to slide away from his hand, which seemed to linger on her waist or shoulder longer than it should have.

Like most people in Devondale, Lara had a tendency to be plain spoken. While she and Jared were alone in the tavern for a few minutes, she tried to prevent matters from becoming more complicated by telling him about her feelings for Mathew. It apparently went in one ear and out the other.

At dinner the previous evening he had asked her to go riding; she refused. The next morning at breakfast, he invited her to visit their family's estate, and she gave him the same response. When Rowena mentioned that Jared would be accompanying them into town, Lara promptly recruited Collin to balance things out.

Stanley Market, as it was called, went on for blocks and blocks. There were literally hundreds of merchants selling every conceivable item, from rugs and jewelry to furniture and clothing. The smells of incense and different foods being cooked on open grills blended together in the air. Paintings and collectibles abounded, and each merchant Lara met assured her that *his* goods were unique, and worth far more than the pittance they were asking. After spotting the same *unique* piece at six different stalls, Lara decided she would have to do her bargaining carefully.

By Collin's estimation, when they turned the corner and started up the fourth or fifth street (he had lost count), he was certain that he had seen every kind of gold chain, jeweled insect, and decorative flower that existed in the world. Why anyone would want to wear a jeweled beetle on their clothing, he couldn't begin to imagine.

People strolled around the marketplace in ones and twos, looking at the various stalls and talking with each other. Some ate sandwiches or snacks sold by vendors, who could be found on every street corner. A number of children were also out with their parents, either being pushed in strollers or running excitedly ahead to see what the next booth contained. On the first block, Collin noted three different artists doing charcoal sketches of people. In each instance, a small crowd was gathered to watch the progress. A few comments could be heard from passersby about how much the sketches looked like, or didn't look like, the person sitting patiently waiting for the end result. Usually, it turned out to be a long-suffering husband, wife, or girlfriend.

On the second street, they encountered several wandering musicians who were more than happy to entertain them. As soon as they were done, however, they promptly took off their hats and passed them around for tips. After making three contributions, Collin eventually got the message and politely held his hand up when they approached. The musicians, disappointed that their new-found source of income had dried up, moved on seeking other prey.

One part of the market contained an enormous array of bolts of cloth and lace, while another was devoted almost exclusively to dolls and plates, though Lara couldn't see what one had to do with another. Jared and Collin dutifully tramped along behind the women as they slowly made their way down the aisles. Both men did their best to appear interested, but after an hour or two a glaze seemed to settle over their eyes. Every so often, when either of them spotted a café, they would inquire whether anyone was hungry, thirsty, or wanted to rest. Eventually, Rowena had enough.

"I don't see how you men can go off on your hunting trips or hike for twenty miles with your friends, but after an hour of shopping you're ready to collapse."

Collin and Jared looked at each other and shrugged.

A brief conference followed and it was decided to deposit the men at the next café, which suited all parties. Rowena told them they would return in about an hour.

When they were out of earshot Rowena laughed and said, "Poor Jared. This is sweet of him, but he absolutely hates shopping."

"So do Mathew and Collin," Lara replied. "I once got them to come with me when we visited Mechlen, but they both looked so miserable, I never bothered asking again."

Rowena smiled and slipped her arm through Lara's. They continued down the narrow streets, past bronze statues, porcelains, figurines, and new furniture which had been made to look old. Eventually, they found the makeup vendors and spent the next half hour sampling various eye shadows, liners, and lip colorings. Lara had never seen so many products in one place. In addition to the more usual colors, there were scents and rouges from Coribar that sparkled when you put them on. While she sat on a tall stool and let one of the saleswomen apply a sample of rouge to her cheeks, Rowena wandered farther down the street to look at some silk scarves. It was so much fun, Lara nearly forgot why she was there in the first place. Unable to decide between two colors, which the woman said were "absolutely perfect" on her, she bought them both and went to find Rowena.

She spotted her standing in the doorway of a building, talking to a man she had never seen before. Lara came to a halt. She wasn't exactly sure why she did, but something about the way they were behaving struck her as odd, almost furtive. Lara watched as Rowena handed the man what looked like a coin purse. He glanced up and down the street and put it under his cloak. Lara turned sideways and pretended to be looking at some lace handkerchiefs in the booth next to her. When she looked again, the man had departed, melting into the crowd. She was debating whether to go back and wait for her friend at the makeup booth, but Rowena rendered the decision academic when she saw her and waved. Like Lara, Rowena had also made a purchase or two and suggested that they take a break from shopping. A small coffee-house a few doors down provided the perfect solution.

While they waited for their drinks, Lara glanced at Rowena. She was a strange mixture of contradictions. Her religious beliefs forbade her to imbibe liquor or eat red meat, yet she was perfectly willing to take her clothes off and pose naked for a statue. Rowena was attentive and affectionate to Gawl, though almost twenty years his junior. And he was clearly smitten with her. Recently, however, Lara had begun to have her doubts. She wondered whether the feelings were mutual and this bothered her a great deal, because Rowena had been more than kind, and she was not a suspicious person by nature. Perhaps it was her imagination, she thought. Then again, perhaps it wasn't.

"You know Jared is very fond of you." Rowena said.

"Yes."

"He told me that he invited you to visit our home. Can I ask why you turned him down?"

Lara took a sip of coffee before answering.

"Mmm . . . this is wonderful," she said. "I didn't mean to hurt his feelings. It's just that I don't think Mathew would appreciate it. On top of that, Jared's a good bit older than I am—ten years, I think."

"Older than you?" laughed Rowena. "Look at Gawl and me. Ten years isn't that much of a difference, you know."

Lara smiled back at her. "I know. It's just that I wouldn't want things to get awkward. I told Jared the same thing, but I don't think he took me seriously."

Rowena nodded. "Well . . . Jared can be a bit thick-headed—all the men in my family are. I seem to be attracted to that type."

The two women smiled again and Rowena said, "I understand Jared's a wonderful lover."

The last comment caused Lara's eyes to widen and she blinked in surprise.

"I got it from Jennifer d'Berge," Rowena said, dropping her voice.

"Jennifer d'Berge?"

"Baron d'Berge's daughter. You met him at the dinner the other night. The one with the curly red beard and the great big tummy." Rowena held her hands out in front of her to illustrate.

"Oh . . . I remember now. He smelled like—"

"Lilacs . . . he scents his beard. They live about fifteen miles from us in Hope Province."

"I see," Lara said. "It's just that I don't want to hurt his feelings."

"Jared? I doubt it." Rowena replied, pausing to add a drop or two of orange flavoring to her coffee. She seemed to find the concept funny.

"Have you and Mathew made love yet?" she asked.

"What?"

"You can tell me," Rowena prompted, placing her hand on top of Lara's.

It took Lara a moment to collect herself. "I don't think it's right to talk about such things. Besides, Mathew would kill me."

"You have!" Rowena said, leaning back in her seat. Lara's color deepened by several shades. "Honestly, I don't know why you Elgarians are so stogy about such matters. It's all quite normal, you know. Gawl and I make love all the time. He doesn't mind my talking about it."

"I guess it's the way we're raised," Lara said, with a weak smile.

"Well, even if you have made love, how are you going

to know if Mathew's right for you unless you . . . ah . . . broaden your experience?"

The last was too much for Lara and she decided to look out the window. A light fog had begun to roll in off the harbor. Warm yellow light from the shop spilled out into the street and a few snowflakes had started falling. She'd never thought of herself as either conservative or prudish, but compared to Rowena she might have well have been raised in a convent.

"If I ever feel the need to *broaden my experience,* I'll be sure to remember that," she finally said.

"Oh, now I've embarrassed you," said Rowena. "I'm sorry, Lara. I didn't mean to do that. My father's always telling me that I should stop and think before I start talking."

"It's all right. I guess we both have to get used to new customs. What did you do while I was trying on the makeup?"

"Nothing really . . . I just strolled around. Now that Gawl's lifting the trade restrictions there's lots of new merchandise to see."

They continued chatting about a variety of subjects. Thankfully, there was no further talk about sex or taking new lovers, which was a relief to Lara. Rowena did surprise her by again bringing up the subject of a visit to their family home. This was very odd because they'd just spoken of it, and Lara had turned down Jared's invitation.

"It would be a wonderful trip," said Rowena. "The mountains are so beautiful this time of year. Besides you'd get a chance to see some more of our country."

"Won't Gawl need you here to help with the banquet?"

"Oh, Gawl . . ." she said, making a dismissive gesture with her hand. "Alexander is perfectly capable of seeing to the arrangements. We'd only be gone for a few days, and frankly I could use a break from the palace."

"I don't know," Lara said.

"Come on. It'll be such fun."

Several blocks away, Collin and Jared sat in the café together, waiting for the women to return.

"I don't get it," Collin said. "I thought you people weren't supposed to drink. No offense."

Jared winked at him, then downed the remainder of his mug and signaled the owner to bring another. "My father and Rowena would go purple if they found out, but I figure I'm old enough to make up my own mind on the subject. Jordan feels the same way."

"Jordan?"

"My brother, the next duke."

Collin nodded and took another sip. With all the dukes, barons, ladies, and other titles running around the palace, he thought it might be a good idea to pay more attention to who was who in the future. The problem was he really didn't care very much what person's title went where, and promptly forgot them as soon as they were introduced.

"Do you think the girls will be gone long?" he asked. Jared glanced out the window at the fog and shook his head.

"Probably not. Unless they decide try on dresses. I think Rowena said something about wanting to get back early."

"I don't see how they can just walk around for hours. It wears me out. This is a nice place, but how many jeweled turtles and dragonflies can a person stand to look at in one morning?"

Jared chuckled. "Why'd you come, then?"

"I promised to keep Lara company while Mat and Father Thomas rode out to the abbey. Besides, I'd like to visit that Felcarin shop you mentioned."

"Sure. I'll show you where it is after the girls get back. So, you and Lara are just friends, then?"

Collin's tankard paused halfway up to his lips and he set it back down on the table again.

"Right."

"Just asking," Jared said, holding up his hand. "God, you Elgarians are a touchy lot. Is she seeing anyone else besides your friend?"

"His name is Mat . . . and no, she's not seeing anyone else. At least not to my knowledge. We pretty much tend to stick with one person at a time. It makes things less complicated."

"So do we," Jared said. "It's just that if she's not spoken for . . ."

"Lara can speak for herself. If you're so interested, why don't you ask her?"

"I did," he shrugged. "That's about the same thing she said. She's a real beauty. Those eyes of hers drive me crazy."

Collin nodded.

Jared leaned back in his chair. "So, what are your plans?"

"My plans?"

"I mean for your future. You have your whole life ahead of you. What are you going to do after you leave Tenley Palace?"

"I'm not really sure," Collin replied. "I guess I'd like to travel and see some of the world. I had it in mind to do that before the war, but I have to help Mat with a problem, and then we'll see."

"You mean the murder charges?"

For the second time that morning Jared's question took Collin by surprise. He marveled at how quickly news could travel, particularly when it was news about someone else's problem.

"Oh, don't look so shocked," said Jared. "It was common knowledge fifteen minutes after the constable arrived. What's his name?"

"Jeram Quinn."

"Right, Jeram Quinn," Jared echoed. "If you ask me, I don't see what all the fuss is about. If some man killed my father then I killed him, everything's evened out. Justice is served, right?"

"Right . . . but then you're the son of a duke, Mat isn't."

"Well, you'd think Delain would put a stop to it, considering everything Mat's done and all."

Collin shook his head and replied, "That's what you'd think."

By the end of the hour Collin had finished his second tankard of ale and Jared was well into his third. Neither Rowena nor Lara had returned yet so they decided to order lunch and wait. With the fog getting thicker by the minute, they decided the chances of finding the women would be better if they stayed put.

"You're a loyal man," Jared said, holding up his glass to Collin. "I like that."

"To loyalty," Collin replied, returning the toast. He was beginning to feel the effects of the ale. "We'd better go easy on this stuff," he added, glancing out the window.

"Agreed. I could use a good man like you. Loyalty is hard to come by these days."

"How so?"

"I've seen you work the batroc at practice and Gawl said you have a good head on your shoulders."

"I think Gawl meant that he wanted to do a sculpture of my head," Collin observed.

The comment made Jared chuckle. "Seriously, why don't you consider throwing in with me . . . after you've helped your friend, of course. You can come up and visit the castle with Lara. My father and brother will be there, and I have a younger sister about your age. Her name is Gabriele. Lara's coming."

"Lara didn't mention anything about it to me," Collin said.

"She and Rowena are going up to visit for a few days."

"Really? Won't Rowena need to be here for Gawl's

meeting?" Collin asked, voicing the same question Lara had.

"The meeting," Jared said disgustedly. "A fat lot of good it's going to do him. Half the barons and dukes are dead set against it. So's the church."

"The church? What do they have to do with politics?"

"More than you'd think. Our region produces some of the best wines in the world . . . as well as oranges and copper. For the last three hundred years, we've been able to control the economy by keeping competition out and importing only what we need. Now Gawl wants to open all the doors and drop trade restrictions."

"But won't more trade be good for the people?" Collin asked.

"The people . . . not the producers," Jared said with a wink.

"We'd better start back," Rowena said. "The men will think we're lost. I'm so glad you said yes. Do you think your friend Collin would like to come with us?"

"It won't hurt to ask him."

On the way back to meet the men Lara received much the same speech as Collin had about Sennian economics. The snow was coming down more heavily, then. Large dry flakes stuck to the hood of Lara's cloak and the fog had turned the city into a world of gray and white.

In truth, Lara had little desire to visit Rowena's estate, however pretty it might be. But she was curious about the older woman's insistence and convinced she was hiding something. It was true, she conceded, there might be any number of reasons for her behavior earlier, most of them perfectly plausible, but she was certain something was wrong. On each occasion Rowena had brought the subject of a visit up, she got a little more forceful. Lara knew how her departure would appear to Mathew, but that couldn't be helped at the moment. What disturbed her the

most were the casual questions Rowena kept asking
about where Mathew kept his ring when he wasn't wearing it, all on the pretext that it was better to be safe than
sorry in case someone tried to steal it. In truth Lara
couldn't imagine too many places safer than Tenley
Palace. She told Rowena that he kept it in his room. And
regretted it as soon as she did.

There was more than a foot of snow on the ground when
they arrived back at the palace. Trees coated with ice glis-
tened sharply through the fog and the horses' hooves
crunched noisily as they entered the courtyard. Lara
handed the reins of her horse to a groom who informed
them Mathew, Ceta, and Father Thomas had still not returned from the abbey. She thanked him, said goodbye to
the others, and promised to meet them in an hour, then
went up to her room to pack.

    According to Rowena, Camden Keep was about four
hours away to the northeast. She suggested they take one
of the coaches in view of the weather.

Lara's room was easily the most opulent one she had ever
been in. Her previous accommodations at the abbey had
tended to be a little on the worn side. Sometimes things
worked and sometimes they didn't. After sleeping in tents
and in taverns during their trip from Devondale, she'd
been more than grateful for a clean bed and a roof over
her head. Gawl's generosity however, surpassed her
wildest expectations. Not only was the room spacious, it
had a crystal chandelier and raised-gilt moldings on the
walls. There was also a balcony and a separate sitting
room where she could read by a fire. A four-poster bed,
complete with a canopy, was so impossibly high, she
needed a small step to get into it. The mattress was soft
enough to make her feel like she was floating.

    I could get used to this, Lara thought. The room's total

effect, with its view of the garden, almost always surprised her each time it caught her eye.

The balcony overlooked the pond where they were planning to put her sculpture. At least that was the way she had come to think of it. Where she ever got the nerve to take off all her clothes and pose naked was simply beyond her. But with Gawl it didn't seem improper. He was so serious about his work. He never once did anything to make her feel self-conscious. She giggled, recalling the look on Mathew's face when he first saw the sculpture. It was almost as good as his expression after she took off her dress in the studio.

Mathew, she sighed.

They had been getting close to making love with each other for over a year, but something always seemed to get in the way, and Mathew was not a person who moved hastily.

He kept approaching the lake, but never took the plunge.

She smiled at the memory of that day in the woods, as he tried to undress her and be charming at the same time. Ceta told her the bustier she had borrowed was supposed to be sexy. But, according to Mathew, it could have doubled for a suit of armor. In retrospect, she had to agree.

The whole thing *was* funny.

Their relationship had changed; there was no denying that. She wasn't the same little girl who used to scramble over rooftops with him and throw down hickory nuts at people passing by. In fact, as she looked at her body in the full-length mirror, she had to acknowledge there wasn't anything little about it anymore. Her stomach was flat as a board and the definition of her muscles stood out, though not to excess. Her legs were long and firm and her breasts, well . . . no complaints there either.

She knew that she had hurt his feelings by flirting with Jared at dinner, but it couldn't be helped. She even thought about explaining the situation to Mathew, but never got the opportunity, and if she did, he would probably have made fun of her. Lara trusted her intuition, which was more often right than wrong, at least in her opinion. All those clever little questions Jared kept throwing in about Mathew's ring were the same ones Rowena had asked. *As if she was too stupid to pick up on it.*

Typical man, she thought.

It was easy to tell that Jared had little respect for women by the way he looked at them. They were more objects than individuals as far as he was concerned, and that attitude made her angry. In addition to a toned body, she also had a toned mind—one which didn't appreciate being taken for a fool. Something *was* wrong—though she couldn't say what it was. And she'd be damned if she would let anyone hurt Mathew. Curious to hear Rowena's response while having coffee in the market, Lara had asked Rowena what she was doing while she looking at makeup. The answer she got was deliberately evasive and Rowena made no mention of the man in the market. Perhaps the pointed questions she and her brother had been asking were just coincidence, but Lara didn't think so.

A quick check in the mirror assured her that everything was in place. She left her room and went across the hall to see Collin, knocking on the door softly. A voice inside said, "Come on in, it's open."

Lara shrugged and opened the door.

Collin was standing in the middle of the room in a pair of dark brown pants, barefooted and bare-chested.

For a moment they were both so surprised, neither knew what to say. He was the first to recover.

"I'm sorry," he laughed, "I thought you were the chambermaid."

Lara raised her eyebrows. "Really? Is this how you dress for the chambermaid?"

Collin continued chuckling to himself, picked a fresh shirt out the drawer, and pulled it over his head.

"Elona was right. You do have big shoulders."

"Oh, right . . . absolutely," he joked. A second later he grew silent.

Lara noticed the change in his expression. "I'm sorry, I . . ."

"It's all right. I get a little twinge about home every now and then."

Lara took a deep breath and turned away to watch the snow falling outside his window.

"I hate this place," she said quietly. "Every time someone tells me something, I get the impression there are at least three different meanings behind what they're saying."

Collin watched her for a moment, then walked over and put his hands on her shoulders. Her comments echoed the way he'd been feeling for the past few weeks. A variety of different thoughts and emotions were going around inside his head. All the things he thought were clear were becoming more and more fuzzy. He knew that he had to get on with his life, but he couldn't leave Mat until the business with Jeram Quinn was finished. Competing with everything was Jared's offer of employment. He had to admit that it intrigued him, but he decided to keep it to himself for the moment.

"Collin . . . do you think Mathew will go to jail?" Lara asked.

"I don't know. I can't see how, but I'm not a lawyer, and I'm also not Jeram Quinn. The whole thing's crazy. I wish Delain would do something to put an end to it."

"I know," she said, resting her head against his chest. "I'm going to visit with Rowena for a few days. Would you tell Mathew when he gets back?"

"I guess someone else will have to do it. I'm going along with you."

"Hmm?"

"Jared invited me to come up and see their home. I figured I was just in the way around here, so I said yes."

Lara frowned. "I didn't know they'd spoken to you too. She was pretty pushy about it."

"Jared and I talked about it while we were waiting for you. What do you mean Rowena was pushy?" Collin asked.

"I don't know, but it's not the first time she's brought the subject up. With all the decorating, you'd think she'd want to stay here and help with the arrangements for Gawl's meeting, but she said Alexander would handle it."

"Maybe they're just being friendly," he suggested.

"Maybe."

After a few seconds Collin turned her around by the shoulders to face him. "What's bothering you?"

"Rowena. She lied to me when we were in the market earlier today. She said she was just wandering around waiting for me and I saw her talking to a man. They were acting odd . . . like they didn't want to attract any attention to themselves. She's also been asking a lot of questions about Mathew. It's nothing I can put my finger on, but Jared's been doing the same thing."

"What sort of questions?"

"She wanted to know where Mathew kept his ring . . . things like that."

"Now that *is* odd, because Jared asked me the same things. He also wanted to know if you were spoken for."

One of Lara's eyebrows arched. "I've already had a talk with him about that. He doesn't take no for an answer very easily."

"Do you suppose they're up to something?" Collin asked.

"I hope not. I really do, because I like Rowena."

"I can't imagine them wanting to harm Mat, can you?"

They spent the next ten minutes debating the issue while Collin finished getting dressed. He packed a bag and threw in some toiletries, along with another pair of pants and two fresh shirts. Then they both went down the stairs together. For the time being they decided to give Jared and Rowena the benefit of the doubt and to simply watch and listen.

18

Sennia, Tenley Palace

WHEN MATHEW GOT BACK TO TENLEY PALACE, HE learned from Alexander that Collin and Lara had left for Camden Keep. The weather had worsened considerably and their ride back through the blowing snow and cold had left him exhausted. Damp and tired, he went upstairs to his room, took a hot shower, then lay down on the bed and fell asleep instantly.

Three hours later, he suddenly awoke in the dark knowing two things at once. He knew who had been in Brother Walker's office; and he knew that someone was on the balcony outside his room. There was barely enough light to see, but silhouetted against the evening sky were the shapes of two men. A slight creak of the door handle told him that it was being tried. He couldn't remember if he had locked it or not.

He realized that whoever was out there probably couldn't see him yet because of the way his bed was positioned in the room. Both his sword and belt dagger were on top of his desk, fifteen feet away, as was his ring. He had taken it off when he got into the shower. If he tried to reach them it would let whoever was outside know that he was awake. Mathew slid out of bed and moved behind the draperies.

A click of the door lock was followed by an angry whisper from outside. He stayed frozen, listening, his heart was pounding. A cold draft on his ankles told him they had the door open.

"Come on, we don't have long," a voice whispered.

"They're all at dinner," a second voice answered.

"Fine. Let's just find it and get out of here."

The accents were strange and he couldn't place them. Mathew moved the curtain back an inch, careful not to make any noise, and peered out. Two men dressed in black were searching his room. For the moment he had the element of surprise, but that would only last until they noticed he wasn't in bed and his sword was propped up against the chair. Across the room he could hear a drawer being opened.

"Keep it down," one of the men whispered fiercely as his companion rattled a glass.

"Sorry."

"Look in all the drawers," the first voice said. "I'll check in here."

The ring. In another moment they'll see it lying on the desk. *Now or never,* he thought.

With a roar, Mathew threw aside the heavy curtain and charged headlong into the first man, his shoulders lowered. The intruder let out a surprised grunt as they hit and careened backward through the double glass doors and out onto the balcony. There was loud crash as they shattered, covering both of them with glass.

The man slammed into the wrought-iron railing, cursed, and began to straighten up. Suddenly, his eyes opened wide and his arms started to flail as the balcony railing gave way. Metal supports tore loose from the cement and a whole section suddenly collapsed. The expression on the intruder's face was replaced by a look of terror. For a moment their eyes met, and time seemed to stand still. Then, in horrifying slow motion, the man began to topple backward. Mathew lunged trying to catch him, but was too late. The man screamed as he fell. He hit the ground with an awful thud, a sound that Mathew would remember for the rest of his days.

He stepped away from the edge in shock, but before he had time to recover, a heavy blow between his shoulder blades drove him to his knees. It was followed by another and then another. The world began to spin around him. In desperation he tried get to his feet, but his legs didn't seem to be working properly. He managed to twist his body around in time to deflect a punch aimed at his face. Strong fingers immediately closed around his throat and began to squeeze, cutting off his oxygen. Colored lights exploded in front of Mathew's eyes as he struggled to break the second assailant's grip. A part of his mind told him that he had only seconds to live.

With all of his remaining strength Mathew struck backward with his knee hitting the man squarely in the middle of his back. The hold on his throat slackened a little, but not enough. Shooting stars began to replace the colors he was seeing. Mathew struck with his knee again and finally the man's grip slackened enough for him to drag a tortured breath into his lungs. Mathew threw a punch and connected with the side of his assailant's head knocking him off. He immediately rolled to his side, pulling in another breath, and began to push himself up onto his knees, still fighting to clear his brain. No more than a second elapsed before the man launched himself at Mathew again, bowling him over and reaching once more for his throat. Out of the corner of his eye, Mathew caught the glint of something shiny and realized that the man had a dagger. In desperation, he crashed another blow to the assailant's nose and felt it break. Scrambling backward on his hands and heels, he bumped into the wall, and drew himself upright. The man also rose, felt his nose, and spat out an oath in a strange language. Then he charged again, the dagger raised above his head. Mathew thrust his arms up, wrists crossed, trapping the would-be murderer's arm as it came down. But instead of fighting against the blow, he yanked forward, using the man's own momentum against him. The dagger continued unchecked and imbedded itself in the man's thigh. He screamed.

From somewhere in the corridor Mathew heard raised voices and the sound of running feet. People were pounding on his door, but he had no time to think. He was forced to leap backward to avoid a wide slashing stroke aimed at his stomach. Mathew backed up again as the man came forward, dragging his injured leg and leaving a trail of blood on the floor. With nothing else to defend himself, Mathew grabbed the drapes, tore them loose, and threw them over the assailant's head. The man yanked them away and lunged. A brief struggle followed and Mathew succeeded in trapping the man's arm against his own body. Both of them fell to the floor, the assailant trying to free his arm and Mathew desperately hanging on to it.

He had no idea how long the struggle went on, but at some point his hand came into contact with one of the ropes that had been used to tie the drapes back. By now both men were on the balcony, rolling back and forth as they struggled with each other. Twice, they nearly went over the edge. Mathew's breath was coming in ragged gasps, and he was beginning to tire badly. He knew his attacker sensed this. Even with the wound in his leg, the man was stronger and heavier than he. In another second he would pull his arm free.

Mathew slammed his elbow into the side of the man's head, momentarily stunning him, then brought his forearm down across the attacker's wrist. The last blow succeeded in knocking the dagger loose.

The attacker responded by lowering his shoulders and forcing Mathew back toward the edge of the balcony an inch at a time. Out of balance Mathew was unable to stop him as the edge loomed closer. In desperation, he looped the drapery rope around the man's neck and, with the last reserves of his strength, threw him sideways. The attacker went over the edge of the balcony, arms and legs wheeling in the air. A loud snapping sound followed as the rope went taut. Mathew looked down to see the man's body swinging back and forth with his head at an impossible angle. Nearly blind with fatigue, he slumped back against the wall, trying to catch his breath.

The door finally burst open and light from the corridor streamed into the room. Father Thomas helped him to his feet. Gawl and Jeram Quinn were both there, as was Alexander, and three palace guards.

"Are you all right?" Father Thomas asked, taking him by the shoulders and looking for any sign of injuries.

Mathew bent over, drew a gulp of air into his lungs, and nodded his head

"What in God's name happened?"

Mathew took a few more deep breaths, then stood up. "I don't know. I was sleeping when I heard them trying to break in.

"Somebody get a light in here," Gawl snapped.

One of the soldiers left the room and returned moments later with a lamp. Alexander righted Mathew's desk, took the lamp from the soldier and lit it. The room was in a complete shambles with furniture thrown everywhere.

"Who are these people? Does anyone know?" asked Quinn.

"We saw them yesterday in Bexley," Father Thomas said. "They were with a priest from Coribar."

Gawl looked at Alexander and gave a curt nod. The Chief of Staff motioned for one of the soldiers to follow him and promptly left the room.

"Did you have some problem with them?" Gawl asked as he walked to the edge of the balcony. He looked down at the figure lying on the ground, then at his companion hanging from the rope and gave a nod of approval.

"Actually, yes," Mathew replied. "They tried to start a fight there."

"A fight?" Gawl said. He turned to Father Thomas, who nodded.

Jeram Quinn studied the room for a few seconds then walked out onto the balcony and bent down to examine the broken railing.

"This is goddamn strange, Siward," said Gawl. "Why would these two want to attack Mat?"

"I suspect for the same reason the statues came to life the other day. Someone or something wants him dead."

"Or wants his ring, more likely," a voice said from the hallway.

Mathew recognized the speaker at once. "Teanna!"

A tall dark-haired woman of about twenty stepped into the light and crossed the room to them. Right behind her were two soldiers wearing Nyngary's colors. The Sennian soldiers moved aside to let her by, but stepped back in front of her guards.

Teanna d'Elso was wearing a long yellow gown that came nearly to the floor with a thin gold belt around her hips. Her dress was cut low in the front, accenting a slender, athletic figure. It was the second time she and Mathew had met face-to-face. Framed in the light from the doorway, she was every bit as beautiful as he remembered.

"Are you all right, Mathew?" she asked. "This is horrible."

"I'm fine . . . thank you."

"Well," she smiled, "I was looking forward to making your acquaintance again, but not in this manner."

Gawl and Father Thomas looked at each other.

"Mathew and I are old friends, your majesty," she explained, brushing Mathew's hair back off his forehead.

He blushed, as much from embarrassment as from the looks he was getting from Father Thomas and Gawl. Before he had a chance to say anything, Teanna stepped around him and walked out onto the balcony. She looked over the edge just as Gawl and Quinn had done.

"Oh, dear," she said, shaking her head, then turned

back to the people in the room. "Do you have any idea why these men attacked you?"

"I was just asking the same thing," Gawl said.

"We had a fight . . . well, almost a fight with them in a nearby village yesterday. I thought it was just coincidence at the time. Obviously, I was wrong."

"Obviously," Gawl said.

"I'm glad to see that you are well, your highness," Mathew said to her. "I was told you weren't expected to arrive until later in the week."

"Teanna will do," she said. "I think we can dispense with formalities for the time being. Our ship arrived early and we came directly here."

Mathew noticed that Father Thomas was closely observing the entire interchange but kept it to himself. Out on the balcony, Jeram Quinn moved to the other side, bent down again, and closely looked at the remains of the wrought-iron supports.

"I suppose we'll have to sort all this out later," Gawl said. "I'll have Alexander move you to a new room as soon as he returns. In the meantime, let's go to my study. There are a few things I'd like answered."

"As would I, your majesty," Teanna said.

She and Father Thomas briefly made eye contact as they were leaving, but it lasted for only a second before Teanna looked away. Gawl posted two men at the door with instructions that no one was to enter the room without his express permission.

When they reached Gawl's private chambers, he paused and held the door open for Teanna and instructed her guards to wait in the corridor.

The study was a warm, comfortable room that Mathew had never been in before. It was decorated with cherrywood paneling and a large granite fireplace. Two double doors opened to a terrace from which the king could look out at the surrounding countryside. A four-tiered crystal chandelier dominated the room's center, and two leather couches sat facing each other on either side of the fireplace. Several beautifully crafted rugs were scattered across a stone floor.

Gawl's desk was actually a writing table, and had a black leather top and intricate brass castings down the legs. It was positioned across the room facing the fireplace. Behind it were a series of built-in mahogany bookcases. A few delicate porcelain figurines and bronzes, strangely at odds with their huge owner, sat on the shelves between the books. One tiny porcelain, Mathew noted, bore a striking resemblance to the sculpture he saw in Gawl's studio. He stared at it for a few seconds, marveling how so large a man could be capable of producing such a finely detailed piece of work.

After they were all seated a servant brought hot spiced wine for everyone. Only Jeram Quinn, there at Gawl's request, declined and asked for cold water instead. The constable took a seat to one side of the room. Teanna sat on one couch and Mathew sat on the opposite one alongside Father Thomas. Gawl picked up a carved highbacked chair in one hand, as if it weighed nothing, and set it down in the middle of the two couches.

"I'm sorry for what happened, Mat," he said. "You seem to be attracting a great deal of attention these days. I don't know how those two got in here, but you have my word we're going to find out. Do you agree with what Siward said upstairs?"

"That someone wants to murder me? Yes," he said.

"Why would those men want to kill Mathew?" Teanna asked.

"For the same reason that you might also be in danger, princess," Father Thomas answered. "It's my guess that Coribar wants Mathew's ring. Since you also possess one of the rings, it would be naive to assume their attentions will be confined solely to him."

There was a pause before Teanna replied.

"I see." Her expression was serious, but she showed little reaction to the possibility that she might also be in danger.

"This is the second time Mathew has been attacked," Gawl explained.

"The second?"

"The first was three days ago here at the palace. Two of my statues came to life, and decided to try and shorten Mathew's in the process."

"What do you mean, your 'statues came to life?' " Teanna asked, putting down her wine.

"Quite simply . . . they got off their pedestals and tried to kill him."

Teanna looked at Gawl for a second and said, "That's impossible, unless . . ."

"Unless someone with the ability to use one of the rings did it," Mathew finished the sentence for her.

Teanna's eyes flashed and she stood up, but Mathew held his hand up, stopping her.

"I don't think it's you," he said. "In fact I'm positive it isn't. Several days ago I told Father Thomas and Gawl that I think someone else has one of the rings. We confirmed it when we visited the abbey yesterday."

"How?" Teanna asked, sitting down again. "There are two in Alor Satar besides mine, but I thought all of the others were lost or destroyed."

Father Thomas related what they learned during their visit to the abbey. When he finished, Gawl said, "Are you certain about this, Siward? No offense, but sometimes you have to look carefully at what some priests tell you."

"Paul Teller has been a friend for many years. If he was making the story up, he'd have to be an extraordinary liar to act as convincingly as he did. No . . . I'm positive he was telling the truth. The abbey has been guarding this particular ring since the ancient war."

Gawl's heavy eyebrows came together and he frowned at the last statement.

"Three thousand years is a long time, my friend. If I'm

not mistaken, there have been at least four abbeys built on that site since the destruction. The present one can't be more than eight or nine hundred years old."

"I'm aware of that," Father Thomas replied. "The ring has been one of the most closely guarded secrets the church has maintained down through the centuries. Teller said it came to the abbey eight hundred years ago. The trust to preserve it has literally been passed down from abbot to abbot. Paul Teller is the latest in a long line. Just recently, someone killed two priests there, then broke into the crypt where it was kept. Whoever it was has it in their possession now."

"If what you say is true, I can hardly imagine more than a few people knew of its existence in the first place," Jeram Quinn said, speaking for the first time.

Everybody turned to look at him.

"That's precisely correct, Jeram," Father Thomas replied.

"And it would account for my statues wandering around the palace," Gawl added.

"Do you have any idea who's responsible?" Teanna asked, looking at Mathew.

"I think so. I'm not positive yet, but tomorrow I'd like to take a trip up to Argenton and have a word with Father Kellner."

"Kellner?" Gawl said, surprised. "The priest who was here the other day? What makes you think it's him?"

"I'm not ready to say that," Mathew replied. "When I was in Brother Walker's office, I saw some marks on the floor. At first, I thought they were blood. It didn't come to me until a little while ago, but I think they were red clay streaks. You told me yourself the only place the earth is that color is in Argenton. It might be nothing, but I'd like ask him if he knows anything about what happened."

Gawl leaned back in his seat and looked at Mathew, then at Father Thomas. A second later the king made up his mind.

"All right, we'll leave first thing in the morning."

"Where is this Argenton?" asked Teanna.

"It's a small town about a half-day's ride up in the foothills," Gawl explained. "The church has been conducting excavations there."

Teanna nodded slowly. "I see. What time should we be ready to leave?"

Her statement brought an immediate reaction from nearly everyone in the room.

"That's very kind of you, princess," Gawl said, "but it would be better if you remain here. The north country can be challenging. It won't take us long."

"I appreciate your concern. Nyngary is also a mountain country, and I'm willing to wager I can ride a horse as well as anyone in this room. On top of that, if this Father Kellner *does* have one of the rings, you may need my help more than you know."

"Why?" asked Father Thomas.

"That should be obvious, general . . . excuse me—Father. I think we both know how strong Mathew's abilities are—but the fact is, I'm probably stronger. Second, we don't know what this man can or can't do, and two against one would give us a much better chance for success. As unbalanced as he was, my uncle was a cautious man. One of the few things he taught me was not to leap into a pond before I knew how deep the water was. It's all quite well for you men to go gallivanting off, but I point out that you may not be dealing with an ordinary man."

When Teanna finished, she folded her hands in her lap and calmly waited for their response. Gawl stared at her for a moment, then turned to Father Thomas. Jeram Quinn simply looked at him and raised his eyebrows.

"What are your thoughts?" Gawl asked, directing the last question to Mathew.

Mathew still felt awkward around Teanna, but he had to admit that what she was saying made sense. He knew so little about her.

That bothered him. Still, she seemed genuine enough, just as she had when they first met. And, as she had pointed out then, if she wanted to harm him, she could have easily done so.

"I think Teanna's right," he answered. "If Father Kellner is involved, and he does have a ring, he would be an extremely dangerous opponent. Having both of us there makes more sense."

"Then we're agreed," Teanna said. She got up in one fluid motion, said good night, and left the room.

"An interesting woman," Father Thomas observed, looking at the closed door. "Do you believe her?"

Gawl blew out a long breath. "I don't know what to believe." The king stretched his legs out in front of him and crossed his ankles. "You knew Marsa d'Elso. Do you think her daughter can be trusted?"

Father Thomas shook his head. "Yes . . . I knew Marsa d'Elso. With respect to Teanna, I'm not sure. If it weren't for Teanna's intervention, Alor Satar would have overwhelmed us at Ardon Field. I confess the girl is a mystery to me. She also seems to be taking her mother and uncle's deaths rather well, wouldn't you say?"

"True," said Gawl, "but they were both crazy. She appears quite sane. All things considered, it was a lot easier being a soldier than a king."

Throughout the discussions, Jeram Quinn had remained quiet. For a moment it appeared that he was going to say something, but then he changed his mind and bid them all good night.

Mathew also excused himself, leaving Father Thomas and Gawl alone.

19

Sennia, Tenley Palace

A SERVANT LED MATHEW UP TO HIS NEW ROOM, WHICH was three doors down from his old one. Except for the layout it was decorated in much the same manner. His sword and dagger had been discreetly placed on the desk, and his clothes were all neatly folded away in a chest of drawers.

Two things about it immediately appealed to him. The first was that it was on the opposite side of the hall and faced the garden; the second was that it had no balcony. A grisly image of the would-be assassins' dead bodies flashed into his mind once again, sending a shudder up his spine.

Mathew walked over to the window and looked out across the landscape. In the distance he could make out the lights of Barcora on the horizon. Snow was still falling, blanketing the hedges and the statuary. The footpath was lit by flickering oil lamps. In contrast, four bronze lampposts at various points along the path burned more brightly, casting shadows on the statues there. Another shiver went up Mathew's spine, and he slid the curtain back in place.

He had no idea what time it was, but the rumbling in his stomach reminded him that he hadn't eaten yet, and dinner was already over. With few options available, Mathew decided to try his luck in the kitchens. He went to the dresser, found a fresh khaki-colored shirt, put it on, and tucked it into his breeches.

Just before locking the door to his room, he opened it again, stuck his head back inside, and made a mental note that the color of the walls was beige.

He thought about Collin and Lara as he walked down the stairs, wishing he could talk to them. It had annoyed him to learn that they had both left without so much as a word. Teanna was also on his mind. At some point he knew they would have to talk. Ever since he has learned that she was going to attend Gawl's conference, he had been mentally rehearsing what he was going to say to her. He wanted to explain . . . needed to explain about what had happened between Karas Duren and her mother, but the first time they'd met, he was so much on guard he never managed to get the words out.

How do you talk about killing someone's mother and uncle? he thought. *By the way Teanna, I apologize for killing your relatives. So sorry.*

Each scenario he practiced sounded more idiotic than the one before. He gave up. He decided to ask Father Thomas the best way to handle things. The priest always seemed to know exactly what to do.

Mathew turned the corner, went down two flights of steps, and found himself in a narrow corridor. Unlike the sleeping wing it was plain and unadorned, with no paintings or tapestries lining the walls. From a prior late night excursion with Collin, after they had first arrived at the palace, he knew this was the servants' area.

The kitchens should be at the far end, he thought.

A light was on, and the clink of a glass and a shadow moving against the cupboards told him someone else was there as well. For a moment Mathew considered turning back, but then decided against it and poked his head inside. Teanna was seated at the end of a long table, sipping a cup of tea.

She looked up when she heard his footstep and smiled. "Good evening, Mathew."

"I-I'm sorry," he stammered. "I didn't mean to . . . I was just . . . ah . . ."

"It's all right. Sit down and I'll make you something to eat. I assume that's why you're here."

"Well . . . actually . . . yes."

Teanna put down her cup, got up, and went to one of the iceboxes, took out a roast and began fixing a sandwich.

"I usually have a cup of tea before bed," she said, over her shoulder. "It helps me sleep. Can I make you one?"

"Yes, thank you. That would be nice."

"And stop standing there like a big ninny. Sit. I promise I won't bite."

Mathew cleared his throat and took a seat next hers. "I'm sorry we didn't have a chance to speak earlier," he said.

"Well . . . under the circumstances, I'll forgive you. Are you all right now?"

"Oh, yes."

"Mustard?"

"Excuse me?"

"Mustard," Teanna said, holding up a sandwich.

"Oh . . . sure."

She returned to the table a moment later, having fixed herself a sandwich, as well.

"Thank you," said Mathew, tearing off a large bite.

Teanna watched him with an amused expression on her face, shook her head, and took a small bite of her sandwich.

"My cousin Armand eats the same way."

"This is very good," said Mathew. "I guess I was hungrier than I thought."

Teanna inclined her head in acknowledgment.

"What is it now?" she asked, noticing that Mathew was looking around the room.

"Oh, I was just wondering if there was anything else to drink here beside tea. I mean it's very good tea, but . . ."

"I imagine we can come up with something more to your liking, Master Lewin."

She pushed herself back from the table, went to the large walk-in icebox, and opened the door. She surveyed the contents for a few seconds, then spotted what she wanted.

"Ah . . . there we are," she said disappearing inside.

Teanna emerged a second later with a mysterious smile. She was carrying something behind her back. Mathew looked at her puzzled.

"Ta-da!" she said, producing two large tankards of ale.

Mathew laughed as she sat back down to join him.

"And I didn't even have to use my magic ring," she smiled. "Better?"

"Better," he answered, taking a long swallow.

The contents of his mug were half gone when he put it back on the table. Teanna looked at it for a moment, arched one eyebrow, then picked up the second tankard and very nearly drained it. She set it down, with a brisk nod of her head and a satisfied "hmph."

"You drink like a man."

"I'll take that as a compliment. My father says the same thing. Most Nyngarians are good drinkers. We make excellent wines. Have you ever tried them?"

"A few times," Mathew conceded. "I'm not much of a drinker. One or two drinks and I'm reciting poetry."

This time it was Teanna's turn to smile.

"Not me. I once drank my cousin Eric and two of his aides under the table."

The image caused Mathew to start chuckling. The laughter however, slowly drained away and he grew quiet.

"What is it?" asked Teanna.

He looked down at his feet but didn't answer her.

"Mathew?" she prompted.

After a moment, he pushed the mug back a few inches and looked into her dark eyes.

"There's something I want to say. We never really had a chance to talk before. And I just wanted to tell you how sorry I am about your mother and your uncle. I swear to God I didn't have a choice."

Teanna's expression grew unreadable and she didn't reply immediately. Instead, she looked at him closely. He held her gaze for a second before turning away. What happened next surprised him; she reached out and put her hand over his.

"I was never particularly close with my family, Mathew. My uncle Karas was insane. Some of what he said made sense, but he was an evil person. You were right when you told Delain he hated for hate's sake alone. Mother wasn't crazy, but she was just as obsessed as he was about fulfilling the family destiny. *One nation . . . one rule*. Their father and their grandfather drilled the idea into their heads from the time they were children.

"Our countries were at war, but at some point the killing had to stop. I know how much you were hurt by it. Really, I do. It came down to your life or theirs. I may be the only one in the family who's forgiven you, but you should know that I have." When Mathew looked back at her, she could see his eyes were bright with tears and she squeezed his hand. He turned away again and used the back of his sleeve to wipe them.

"Thank you," he said quietly.

Teanna responded with a smile.

They talked for almost two hours. She told him about Nyngary and what it was like growing up in a palace, and he told her about Devondale. The conversations were tentative at first, but in time they both began to relax as they grew more comfortable with each other. It surprised him to learn that she had once been a tomboy and enjoyed climbing trees, to the dismay of her governess and annoyance of her mother. He looked at her elegant features, trying to imagine what she was like as a child. She asked a few questions about his ring, the things he felt or did when he used it, and responded with candor to his questions. In spite of his own reticence, he found himself drawn to her. She had a wonderful smile, not to mention a provocative figure, which he found himself admiring more and more as the evening wore on.

In truth, Mathew felt slightly guilty about not mentioning Lara, but he was still angry with her for running off to visit Rowena and not talking to him first. At least that was how he rationalized it. On top of that he was certain she'd been flirting with Jared at dinner earlier in the week.

"You said something before about being the only one in your family who forgave me."

Teanna folded her hands on the table. "Armand is an excellent general, but he's also a man. His father's death was particularly hard on him. Eric is another matter. It's hard to tell *what* he's thinking. My mother was a lot like that. He'll be here at the end of the week you know."

"Oh, that is marvelous," Mathew said, slumping down in his chair.

"Don't worry," Teanna said. "Eric is quite practical. He knows there has to be peace between our countries, and he'll put that ahead of his personal feelings."

"Before he decides to kill me, you mean."

Mathew made the last remark hoping to lighten the conversation, but it had the opposite effect. Teanna's face grew very serious and she didn't speak for several seconds.

"You don't really believe that, do you?"

"I was just trying to . . . what I meant was . . ."

Mathew took a deep breath and said, "No . . . I don't think Eric is capable of killing me. If I didn't have the ring and it was one-on-one combat, that might be another matter. Anyway, I don't want to fight him. I lost my father too and I know how he feels. Maybe we can talk."

For whatever reason that seemed to satisfy Teanna, and her expression relaxed again.

"You and I, we're very different," she said. "You understand that, don't you?"

The first time they met she had said something very much like that.

"I understand," Mathew said. "I didn't ask for any of this. I suspect you already know that. I'd like things to be the way they were, but I'd have to be completely blind to think that's possible now. I've considered pitching the ring into the ocean, or melting it down, but I guess I don't have the nerve."

Mathew spoke without guile or pretense, and Teanna didn't interrupt; her face was without judgment. Oddly, he felt himself somehow drawn to her, which was ludicrous considering their different backgrounds and positions. Yet one inescapable fact remained: they *did* share something in common—the rings.

"Do you mind if I ask you a few questions?" Mathew said, changing the subject.

"Go ahead."

"You said a couple of things that confused me. A moment ago you spoke about a conversation I had with Prince Delain, though I guess I should call him king now."

"Um-hmm."

"That took place in Tremont at their inn. You weren't anywhere around. How could you possibly know what I said?"

"And the other is, how can I know how you felt about having had to kill my mother and uncle?" Teanna said. "I think you already know both answers, Mathew."

"You can read my mind?" he said, shocked at the concept.

Teanna closed her eyes and took a deep breath.

"Not really. At least not in the way you mean. Some thoughts are more obvious than others. It's an ability that

I acquired shortly after I put the ring on. It's not always consistent, but I've been able to sense certain things about you from the very beginning. When I spoke to my uncle about it, he thought the effect was confined only to family members, but I think it applies to anyone who wears the rings."

"But I can't tell what you're thinking."

"Good," Teanna said, the smile returning to her face. "The fact is you haven't tried, and if you did, I'd block you."

"Block me?"

"Mm-hmm."

While she was talking it suddenly occurred to him where his thoughts had been straying for the last few minutes. Teanna's dress was cut low in the front revealing her cleavage. Mathew promptly averted his eyes, which had been wandering in that direction. She followed his glance and sat a little more upright in her chair.

"I suppose you don't have to be a mind reader for some things," she added, making a small adjustment to her dress.

Mathew did his best not to look guilty and returned to the previous subject. "I don't understand all this about thought reading and blocking," he said.

"The fact is that you've probably done it already—at least I think you have," she said. "In the beginning when you first made contact with us, we were in my uncle's garden in Rocoi. You were on a ship somewhere, as I recall. I knew it was you the second the connection happened. I don't understand everything about the process myself, though I have learned to control it. It's just a matter of concentration, really."

"How did you know about what I said to Delain?"

"I listened."

"Hmph," Mathew said, sitting back in his chair.

"What does that mean?"

"I didn't know you could do it, that's all," he answered, slightly miffed.

"There are a lot of things I can do that you don't know about," she said, giving him an enigmatic smile.

"Really? Like what?" Mathew asked, leaning forward on his elbows.

Instead of answering, she pushed her chair back from the table and stood up.

"It's late. We can talk about it on the ride tomorrow. Would you like to walk me back to my room?"

"Sure."

For the second time that evening Teanna surprised him when she slipped her arm through his as they strolled back together. Her comment about sensing his thoughts was still fresh in his mind, so he made a deliberate effort to keep the conversation as neutral as possible. That fact that she was a very lovely young woman didn't make matters easier. Neither did her perfume. He was so much aware of their proximity to each other, he decided to think about something else, anything else, while they walked. It surprised him how tall Teanna was. He didn't realize it until she was standing next to him. He was at least six-foot-two and she was almost on eye level with him.

Her guards were on duty at the entrance to the apartments Gawl had assigned her. They both came to attention when they saw them approach. Teanna nodded but didn't remove her arm as they passed.

When they reached her room, she put her hands on his shoulders and gave him a light kiss on the cheek. Perhaps his hands remained on her waist longer than they should have. There was a tiny smile at the corners of her mouth when she said good night. Mathew stood in the hallway for a moment trying to decide exactly what that meant before he turned and headed back to his room.

Pleased with himself, he even said good night to Teanna's guards. Neither responded. And from the cold stares he received, there was little question in his mind about what their looks suggested.

After she closed the door Teanna leaned back against it and closed her eyes, then walked across the room and began to unbutton her dress. By chance, she glanced up and caught a reflection of herself in the full-length mirror. She stared at her face for several seconds before turning away. A mixture of emotions came and went in her mind. She continued wrestling with them as she lay down on the bed, still fully dressed. Mathew was very much the same as she remembered him—open, unpretentious, and with the most wonderful blue eyes. She lay there thinking for a long time before she leaned over and blew out the candle.

20

Tenley Palace

THE FOLLOWING MORNING, MATHEW WOKE EARLY, STILL in good spirits. He put on a heavy blue wool shirt, a sturdy pair of black breeches, and went down to breakfast. Through the window on ground floor he could see the snow had stopped falling during the night. The ice-covered branches looked like they were encased in glass.

Except for a pair of servants, who bowed when he entered, the breakfast room was deserted. A fire was already going in the fireplace, spreading warmth throughout. Mathew walked over and stood in front of it. The mantel consisted of two different kinds of marble; a dark maroon stone and a pale yellow one with gold veins. The heat felt so good he flopped into a big wing-backed chair and sat back to enjoy the quiet. The world always seemed fresh and new at that hour of the day, like it was reborn.

He stretched out his legs and stared into the fire. After a little while he found himself thinking about Lara and the day they finally made love together. It wasn't the first time for him. That had come two years earlier when he, Collin, and their fathers were returning from a hunting trip to Broken Hill in Elgaria. There were two sisters who were staying at the inn with their family before going on to Rockingham. The younger one was a girl named Lisa. He took a deep breath and wondered what she was doing.

Ultimately, images of Lara and Teanna both appeared in his thoughts. He admitted to himself that he was attracted to Teanna, though how much of it was due to his being annoyed at Lara for leaving he couldn't say. He didn't want to think about this. It made him feel uncomfortable. But something was definitely there. He thought the attraction might even be mutual, judging from the coquettish way she had returned his glances the night before.

Mathew's reflections were interrupted by one of the servants.

Without being asked, the man brought him a cup of dark mint tea, just as he had done each morning since Mathew arrived at the palace. His casual assumption rankled slightly, but Mathew thanked him and made a mental note to order something different the next time, for the sake of principle if nothing else.

He yawned and put his feet up on a stool in front of him, sinking deeper into the chair and enjoying the moment. Mornings were definitely his favorite time of day. In the fireplace a log fell from the grate sending a shower of sparks up the chimney.

Gawl had told him Argenton was a little over a half-day's ride from the palace. In truth he was not looking forward to meeting Father Kellner again. In the first place, he rather liked the man; and in the second, asking a priest if he was involved with murdering anybody was not going to be pleasant. Mathew closed his eyes and reviewed what he knew about Father Kellner.

He was an odd mixture of curiosity and nervous energy, very clearly enthused about his work, and quite intelligent. Mathew recalled Father Kellner several weeks ago had asked about the mental process that had to be employed to make the ring work. At the time he'd attributed the questions simply to scholarly interest, but now he wasn't so certain.

The lightest of touches to his earlobe pulled him back into the present. Assuming that it was a fly he brushed at the air to shoo it away. A second later it happened again and he brushed the air more vigorously. Mathew was about to do so for a third time, when he heard someone trying their hardest to keep from giggling directly behind him. Puzzled, he looked over his shoulder and saw nothing there. When his opposite ear was tickled he quickly twisted around in his seat. Teanna was standing in the doorway thirty feet away with a mischievous smile on her face.

Mathew raised an eyebrow, which only caused her smile to widen, showing a set of even white teeth. The sunlight bathed her in a warm yellow glow and made her look even lovelier than she had the night before. She came over, kissed him on the cheek, and took a seat in the big chair opposite him.

"Good morning," she said. "Sorry, but you looked so serious sitting there staring into the fire."

"Good morning. Did you sleep well?"

"Wonderfully. And you?"

"Fine, though I imagine the beer may have had something to do with it."

One of the servants came in carrying a porcelain tea service on a silver tray, but stopped in mid-step. His mouth fell open in shock as both the cup and teapot lifted off the tray and floated to Teanna, setting themselves gently down on the table. She appeared not to give it a second thought. The flustered servant turned and quickly disappeared in the kitchen, no doubt to tell a companion about what had just happened. Mathew chose not to comment.

"Would you care for some milk with your tea?" he asked.

"Yes, please," Teanna said, looking out the window. "Everything is so pretty this morning."

The pitcher of milk was sitting across the room on a sideboard. Mathew started to get up but sat back down. He glanced at the pitcher and formed the thought as Teanna had done, then watched it lift up and float to her. She plucked it gracefully out of the air and gave him one of her looks again.

It was a simple, silly trick, he knew, but for some reason he hoped it would impress her.

"Have you eaten yet?" she asked.

"No. I thought I would wait for the others . . ."

Like the startled servant, Mathew's eyes opened wide as a plate with two eggs and toast materialized on his lap, complete with a roll and butter. When he glanced up he saw that Teanna had a smug expression on her face.

"Why thank you," he said. "May I get you something as well?"

She inclined her head graciously and started to reply, but let out a small gasp as a single red rose materialized on the table next to of her.

"Thank you, kind sir," she said, picking up the rose and smelling it. "Such a strong fragrance for a single . . ."

Her words trailed away, replaced by a puzzled frown. Smiling, Mathew looked every bit as smug as she had only a moment ago. Teanna followed his gaze and drew her breath in sharply when she saw the main dining room table was covered with well over a hundred roses of every imaginable color. Some were even blue. Mathew conceded later that that color might not have been the best of choices.

For the next fifteen minutes, to the utter amazement of the servants, Mathew and Teanna played a game of Can You Best This? with each other. Flowers came and went, as did a plum tree, fully laden with fruit that appeared in the middle of the room in a large pot. A moment later it vanished, only to be replaced by a dragon, nearly seven feet tall with luminous gold eyes. All of it was pure illusion, of course, and the servants stood there gaping in awe while the two young people laughed uncontrollably.

The merriment might have gone on awhile longer but for the untimely appearance of Gawl. The king walked into the room and came face-to-face with the dragon which sat there calmly looking at him.

"God!" he exclaimed, nearly falling over his feet as he backed away.

The dragon tilted its head to the side, blinked at him, and promptly dissolved into smoke.

"What the hell was that?" Gawl demanded, pointing at the smoke, and trying to catch his breath at the same time.

"Just a dragon. Mathew was showing me some things he can do with his ring."

"A dragon?" Gawl sputtered.

Mathew's mouth fell open because it was Teanna who had created the illusion in the first place. She stuck her tongue out at him and turned back to Gawl.

"He's very talented, don't you think?" she said, in an innocent voice.

"Immensely," Gawl growled, recovering his composure and straightening his clothes.

Mathew looked at the servants for support, but they were both studiously staring straight ahead.

"We'll meet in an hour in the courtyard," Gawl told them. He cast a baleful glance at Mathew, picked up a loaf of bread and a large piece of yellow cheese from the table, and stalked out of the room, grumbling to himself about dragons and magic rings in his house.

Mathew put his hands on his hips and turned back to Teanna, who wisely decided to place the dining room table between them for her protection.

"I think I'd better go up and change," she said, moving to the opposite end of the table as he started coming around it. A second later, seeing her opportunity, she lifted her skirt and fled out into the hallway, past a surprised Jeram Quinn. Mathew waited for a second, then fixed the image of her shapely derrière in his mind, and "pinched."

There was a small squeal from out in the corridor.

Pleased, Mathew strolled over to his chair, picked up his tea from the side table, and took a sip.

* * *

Teanna d'Elso was still laughing to herself when she got to the top of the stairs and nearly ran into Father Thomas.

"Princess," the priest said, nodding to her.

The smile evaporated from Teanna's face, replaced by the mask she generally wore in public.

"Good morning," she said.

"Good morning. You seem in high spirits today."

"I was having some fun with Mathew," she explained, brushing a strand of hair away from her eyes.

"Ah."

"He's very nice," Teanna said.

"Yes, he is," Father Thomas agreed.

"Have you known him a long time?"

"Oh, yes, ever since I came to Devondale . . . about thirteen years, I should say. He's a fine person."

"He seems that way," Teanna said. "We found out that we have a lot in common."

"Indeed."

Teanna started to say something, stopped, and appeared to change her mind. "I can see that you don't think so, but we do."

"Princess, I've said nothing to the contrary."

"But you don't believe it, do you?"

"What I believe, or don't believe, is not terribly relevant. It's what Mathew believes that counts."

Teanna folded her arms across her chest and leaned back against the wall. "Do you think it's so odd for us to be attracted to one another?"

Father Thomas regarded her, but didn't answer immediately. "Is that what you really want to discuss, Teanna?"

"I don't want to discuss anything with you, any more than my mother did."

"I see," Father Thomas nodded. "Then, if you'll excuse me, my child."

"*Don't* call me that," Teanna snapped, her eyes flashing.

Father Thomas stopped and turned around. They stared at each other for several seconds. "I understand," he said.

"You understand *nothing*," Teanna spat at him.

"Quite possibly," he replied. "You are not your mother and we hardly know each other, but believe this, Mathew Lewin is very dear to me. I made a promise to protect him and I intend to honor that promise."

"You haven't trusted me from the moment I arrived," Teanna said.

The priest took a deep breath. "Trust is something that is earned. Nothing would give me greater pleasure than to trust you. That, you may believe."

Teanna's lip curled back in contempt. "I could destroy you with a single thought," she said.

"You could . . . though it would hardly be a way to inspire trust."

"Mother could have as well."

Father Thomas smiled. "I know, but she didn't," he said quietly. "Perhaps we can get to know each other a little better over the next few days."

Teanna watched Siward Thomas for several seconds before her face gradually softened.

"Perhaps," she said. "I have to change now."

And with that she continued across the balcony to her apartment.

21

Camden Keep

LARA PALMER WANDERED DOWN THE LONG GRAY CORRI-
dors of Rowena's home, looking at paintings and tapestries. It had been two full days since the snowstorm
subsided and she was bored. Jared and Rowena were
courteous and attentive hosts, but they told her it would
be at least another day until the road back to Tenley
Palace was clear enough to travel. For the fifth time she
kicked herself at not leaving a note for Mathew, but the
last thing she wanted was for him to come charging after
her, particularly if it might have endangered him.

Although Devondale wasn't located in the mountains
the way Camden Keep was, and it certainly got snow
there as well, but it was the first time she'd ever heard of
roads being blocked for *three days*. There couldn't have
been more than a foot of snow on the ground, and most of
it must have already melted. She found herself in an awkward situation. Unless she personally went to see, she
would be forced to call Jared a liar and that wouldn't be
good.

It was obvious they were trying to keep them there, but
for what reason? At first she thought it was because Jared
was attracted to her. Now she wasn't quite so certain. His
attentions were flattering of course, but then Jared appeared to be interested in anything wearing a dress. It
made no difference to him whether they were serving
girls or Rowena's nearest neighbor, Katherine Chartraine.

Lara continued to rebuff his advances, just as she had
done since they met. She was certain Rowena was aware
of the situation, and even considered discussing it with
her, but in the end decided against it. As a guest in someone else's home it wasn't proper to create an embarrass-
ing situation. Lara knew that she could handle herself,
and Jared too, if the need arose, so for the time being she
decided it would be better to keep matters as simple as
possible.

Camden Keep, as Rowena's estate was called, was really three buildings connected together. According to
Jared, his family had lived there for more than six hundred years, with one generation simply adding on to what
the others had created. The end result was an unbalanced,
disconnected structure that put the living apartments at
one end and kitchens and dining area all the way on the
opposite side. During her first day, while giving her a tour
Jared told her that the Keep once housed many of the
Sennian government's administrative offices. Bewildered, she asked why, since it was not exactly in the center of the country.

Jared explained that his father had been the regent of
the country, just as his grandfather and his great-
grandfather had before him. In fact, Jared said, his relatives had held the regency for over two hundred years.
After Gawl took the throne he moved everything back to
Tenley Palace, which didn't sit well with them.

Lord Edward Guy was a slender, dour-faced man, with
snow white hair. Though well into his sixties, he possessed a pair of intelligent blue eyes that missed nothing.
Lara quickly found that Lord Guy said very little himself
and was not given to idle conversation. When he did
speak, his questions tended to be concise and to the point.
Most of what he asked at dinner the night they arrived
centered on what the conditions in Elgaria were like after
the war. He also wanted to know what the new king was
doing to rebuild the country and its armies. Lara tried her

best to answer him, though as she pointed out, she was far from an expert on those topics.

"Clearly," Lord Guy replied, and promptly turned his questions to Collin, who had overheard his comment. Collin suggested his host compose a letter to King Delain on the subject and added that he would be happy to deliver it in person. Fortunately, Collin was polite enough in his speech so that no offense could be taken. Lara reached down and squeezed his hand under the table for coming to her rescue.

Lord Guy had looked at Collin sharply, as the meaning of his words became clear. Also having heard the exchange, Jared's face colored and he started to say something, but a look from his father silenced him. Thankfully, the rest of the meal went quickly after Lord Guy excused himself on the pretext of having to review some papers in his study. Jared left with him.

"You shouldn't have done that," a young lady seated next to Collin whispered, "Lord Guy is an ill man to cross."

"So am I," he muttered.

He gave Lara a quick wink and went back to flirting with his companion, who seemed receptive, if not actively interested in furthering their relationship.

That was three days ago, and except for occasional glimpses, Lara hadn't seen Lord Guy again, which suited her quite well.

Lara continued to wander down the confusing, twisting corridors and ultimately turned left instead of right as she should have. She found herself facing a pair doors. Out of curiosity, she turned the handle on one of them and opened it just a crack. There were voices coming from within, but they seemed distant. She opened the door a little more and peered in. Blinking in surprise, Lara pulled her head back, because instead of seeing a room as she expected, she found herself looking at the back of a set of heavy brocade drapes. Cautiously, she moved them aside and found that she was at the back of a balcony in a chapel of some kind. It was not especially large, and was made up of eight rows with approximately twenty seats on either side of an aisle that went down to a brass railing. In the main gallery below were five men; three were seated and two were standing. Lara recognized one of them immediately.

"Do you think they'll come?" Lord Guy's voice drifted up to her.

"There's very little question about that. Kellner left enough clues for a blind man to follow," another man answered. Father Kellner looked at him, but didn't respond.

Lara didn't recognize the voice of the speaker, clearly a stranger. He was leaning against one of the marble columns, slender and elegantly dressed in green and black silks.

Her eyes darted to the next man, seated across from him, at the end of the first row, lounging casually in his seat with one arm resting on the bench back. Though he was facing away from her, the clothes and arrogant bearing left little question that it was Jared. To his right was Bishop Willis.

"You think this has been easy?" Father Kellner snapped, "I'm the one who'll have to face him."

Intrigued, Lara eased herself into the room and slipped behind the curtain.

"Courage, Aldrich," the bishop said. "God is on our side in this matter—we cannot fail."

Kellner gave the Bishop a sour look and turned away.

"Understand this," Lord Guy said, "the young man is only one factor in a complex equation. We know he is unlikely to come alone, that's why we must be certain everything is in readiness."

"But, are we sure the others will come?" the bishop asked.

"The priest certainly will," Jared replied. "He watches over him as if he were his own child. And unless something happens to prevent the king from doing so, he'll accompany them. Gawl and Siward Thomas have been friends for over twenty years. Our only problem is we don't know what the size of their escort will be."

Jared's last comments were addressed to the man in green and black, who listened with an amused smile on his face.

"Whether the king brings ten or twenty men, it will make no difference. I have five thousand soldiers camped in the vale, three miles from here. As long as we can count on the full support of the church and your barons, Sennia should have a new king in two days."

He punctuated his speech with a bow in the bishop's direction

Ferdinand Willis inclined his head in acknowledgment.

"Does you cousin know about the invasion?" Lord Guy asked.

The man flicked a piece of lint off the sleeve of his doublet and said, "I have found it best not to share my plans with too many people. That includes family. For reasons I have yet to understand, Teanna seems to be attracted to the young man. Nevertheless, an alliance between Alor Satar and Sennia is in the best interests of both our countries, my lord, as you have so intelligently put it."

Lara nearly gasped when she heard what they were saying. *New king! Oh, my God . . . they're going to kill Gawl!* It occurred to her the same moment that Father Kellner wasn't referring to "facing" Gawl, as she first thought—he was referring to *Mathew*. So was the man who had just spoken.

She got down on her stomach, wishing she had decided to wear pants instead of a dress, and crawled to the far side of the aisle behind the seats. With a quick glance to make sure no one was looking, she carefully moved to the edge of the balcony where she could hear better. Lord Guy was speaking again.

"Many are still loyal to the king, Lord Duren, but the majority of power lies in the hands of a few families. Where they lead, the rest will follow. I assure you no one will be terribly upset to see him go. Lowering the trade tariffs and opening the borders has angered a lot of people."

For the second time in less then a minute, Lara's heart missed a beat. *Duren! It wasn't possible—the man was dead!* She'd seen it happen with her own eyes. Something was terribly wrong. Ever so slowly she peered over the edge of the balcony at the stranger. The man had hooded eyes that fit the descriptions she'd heard about Karas Duren, but he was much too young. Father Thomas once told her Duren was in his sixties. Whoever this person was he couldn't be much more than thirty-five or thirty-six. Then she remembered Duren had two sons, Armand and Eric. Armand was supposedly large, with a full red beard, so she guessed the man in green silks was his brother, Eric.

"Gawl may be misguided and corrupted by young Lewin, but the people seem to love him," Father Kellner said across the aisle.

"False heroes, like false prophets, have the longest way to fall," Lord Guy answered. "The people love whoever captures their imagination for the moment. In the end, their loyalty will go to those who put food on the table. That great hulking fool will be forgotten in a month's time."

"How soon do you think they'll arrive?" Eric Duren asked.

Lord Guy looked out the window before answering. "Tomorrow probably . . . Barcora is nearly a hundred miles to the south of us, and they usually don't get the same snowfall we do."

"And what about his companions?"

"My sister's *guests* are here to visit and see the country for a few days," Jared replied. "I'll find some way to keep them occupied until he arrives . . . particularly the girl. She amuses me."

Lord Guy turned to his son and gave him a flat look.

"You'd do better to think with the head *above* your shoulders," Eric Duren told him. "We can't afford mistakes at this point."

The smile vanished from Jared's face and he started to get up, but his father put a hand on his shoulder and stopped him.

"He's right," Lord Guy said. "They are here as bait— or perhaps additional security would be a better way to put it. You will see no harm comes to them. Do I make myself clear? Your sister is also very fond of the girl."

"Would that Rowena never directs such affection toward me," Eric Duren remarked. "I'm curious my Lord, was she really prepared to marry Gawl? I still can't believe he accepted her so willingly. For an intelligent man, his naïveté astonishes me."

"My daughter wholeheartedly believes in our cause. Of course, it helps that she is also quite beautiful. Once smitten, our monarch has given little thought to the difference in their ages. He sees only a young girl in love with him . . . infatuated by his muscles and position, no doubt. Gawl d'Atherny is content to do his carvings and make his silly pronouncements, as if he were fit to do so, or was capable of understanding their ramifications. No, our king goes blithely along hoping the country will run itself. Love, I'm afraid, can blind even the most astute of us."

Duren laughed to himself and turned to the bishop. "And you, my lord bishop, are you of the same mind?"

"The king is a foolish and willful man. I believe that he means well and loves his country. But as I have told you, Gawl is blinded not only by love but by the greater evil Mathew Lewin subtly works upon him. That is why he must be stopped. The country's moral fiber—if not its very survival—is at stake."

"Indeed," Eric Duren said. "Not to mention your own fortune, which will take a large leap forward once you are named the head of the church, eh, your Eminence?"

"That has nothing to do with it," the bishop said. "I am commanded by a higher authority, not by avarice or love of position."

"Of course, Eminence. Forgive me," Eric Duren replied. His words said one thing, but the mocking smile on his face said another.

"Enough of this," Lord Guy cut in. "We each have our tasks to perform. Let us drink to success and be about them."

He walked over to the altar, picked up a bottle of wine and poured a glass for each of them.

"To God and Sennia," he said, raising his glass in a toast.

The others joined him, including Father Kellner, who appeared to do so with less enthusiasm than his companions. A second later they were gone and Lara found herself alone in the chapel.

22

Camden Keep

AS SOON AS THEY WERE IN THE HALLWAY FATHER Kellner touched Ferdinand Willis on the arm and motioned for him to wait. The bishop's brows came together, but he stepped aside allowing the others to pass.

"I need to speak with you," Kellner said under his breath.

"Is something the matter, Aldrich?" he asked once they were alone. "I noticed that you barely touched your wine a moment ago."

There was a pause before Kellner answered.

"Is there no other way to do this, Eminence? I'm not a violent man. I think we should speak with the king and let him know what we know about Mathew Lewin. If Gawl realizes that he's being used, perhaps we can turn him from the path he's on. A revolt will only lead to bloodshed with many innocent people killed."

Willis had been expecting as much since he had observed the young priest's reaction in the chapel, and already knew what he was going to say.

"Who said anything about a revolt, my son?"

"Lord Duren. He said five thousand men at arms camped near here."

"They are only to insure the transition will be an orderly one, Aldrich. No one wants to see anyone harmed."

"But it *will* come to that," Kellner insisted. "Gawl is not going to abdicate without a fight."

The bishop held up his hands to calm the priest. "I have spoken to Lord Guy and he assures me they will do everything possible to avoid bloodshed . . . everything."

Kellner however appeared unconvinced.

"Holy Father, we're men of God. The sacred writings tell us that to kill another is a sin. If I do this, I'll be damned to hell. My eternal soul—"

"Your soul will be forever blessed, Aldrich, as will any who die in the service of the Lord. We pray there will be no deaths, but if there are, it will be among the servants of evil. You've studied the scripture. Do you recall the story of the angel who fought for the Lord using a flaming sword to smite his enemies?"

"Yes, Eminence."

The bishop slipped his arm through Father Kellner's and they began walking.

"It is no accident this parable is there. It is a lesson. The error many young priests make, my son, is that they interpret the scripture too literally. Do you also remember Saint Ellias's greatest teaching?"

"Of course . . . *the letter killeth, but the spirit giveth life*, but—"

"*Exactly*, my son. When the writings speak of *flaming swords* they do not mean a burning piece of metal. No, Aldrich. These are only representations. The men angels recruit *are* those swords. *You* are that sword."

Father Kellner stopped walking and looked at his mentor. "I don't understand, Eminence."

The bishop took a breath. Pleased with the analogy he had made, he continued in a patient voice. "It is a sign from God that you have been blessed with the ability to fight for him. Such an honor could only go to one whose heart is pure and free of evil."

"Eminence, I—"

"This is no mere conjecture, Aldrich. Alarice came to me in a dream two nights past and told me as much herself. Once I am restored as head of the abbey, we will do great things together, wonderful things. We will uncover such secrets as the world has not seen for three millennia. *You* will be the sword that leads us . . . the implement of the Lord, my son."

There was a pause as the bishop's words sunk in.

"Alarice spoke to you of me?" Kellner whispered.

"Yes, my boy," Bishop Willis lied. "You have made the church very, very proud. Doubt can weaken even the boldest man, but if we hold fast to one another, there is nothing that can stand against us. Do you trust me?"

"Of course, Eminence."

"This is a task that Alarice laid before me. She foretold that doubt would overcome you. Know that it has fallen to me to guide you through the rough waters, and guide you I shall, for you are not alone. I am with you always."

The bishop pulled Father Kellner to him and hugged the young priest. While the two men embraced, Ferdinand Willis made a mental note to have his cassock replaced because one of the sleeves was becoming frayed at the end.

Tears began to roll down Kellner's face.

"Go now, Aldrich," the bishop told him. "The time grows short and everything must be in readiness."

"Yes, Eminence," Kellner said, kissing the bishop's ring. "I will not fail you. Forgive me for my weakness."

"There is nothing to forgive. Nothing."

Ferdinand Willis watched Father Kellner's receding back for a moment, then took a deep breath.

Well, that was easier that I thought, he said to himself. *A few more weeks and the abbey is mine again.*

The bishop straightened his robes and strolled down the hallway, whistling as he went.

23

Camden Keep

LARA PALMER'S MOUTH WAS DRY AND HER HEART WAS beating so fast she had to take several breaths to slow it down.

So . . . Jared is amused by me. And Rowena is part of the conspiracy too. Lovely . . . just lovely!

The first thing she had to do was to find Collin and let him know what was happening. Gawl was probably on his way to Camden Keep at that very moment. He had to be warned. It was all the more insidious and horrible that the trap was being set by people he loved and trusted. Her blood boiled at the treachery. To make matters worse, Mathew was also in danger.

Kellner's comment about having to "face him" hung in Lara's mind like an axe waiting to fall as she walked back toward the living quarters. She was still trying to decide what he meant or thought he could do to Mathew when she rounded the corner and ran directly into Rowena.

"My goodness," Rowena said, catching her. "Where are you off to in such a hurry?"

"Oh, I'm sorry," Lara said, resisting the temptation to hit the taller woman. She managed an embarrassed laugh instead and straightened her dress, "I don't know where my mind was. I thought I'd find Collin and see what he's up to."

"Um . . . it might be best to wait a little while before you try his room," Rowena suggested tactfully.

"Why?"

"I think he has company," she said, dropping her voice discreetly.

"Company? But . . ."

Lara was about to say something else when she recalled the clingy way the girl next to him had been hanging on to Collin's arm the night before.

"Katherine and Nadia decided to stay the night," Rowena explained. "My guess is—"

"Yes, I understand," Lara said, her face reddening slightly.

Rowena laughed and took her arm. "Come and walk with me," she said. "I know being cooped up here the last few days must have been a bore for you, so I've planned a little trip for us to Argenton today."

"The town where the ruins are?"

"Um-hmm. It'll be a lot of fun. Father Kellner told me they've made some new finds there recently. Something about light tubes that still work and all that. They also found a strange coach of some kind that can move without out a team pulling it."

"Really?" Lara said. "That does sound like fun. I'll have to change my clothes, though. When do you want to leave?"

"Let's go after lunch. The town's just a short ride from here. I'll finish writing my letters and meet you at the stables."

Lara watched Rowena disappear around the corner and was glad that she resisted the urge to punch her. At the moment it was more important to speak with Collin and let him know what was happening.

Of all the times for that big lummox to get romantic. And with that little chatterbox, Nadia. The stupid woman didn't shut up all evening. It would serve him right if I did bang on his door!

She went to her room and quickly changed into a sturdy pair of shoes and a heavier dress. A white wool

sweater, sheepskin cloak, and gloves completed her out-
fit. Midday meal wouldn't be for another two hours yet,
and she *had* to speak with Collin.

Lara walked down the hall to his room and stopped in
front of his door, debating about what to do.

When she thought about it later, she conceded it might
have been mean-spirited on her part, but the opportunity
was just too good to pass up, and she had to get him
alone. Her knock set off a mad scrambling of feet from
inside the room.

"Collin, it's me. I need to talk with you."

"What? Uh . . . just a moment," a groggy voice answered.

It was followed by the sound of frantic whispering. A
moment later, she heard the latch turn and the door
opened slightly to reveal a sleepy-looking Collin Miller,
who was standing there bare-chested with just a sheet
wrapped around his middle.

"Good morning, lazy bones," Lara said brightly.

Collin leaned forward and lowered his voice. "Lara,
this isn't . . . uh . . . exactly the best time to—"

"I'll bet you don't even know what day it is, do you?"

"What day? Well, I don't . . . that is . . . I—"

"Oh, you men are all alike. But I forgive you."

Lara leaned forward and gave the startled Collin a kiss
on the lips, then pushed her way past him into the room.

"What the devil are you talking about?" he hissed.
"Listen, I was trying to tell you—"

"Close the door you silly thing. Do you want someone
to see you standing there half dressed?"

"What? Oh . . . sure," he replied. "But see here, why
don't you wait for me in the hall and I'll be dressed in a
jiffy? I don't get what you mean about today. I—"

"It's our anniversary, darling," Lara said, stepping
close to him and putting her arms around his neck. "You
didn't forget, did you?"

"Anniversary? What the hell are you—"

Collin never got the chance to finish his sentence because Lara pulled him close and kissed him again. Directly over his shoulder, she could see someone's shadow moving behind the closet door that was slightly ajar. Collin must have thought she'd taken leave of her senses. When their lips parted, his eyes were as wide as saucers.

"Now hurry and get dressed, dear. Rowena will be up any minute. She's taking us to Argenton to see the ruins. Isn't it exciting?"

The shadow behind the door moved again, and a hand snaked out to grab a woman's slip hanging on the knob.

A small crease appeared between Collin's eyebrows and he took Lara by the shoulders searching her face. After a second or two he glanced over his shoulder at the closet and turned back to her.

"Yes," he replied, drawing out the word. "It does sound fascinating. I can hardly wait."

"Do you know, dearest, I believe there's a draft coming from that closet. I'll just close it so you won't catch cold."

"Your consideration overwhelms me," Collin said, folding his arms across his chest. Lara crossed the room and kicked the door. She locked it and mouthed, *get dressed* to him.

He silently replied *turn around* to her, and punctuated it with a hand gesture.

Lara shrugged and sat on the bed, obediently facing the wall, while Collin found his clothes and changed into them, still muttering to himself. Later, she firmly maintained being totally unaware of the mirror that was hanging there.

24

Camden Keep

"WHAT THE HELL WAS THAT ALL ABOUT?" COLLIN asked, as soon as they stepped into the hallway.

Lara started to answer, but held her reply as a clerk carrying an armload of papers came around the corner. She and Collin nodded pleasantly and said good morning as they passed.

"They're going to kill Gawl," she whispered, glancing over her shoulder.

Collin nearly missed a step. "Kill Gawl? Who's going to kill Gawl?"

"Lord Guy, Jared, Father Kellner, and the bishop. They also want to hurt Mathew. Duren's in on it too."

Collin stopped in his tracks, looked at her sharply, then stepped into an alcove and pulled her with him.

"Maybe you'd better tell me what's going on—slowly. And what's this about Karas Duren?"

"Not Karas—it's his son, Eric."

"How do you know?"

"Because I *saw* him and I overheard them talking."

Lara proceeded to recount what went on in the chapel while Collin's face grew more and more grave. She was interrupted once more by two workers who were walking by. She was in the middle of filling in the rest of the details and was not prepared when Collin suddenly grabbed her, pulled her close, and kissed her, nor was she prepared for it when his hand squeezed her buttocks. Lara didn't pull away, but she decided she was going to hit him if he looked the slightest bit smug when they separated. Fortunately he didn't. She smoothed her dress, stepped back into the hallway, brushing a wisp of hair away from her face.

For his part Collin half expected to have to duck and was pleasantly surprised when that didn't happen. Lara gave him an odd look but didn't say anything. Until that moment he had never really thought of her in a sexual way. They were just friends. Good friends . . . but friends. On top of that she was Mat's girl. They'd known each other since they were children and he could remember dashing through the streets with her after they stole an apple from Enoch Ruffin's store. The kiss was to get even for what she did to him in the room. The buttocks thing . . . well, just sort of happened on its own, but instead of feeling better for getting even, he felt worse.

"Uh . . . sorry," he mumbled.

"Maybe Elona and I ought to have a talk when we get home," she said.

Collin felt himself go red in the face. "Listen, I'm sorry about—"

"Forget it," she said. "Let's go down to lunch. Oh, I apologize, it's still breakfast for you isn't it?"

"What about Nadia?" he asked, ignoring her jibe. "You locked that poor girl in the closet."

Lara raised an eyebrow. "I suppose one of the maids will be along later this afternoon and let her out. Meanwhile, you and I have to find a way to get out of here. We need to warn Gawl and Mathew."

"That's not going to be easy," he said. "There always seems to be at least one or two soldiers around wherever I go in this place. I thought it was just a coincidence, but after what you've just told me, it's obvious they're trying to keep track of us. Who's coming to Argenton today besides you and me?"

"I don't know," Lara said. "Rowena, definitely . . .

probably Jared too. He usually finds an excuse to hang around."

"That's because he finds you desirable," Collin grinned.

"I seem to be having that effect on a lot of people lately."

Collin cleared his throat. "Ah . . . yes . . . well . . . what do you think we should do? From what you told me, Gawl is probably on his way here right now."

"Argenton's going to be our best chance," Lara whispered, while they walked. "We can slip away when we get there."

When they arrived at the dining room, Lara expected that Lord Guy would be there, but he was nowhere to be seen. Rowena was, and so were Jared and Bishop Willis.

"I understand everyone is going to Argenton today," the bishop said.

"Yes," Lara answered.

"Would you mind terribly if an old man accompanied you? I've heard so much about what they've been finding there, I'm excited to see it for myself."

"Of course not, bishop . . . or is it, Eminence? I never can tell the difference," Lara said, giving his hand an affectionate squeeze. "More company would be wonderful."

"Either is quite correct, my child. It hasn't been that long since I was a regular priest, and to tell the truth, I sometimes miss the duties of having my own church to watch over. Bishops do the same thing as priests, but on a larger scale. When one becomes a bishop they are generally referred to as 'Eminence,' but we try not to stand on too much ceremony whenever possible."

"I don't even know if we have bishops in Elgaria," Lara said.

"You do . . . or at least you did. Unfortunately, they were both killed in the war. Bishop Morelli was a good friend of mine. So was Bishop Vernon."

"Oh . . . I'm very sorry," Lara said.

"Thank you, my dear. Have you been enjoying your stay here?"

"Oh, yes . . . Rowena is a very considerate hostess."

"And you, my son? Are you also enjoying yourself?" the bishop asked Collin.

Collin was aware that Rowena and Jared were both listening to the conversation, though each was pretending not to. "It's a nice change from Tenley Palace," he replied, "but with all this snow and the roads being closed, I'll be glad to be getting out."

"I take it neither of you have been to Argenton before?" Ferdinand Willis asked.

"Nope," Collin answered.

"From everything I've heard, I think you're going to enjoy it. Father Kellner tells me there's an entire city buried under all that rubble. Apparently, it's going to take quite some time to uncover everything, but hopefully what we'll learn will be worth it. Rowena said she already mentioned the horseless coach and the light tubes to Lara."

"Mmm," said Collin, taking a sip of wine. "Maybe the road will be clear by the time we finish our visit. We really need to be getting back, you know."

He saw the quick glance Jared shot Rowena and ignored it.

"Another day should do it," Jared said, cutting up the chicken on his plate. "One of our patrols reported in this morning and said things are getting better, but the main road is still blocked."

How convenient, Collin thought. "What do you need patrols for?" he asked. "We're not at war."

Jared's knife paused. "Brigands."

"Brigands?" Lara repeated.

"Bands of roving thieves," Rowena explained. "They've been plaguing this area for years. But they seem to have gotten much worse in the last few months."

"I know what brigands are," Lara said. "No one ever mentioned them before."

"Well, I'm sure Jared and Rowena didn't want to worry you," the bishop told her. "They've been quite a problem in the past. Neither Rowena's father nor the king have been able to do anything about them. Generally they prey on unarmed citizens and merchants traveling by themselves, but since we're taking an escort along I'm sure we'll be more than safe."

"I'm sure," said Collin.

"Besides, we'll have two strong men to protect us," Rowena smiled. "Jared's coming with us today, aren't you dear?"

"Sure. I'd like to see what all the fuss is about," he said. "I can't imagine anything surviving for three thousand years, much less still working."

The rest of the meal passed quickly in idle conversation and speculation about what the Ancients were like. Lara managed to catch Collin's eye once or twice, but his expression was impossible to read.

She was thinking about several things at the same time. In all likelihood Gawl was already on his way, riding into a trap, unless she and Collin could get word to him in time. Also, a knot was beginning to form in the pit of her stomach over several things. Father Kellner said, *he would have to face Mathew;* and, although it was nowhere on the same level of importance, she felt guilty about having let Collin kiss her. She could have stopped it of course, but she didn't, and that only made matters worse. She knew a lot of girls found him attractive, but that was no excuse.

Obviously Nadia did, she thought. She acknowledged it was mean to barge in on them like that and lock her in the closet. The whole situation was very confusing, she thought, even though the memory did make her smile. In the end she decided it was curiosity that prompted her to accept the kiss—at least, she thought it was curiosity.

She was spared further reflection when Bishop Willis asked her a question.

"Excuse me?" Lara said.

"I asked if there were any ruins in your country."

"Oh, yes . . . quite a few. There aren't many around Devondale, where Collin and I are from. It's about a week's ride south of Anderon if you're not familiar with the area. The old cities are all gone of course, but we did see parts of the roadways and some old building foundations on our way here."

"There were a lot more in Tyraine," Collin added. "Father Thomas pointed them out. Did you know he once rode in one of the coaches they found on Coribar?"

"Ah . . . Siward Thomas . . . an interesting fellow," said the bishop. "He wants us to intercede with King Delain for your friend—Mathew, I think his name is?"

He knows damn well what Mathew's name is, Collin thought. *So do half the people in Elgaria and Sennia.*

"Why, yes . . . I believe that is his name," Collin replied. It immediately earned him a sore shin when Lara kicked him under table.

"Collin's teasing you, your Eminence. He and Mathew have been best friends since they were children."

The bishop smiled and nodded, but Lara noticed that Jared didn't seem amused.

"Tell me, are all those fantastic stories I've heard about his ring true? You know how people tend to exaggerate," the bishop asked.

"I suppose so," said Collin. "To be honest, I don't really understand much about it myself. I was there at Ardon Field when he fought Duren. The fireworks were very impressive, but as to how he does those tricks . . . well . . . frankly the whole thing is beyond me. I prefer a quarterstaff to balls of fire."

"Tricks? Are you saying those things he did were tricks?"

"Mat and I are friends, but he doesn't tell me everything. Personally, I think he enjoys keeping people guessing, if you know what I mean. That's just the way he is."

The bishop's frown deepened. "This is certainly very confusing. What sort of person is he?"

Collin shrugged. "Just an ordinary fellow."

"I heard he killed a man," Rowena said. "Strangled him to death with his bare hands or something like that."

Collin waved away the comment. "It was a fair fight. I was there when it happened. The man he killed was a fellow named Berke Ramsey who had it in for Mat. I won't bore you with all the details, but things got out of hand, and Berke, who was nothing but a no good son of a snake, tried to kill Mat with a crossbow. Instead, the fool missed and killed his father, Bran. Mat went after him. Anybody would have done the same. Isn't that right Lara?"

"He was a horrible person. He got exactly what he deserved," Lara answered.

"Then why is that constable person here to arrest him?" asked Rowena.

"Quinn? He's just doing his job," Collin answered. "He's a stickler for the rules. Nothing is going to come out of it, you mark me."

"I still don't understand why Gawl prevented him from taking your friend back and getting the thing cleared up if it's so simple," Jared said.

"Yes," the bishop agreed. "You would think the young man is exercising some kind of influence over him."

"Mat?" Collin laughed. "That's a good one. Can you see Mat making Gawl do anything he doesn't want to?"

Collin looked at Lara, who shook her head and smiled.

"I think the only reason Gawl hasn't sent us home already is that he and Father Thomas are friends, and they're not through visiting yet," she said.

The discussion about Mathew went on for another twenty minutes before Rowena reminded everyone that it was time to leave. The questions the bishop asked, however subtle he tried to make them, all centered on what kind of person Mathew was. Did he covet power? Was he a religious person? An honest person? Did he and Gawl spend a lot of time talking with each other alone, and so on.

Though Collin and Lara answered them all without providing anything in the way of real information, her concern for Mathew's safety deepened with each question the bishop asked and it was a relief when they all finally got up from the table.

25

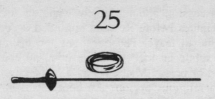

The Argenton Ruins

IT CAME AS NO SURPRISE TO COLLIN WHEN THEY REACHED the stables and found that Rowena had ordered a coach for them. Fortunately, since five people were going, it gave him an excuse to take his horse, Cloud. The problem, he thought, was what to do about Lara once they finally made their move to escape. A quick glance at the eight soldiers who were riding along for their *protection,* did nothing to allay fears. The men were tough-looking, professional, and not given to conversation. Four of them rode about fifty yards ahead of the coach and the other four were following behind it. Collin stayed with the first group. While the men responded to his questions, none of them initiated any conversation, and the answers they gave were either evasive or downright lies. It was a sharp, cold day and there was still snow on the ground, though it was now hard-packed and brown from use. Looking at it, he had little doubt that the main road back to Barcora was no longer blocked. Twice during the trip he spurred his horse ahead only to be accompanied by two of the soldiers, who suddenly decided to ride with him. It was clear that he and Lara were on a leash, a long leash but a leash nevertheless.

The town of Argenton became visible after they crested one of the last hills. The village wasn't much larger than Devondale. The Camenon Mountains, rose up like a wall to the east of it, solemn and silent. Surprisingly, there was almost no snow in the valley. One of the soldiers noticed Collin looking out over the scene. In a rare burst of talkativeness, he began explaining that the region was drier due to the shelter provided by the mountains.

The ruins bordered on a river, the same Deeprun River that ran past Tenley Palace. It was almost five miles from where the townspeople lived on the other side of a forest. They appeared to have been stuck in the middle of nowhere, as far as Collin could discern.

In a clearing nearly half a mile across lay the remains of a city dead more than three thousand years. Few of the records from that period had survived, and its original name remained a mystery, the bishop told them. For lack of anything better, the locals also referred to the ruins as Argenton, as though they were simply an extension of their town, even though it had been built 1,800 years after according to the artifacts that had been unearthed.

Though most of the digging had been shut down for the winter, a few small crews of workmen still remained. The first thing Collin noticed about the city was that it had a wall surrounding it. Seconds later he saw a company of soldiers wearing Lord Guy's colors, camped near the wall and front entrance. The ruins were far larger than he expected. They had seen remains of old buildings while traveling through Elgaria, but those tended to be isolated. Most were crumbling, weatherworn shells that forced people to use their imagination in order to picture what the original structures must have looked like. That was not the case in Argenton. More than fifteen buildings had survived almost completely intact down through the centuries. Most were taller by several times than Barcora's central watchtower. Collin saw at least two buildings that would have easily stretched from one side of Devondale to the other.

The streets themselves were wide, though badly pitted and broken. He thought they must have once made an impressive sight. Uncertain what to expect or feel about the place, he looked around. He finally decided the word he was looking for was "sad."

How could people who had built something like this have destroyed themselves? he wondered.

For almost eight months, he had watched his friend study the ancient texts at the abbey trying to find some clue as to what had happened to them. Mat said he was certain that the rings were involved, but didn't know in what way. It was all very confusing. The city lying before him, silent and still, was an impressive sight, but as much a mystery as most things about their ancestors were.

He was not to learn until much later it was not quite as dead as it seemed.

Collin dismounted and tied his horse to a lamppost near the first building, then walked around to help Lara and Rowena down from the coach.

"This is astonishing," Bishop Willis said, turning slowly around and taking in the scope of the place. "They told me the ruins were extensive, but I never thought they would be this large."

"They're amazing," Lara agreed.

"I'm so glad you could all come," a voice behind them said.

Everyone turned to see Father Kellner standing there. He was not dressed in a priest's garb, but was wearing a heavy wool cloak over dark blue pants and boots. His hands were thrust deep into his pockets.

"Aldrich, I believe you've already met Collin Miller and Lara Palmer," the Bishop said.

"Of course," he replied, coming forward to shake their hands.

"And you know, Rowena and Jared Guy."

"Yes, yes we've met," the priest replied.

Lara had to bite her tongue to keep from saying anything while the others went through the charade of being introduced. It was incredible how easily these people could lie. She noticed Collin's eyebrows lifted a little, but was glad when he showed no other reaction.

"I know how exciting this all appears," Father Kellner told them, "but for the time being it might be best if we all stay together. This way I can show you around and point out the areas to avoid."

"Why is that, Father?" asked Collin.

"Well, to put it simply . . . certain parts of the city are still active."

That statement brought puzzled stares from everyone and Father Kellner held up a hand to forestall their questions.

"I don't mean to sound mysterious," he laughed, "but I'm not exaggerating very much. We have found a number of fascinating things here which I'll show you in just a moment. I think you'll find them as amazing as I did . . . and still do. Every once in a while, though, we come across something that looks quite innocuous . . . but isn't. Such things can be dangerous."

"What do you mean, Father?" asked Jared.

"Well . . . for example, one of the workmen, a fellow named Townes, was examining a sink in that black building on the left. From all outward appearances the sink appeared to be most ordinary, except it was made of some kind of ceramic material that is incredibly strong and completely resistant to scratches. When Townes looked in the drain, he saw what appeared to be a four-bladed object sitting at the bottom of it. He stuck his hand in to retrieve it. Unfortunately, it was a machine of some sort the Ancients used—though, why they would do so is beyond me. It immediately came to life and severed two of his fingers and a part of another."

Rowena and Lara both gasped.

"My God!" exclaimed Jared.

"Is the man all right?" Lara asked.

"Yes. He's fine now, or as well as he can be under the circumstances. We sent him home to his family to recuperate, of course."

"I don't understand, Father. Was it some kind of a trap?" Jared asked.

"I think not, my son. In all likelihood, the Ancients had a use for the device. We found similar ones in other buildings. They don't appear in every sink, just those in the kitchens. I instructed our men to take greater precautions with anything they come across, no matter how harmless it might appear. That's why I ask that we all stay together, at least initially. Afterward, you can go exploring on your own. We've marked the unsafe areas off with yellow rope, so you'll be in no danger. I feel very badly about Townes."

"I don't get how anything could be working after all these years," said Collin.

"It *is* incredible," Father Kellner agreed. "What we have learned is that there's still a power source at work, though we haven't been able to identify where it comes from, or even how it makes the machines function. I believe whatever caused the machine that injured poor Townes to come to life is same thing that powers the lights we found."

"I'd love to see them, Father," the bishop said.

"So would I," Jared agreed.

"Very well—if you'll all follow me."

As they walked down the street, Collin lagged behind and Lara dropped back to be with him.

"I don't know when we'll have the opportunity," he whispered, "but we both won't be able to get away. I'm going to create a diversion. When I do, I want you to get to my horse. If you're quick enough about it, I think you'll be able to get past the soldiers."

"*No.*" Lara hissed. "We both go together."

"The important thing is to warn Gawl and Mat. Cloud is the only horse available except for the ones Lord Guy's men rode in on, and they're all tethered in a group, plus they've got two men guarding them. If we take the coach, they'll ride us down in a couple of minutes. I've thought about this, Lara. It's the only way."

"Collin, I can't—"

"*Yes,* you can," he whispered fiercely. "Just do as I say. You're a good rider—maybe better than me. When the time comes, slip away, then go like hell."

"Collin—"

"Stop arguing. One of us has to get through. You know I'm right."

Lara did know, though it didn't make her feel any better. Before she could think of anything else to say, Rowena turned around and glanced at them, which effectively cut off any further conversation.

The building Father Kellner led them into smelled old. Despite the sweeping marble lobby, a gray-green mold was growing on the walls and a dank smell hung in the air. It got worse as they approached a staircase tucked away in the corner.

Father Kellner pointed out a series of gleaming metal doors located in the center of the lobby. Two of them had been pried open to reveal a small cubicle-like room about the size of a closet, no more than seven feet square. A yellow rope had been placed across the entrance to prevent anyone from going in. One of the little cubicles was only partially visible with two-thirds of it below the floor line. From what Collin could see it appeared to be suspended by two thick metal cables that ran up a dimly lit shaft all the way to the top of the roof.

He craned his neck in, looked up and whistled, the sound echoing off the walls.

"My theory is this machine is some kind of conveyance the Ancients used to transport themselves up and down the building. There are more metal doors just like these on each of the other floors. Since it no longer works, we will have to negotiate the steps the old-fashioned way," Father Kellner said.

Lara and the others each looked in before following Father Kellner to the staircase. A thick blanket of dust lay on the floor, disturbed only by workers' tracks. A number of oil lamps had been hung from the walls to make the going easier.

When they were about halfway up, Father Kellner told them, "There are two rooms in this building I think you'll find interesting. They both contain different types of lights. The first, which I will show you in a moment, contains globes that produce a yellowish kind of glow; the other has long glass tubes which give off a very bright white light."

In deference to the bishop, they kept the pace moderate. He appeared to be struggling but made the climb without complaint. A few minutes later, they emerged through a door on the tenth floor.

"Why did you bother to take that thing with you?" Jared asked, looking at Collin's quarterstaff.

"I listened to Father Kellner. If I have to stick anything down a hole, it's going to be this or something else I wouldn't care to lose."

Jared laughed and clapped Collin on the shoulder.

At the end of a hallway, Father Kellner waited for them beside a pair of double doors. They were not made of wood, but neither were they of the same material as the doors in the lobby. The priest used his right hand to pull one open, then used the same hand to open the other door. When he did, it occurred to Collin that the priest had been keeping his left hand in the pocket of his coat since they arrived.

"What the devil is that fellow hiding?" he thought.

He found out a moment later when Rowena missed a step and slipped on the dusty surface. Jared and Father Kellner both reached out to steady her at the same time. That was when Collin saw the rose-gold ring on Father

Kellner's left hand. He averted his eyes just in time as the priest looked back at him. Kellner quickly placed his hand back in his pocket.

The room contained a long granite table with eighteen chairs around it. Both the seat cushions and draperies that once hung on the walls were long gone, having disintegrated into dust with only tattered fragments remaining. Above the center of the table was a brass chandelier. There were no candles in it, but in their place were small oblong-shaped glass bubbles in which candles could have been. High up in the ceiling, a series of round black holes contained different shaped glass globes. At that point the only illumination was provided by mid-afternoon sunlight streaming through a window that covered one entire wall—until Father Kellner threw two switches near the door.

Suddenly the room was bathed in a bright yellow light from the chandelier. A moment later the globes in the ceiling came on. They were so bright Collin was unable to look directly at them for more than a few seconds. It was an incredible thing to see.

"Amazing, is it not?" Father Kellner asked.

They were all so dumbfounded no one answered. They could only stand there and shake their heads in wonder.

"I never thought to see anything like this," said Bishop Willis.

"I just can't believe it," said Rowena.

Jared just stared up at the lights openmouthed.

"I felt the same way the first time I saw them," Father Kellner explained. "The odd thing is that the lights in some of the rooms work, but don't in others. This is the first building we've fully excavated, and we're still discovering new things about it every day."

While the others were occupied Collin nodded to Lara, then walked over to a painting on the wall and began examining it. The scene depicted there was more impressive to him than the light globes and there was something

oddly familiar about it. It took several seconds before he
realized that he was looking at an artist's rendition of the
city itself, at least the way it used to be. Gleaming buildings reached into the sky, untouched by the years and the
war his ancestors had fought. A quick glance out the window confirmed he was right. Though there were differences and a great number of buildings had yet to be
unearthed, there were enough to convince him that the
scene in the painting and the city below were one and the
same. It was like looking back in time.

Ancients strolled along the avenues. The figures were
too small to make out any detail, but he could tell that
their clothes were different from the way people
presently dressed. Carriages with no horses cruised the
thoroughfares, and most unbelievable of all—some hung
suspended in the air several stories above the ground.

Eventually Jared and Rowena noticed the painting and
came to join him along with Father Kellner and the
bishop. With the exception of Father Kellner, none of
them had seen anything remotely like it before.

"Their vehicles flew?" whispered Rowena.

"If you look back here," Collin said, pointing to part of
the painting, "you can see one of the airships just over the
top of the mountains."

"That's a bird," said Jared.

"No, look. The lines are too straight, and this part
looks like smoke's trailing behind it," said Collin. "I've
never seen a painting like this. You can't even see the
brushstrokes."

"Incredible," agreed Bishop Willis.

"That is because it's not a painting, my son," Father
Kellner explained. "The Ancients called this a photo-
graph. They had a machine that could freeze an image in
time—if I'm explaining it correctly. Whatever the user
was looking at was captured in the blink of an eye just by
pressing a button. We actually found several books . . ."

The priest's voice trailed off and he glanced around the room frowning. "Where is Lara?" he asked.

"She probably just wandered down the hall to see the other rooms," Collin said. "I imagine she'll be back in a second."

He saw the look that passed between the bishop and Jared.

"I'll go find her," Jared said. "We wouldn't want her to fall down one of those shafts."

"Hang on for a second," Collin said, taking his arm. "You know you might be right about this being a bird. See here—"

"Find her," Bishop Willis snapped.

Jared stared at Collin for a second before he realized what was happening, then jerked his arm away and started for the door. A second later he was flat on his face when Collin's quarterstaff caught his ankle and tripped him. A sharp blow behind the ear rendered him unconscious.

Rowena screamed.

A look of shock appeared on Father Kellner's face and he took a step forward only to be hit between the eyes by the butt end of Collin's staff. He crumbled to the floor next to Jared.

Collin jumped over the prone bodies and started for the door. Bishop Willis's face was contorted with rage, and he grabbed the back of Collin's cloak. A sharp backward swing with the staff caught him just under the rib cage. The bishop grunted and went down on one knee releasing his hold. In three more strides Collin was in the hallway. He slammed the door shut and wedged his quarterstaff between the handles.

Inside the room he could hear shouts, cursing, and things being banged aside. It took a minute before someone, Jared he assumed, tried the door. The quarterstaff was made of stout yew wood and held its place. Collin helped by bracing his back up against it. He only had time to issue a quick silent prayer that Lara would be all right before a heavy thud from inside the door shook his body.

Collin quickly looked around for anything else he could use. There were nothing but empty walls and dust. Another thud shook him again. On Jared's third try, a small crack appeared in the quarterstaff and Collin knew it was about to go. Even with the addition of his weight, he couldn't hold on much longer. Then from the inside of the room, he heard Father Kellner yell something.

Calculating quickly, Collin thought that Lara had probably gotten to Cloud by then, but decided to give her a few more seconds.

The impact of Jared's next blow knocked him back a half step. He grunted and threw his shoulder back against the door. A glance at his staff told him it was all but finished.

Time to go, he said to himself.

With one deep breath, he pushed himself off the door and sprinted for the staircase at the end of the hall.

If I can just make it out of the ruins and into the hills . . .

The doors exploded outward with a deafening bang. Bits of metal and splinters struck him in the back and legs and a hot blast of air roared down the corridor, lifting him up and slamming him into the wall face-first. The impact knocked the air out of his lungs and Collin crumpled to the ground, only dimly aware that the red dripping down his hands was his own blood.

The last image he saw was Father Kellner standing in the doorway, framed in yellow light from the ancient globes. Then a dark curtain settled over his eyes.

Lara heard the explosion as she raced down the street toward the soldiers.

"Help!" she screamed. "There's been an accident, Father Kellner's hurt. Come quickly."

Both men leaped to their feet.

"What is it girl?" one of them asked, catching her by the shoulders.

"An accident," she answered, gasping for breath. "They're on the fifth floor. You've got to hurry."

"I'll go," the man said. "Gerald, get the others in case we need them. Wait here girl."

The first man sped off down the street and his companion started running up the block in the opposite direction. Lara waited a moment, then dashed to where Collin had tethered Cloud, jerked the reins frcc, and leaped into the saddle. They would figure out what happened in another minute. There was no sign of Collin, and what she did see wasn't good.

At the opposite end of the block Jared came charging out of the building, followed by Father Kellner and Rowena. They started pointing in her direction and yelling. The soldier who was running toward them came to a halt, turned, and started back to her. He was coming fast. Their shouts also attracted the attention of the second soldier.

Damn, she thought.

Lara wheeled her horse to the right and galloped toward the main gate at full speed. The second soldier stopped and began waving his arms, trying to get her to do the same. He was standing directly in her path. She pulled the reins and tried to go around him, but he managed to catch hold of the bridle with one hand yanking Cloud's neck to the side. Lara kicked out with her left foot and the toe of her boot caught him squarely under the jaw, knocking the soldier unconscious. Cloud went down at the same time, still held by the bridle, pinning her leg under him. The crushing weight caused her to gasp. In desperation, she tugged the reins in the opposite direction, fighting with all her strength to remain in the saddle. By what effort she never knew, but the animal succeeded in regaining its feet with her still in place.

The first soldier was now barely ten feet from her, with Jared and Rowena right behind him. In a flash, Lara pulled the dagger from her coat sleeve, turned in the saddle, and threw it. The man slowed and staggered forward, a puzzled expression on his face, as he looked down at the hilt of a weapon sticking out of his chest. For a moment their eyes locked before he collapsed to his knees and fell face-down in the street.

Lara and Cloud burst out of the main gate past Lord Guy's soldiers, who had to dive out of her way to avoid being run down. Behind her she heard the sound of horns being blown. It was better than five miles across the valley to the top of the rise and the forest. She bent low over Cloud's flank, urging every ounce of speed she could out of him. They were moving so fast, her eyes began to tear from the wind and cold. When the horns sounded again, she looked back over her shoulder. The pursuit was coming. The trees were closer, and Cloud, sensing his rider's urgency, stretched his neck forward, his huge muscles and sinews straining with effort.

She almost saw the returning patrol too late as they emerged from the forest on her left. Professional soldiers, they immediately began riding on a diagonal line to intercept her. Without pausing to think, Lara cut sharply to the right for the nearest trees. She reached them seconds before the patrol did.

For the next few minutes a game of cat and mouse took place. Lara crashed through the underbrush, twisting and turning, trying to avoid the soldiers who were reaching for her. Using her knees and hands to guide the horse, she negotiated the trees at a frightening pace. Twice she came within inches of a soldier's grasp, and twice she avoided it at the last second. She saw a clearing about fifty yards ahead and made directly for it. From the shouts, she knew that Jared and the first group of soldiers had entered the forest.

If I can just get to the other side of the river, she thought.

For a moment it seemed there were angry bees buzzing around her left ear, but the sounds became louder as four arrows embedded themselves in the nearest tree. She had less than a second to register the still vibrating fletching in the truck before she spurred her horse forward again. A path at the side of the clearing appeared to go in the right direction. If she guessed correctly, the river would be beyond that.

A second after she reached it, she knew she had made a mistake. Instead of descending, the path went up. Lara dug her heels into Cloud's flank and the stallion responded. With his speed he began to pull away from her pursuers. Though many parts of the path were still covered in snow, it turned out to be little more than a single dirt track. Thoughts of Collin began to creep back into her mind. *What if he couldn't get away?* In a short while the path leveled out and Lara found herself atop an escarpment. She turned Cloud in a circle trying to determine which way to go. The soldiers were less than two hundred yards below her, winding their way up.

Left, she decided.

Another hundred yards and her heart sank. The path abruptly ended at the lip of a ten-foot-wide crevass with a two-hundred-foot drop straight down. To her right, the crevass widened; left was worse. Far below, the Deeprun River meandered its way through a rocky canyon. On the other side of the crevass she could see a path disappearing into the trees and reemerging at the bottom of the cliff by the river.

Lara made her decision.

She turned Cloud around and walked him about thirty yards away from the ledge.

"There she is," one of the soldiers called out from farther down the trail.

Lara reached out and patted the stallion's neck to calm him, then leaned forward and whispered softly, "I hope you're up to this."

The horse snorted and stamped his foot.

Without further hesitation, she spurred Cloud forward. The stallion accelerated to a full gallop in a matter of strides, with Lara holding her breath as the ledge loomed closer. She prayed her timing would be right. For some reason memories of leaping three rail fences on her brother's farm suddenly popped into her mind, and she gritted her teeth in concentration.

The bond between rider and horse is a funny thing. As soon as Cloud felt Lara's weight shift forward, he knew what she wanted. He never broke stride, and with a mighty thrust of his back legs, the horse launched himself into the air.

They landed on the opposite ledge in time to see the first riders arrive. Two of them stood up in their saddle and fired their crossbows at her. Both arrows went wide. She decided not to wait to see if their aim would improve. Lara patted Cloud's neck and they started down the path.

"That earned you a carrot," she told him.

It took fifteen minutes to make the descent. When they reached the bottom, she dismounted and took a moment to regain her breath. Flows of ice and snow drifted by on the river's swift current. The bed of the Deeprun was nearly a hundred yards wide and strewn with smooth white and gray stones. Of her pursuers there was no sign.

Lara had no idea where she was, but she knew the important thing was to keep moving, and put as much distance between herself and the soldiers as possible. The main road was out of the question; and even if she could find it, they were sure to be watching. She thought for a moment and decided that if she was to reach Tenley Palace, she would have to find a way around Argenton using the forest for cover. She prayed Gawl and Mathew hadn't left yet, but a little voice in the back of her head told her that Jared's statement in the chapel was correct—they would come, and Father Thomas would be with them.

Lara stooped down, cupped some water in her hands, and took a drink. It was achingly cold. She splashed the rest on her face and behind her neck then swung back up into the saddle and began negotiating her way along the rocks.

A loud crack that sounded like lightning almost caused Cloud to shy as a tree a few feet from them suddenly burst into flames. Seconds later another tree exploded, and then another. On the other side of the river the same thing was happening.

Lara's mouth fell open in shock when a line of fire actually began moving across the water. In moments it reached the edge of the bank where she was fighting to keep her horse under control. Incredulous, she watched it rise up to a height of twenty feet, blocking her path.

Cloud whinnied and stamped his feet nervously.

Lara pulled the stallion around and started in the opposite direction. She only got a few yards before another wall of flame sprang up in front of her. The horse was close to panicking; his eyes rolled back in its head until the whites could be seen. Lara patted his neck and tried to calm him.

Only once before had she ever seen anything like this, and that was at Ardon Field when Mathew had fought Karas Duren. Knowing that the fire in front of her was no natural thing, Lara got down off the horse, put an arm around Cloud's neck, and waited.

The wall of flames continued to crackle and dance, hemming her in. Though they moved no closer, she could feel the heat on her face. *There might still be a way out by fording the river,* she thought. *It was sure to be freezing cold, but if they could get across quickly . . .*

Lara didn't get the chance to test her theory.

An opening appeared in the flames and Father Kellner

walked through, followed by Jared Guy. Neither of them looked happy. The priest had a large purple bruise in the middle of his forehead and both of his eyes had started to blacken. Jared's jaw was swollen and his face was smeared with dirt, as were his clothes. He walked directly up to Lara and struck her across the face with the back of his hand.

26

Sennia, The Road to Camden Keep

MATHEW LEWIN STOPPED IN MID-CONVERSATION, HIS head coming up abruptly. Although they were still over thirty miles away, he knew almost immediately that Aldrich Kellner had just done something. For an instant, the priest standing in the room of an old building became crystal clear to him. Teanna d'Elso knew it as well.

Father Thomas was speaking with Jeram Quinn at the time and saw the change of expression on Mathew's face. "What is it, my son?"

"Kellner. He's just unleashed something—an explosion I think. I could only see him for a second, but . . ."

Mathew's eyes took on a distant look again and seconds passed.

Gawl, Father Thomas, and Jeram Quinn all exchanged puzzled glances as Mathew's face darkened. Then, without warning, he spurred his horse forward.

Father Thomas immediately set off after him and eventually succeeded in pulling his horse alongside of Mathew's.

"Listen to me," he shouted. "We cannot go blindly charging into Camden Keep like this. You must tell me what's going on."

For the first time that he could recall, the expression on Mathew's face frightened him. Only once before had he seen anything similar and that was after Berke Ramsey had killed Bran Lewin.

"Mat . . . Mat," he called. "*Mathew.* I want you to stop and tell me what happened. *Now.*"

Mathew gradually slowed his horse, and his eyes, which were as hard as agates, slowly began to calm. Gawl and the others came riding up.

"I think Collin is dead, Father," he said, breathing heavily. "I saw his body lying there. He was bleeding and the back of his clothes were burned. He wasn't moving."

The words came out in a rush.

"If he is bleeding, then he's still alive," said Jeram Quinn. "It's important that we know what you saw. Just try and tell us . . ."

The constable let his words trail off as Teanna caught up to the group.

"Mathew's friend may be dead," she explained, without preamble. "There was an explosion of some type as Mathew said—and it was caused by the priest . . . this Father Kellner. I'm positive about it. This is obviously a dangerous man we're dealing with. Have you got control of yourself?" she asked, looking straight at Mathew. "This could be exactly what he is trying to accomplish."

"An explosion? At Camden Keep?" Gawl asked. "Was anyone else hurt?"

"Not at Camden Keep," Mathew told him. "It was someplace else. Someplace with old buildings. I've never been there, but I think they're at the ruins in Argenton."

Gawl blew out a long breath and rubbed his face with his hands. "How do you know?"

"Because of where Collin was lying. It was in a narrow corridor covered in reddish dust, and it's not like any place our people live in today."

Teanna slowly nodded her head in agreement and explained, "Sometimes when a person uses one of the rings a link can form with the other users. It happened that way with my uncle and mother, and it happens sometimes between Mathew and me. It's difficult to describe."

"But why would this man want to harm Collin?" asked Father Thomas.

"There could be any number of explanations," Jeram Quinn said. "If he is the same person who murdered the priests it would follow that he might not hesitate to kill again."

"But that doesn't answer why," Father Thomas said.

"Do we know if the boy's dead?" asked Gawl, looking from Teanna to Mathew.

Both shook their heads.

Gawl thought for a few seconds. "Then I suppose we should go have a talk with this priest."

"I agree," said Father Thomas. "But we need to exercise caution. If the princess is correct, this *is* a very dangerous man. Quite probably he has already killed twice in order to get what he wants. It's equally clear that Mathew has been the object of his attacks on two different occasions. Personally, I don't believe he's acting alone. Would you agree, Jeram?"

Jeram Quinn looked at Father Thomas and hesitated before answering.

"People kill for all kinds of reasons—anger, greed, jealously. None of these really seem to apply here. You told me last night," Quinn said, turning to Mathew, "that you've only had contact with him a few times—while you were studying at the abbey, at the dinner several days ago, and at the tavern after the Felcarin match. Since there were no harsh words or ill feelings, that would leave us with the question of motive."

"And obviously," Gawl said, "with Mat out of the way, there would be no one to stop him from doing anything he wants to do, except—"

"No," Teanna said, shaking her head. "I don't think he knows I'm here yet. I only arrived yesterday, and I've never met him. I also don't think he's aware that I possess one of the rings, unless Mathew told him."

Mathew shook his head.

"That leaves us with more questions than answers," said Father Thomas.

"Such as?" asked Gawl.

"Such as how does a priest—predominantly an academic—come to have contact with Coribar? The men who tried to kill Mat yesterday came from there. I believe Kellner may be in league with them. Further, how did he even know of the ring's existence, and get it to work if each of them is unique as Mathew has told us?"

"Well, we're not going to find the answers sitting here," Mathew said. "Collin may be hurt or . . ."

He went quiet again and stared off in the distance. At the same time Teanna put her hand to her throat and gasped.

"What now?" Gawl asked.

"Fire," Mathew answered absently, still looking to the north. "It's Lara . . . she's unharmed, but . . ."

"Lara?" Teanna repeated.

"A friend from Mat's village back home," Father Thomas answered. "Is she all right?"

"She's been taken prisoner," he replied.

"Did you just see the same thing he did?" the priest asked Teanna.

"Yes," she replied, nodding her head.

Mathew tugged on his horse's reins and started back up the road again at a half-canter. Gawl shook his head and signaled the rest of the soldiers in the party to follow. Several glances were exchanged among the men, but no one commented on what was happening.

After a while Father Thomas drew alongside Mathew and spoke, keeping his voice down. "I need to ask you a question, my son."

Mathew looked at him.

"Last night, Teanna said something that puzzled me. She said she was stronger than you."

"Yes."

"Is that true?"

There was a pause while Mathew thought about it. "No. She can certainly do some things that I can't—at least not yet, but I don't think that equates with strength, Father."

"I see. In the past when we've have talked about your ring and what you can do with it, you explained the power comes from a machine the Ancients built."

"Right."

"And you've told me that you do not know the location of this machine. Is that correct?"

"Yes. Why?"

"Is it possible the machine is in Argenton?"

"I don't think so," Mathew said slowly. "I believe the Ancients hid it deep in the earth in a town called Henderson."

"This was the town you told us about the other day?"

"It was like no town I've ever seen before. There were no ruins and everything looked perfectly new, but there was something very odd—apart from its being underground. I saw a giant crystal there that reached up hundreds of feet. Not a soul was anywhere except for Teanna and myself. It was eerie. We talked for a long time."

"About what?"

"That she and I are different from other people—at least the way she sees it. She told me there are a lot of things I needed to learn. She said there was power in the town, which is why I'm guessing the machine is there. I wasn't sure what she meant at the time, Father, but she may be right about our being different . . . except I don't feel different. When I look in the mirror, I still see myself there."

"Mathew—"

"It's the same way with people. Some are physically stronger than others—like Gawl. The mind works the same way. Being able to do a thing that someone else can't doesn't mean you're stronger, only more versatile."

Father Thomas smiled. "An intelligent observation, my

son. I'm not trying to pry, but I don't need a ring to see you are disturbed."

"I knew why Karas Duren wanted to kill me, but I don't understand what Father Kellner is doing. I barely know the man. Just having one of the rings doesn't turn someone into a murderer."

Father Thomas heard the hurt and confusion there. Until quite recently, Mathew's entire life had been spent growing up in a small town where he knew everybody and everybody knew him. There were likes and dislikes among the citizens of Devondale, just as there were in other towns, but hatred rarely became an issue. Dealing with such things was daunting enough for those with more worldly views, but to a young man of nineteen, possessing no frame of reference for such things, it must be especially difficult, thought the priest.

"Mathew, what you say has been troubling me too. If a man is moved to commit murder usually there is a reason for it. I've met Kellner several times and he seemed neither ambitious, nor arrogant. Intense in his views, yes, but certainly not a man who would go to such extremes. No . . . I believe there is something else at work here. Jeram feels the same way—we spoke about it earlier. At any rate, we'll soon have our answers. Right now the important thing is not to lose our heads. The actions we take must be measured ones. Do you understand me?"

"I understand. I understand that Collin might be dead, and if Kellner's done anything to Lara . . ."

Father Thomas glanced down and saw that the knuckles of Mathew's hand were white.

"I feel the same way you do, but I don't want any more of my flock injured. We'll deal with Aldrich Kellner when the time comes. Maintaining a clear head gives us the greatest chance for success."

"Is your head clear right now?" Mathew asked.

"No . . . not very," the priest admitted. "I don't like having left Ceta at the palace by herself, or knowing that

Collin could be hurt, but by the time we ride into Argenton my mind will be clear."

"Can I ask you something, Father?"

"Certainly."

"When you first met Teanna, she referred to you as 'general,' then she corrected herself. That wasn't an accident was it?"

A rueful smile appeared on Father Thomas's face before he answered.

"No . . . it was not an accident. Her slip was quite intentional. I suspect it was more to let me know that she is familiar with my background. You are aware that before I become a priest, I served in the army with your father?"

"Yes."

"It's been many years . . . certainly before you and the princess were born, but at one time I commanded Elgaria's western army. The work was less satisfying than it is now, although the pay was slightly better."

Mathew smiled in spite of himself. "Thank you, Father. I didn't mean to pry."

"It's not a secret, my son, though I can just imagine Ceta's reaction when I tell her."

"Do you know when you two will marry?"

"No. We've discussed it of course, but several things have to be worked out first. Devondale is my home and there are many customers there waiting for my services." The priest smiled. "Ceta lives in Elberton. I suppose it will all become clear in time. Such things usually do. I trust we'll be enjoying your company on the return trip."

Mathew's lack of an answer didn't concern the priest as much as the expression on his face and the set of his jaw.

Two hours later, Gawl and his party rode through the gates of Camden Keep. One of the soldiers accompanying them was a tough-looking old colonel named Shelby Haynes, who was in charge of the king's personal bodyguard. Also with them were Sandy Johnson and his second in command, Rodney Blake. Mathew had taken a liking to Blake the first time they met. He was a quiet, intelligent man, not given to boastfulness. Unlike Jared, who enjoyed recounting his exploits, Blake had simply nodded or said thank you to the compliments he received about his performance during the match. Mathew was glad to have Johnson along.

Rowena was the first one out to meet them, with her father following closely behind.

"My dear," she said. "This is such a surprise. What brings you here?"

"Grave tidings," Gawl said, getting down off his horse. He and Rowena quickly embraced.

"What's the matter?" she asked.

"Not here," Gawl whispered under his breath.

"If I only had some word you were coming, your majesty, I could have made better preparations," Lord Guy said. He signaled for a groom to take the king's horse.

"We're not staying, Edward," Gawl told him.

"Is something wrong?" asked Guy, feigning concern.

"Two priests were recently murdered at the abbey. We think Father Kellner may have had something to do with it. Also, do you have any idea where Collin Miller and Lara Palmer are? Are they here?"

Rowena let out a gasp and put a hand over her mouth, but recovered quickly.

"Collin and Lara are with Father Kellner. They went with him to Argenton to see the ruins."

Lord Guy's face became serious. "Why would Aldrich Kellner murder two of his fellow priests?" he asked.

"Well, Mathew saw—"

"How far are the ruins?" Teanna asked, getting down off her horse.

"Forgive me," said Gawl. "My manners seem to have deserted me. May I present Teanna d'Elso, crown princess of Nyngary. Your highness, this is Lord Edward Guy and his daughter, the Lady Rowena."

Lord Guy executed a formal bow and kissed Teanna's hand, while Rowena curtsied. He glanced at the others still on horseback and added a curt nod acknowledging them.

"It's a pleasure to have you as our guest, your highness," he said, turning back to Teanna.

"Thank you. But Gawl is quite correct. We have to get to Argenton at once. How far is it?"

"Approximately ten miles," Rowena answered. "The ruins are perhaps five miles beyond that. Is there anything I can do to help?"

"It would be best if you wait here for us." Gawl smiled at her. "Edward, with your permission I will leave two of my men in case Kellner returns. The rest will come with me to Argenton."

"Of course," Lord Guy said. "If you need additional troops, I would be happy to supply them."

"No . . . thank you, my friend," said Gawl. "I think we have enough people. This shouldn't take long. Right now all we want is to talk with the man."

Before anyone could respond, Jared Guy rode through the gate and saw the people assembled in the courtyard.

"What goes on?" he asked.

Rowena took it on herself to recount what Gawl had just told them.

"I don't believe it," said Jared. "I know Aldrich Kellner. He's not capable of anything like that. There has to be some mistake. I'm coming with you."

"We hope so as well," Father Thomas said, from horseback. "But it would probably be best to limit the number of people. That way there'll be less chance for anyone to get hurt if there are problems."

"I wasn't addressing you, priest," Jared snapped. "I was speaking to his majesty. If I want your opinion, I'll ask for it."

The expression on Father Thomas's face changed and for a moment he looked as dangerous as he was. It disappeared almost as quickly, replaced by a faint smile.

"You will have to forgive my son," said Lord Guy. "He tends to be overly loyal to his friends."

"An admirable quality," Gawl replied, placing a hand on Jared's shoulder. "But I think Siward is right. I don't want to risk anyone else, particularly future relatives."

The king's comment helped to break the tension, and as he remounted a look passed between Father Thomas and himself. Gawl rolled his eyes up and gave a slight shake of his head. Father Thomas kept his face neutral.

Rowena came forward and put a hand on Gawl's leg. "Promise me you'll be careful," she said.

Gawl reached down, touched her face, and smiled. "We'll be back shortly, Row."

"You shouldn't have interfered," Jared said, after the party rode out. "I wanted to be there in case something went wrong. If it wasn't for that meddlesome priest—"

"Your temper is going to get you killed one day," Lord Guy said, under his breath. The pleasant smile never left him as he continued to wave. "I probably just saved your life."

"What?"

"That *priest* would have eaten you alive. He's the last person you want to pick a fight with."

Jared looked at Father Thomas's departing back and said, "Ridiculous."

"You have a lot to learn," Lord Guy said, shaking his head. Then he turned and walked back into the castle.

27

Argenton

By the time Gawl's party reached Argenton it was early in the afternoon. No one was in favor of stopping to eat so they decided to proceed straight through to the ruins. Several people recognized the king as he rode by. Most bowed or waved, and Gawl returned the greetings. At seven feet tall he was not an easy figure to miss. More interesting to Father Thomas was that an almost equal number recognized Mathew. Some pointed at him or plucked at the sleeves of their friends and whispered to each other as he passed. The priest glanced at Mathew, noting that his face remained neutral throughout.

A few scudding clouds appeared in the sky and the horses' hooves crunched over the snow-covered ground without difficulty. As soon as they reached the forest, on instructions from Colonel Haynes two of the soldiers moved to the head of the column and two others dropped back to the rear. Mathew noticed the men loosening their swords and followed suit. The sword he carried, from Randal Wain's shop, was given him by his father before they rode out to rescue little Stefan Darcy. That day ended badly, with more friends killed than he wanted to remember, and the boy was never found. It felt distant to him now, though the events happened barely a year ago.

Teanna saw his expression and nudged her horse closer. "Your friends will be all right," she said softly.

Mathew nodded, tight-lipped.

"It's important for us to remain calm, Mathew," she said echoing Father Thomas's advice. "We don't know much about this man. Between the two of us, I don't think we will have a problem, but it pays to be cautious. If it comes down to it, we can link."

"Link?"

"My mother and uncle managed it several times and I did it with her once. It's a way of combining our strength. I can teach you, if you like."

A brief image of himself standing on a windswept cliff and looking at the approaching Nyngary and Cinar fleets flashed through his mind. So did the recollection of Karas Duren and Marsa d'Elso's combined attack that nearly killed him.

"I've never done anything like that before," Mathew said.

"It's simple. Imagine you and I are standing alone in a field together. We're facing each other and there's nothing else around—just the two of us. Now relax. There are no trees . . . no grass. Absolutely nothing to distract you. Just concentrate on me."

Mathew tried it.

A picture of Teanna formed in his mind and her voice seemed to recede in the distance. She was still talking, but he realized she was no longer doing it aloud. Her voice was inside his head. In seconds, it grew stronger and more distinct. Her features also became clear. She had such large brown eyes—intense eyes. Mathew sensed strength there immediately; incredible strength. He could almost feel it radiating from her. The gossamer world he had entered continued to resolve itself, forming shapes and sounds. Teanna stood before him, a warm glow of light radiating around her. An invisible wind blew her long hair away from bare shoulders, and her breasts rose and fell in time with her breathing. He could almost see the muscles in her stomach and legs, tense and firm. Her hips . . .

Suddenly Mathew was back in his saddle as the link terminated. Teanna was staring at him, her mouth open in surprise.

"What in the world were you just thinking about?" she whispered.

Mathew blinked and said, "Well, I . . . that is . . . I was just . . . uh . . ."

"Oh, for God's sake."

The color in his face rose as Teanna's eyebrows went up. He looked away, trying his best to keep from smiling, which he deemed might not be in his best interest at the moment.

"Just keep your mind on business, Master Lewin," she said, but then added, "time enough for all that later. . . . You're terrible."

"Uh . . . sorry."

"Sorry." She muttered it under her breath, then spurred her horse forward to speak with Gawl.

Mathew couldn't be certain, but he thought he saw the ghost of a smile on her face before she went. A minute later his mind did return to business as the skyline of the ancient city came into view.

The room Lara was in was dark and cold. She lay on a bed with her lip throbbing from where Jared had hit her. She touched it lightly and winced. She was in a home of some kind, but all the windows were sealed. Try as she might, she had been unable to open them or the door, which was also locked.

She decided to search the other rooms in the hope of finding some way out. There were eight in all, with a collection of different furniture. One contained the most unusual table Lara had ever seen. It was covered in a soft green material and had four holes cut into the corners. Two more were cut in the center of the table along its sides. She looked in one of the holes and found a heavy white ball there. Out of curiosity Lara checked the other holes and found more balls, some with solid colors and some with stripes; all of them had numbers. She picked one up, rolled it the length of the table and watched it disappear into the corner hole. Bewildered, Lara stared at the table for a moment, trying to figure out its function, because it didn't seem to have any purpose at all.

She found the kitchen next. All of the knives were gone of course, and there was nothing around that would make a decent weapon, so she left the room and moved on. In the next room, to her surprise, she discovered a painting of the people who once had lived there, on the mantel above a fireplace.

A man, woman, and two children, dead for three thousand years, looked back at her. The man was seated in a large armchair with the woman standing next to him, one hand resting gently on his shoulder. A boy, about nine years old, and a girl perhaps a year younger, sat on the floor cross-legged in front of the couple. They were all smiling. The girl had blond hair like her mother, and the boy's hair was brown and wavy like his father.

He reminded her of Mathew.

Lara looked at the painting for a long time.

What did you people do to yourselves? she thought.

She continued searching the home, trying to locate anything that might help her. From where she standing she could see a dining room complete with place settings and glasses, making it look for all the world like the couple in the painting had just left for a walk and might return at any moment.

But they weren't going to return—*ever*. This was all that was left of people who once flew machines through the air; who laughed at each other's silly jokes and built enormous buildings. People who once lived in these rooms. She looked down at the chair she was standing next to and realized with a small shock it was the same one in the painting.

She must have stood right here, Lara thought. *So sad . . . so terribly, terribly sad.*

A click of the front door lock made her jump. She whirled around to see Father Kellner standing there.

"I came to see if you are all right," he said.

"I'm fine, thank you."

"I know what you must think, but I hope you believe how sorry I am for what happened. I meant no harm to you. Does your lip hurt?"

"I'll survive."

"I've brought some water and something to eat," he said, placing a small package wrapped in paper on the table.

As soon as he took a step toward her, Lara backed away. Oddly, her reaction seemed to pain him.

"Please do not be afraid, my child. I'll see to it no further harm comes to you. I apologize again for Jared's actions. There can be no excuse for striking a woman. I'm extremely sorry."

"I'm not your child, and you are a traitor. What is it you want?"

Father Kellner hesitated. "All right . . . Lara. I would like you to understand why I'm doing this. I am no traitor. This is something I must do. I love my country and its people. Violence is not my way; it never has been. I'm a man of God. But sometimes one must be strong to fight evil, and that strength can be misinterpreted."

Lara looked at the priest and shook her head.

"Is that what you call it—fighting evil? How convenient. You woke up one morning and discovered that Gawl was evil. As I recall he took the throne with the blessing of the church. Or have they turned evil as well?"

"Gawl is only partly responsible for his actions. The young man you are friends with has corrupted him—turned his mind. I know this is difficult to accept, but I swear it's true."

Lara's eyes opened wide. "Mathew? You're talking about Mathew?" The concept was so ludicrous that she started laughing.

"You mock me," he said, sadly. "I was told this would happen. Listen to me, Lara. I have been visited by the lady Alarice. You are not of this country, but perhaps you've heard the name. She is an angel . . . sent from God himself. I know it is difficult to accept, but I assure you that I am not the only one who has seen her. Alarice told me that a cloud has descended over the king's eyes—a cloud of your young man's making. Mathew Lewin is strong, I know, but Alarice has given me strength as well."

Father Kellner slowly held up his hand to show Lara the rose-gold ring on his finger. It glinted dully in the light before he put his hand down again.

It took some effort for Lara to contain her surprise. "Father, I've known Mathew Lewin all my life. We grew up together; there isn't an evil bone in his body. What you're saying is not possible. I don't know who—or what—you saw, but you are mistaken . . . sadly mistaken."

"I told you Alarice visited not only me, but his Eminence as well, Ferdinand Willis. He was with me when she appeared. She floated in a circle of light upon the waters of a lake, the most beautiful thing you can imagine. From deep under the earth she called to me and we spoke with each other for hours, Lara. Each time we met, the lady revealed more and more about what has . . . what *is* transpiring even as we stand here.

"At first I did not want to believe her words. I thought to go to the king and counsel with him. But then I learned what he plans to do. Gawl wants to open our borders to the whole world. Can you understand that? The morals and values our people have held so dear for thousands of years will be lost forever. Foreigners with their evil ways and values—"

"Foreigners? Such as all the evil Elgarians like me?"

Lara asked sarcastically. "I see. What about Father Thomas? If I recall correctly, he's a priest too, or has he turned evil as well?"

Father Kellner rubbed his face with his hands and took a deep breath. When he spoke again his voice sounded tired and drained.

"I do not have all the answers. I only know what I must do. You seem like good people to me, but the devil is clever and can deceive even the best of us."

Lara noticed that the more he spoke, the more forceful the priest's voice became. It was as if he was rehearsing, or trying to convince himself that his words were true.

"By the way, where is Collin, Father?"

"He's been taken back to Camden Keep."

Lara noticed the priest didn't meet her eyes when he answered, and she felt her chest start to tighten.

"That explosion . . . is Collin all right?"

Father Kellner held up his hands to calm her.

"Is Collin all right?" she repeated.

"I'm certain he is," Kellner answered, a little too quickly. "You must understand we had to get out of that room. I am still learning about the ring and the results are not always predictable. Saint Alarice has given me ability to fight for our people, and fight I will if compelled. It is something I cannot turn away from. In a holy war, injuries are inevitable. I did not mean to harm the boy."

Lara looked down at the floor, waiting for her anger to subside. After a moment her head came up slowly and she locked eyes with the priest.

"If you plan on fighting Mathew, Father, I suggest you practice a bit more. I was there at Ardon Field . . . and I've see what he can do."

The expression of fervor on the priest's face slowly faded and he seemed to go a little pale.

"Come with me," he said, grabbing her by the wrist.

When they got to the street a soldier was waiting for them with two horses. Several more soldiers were entering the buildings across the way, as another group headed down one of the side streets. A movement at the corner window on the second floor caught Lara's attention. Three more soldiers, all with crossbows, were positioning themselves there.

"Thank you, my son," Father Kellner said to the man. "You have your orders?"

"Yes, Father. Good luck."

He saluted and left without another word.

Lara shook her head in disgust.

"Those men are patriots," Father Kellner said, pointing at them.

"How clever of you. We call them assassins in Elgaria," she answered coldly.

The priest's face flushed and he opened his mouth to say something, but then changed his mind.

"Get on your horse," said Father Kellner.

Their passage through the town of Argenton excited no particular comment from the townspeople. A few waved at the priest and he waved back. Lara thought about calling for help, but decided against it for fear that others would get hurt. At the end of the town, they tethered the horses and began to climb a hill, with Father Kellner insisting that she precede him. The farther up they went, the steeper the going became. Twice Kellner reached out to help her, and each time she pulled her arm away. At last they found themselves on a small tree-covered plateau. The hill continued to merge into more mountainous terrain. Lara watched as the priest walked to where three bushes stood, took hold of the one in the center and pulled it aside, revealing a narrow opening in the rock. He gestured for her to go in, but she stood her ground.

"What is it you want from me, Father?"

Kellner took a deep breath before answering. "Your young man is on the way, as you've probably guessed. I don't want to hurt him. I hope you can believe that. It occurs to me that without his ring, Mathew Lewin poses no real threat. I may be able to counsel with the king and convince him to choose a different path from the one he is presently on. As far as Mathew is concerned, I suspect . . . I truly hope . . . it is only the lure of power that has corrupted him, and not something in his nature. If this is the case, he could still be saved—assuming he is willing to seek the aid of the church."

"Your conceit amazes me," Lara shot back. "Did you think of this by yourself or was it one of your divine messages? You expect Mathew to simply hand his ring over to you and go his merry way?"

The priest shook his head slowly. "I thought perhaps, if *you* asked him . . ."

"Father, I have no intention of helping you," Lara said slowly. "You can do what you want to me. Despite what you said earlier, I think you *did* hurt Collin. You're a fine one to talk about evil. You should take a good long look in the mirror at yourself if you want to see what it looks like."

As Lara stood there watching the cleric on that wind blown cliff with the town of Argenton stretching out behind him, it occurred to her that the priest was either completely insane or he actually believed that Mathew was evil and had somehow placed Gawl under a spell. It made no sense.

In a little under two hours, she and Father Kellner found themselves standing on the shores of the cavern lake. During the entire trip through the winding passages with their strange glowing rock formations, the priest had said nothing, but even in the dim luminescence Lara could see fervor and passion painted on his face. She could also hear him muttering to himself. Once they arrived, he fell to his knees, closed his eyes and began to pray.

To her amazement, the water in the lake began to boil.

28

Argenton

SHORTLY AFTER THEY ENTERED THE FOREST THAT SEPA-
rated the town of Argenton from the ruins, Mathew's
party came upon an elderly woodcutter leading a horse
and wagon along the road. Gawl stopped him and asked
if he had seen Father Kellner. The man was so taken
aback by the sudden appearance of the king and a group
of soldiers that he could barely speak, but after recovering his composure he told them he had seen a man answering Father Kellner's description heading in the
direction of the ruin about two hours earlier. He added
that the person he saw wasn't dressed like a priest, so he
couldn't be certain it was him.

A brief conference was held on horseback. It was decided that Father Thomas and Rodney Blake would proceed to the ruins with six soldiers in case the man was
Aldrich Kellner. Gawl and the others, including Mathew
and Teanna, returned to the town and searched for him.

When Mathew's party arrived in town, they located a
blacksmith's shop and inquired further. Its owner was one
Angus Cates, who, unlike most smiths Mathew had met,
was neither a big man nor did he have brawny arms. In
fact he was slender, wore glasses, and reminded him of
his friend Daniel. Cates was in the process of shaping a
horseshoe when they rode up. He told them that he had
seen the priest and a woman heading up the hillside toward the mountain a little over an hour ago

"What did she look like?" Mathew asked.

"I didn't pay much attention, but I'd say she was pretty and had chestnut-colored hair, if I remember right. Never seen her before."

Jeram Quinn looked up at the hill and frowned. "Why would they go up there?"

Cates shrugged. "I don't really know. The only thing up there is a cave. You can't see it from here, but it's about fifty yards to the right of that outcropping. The children play up there occasionally. It doesn't sit too well with their mothers, though, because it's supposed to be haunted."

"Haunted?" said Gawl.

"You know how rumors get started, sire."

"Aren't you worried living so close to something like that?" asked Teanna.

The smith looked at her and pointedly brought the hammer he was holding down on the anvil with a re-sounding clang that sent sparks flying.

"Not really, my lady. I'm not much for ghosts. Is something the matter, sire?" he asked, turning back to Gawl.

"No. We just want to talk with Father Kellner. How far can we take the horses?"

"Another quarter-mile or so. There's a place where you can tie them up at the bottom of the hill, or you're welcome to leave them here if you wish."

Gawl nodded and got down; so did the rest of the group.

"Thank you, Cates," he said, clapping the smith on the shoulder. "We shouldn't be too long."

He turned to one of the soldiers accompanying them and said, "You and another man stay here and enjoy the town. If Father Kellner returns this way, ask him if he wouldn't mind waiting for us. Don't do anything to provoke him—just ask him to wait." The departure of the soldiers left Mathew, Gawl, Teanna, Colonel Haynes, Sandy Johnson, and Quinn to go on.

Along the way to the cave, they passed two horses. Mathew said nothing when he saw them, but began walking faster and twice Gawl had to find an excuse to speak with him to prevent him from getting too far ahead of the group. From the description Angus Cates had given of the woman, he was fairly certain it was Lara. He was equally confident Mathew was thinking the same thing. The king and Jeram Quinn exchanged glances, but the constable just shook his head.

They located the cave entrance with no problem. Once inside, they began checking for any sign that Lara and Father Kellner had been there. They searched for almost five minutes and found nothing. Then Teanna spotted the light at the back of the cave. The moment she pointed to it, Mathew started walking.

"Slowly, Mat," said Gawl. "I'm just as anxious about Lara as you are, but let's use our heads, all right?"

"Exactly who is this Lara?" asked Teanna.

"Mathew's friend," Gawl replied over his shoulder.

"Really?"

There was something strange in Teanna's tone that made Jeram Quinn look at her, however it was too dark to see her face clearly.

"The light's coming from those rocks," Mathew said.

"It's called phosphorescence," Quinn explained, "I've seen it before, though never as bright as this."

"Look, there's a path there," Colonel Haynes pointed. "Your majesty, I would feel better if we could wait until I can get some more men here."

But Gawl shook his head and replied, "We're going."

For the next hour they had to squeeze their way through crevices and around boulders as they followed the path. Haynes insisted on going first and told Sandy Johnson to bring up the rear.

Some of the passages were uncomfortably tight for a person of Gawl's size, but with some muttering under his breath, and with an occasional push from Jeram Quinn, the giant managed to get through. Eventually they reached the strangest room any of them had ever seen. It was roughly circular and had three doorways facing them. Fifteen feet above their heads a ridge ran around the perimeter of the room with two more levels rising above that one. Unlike the bottom level, the other two had at least twenty separate doorways. It reminded Mathew of a beehive. All of the doors were dark save for one, which pulsed with an emerald glow.

They stood there in the semi-darkness staring at it.

"I don't like this," said Quinn. "It's too convenient. If he's running from us or trying to hide, he's being unusually accommodating."

Gawl nodded and slowly pulled his broadsword from its scabbard.

"Maybe this will help," said Teanna.

A second later a ball of blue light appeared just above her hands, illuminating the walls and ceiling. Everyone was surprised, not only at what she had just done but at the array of colors that suddenly became visible all around them. Mottled shades of red and yellow flecked with silver appeared on the surface of the rock. Deeper and more vivid colors could be seen high above them in the ceiling. Even the two soldiers were impressed.

Mathew looked at Teanna who smiled back at him and winked.

Gawl stood there staring at the glowing doorway for a moment, then said, "It would be rude to ignore this invitation, and I'm a very polite king."

He punctuated the sentence with a smile that did nothing to make him appear any more pleasant. In fact, it gave him a distinctly feral appearance. He began walking toward the green light, but stopped when Colonel Haynes cleared his throat.

"If your majesty will allow me," the colonel said.

Gawl drew a long-suffering breath. Nevertheless, he

went along with Haynes's gentle bullying. The colonel nodded to Johnson, and they started forward together.

Neither man had taken more than a few steps when Mathew said, "Stop."

Something about the situation had pricked his memory. Many months past, in a smoke-filled forest, a raiding party of twelve Orlocks that had been following them for over a week were finally preparing to attack under the cover of darkness. At the time Mathew had no idea what the ring was or what it could do. Outnumbered and scared, he had hidden in the trees, desperately wishing he could see into the night. Moments later his vision turned green and he was able to see detail with astonishing clarity. It nearly scared him to death at the time because he thought he was going insane. As bizarre as it was, the incident marked the first time he had accessed the ring. Although he wasn't aware that he was doing so then, it had saved his life and the lives of his friends. Since that night Mathew had never tried to duplicate that particular feat again and he wasn't certain he could do it now even if he wanted to.

No harm in trying, he thought.

Everyone was looking at him, which did nothing to help his concentration, so he took a breath, shut everything out, and turned his thoughts to the darkness.

In a split second, the green light returned so abruptly he took a step backward.

"What is it Mat?" asked Gawl.

Mathew held up his hand and didn't answer. Instead, he carefully began looking around the room. Details hidden before were suddenly visible to him. He could see the rough texture of the stalactites hanging from the ceiling and the grains of sand covering the floor . . . and he could see the thin line directly in front of the glowing doorway.

Mathew stared harder and discerned a faint rectangle shape partially covered by the sand.

Strange, he thought, taking a step closer

"Are you all right?" asked Jeram Quinn.

Again he didn't answer, but picked up a rock lying on the floor and tossed it at the doorway. The second it hit, a ten foot section of the floor fell away and the arch collapsed inward, sending a cloud of dust into the room.

Everyone jumped backward in shock.

Gawl spat out an oath and spun around looking for an attack. Jeram Quinn and the soldiers followed suit. Only Teanna didn't react.

"You're wonderful," she said, giving Mathew a hug. "You saved our lives. How did you know?"

"Yes . . . how *did* you know?" said Sandy Johnson.

"I didn't," Mathew replied. "I noticed a line on the floor and figured it wasn't supposed to be there."

Haynes and Johnson frowned at one another, then glanced back at the gaping hole in front of the doorway and the pile of rubble behind it.

"Lucky for us you did, young man," the colonel said. "Thank you."

Johnson clapped Mathew on the shoulder. "Good job, Mat."

"Well, now that the way is blocked, I suppose we'll have to find another," said Gawl.

"But which?" Quinn asked, looking around the room at the other doors. "And are there any more surprises waiting for us?"

"I'm becoming very annoyed with this priest," Gawl rumbled. "Mat?"

Mathew took a moment to examine the other doorways, but none appeared to contain anything unusual.

"I don't see anything out of place," he said. "I suppose one is as good as another. Do you have any idea?" he asked Teanna.

The Nyngary princess closed her eyes and concentrated. A minute passed before she opened them again and she pointed to a door on the next level.

"There," she said.

A narrow set of steps on the other side of the room led up to the second floor.

"Let's go," Gawl said.

The king began to walk toward them, then stopped and looked at Colonel Haynes, who stood patiently waiting in his place. Gawl shook his head and made a sweeping theatrical gesture with his right hand, for Haynes to precede him. The rest followed in the same order as before.

"I'm impressed," Mathew whispered to Teanna as they climbed the steps. "Can you teach me to do that?"

"No," she whispered back.

"How come?" he asked.

"You'd have to change sexes."

"Excuse me?"

"Woman's intuition."

29

The Argenton Ruins

FATHER THOMAS WATCHED THE SKYLINE OF THE RUINS as they approached. It was already late in the afternoon. The sun hovered just above the treetops, and long black shadows were beginning to creep into the dead town. Near the main gate he counted four large tents that Lord Guy's men were using as their temporary barracks. From experience he knew each tent probably housed four or five men.

The military part of Siward Thomas's mind noted that sixteen or possibly twenty soldiers was a lot of manpower to devote to something so mundane as guarding old ruins, though the fact didn't seem terribly important at the time. Three of the soldiers were outside playing pitch-coin against a wall, while a fourth looked on. The scene brought a smile to Father Thomas's face. He remembered playing a similar game as a young man. In his version, cards were used and each person put up an ante, with the closest to the wall winning the pot. Despite the differences, he concluded the principles were about the same.

"Good afternoon," the priest called out when they got close. "Who's in charge here?"

The soldiers stopped playing and looked up. The fourth man, a burly fellow with a scar over his right eye, pushed himself off the wall and came forward. An insignia on his left breast indicated that he was a sergeant.

"I expect that'd be me. What can I do for you?"

"We're looking for Father Kellner. Have you seen him?"

The man's eyes shifted to the priest's companions, dressed in the king's uniform, and then back to Father Thomas again.

"He's probably at the end of town in that low gray building," the soldier said pointing. "That's where they've been working. Is anything wrong?"

"No sergeant, why do you ask?"

"We don't usually get many of the king's men calling on us. Argenton isn't exactly in the middle of Sennia."

Father Thomas chuckled and so did Rodney Blake, who was seated on his horse next to him.

"No . . . no, nothing's wrong," Father Thomas assured him. "We just want to ask Father Kellner a few questions. Something about that machine you found. Where is everyone else?"

"Out on patrol since this morning. They left us here to mind the store."

Blake shook his head in commiseration. "A soldier's work is never done, eh?" he said.

"At the end of town, you say?" Father Thomas asked, looking down the street.

"Right, Father."

"Well," Father Thomas said, "I imagine his majesty will be along presently. He's visiting Lord Guy at the moment . . . or I should say he's visiting Rowena. He may need a while to, ah . . . finish his business."

That produced a burst of laughter from the soldiers.

"Thanks for the help, friend," Blake said. "When the king gets here, let him know where we are, would you?"

"Right, sir," the sergeant said, with a salute.

Sharp boy, Father Thomas thought as they rode on. Blake had picked up on the man's lie quickly. It was possible the blacksmith they met was mistaken about seeing Father Kellner going the other way, but he didn't think so. More interesting was that none of the four soldiers saw him leave and none of them saw him return. According to them, the priest had been there all day, which wasn't possible given the circumstances. Either it was a case of selective blindness, or something worse, but what?

When Rodney Blake pulled his horse alongside Father Thomas's mount, the first thing he noticed was that the priest's eyes were carefully scanning the buildings on both sides of the street.

"Sir, I assume you heard—"

"Listen carefully to me, my son. We have ridden into a trap," Father Thomas said, keeping his voice low. "How many men would you say are stationed here?"

"Between sixteen and twenty."

"That would be my guess, too—and there are six of us."

"Not very good odds, Father, but attacking the king's soldiers would be an open act of treason."

"Or rebellion," said Father Thomas.

"Rebellion?" Blake pulled up on the reins of his horse. "You think—"

"Please keep riding. What I think is irrelevant for the moment. The important thing is getting out of this place alive. I have no idea what's waiting for us down this street, but if we act as a unit we stand a far better chance of succeeding. How well trained are your men, lieutenant?"

"Very well, Father." There was no hesitation in Rodney Blake's answer.

"Excellent. Let us dismount and walk the horses for a bit."

The young lieutenant stared at Father Thomas for a second, then gave the order. Siward Thomas got down off his horse, then causally strolled over to one side of the street for a closer look at a shop window. He stood there with his arms folded across his chest examining it . . . or at least he gave the appearance of doing so. Lieutenant Blake and his men exchanged puzzled glances at his behavior, but walked over to join him.

"Father, may I ask what you are looking at?" Blake said.

"Why, this very excellent window of course."

"But it's empty," a corporal named Billy Baxter pointed out.

"Perhaps the interior is vacant, but the glass can tell us a lot of things. Fine workmanship, wouldn't you say?"

"I guess," the corporal replied, looking at his companions. It was obvious that he thought Father Thomas had taken leave of his senses.

"I quite agree. However, I'll wager though it's not nearly as good as the one across the street. Perhaps you men would care to join me?"

Without waiting for their answer, Father Thomas turned and crossed to the opposite side of the street, stopping briefly in the middle of it to tie his bootlace. The window he pointed to was bay shaped, and like the first one, it was quite empty, except for a few broken pieces of colored glass and a pan lying at the bottom of the case. The consternation on the soldiers' faces increased, but they followed. When they got there, Father Thomas lowered his voice and asked Rodney Blake, "Did you note anything interesting about this street, my son?"

"No, sir, it appears quite empty."

"Like the window," Baxter supplemented, then added, "Sorry," when Father Thomas looked at him.

"The window *is* quite empty, except for that trash on the bottom, but that's not what makes it interesting . . . Baxter is it?"

"Uh . . . yes, sir."

"Look more closely young man, but please oblige me by not turning your head."

The corporal looked as did the other men, and to anyone watching it appeared they were merely examining artifacts. A second later, a stocky sergeant named Mickens, let out an oath.

"An ambush," he exclaimed.

"Exactly," Father Thomas agreed.

In the reflection of the glass were the unmistakable forms of two soldiers hiding in a window on the second floor of a building on the next block.

"Three are more concealed on the opposite side," Father Thomas told the men. "Who is the best tracker among you?"

"That would be Baxter, sir," said Blake.

"And the best shot?"

"Mickens."

Father Thomas looked at the grizzled soldier, who nodded in agreement.

"Can you move quietly as well?"

"Quietly enough," Mickens replied.

"Excellent. Then why don't you and young Master Baxter tether the horses to that fountain over there, then circle around and use the back streets to enter those buildings. The rest of us will enjoy a leisurely stroll."

Father Thomas was about to say something else when he stopped to wave at the one of Lord Guy's soldiers, who was walking past the archway at the main gate and very obviously checking on their progress. The man waved back and crossed to the other side.

"Lieutenant, would you care to join me?"

Blake swallowed, but nodded his head and started down the street with the priest. After putting up the horses, Billy Baxter and Sergeant Mickens disappeared around the corner.

"The rest of you men split up. Two of you take one side of the street and the others take the opposite side. Keep out of any direct line of fire. You're to take no action before Father Thomas and I do," Blake instructed them.

Father Thomas listened to the lieutenant's instructions and smiled to himself. The young man was nervous, but he was giving his orders competently and without hesitation.

A good officer, he thought.

His own heart was beating rapidly, and he managed to conceal it by making light conversation as they walked.

"They tell me you are quite the Felcarin player," Father Thomas said.

"What? Oh . . . uh . . . not really. I do play on the team, though," Blake replied.

"Marvelous game, Felcarin."

The lieutenant nodded. "Yes."

"Did you know, Mr. Blake, the accuracy of a bolt shot from a crossbow drops off radically after sixty feet?"

"Really, Father? I had not heard that."

"Oh, quite. And it would take an extraordinary shot to hit anything beyond ninety feet."

"Well, I am certainly relieved to learn it. I suppose having a sharp breeze makes matters even more difficult."

"Absolutely," Father Thomas agreed.

"Are you quite certain about that?"

"I have it on the best authority, lieutenant," Father Thomas said, slipping his arm through Blake's.

"You seem unusually well informed on such subjects, for a priest, Father. If you don't mind my saying so."

"Not at all, Rodney," the priest said. "The church is an excellent means to expand one's knowledge. Have you ever considered it as a profession?"

"Not so far, although I admit it's looking more attractive every minute."

Both men continued their banter as they walked along, and to Lieutenant Blake's surprise, he began to relax, even though his stomach was in a knot as they approached the buildings on the next block. All the while Father Thomas was speaking, the priest's eyes never stopped moving.

"Tell me Rodney, I've noticed most Sennians tend to favor short swords over the longer weapons such as mine. Are you of the same opinion?"

"What? Oh . . . well . . . yes under certain circumstances."

The color of the lieutenant's face was beginning to heighten and it was obvious to Father Thomas that it was taking some effort for him to maintain his composure. Beads of sweat had broken out on Blake's forehead and his breathing was becoming more rapid. A small noise off to their right caused the lieutenant to jump.

"Rodney, would you look at me, please?" Father Thomas said, stopping. "I would prefer not to let them know we're aware of their presence."

The rapid change in his tone stopped the lieutenant from turning toward the doorway they were passing.

"I'm sorry, Father . . . nerves."

"Quite understandable," said Father Thomas. "I'm as scared as you are, my son, but let's keep that fact to ourselves. How much longer before your men reach their goal, would you say?"

"A minute or two. No more."

"I agree. May I see your weapon for a moment?"

"Oh . . . of course," Blake said, removing his sword from the sheath and handing it to Father Thomas.

The priest hefted it in his right hand a few times and circled the point in the air testing its balance.

"An excellent weapon."

Rodney Blake was not prepared for what happened next.

In one smooth motion, Father Thomas flipped the blade over and caught it about six inches down from the point between his thumb and forefinger, then spun around so suddenly, Blake could barely believe his eyes. A buzz cut through the air as Father Thomas threw the sword at a soldier in the doorway who was bringing his crossbow to bear on them.

The man let out a strangled sound and clutched for his throat as the blade buried itself in his neck. It all happened so quickly Blake had no time to react. A second later chaos broke loose.

A scream from the window on their right was followed

by glass shattering and a body tumbling out of it. Whoever the unfortunate soldier was, he hit the ground with a thud and didn't move again. Blake recovered his composure quickly and ran toward Father Thomas who was removing his weapon from the dead soldier's throat.

"Behind you!" he yelled.

Another soldier came charging out of the building with a halberd leveled at Father Thomas's chest. The priest pivoted to his right and parried the weapon over his shoulder, then stuck out his foot tripping the man. A looping swing of Father Thomas's sword all but severed the man's head from his shoulders. One of Gawl's men came rushing to aid them when he heard the commotion, and froze in mid-stride. His back suddenly arched, he opened his mouth, then fell face forward with an arrow between his shoulder blades.

Father Thomas tossed Blake his weapon and started into the building, but only got a few steps before Sergeant Mickens suddenly reappeared. The front his uniform was covered in blood and for a second the priest thought he had been wounded, but Mickens signaled he was all right. He held up two fingers and made a cutting motion across his throat.

"I'm asking Gawl for a raise when I get back," Mickens said, breathing heavily as he trotted up to them.

Father Thomas smiled and clapped him on the shoulder. "Still in one piece, my son?"

"This was a lot easier twenty years ago, Father," he replied.

The other three soldiers in their party came running to join them.

"We lost Wallace," a corporal named Jones said, looking back at the body of their companion lying in the street.

"When we get to the end of the street, Jones, you and Hudson cross over and see if you can find Baxter," Blake told them. "Francis . . . you're with us."

"Yes, sir," Jones replied.

"Not counting the men we saw on the way in my guess is there are at least between eight of them still left, maybe more," Blake said.

Father Thomas nodded absently. He was looking down the street at a shop that had partially caved in. He was about to reply when Baxter staggered out of a building across the way. Hudson and Jones, who were trotting down the street saw him at the same time and dashed forward to help. They got there just as he collapsed against the side of the door and slid to the ground. Even from where Father Thomas was, he could see the dark red stain across the front of Baxter's doublet and the arrow sticking out of his chest. The others raced toward the fallen soldier, but the priest hung for a moment, still looking down the street before joining them. By the time he got there, Rodney Blake was down on one knee pressing a handkerchief against the boy's chest.

He's not much older than Mathew or Collin, the priest thought.

Blake looked up and shook his head slightly. Hudson, a grizzled-looking veteran with gray hair, disappeared into the building only to reemerge a minute later carrying two crossbows.

"He got all three of 'em," he said, handing a bow to Jones. His voice was shaking with emotion. Hudson dropped down next to his lieutenant and took Baxter's hand. "Good work, lad. We'll make a soldier of you yet."

Baxter gave him a weak smile and opened his mouth to speak, but before he could get the words out he began gasping for air—once . . . twice . . . three times. A rattling sound starting in his chest followed, and he collapsed back to the ground, his eyes staring at nothing.

Lieutenant Blake put a hand over his face and took a second to compose himself, then bent down and closed the boy's eyes.

"Miserable traitorous bastards," Mickens said, muttering under his breath.

The other men expressed similar sentiments, all of their faces ashen.

Father Thomas was the first to recover.

"Gentlemen, they have to know the game is up by now, so time is of the essence. It won't be long before we see a response, so I want you to listen to me carefully. Given the superiority of their numbers, the next action will be a direct one.

"Mickens, do you see that block and tackle by the collapsed building over there?"

"Right."

"I want you to get the rope and secure it to anything you can find, then run it along the ground to the opposite side of the street."

Mickens nodded and left.

Father Thomas grabbed Lieutenant Blake's elbow and helped him to his feet.

"What do you think they'll do, Father?" Francis asked. He was a slightly built young man with blond hair and slender fingers.

"We haven't seen any horses yet, other than those we passed on the way in. I imagine that is about to change, my son."

"A charge?" asked Lieutenant Blake.

"Precisely."

"All right." Blake nodded. "Hudson, you and Jones have the only crossbows. Both of you separate. I want you on opposite sides of the street. We'll catch them in a cross—"

"I would prefer them on the same side of the street for this," Father Thomas interrupted. He watched Mickens disappear into a building about a hundred yards ahead of them carrying the rope he had cut loose.

"Do it," Blake ordered.

The two soldiers took off at a run.

"Well . . . that leaves the three of us," Father Thomas said to Blake and Francis, who looked somewhat pale, but resolute. "Let's wait for a minute to make sure your men are in position."

Francis looked from the priest to his lieutenant and swallowed hard.

"Join the navy my dad kept telling me, but *no,* I was too smart to listen. Excuse me for a second."

Father Thomas and Lieutenant Blake watched as Francis dashed to the other side the street and returned with a pike from one of the dead soldiers.

"I know we have God on our side, Father," he said, "but I thought this might help."

Father Thomas smiled and all three of them started down the street together.

They had only gotten sixty yards when the sound of hoofbeats reached them. Nine riders burst around the corner at a full gallop, yelling at the top of their lungs.

"Here they come," Lieutenant Blake said.

"Single column behind me when they're at twenty yards," shouted Father Thomas, "then wheel right and charge the flank."

The three of them halted, standing their ground, as Lord Guy's soldiers bore down on them, dust and earth flying from the horses's hooves.

"On my command . . . steady . . . *now!*"   Father Thomas yelled.

Francis and Lieutenant Blake fell back behind Father Thomas. At almost the same time, two buzzing sounds from the building on their right split the air as arrows fired by Hudson and Jones found their marks in the nearest riders. Father Thomas saw the men go down. A moment later, concealed inside a doorway directly across the street, Mickens yanked hard on the rope lying on the ground and wrapped it around the base of a lamppost. The lead horses struck it and went down amidst a tangle of bodies, hooves, and screams.

The first soldier was just getting to his feet when Lieutenant Blake reached him.

Without breaking stride, Blake slashed upward with his sword, splaying open the man's abdomen, then spinning backward and striking the side of his neck. The same fate awaited his companion, who looked up to see Francis running at him at full speed with his pike. The man screamed and held his arms out in front of him as the young soldier drove him backward into the ground, the force of the collision snapping the pike in two. Mad with the heat of battle, Francis pulled the dagger from his belt and plunged it into the man's heart.

The moment the horses fell, Mickens left his hiding place and raced across the street to help his companions. Jones and Hudson did the same, but were unable to shoot for fear of hitting their own men.

Mickens was still about fifteen yards away when he saw Father Thomas go on the attack. The man he was facing was easily half a head taller than the priest and was wielding an axe. Father Thomas had a short sword in each hand. After sidestepping a vicious blow aimed at his head, he immediately counterattacked. To Mickens it appeared that the blades were coming at the soldier from everywhere at the same time. Father Thomas drove the man back, parried another blow wide of his body, and killed him with a thrust through the heart.

Jones died when one of Lord Guy's remaining soldiers ducked under his guard and plunged a sword into his chest. Unable to reach his friend in time, Mickens saw Jones's knees collapse and watched him fall over sideways. He lowered his shoulders and charged the man like a bull, slamming him backward against the side of a building. Both men fell to the ground grappling with each other until Mickens took hold of the other's head and with one violent twist broke his neck.

Hudson got to Francis first and helped him up. Off to

his left, Rodney Blake was in the midst of fighting a bearded soldier when his foot went out from under him and he stumbled backward. The soldier raised his sword above his head with both hands and moved in for the kill. Without hesitating Hudson grabbed Francis's pike and hurled it a good thirty feet through the air. The snarl on the soldier's face changed to shock as he looked down to find a spear sticking out of his chest. A moment later the sword fell from numb fingers and he collapsed to the ground, dead.

Now outnumbered five to two, one of Lord Guy's remaining soldiers turned and fled. Francis set off after him, both men rounding the corner running at full speed. A moment later a piercing scream ripped the air ... followed by silence. Francis reappeared and trotted back to join his friends.

The remaining soldier was desperately trying to remount his horse when Hudson and Father Thomas pulled him from the saddle. Wild-eyed, Hudson cut the man's throat before the priest could stop him. The soldiers at the gate, seeing what was happening, did not attack. Instead, they got their horses and fled.

Father Thomas was bent over double, trying to catch his breath, when Mickens and Blake reached him.

"Are you all right, Father?" Lieutenant Blake asked.

All the priest could do was to nod. "I'm afraid I'm getting too old for this," he said. When Mickens put a hand under his arm to help him up, "Why thank you, my son," he added.

Mickens looked at the priest and shook his head in admiration. "They must have a tougher training program at the abbey than I was told. I've never seen anyone fight like that."

"Ah ... well, the spirit was upon me," Father Thomas replied, rubbing the small of his back.

"Remind me not to get crossways of the spirit," Mickens mumbled in reply.

"I doubt if we'll find anyone left here," Blake said, "but we should check out the rest of this area anyway."

The lieutenant turned to Hudson.

"Get back to Argenton as fast as you can and let the king know we have a rebellion on our hands. Francis, you will ride to Tenley Palace and return with the garrison. Take Jones's horse and Baxter's too if you think you'll need them. You are to stop for nothing and speak with no one. Do you understand me?"

"Yes, sir," Francis replied. After saluting his lieutenant, the young soldier turned to Father Thomas and added, "See you in church on Saturday, Father. I've decided to convert."

"New customers are always welcome, my son," the priest answered with a smile and slight inclination of his head. "Let us go and see what other interesting sights these ruins hold."

30

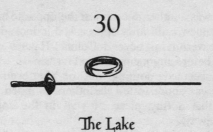

The Lake

GAWL'S PARTY FOUND THEMSELVES STANDING ON THE
ledge of the second floor of the beehive room. Water dripping from the ceiling made the rock surface slippery and
unstable forcing them to proceed cautiously. While they
were walking, a portion of the ledge unexpectedly collapsed with Jeram Quinn on it. The constable would have
fallen had it not been for Gawl, who pulled him back in
time.

"Thank you, your majesty," gasped Quinn, looking
over the edge. Gawl responded with one of his wolfish
smiles.

With Teanna's ball of light floating ahead of them, they
proceeded along the passageway and entered a room approximately twenty feet square. In the meantime Mathew
experimented with his night vision, making it come and
go until he was satisfied that he could control it at will.
He came to a halt when the others did and looked at his
surroundings.

The room they were in appeared to serve no purpose at
all; it was just an opening cut in the cavern rock. Except
for the fact that the walls were perfectly smooth, and con-
structed of some type of light stone colored material none
of them had ever seen before, there wasn't anything even
remotely interesting about it.

Why would someone bother to build a room here?
Mathew thought. *There's no reason for it.*

There was another doorway at the opposite end of the room. Mathew cautiously approached it, looked out, and saw the cavern lying beyond. Colonel Haynes asked if it was safe before anyone proceeded farther.

There seemed nothing out of the ordinary and Mathew was about to tell the others as much when he noticed that a tiny piece of wall in the corner had chipped away.

"What's that?" he asked, moving closer for a better look.

Gawl frowned and tapped on the wall with the hilt of his sword. "Hollow," he said.

"There's a little hole over here," said Quinn. "I don't think this is more than an inch or two thick." For emphasis he stuck a finger in and wiggled it.

Everyone watched while the constable and Gawl carefully began examining the rest of the wall while Colonel Haynes took the opposite side.

"All right. They're clearly hollow, but why?" asked the colonel.

"There's only one way to find out," Gawl said. He stepped back and with one swing of his forearm he hit the wall, caving in a portion of it. But instead of shattering it ripped. Gawl pulled a chunk away and tossed it aside. Two more blows from his shoulder enlarged the hole. On his last attempt, to everyone's surprise, Gawl crashed completely through.

Teanna let out a scream as dozens of skulls and bleached white bones began pouring out of the opening. Skeletons fell from their final resting place, their mouths open in silent screams; black eyeless sockets stared at the intruders.

Gawl let loose a string of oaths, swatted the skulls away, and scrambled to his feet.

Mathew was as shocked as everyone there, though it wasn't the gruesome discovery that caused his stomach to turn; it was the shape of the skulls themselves. These were no human skulls—they were Orlocks.

"We have a problem," said Quinn, staring at a skull that had rolled up next to his foot.

"Orlocks," Colonel Haynes observed.

Quinn looked at him and turned back to Gawl who was still muttering to himself and brushing the dust from his clothes.

"Marvelous, we've stumbled into an Orlock burial crypt," said the king.

"Or we've been led into one," Quinn observed.

"You think the priest knows about this?" Gawl asked, incredulous. "He'd have to be completely insane."

"He's given very little indication of his sanity thus far, wouldn't you say?" Quinn replied.

Gawl surveyed the room slowly before answering and shook his head. "I don't think anyone's been in here for ages," he said. "Orlocks haven't been reported in this area of the country for years, and even during the Sibuyan War, they never came this far west. The last time I recall hearing about them was when I was quite young, maybe eight or nine at most."

The king took a deep breath and looked around the room. "All right, let's do what we came to do and leave."

The lake in the cavern lay silent and unmoving a hundred feet below them. It was impossible to say how large it was because the farthest shoreline was lost in shadow. Immense was the only word Mathew could use to describe it. The rock formations were even more spectacular than any he and the others had seen earlier. Their emerald phosphorescence continued to pulsate making the shadows appear to move with a life of their own. It was like being suddenly being dropped into another world.

"Good lord," Mathew heard Johnson exclaim and turned to see what he was looking at. Startled exclamations come from everyone at the same time. In the distance, at the far end of the lake, stood the giant stone statues. Solemn and foreboding, the tops of their heads rose almost to the height of the cliff Mathew was standing on. Such a discovery would have been disturbing enough, except for the fact that one of the statues was a man and the other was an Orlock.

Mathew stared at them in disbelief. Whoever had made the carvings must have spent years doing so. Situated between them was a large rent in the rock, through which he could see another cavern containing buildings and a large circular plaza. After a minute he returned his attention to the statues. The clothing they wore was odd in appearance and although carved in intricate detail, it bore little resemblance to the way the people of his time dressed.

"Astounding," said Gawl. "Let's go down there and see if we can find this Father Kellner. I'd like a word with him."

A brief search located a path that appeared to lead to the cavern's base. Unfortunately, it was no longer usable because a large section had torn away from the cliff at some point in the past, leaving them with no choice but to climb down. To Mathew's surprise, and that of the other men, Teanna declined their offers of help and negotiated the rocks with surprising ease. When they finally reached the bottom, Colonel Haynes and Johnson began surveying the area. They were aided by the glows coming from the rocks which continued to cast their odd green light throughout the cavern. It was almost bright enough to approximate daylight.

Though Mathew's curiosity was aroused by the mysterious buildings in the second cavern, he forced himself to concentrate on the task at hand and searched along with the others. All the while the silent stone guardians at the entrance watched their progress.

In the interest of time it was decided that Colonel Haynes, Gawl, and Jeram Quinn would take the opposite side of the lake, leaving Mathew, Teanna, and Johnson to check the immediate area. They agreed to meet in a half hour.

Gawl was the first to return. "Nothing," he said, shaking his head.

Mathew looked questioningly at Teanna.

"I get no feeling from this area," she told them. "The sensation was much stronger when we were in the room above, but down here . . . I don't know. This is such a strange place."

No one responded because they were all feeling the same thing. Whatever they had stumbled into, it was decidedly unusual and alien. The bizarre landscape and the statues had a great deal to do with it of course, to say nothing of coming upon buildings and a lake deep under the earth, but there was something else. It felt as if they were intruders. That was the only way Mathew could describe it. None of them belonged there.

Gawl looked up at the cavern roof and slowly turned in a full circle.

"Well, if there's nothing here," he said. "I'd like to get a closer look at those buildings. Looks like this path runs all the way around the lake."

Colonel Haynes nodded and said to Johnson, "I'll take point. You take the rear."

"Right," Johnson responded.

The young soldier had said very little since they began their descent into the cavern. He was slightly older than Mathew and had light brown hair, with a pleasant smile. Like Mathew, he was slender and tall, though perhaps an inch or two shorter. In the tavern after the Felcarin match, he told Mathew that he'd joined the army a little over three years ago, but was assigned to Gawl's personal bodyguard since that time at Rodney Blake's request.

"Do you like being a soldier?" Mathew asked, as they walked along.

Sandy Johnson shrugged. "They give us all the time off we need to practice so it's not so bad."

"Practice for drills?"

"Felcarin. Gawl hates to lose."

The lake was as black as obsidian. A chill breeze skimmed across its surface causing ripples on the water to lap up against a shoreline. Mathew peered into the cavern's recesses as they walked, but even with his extended vision all he could make out were shadows, so he gave up and let his sight return to normal. Teanna looked to be doing the same thing—her head moving back and forth, studying their surroundings.

"You know it's strange," Johnson said. "I've lived in these mountains all my life and I had no idea any of this was down here. What d'you suppose it means . . . an Orlock and a human together? Do you have anything like this in your country?"

Teanna and Mathew both said no over their shoulders at the same time, then looked at each other and smiled.

"We're both foreigners, it seems," she said.

"Now will you look at that?" Sandy Johnson said before Mathew could reply.

Mathew turned back to Johnson and saw that he had stopped and was staring at the lake. He followed the soldier's gaze and blinked at what he saw. The wind blowing through the cavern had suddenly picked up, causing the surface of the lake to form tiny whitecaps. Mathew took a step back to avoid a wave washing over the top of his boots. The closer he looked at the lake, the more he had the feeling that something was wrong. He frowned and stood there watching the water. Then it came to him. Only the water at the center of the lake was moving; the sides were calm.

Impossible, he thought.

Gawl and the others were almost a hundred yards

ahead of them and had also stopped to watch what was happening.

Teanna folded her arms across her chest and stood next to Mathew. It took several seconds before he realized what was bothering him. The wind was blowing across the lake from left to right, yet the waves were coming directly at them. Before he had time to consider the problem further, a diffuse area of white light suddenly appeared under the water's surface.

"What the hell is that?" asked Johnson.

Mathew narrowed his eyes and stared at the light. Seconds passed.

"Get back," he said, half talking to himself. He reached out, took hold of Teanna's elbow and began to more her away from the water. "Sandy, get back," he repeated loudly.

The young soldier gave him a puzzled look and turned back to the lake, drawing his sword. A mist was beginning to form directly over the light.

"Mathew, what is happening?" asked Teanna.

Everyone stood frozen in their places, watching as the mist continued to grow and thicken. In less than a minute it was more than fifty yards across and nearly double that in height. Gradually, its shape began to change, becoming denser and more cloudlike in appearance. At first Mathew thought his eyes were playing tricks on him, because there seemed to be flashes of light coming from inside of it.

Then the voices started. They were faint and indistinct at first, but with each passing second they grew louder. Mathew couldn't tell how many there were, but he could hear whispering, punctuated by shrieks and laughter. Words being spoken in different languages . . . at least he thought they were words.

He glanced at Teanna, whose eyes had gone wide.

The cloud continued darkening until it was almost

completely gray, and with every passing second it looked more and more like a small thunderstorm hovering just over the lake's surface.

Mathew opened his mouth to ask a question, but stopped. He looked up at the cavern walls instead. A deep groaning sound seemed to be coming from all around them, as though incalculable tons of rocks were moving.

This can't be, he whispered to himself.

Teanna, Mathew, and Johnson looked at each other and backed away from the shoreline. On the lake the cloud began to churn and move. The groaning in the walls continued to increase. Whatever was happening, it wasn't good.

Mathew was about to suggest that everyone begin making their way toward the second cavern, in case the storm that was brewing in front of them decided to erupt, but before he could get the words out, a bolt of yellow light shot out of the cloud accompanied by a loud crack. It struck Sandy Johnson in the chest, lifting him off his feet and hurling him backward into the nearest wall. He crumpled silently to the ground. It all happened so fast Mathew had no time to react. A second bolt hit the shoreline five feet in front of him, knocking him down.

Teanna reacted by throwing up a shield over them and deflecting a third bolt in the nick of time.

"Get out of there," Gawl yelled.

Mathew scrambled back to his feet, looked at Gawl, and signaled him to stay away, pointing to the second cavern. Two more columns of light hit Teanna's shield, shaking the ground under their feet.

"Are you all right?" she asked. "It's the priest—I can feel him."

"I'm fine. Can you hold this?"

"I can hold it forever if I have to, but I can't fight back as long as it's up. If we stay here he'll bring the cavern down on us."

She was right. The whole cavern seemed to shake each time a blast hit.

Teanna had to shout to make herself heard because the wind over the lake had picked up to the point where it was blowing at nearly gale force. Everything around them was chaos. A chunk of rock the size of a small house broke loose from the cavern's roof and came crashing down about twenty feet from where they were standing. On the lake the cloud was nearly black and still expanding, moving with a life of its own. Flashes were shooting out of it in all directions, hitting the walls and blasting whole sections away.

"We need to separate," Mathew yelled. "I want you to move away from me and get into the second cavern with the others. It's *me* he's after."

"I'm not leaving you, Mathew."

"We're too easy a target," he shouted back. "We've got to figure out a way to fight this thing."

Teanna held his eye for a second and spun around fixing her attention on the huge boulder that had fallen nearby. She extended her right arm at it, fingers spread wide. Incredibly, the boulder began rise into the air . . . five feet . . . eight feet . . . twenty feet. Beads of perspiration appeared on her forehead and her breathing grew more rapid. Another bolt struck the shield. Mathew flinched, but the princess took no notice, so intense was her concentration. Still churning, the cloud split apart and combined again. Suddenly the voices faded, only to be replaced by the sound of a heavy, bellowlike breathing.

Whether Teanna saw or heard what he did, Mathew didn't know. What he did know was that for a moment the clouds parted and a pair of angry red eyes stared at him from the darkness. He took a step back in shock. The Nyngary princess turned toward the lake with the boulder still suspended in the air, took a deep breath, and snapped her hand closed into a fist. The boulder hurtled forward into the center of the storm. Water exploded out of the lake and the clouds broke apart . . . only to reform moments later.

The power Teanna generated surged around Mathew, strong enough to stand the hairs of his arm on end. An answering bellow of rage came from inside the storm, ringing off the cavern walls. Lightning arched from Teanna's fingers in reply. Whatever was in there roared again and another column of yellow light streaked out of the clouds. It hit the ground with tremendous force, knocking Teanna down and stunning her.

Out of the corner of his vision, Mathew saw Gawl, Colonel Haynes, and Quinn turn and start running toward them. He reached down and helped Teanna to her feet; she was shaken, but unharmed. Before he could ask if she was all right, Teanna screamed and pointed behind him. Mathew spun around drawing his sword. A tail the thickness of a tree trunk and covered in iridescent amber and black scales suddenly lashed out of the storm at Gawl.

"Gawl!" Mathew shouted.

The giant saw it at the same time and slashed upward with his broadsword. Black blood sprayed from the wound and another bellow came from within the clouds, reverberating around the cavern. It was so loud that Mathew was forced to cover his ears. An answering stream of liquid fire exploded on the beach directly in front of Quinn and Colonel Haynes, who skidded to a halt and barely missed being burned to death. As soon as it struck the beach, the fire spread out in both directions until it formed a wall, then rose up to the cavern roof and became a flaming canopy. Mathew and Teanna were isolated.

Gradually, the initial shock at what was happening began to wear off and Mathew collected himself. He took a deep breath, as his mind worked rapidly, weighing various possibilities. Dust filtering into the air mixed with the emerald light from the rocks, giving the cavern a surreal, nightmare-like aspect.

"Teanna, I want you to move away from me," he said, under his breath. "About fifty yards to your left is an outcrop of rock. There's an overhang. Do you see it?"

"Yes, but we can destroy this thing, Mathew, I know we can."

"Maybe we can fight clouds and maybe we can't, but there's more here than just a storm. The only thing I'm sure of is that together we're too easy a target. Now go."

Teanna looked like she was about to argue, but changed her mind and started edging along the lake shore in the direction of the outcrop.

"Mat," Gawl called out, from the other side of the fire wall. "You've got to get out of there—"

"Run for it, son," Jeram Quinn yelled.

Gawl was shouting something else and stopped in midsentence when Mathew held up his hand.

All right, there's a storm sitting over a lake with something inside it that wants to kill me. Fine. Let's just see what you look like.

With that, the air in front of Mathew began to bend and distort itself. In the blink of an eye a ball of red flame materialized in front of him. It was about two feet in diameter and hung suspended in the air at the edge of the lake. On his left another ball of flame created by Teanna popped into existence and rushed forward into the center of the storm. She followed it with another, then another. As each ball struck, more roaring could be heard from deep within the heart of the clouds. They were expanding once again and swirling angrily around each other.

Mathew was aware Teanna didn't understand what he intended to do, but for the moment it made no difference. Given the size of the tail he had just seen, he doubted that whatever was lurking inside there could be destroyed quite so easily. As if in response to his thoughts, a jet of flame shot straight at him, ignoring Teanna and the others. This time he was ready for it and the shield he put in place deflected it. The flame, more liquid than gaseous, bounced off, blasting rock and sand into the air fifty feet from him.

Another second jet of fire, heavier and more intense than the last followed it. One after another Teanna's lighting bolts streaked into the storm. Whether they struck the thing hiding in there, Mathew couldn't tell. The only thing he was sure of was that they were having no effect. He lowered his chin and concentrated on the ball of flame he had created. Slowly, it began to drift forward and disappeared into the swirling clouds. In seconds, a reddish glow could be seen coming from inside the storm, and with each passing moment it increased in brightness until the edges of the farthest clouds were tinged with the same color. Sweat started to run down Mathew's back as the temperature in the cavern climbed. Minutes ticked by and the glow changed, turning yellow in color. The roaring inside the storm trailed away. Unseen by any of the others, Mathew's fireball changed once again, becoming white hot. It continued growing in size until it was more than eighty feet across. Waves of heat radiated outward and the temperature in the cavern rose at a phenomenal rate—the fireball was now a small sun. Gawl and the others were forced to back away, shielding their eyes from the glare. In minutes the lake itself began to boil. Columns of steam rose from it, drifting upward to the cavern's roof and coming back down again in the form of rain.

Then without warning the wall of flame separating Gawl, Quinn, and Haynes from Mathew disappeared. He saw it out of the corner of his vision, noted it, and concentrated harder on the molten ball of fire in the middle of the lake. The clouds were breaking apart, evaporating into steam as the water in the lake continued to boil furiously. The heat was now so intense that Mathew had to take cover behind a group of rocks. Teanna broke off her attack as well.

When the last of the clouds disappeared and the steam

had evaporated Mathew looked up from behind the rocks and blinked in surprise. There was nothing there. He stood up and searched the surface of the lake. Only for a second, deep in the shadows at the farthest recesses of the cavern, he caught a glimpse of a giant black snout sinking slowly under the water.

Good lord, he said to himself.

Whatever it was, the faint tingling in the air that he associated with the rings abruptly disappeared as soon as it went under. A moment later his sun did the same, winking out of existence. Too surprised to speak Mathew stood there looking out across the lake while rain fell from the cavern roof. Gawl and the others came to join him. A few minutes passed and the boiling water grew slower and slower until the lake was calm once more. He was aware that Teanna and the others were back by his side and he felt her put an arm around his shoulders. He also felt it when she kissed him on the cheek and whispered, "You were wonderful."

"Well done, young man," said Quinn, shaking Mathew's hand.

Gawl's face split into one of his broad smiles and beamed down at him.

"An interesting solution to the problem," Colonel Haynes said. "But well done indeed."

"I'm sorry about Sandy Johnson," Mathew told him, looking back to where the soldier's body lay. "I wasn't able—"

"You did more than anyone could have asked for," the colonel said. "Johnson was a good man and you have my thanks. What in God's name was that thing? I saw the tail, but—"

"I don't know," said Mathew.

"Do you think it's still alive?" asked Quinn, squinting at the lake.

"I don't know," Mathew repeated. "I saw something, but it was only for a moment. Kellner's close by, though. He was hiding in those rocks a little while ago."

Everyone looked where he was looking.

"He took off in that direction," Mathew said, pointing toward the second cavern. "I think we should find him now."

"So do I," said Gawl.

"I don't understand why he doesn't just come out and fight if he wants me dead so badly," Mathew said, looking up at the rocks. "The only thing he's done up until now is to attack and hide like a coward."

He was met only with silence and the passage of wind through the cavern.

"We were on our way to have a look at those buildings before we were interrupted," said Gawl. "Let's move."

"After we give Johnson a decent burial," the colonel reminded him.

"What? Oh . . . quite right. Forgive me, Haynes. I don't know where my head—"

Gawl's words were cut off in mid-sentence as the ground under everyone's feet suddenly heaved upward. Mathew felt himself being thrown into the air and landed heavily on his side, dazed. Confused, he shook his head to clear it and looked back over his shoulder to see what had happened.

"Whoa!" he yelled, scrambling backward on his hands and heels.

Fifteen feet off the ground a pair of gold reptilian eyes stared back at him. They were attached to the head of an enormous black dragon that was watching him. A long snout covered in black and amber scales had a horn protruding from the end between its nostrils. Two more horns rose from the top of the beast's head, angling slightly backward. A forked tongue snaked in and out of its mouth, tasting the air directly in front of Mathew.

The dragon was between him and the others.

"Run, Mat," Gawl yelled out.

Slowly, the dragon looked at the king then turned back to Mathew. Its skin was covered in the same thick scales as its face with the neck widening into a charcoal black body, heavy with muscle. Two powerful arms that ended in talons looked like they could tear through solid rock. They were opening and closing in time to the dragon's breathing. A ridge of triangular-shaped spikes ran along the dorsal spine to a tail coiled close beside the creature's body.

"Run," Gawl yelled again.

Mathew continued sliding back along the ground, bumped into a small boulder and used it to push himself up. Meanwhile, the dragon stared at him unblinking with those gold eyes, but strangely the beast made no move to attack. Its head moved closer and Mathew could smell the moist air coming from the nostrils.

He wasn't certain why he didn't follow Gawl's advice; something told him that it would be the wrong thing to do. He looked into the eyes of the dragon. The actions it had taken up to that point gave the impression of intelligence, so palpable that Mathew could nearly sense it.

The head moved closer still . . . close enough so that its tongue nearly touched his face the last time it flicked out.

"Why are you doing this, Kellner?" Mathew said, "I know you're here."

There was no answer, only the bellowlike breathing coming from the dragon's lungs. So he waited, unsure what to do next.

An explosion on his left caused him to jump. Out of nowhere a ball of blue flame exploded against the creature's shoulders as Teanna struck. The dragon recoiled, pulling back its head and letting out an ear-splitting roar. The huge tail lashed out at Teanna and the others, smashing boulders and rocks aside as if they were no more than pebbles. Quinn, Gawl, and Colonel Hanyes all dove out of the way.

For a moment, Mathew refused to believe his eyes. He

saw the tail snap out and everyone scatter—everyone except Teanna. The Nyngary princess stood her ground and struck again with another fireball, larger and more powerful than the first.

"Teanna!" he screamed, trying to warn her.

But to his amazement, the tail passed right though her body. Mathew gasped because it was the last thing in the world he expected. Another fireball materialized in front of Teanna and sped forward hitting the dragon in the middle of its body. Amber scales lit up, briefly becoming iridescent against the different shades of black that were the creature's skin. For some reason he wasn't surprised when the dragon disregarded her and turned back to him. The great mouth slowly opened, revealing two rows of pointed teeth almost as big as he was. Then without warning, it felt like someone had flung open the door to a furnace. A blast of flame came pouring out of the creature's throat, exploding around Mathew and turning the sand near his feet into a green glass.

When he thought about what happened afterward, he couldn't remember feeling anger or rage at the creature. Curiosity was a better description. So intense was the dragon's fire that the air around him grew difficult to breathe. One part of his mind told him that Teanna's fireballs weren't going to kill the creature and another part told him that he had to do something quickly.

Through the burning stream raining down on him, Mathew could see the luminous golden eyes change to crimson. He gathered himself, took a deep breath, and raised his right arm. A column of air solidified in front of him and struck the creature in its chest, hurling it to the other end of the lake. Mathew's shield snapped out of existence.

As soon as it did, the other others came running.

"How do we kill this thing?" Teanna asked. "Fire doesn't seem to have any effect on it."

Mathew didn't look at her. His attention was fixed on

the dragon, who had spread a pair of great leathery wings and was circling near the top of the cavern at the other end of the lake.

"Here he comes again," said Haynes.

Gawl stepped forward raising his broadsword to meet the attack.

"Swords are no use here," Mathew said. "Let me handle this, Gawl."

Before the king could answer, a piercing shriek split the stillness of the cavern. The dragon was diving, its wings folded back against its body. At about twenty feet from the ground, it fired another blast of flame and swooped over their heads, talons stretching out. Mathew deflected the flame away from everyone, but was too late to stop Gawl, who struck at the creature with all his strength. The blade bit deeply into scale and bone. Half-turned by the force of his blow, Gawl struck again. He never saw the tail coming. It caught him in the side and knocked the giant twenty feet away.

Teanna fought back, drawing even more on her considerable strength. A ball of flame bounced off the creature's body like water. Shaken loose by the impact, dust and rock began to skitter down from the cavern roof as the dragon rose into the air once more.

Colonel Haynes and Jeram Quinn ran to help Gawl and were attempting to pull the unconscious king to safety. Mathew's own mind raced as he watched the dragon glide to the middle of the lake and begin a slow turn back toward them.

Thus far everything he and Teanna had done had no more effect than tossing water on a runaway carriage. To make matters worse, he was afraid that if either of them increased their power, they would cause the cavern to collapse. Several large stalactites had already broken away from the roof in warning.

The dragon's wings beat in unison as it closed on the party. Years later, when the scene played over in

Mathew's mind, he was only able to describe what he did
then as a hunch. In a matter of two or three strides, his
long legs broke into a run that carried him past a startled
Jeram Quinn and Colonel Haynes.

The moment the dragon saw him separate from the rest
of the group, it altered its course and went after him. Far
up on the ledge, just above the crown of the human
statue, Mathew caught a glimpse of a man ducking down
behind a rock formation. He had little question who it
was. He knew the priest was somehow controlling the
creature. For the moment things were at a standoff.
Teanna and he could continue to protect everyone, but for
how long? The dragon would effectively block their way
out, and the longer the battle went on the more dangerous
and unstable things became.

The statue of the dead king loomed closer, arms
crossed. Its giant legs formed a solid base at the cavern
floor. A broadsword ran down the length of one leg almost to the ground. Behind him, Mathew felt rather than
saw the blast. Instinctively his shield went up, splattering
the fire in every direction. At the last moment the dragon
veered away to avoid crashing into the statue. Mathew
ducked under the tail that swung around at him and missing his head by less than a foot. He came to a halt under
the statue's legs as the creature completed its turn.

And then a strange thing happened—a second dragon
popped into existence. The first let out a roar of surprise
and pulled sharply backward in mid-flight. It came to
light on an outcrop of rock. Puzzled, it tilted its head to
the side and looked at the newcomer who sat there calmly
on silent haunches, staring back at it. With three great
flaps of its wings, the first dragon glided down to the
shore and waddled forward a few steps. It gave a tentative
roar, different from any of the previous ones. The second
dragon didn't respond; it merely sat and stared. Curious,
the first dragon came closer.

Mathew watched in fascination as its neck stretched

forward. The eyes, red only a moment ago, had resumed their golden color once again. In the middle of the creature's chest, he could see its heart beating and could almost hear the *thump, thump, thump*. The first dragon sniffed at the illusion Mathew had created, oblivious to the blood that continued to drip from the wound Gawl inflicted. Large drops fell to the ground and mixed with the sand.

Suddenly, the first dragon let out a mighty roar and pulled away, taking a vicious swipe at the other with its talon. As quickly as it had appeared, the imaginary dragon dissolved into smoke. Only a long black shadow remained. The first dragon blinked its eyes in confusion and looked left then right, never noticing that the shadow had begun to move. Slowly at first, and then with increasing speed, the statue of the human king toppled forward. When the dragon finally looked up, it was too late. A hundred tons of stone came crashing down on the creature's head.

The impact was so great it nearly knocked Mathew off his feet. Dust and smoke shot up into the air. When it settled, he saw the dragon was dead and silence descended on the cavern once again. Teanna was the first to find him in the haze; she was followed by Jeram Quinn, and Colonel Haynes, and Gawl, who had apparently recovered.

"Oh my God," Teanna said, "when I saw that statue begin to fall, I thought you would be killed. You were magnificent."

"Glad to see you're all right," Mathew told Gawl, shaking the king's hand.

"It'll take more than a little lizard to kill me," Gawl replied.

Colonel Haynes's eyebrows went up at the comment. He glanced up and down the length of the dragon's body and gave an involuntary shudder. "What in the world is a dragon doing here in the first place?" he said.

"I thought they were just something you read about in

books. I never heard of a real dragon before," said Teanna.

"Nor have I," said Gawl. He was looking at where the beast lay, partially buried by the statue. "Did anyone notice anything strange about it?"

"Isn't being a dragon strange enough?" asked Teanna.

"The blood," Mathew answered absently, staring up at the place where he had seen Father Kellner a moment ago. "It was black."

"Right," said Gawl.

"What does the color of its blood have to do with anything?" asked Colonel Haynes.

"Let's just see," Gawl replied.

With the others trailing behind him, Gawl walked over to the creature and raised his broadsword high above his head. The blade flashed in the green light as he brought it down with a mighty swing. It cut through an exposed portion of the foreleg, severing it from the body in a single stroke.

Everyone inhaled sharply, because instead of bone and sinew, what they saw were a series of tubes held together by a pasty-white substance. Embedded within it were dozens of tiny lights blinking off and on. The leg bone, if it could be called that, was made of a thin grayish metal.

Quinn bent down and examined the cut, then reached one of tubes and pinched the end of it. A drop of black blood oozed out. He rubbed it between his thumb and forefinger, brought it up to his nose, and sniffed.

"Oil," he announced.

"What in God's name is this thing?" whispered Haynes.

"A machine," Mathew answered.

"A machine!" Haynes exclaimed, taking a step back. "How in God's name is that possible?"

Mathew stared back at the colonel.

"Oh, I see . . . the rings," said Haynes. "But how anyone would even begin to build such a thing? It can't be."

"I think it can," answered Teanna. "I'm still learning every day—so is Mathew. It appears that Father Kellner may be able to do things we can't."

"He took off in the direction of the second cavern," Mathew said. "Assuming that he doesn't keep running, we can deal with him after we see to Johnson."

"Right," said Gawl.

Mathew started walking, but then stopped and shouted up at the rock, "If you want me, Kellner, here I am."

Only the wind answered him.

31

The Cavern

WHEN THEY REACHED SANDY JOHNSON'S BROKEN BODY, Teanna solved the problem about their lack of tools to dig a grave with by opening a suitable hole in the ground. Mathew felt a slight surge when she drew on the energy source. And he also felt her arm slip through his as Gawl and Haynes lowered the body into the grave with Jeram Quinn's help. When they were through, the colonel stepped back and looked at the king, who realized they were expecting him to say something.

Mathew knew Gawl had not been on particularly good terms with the church since he had won the Sennian throne, and he wished he could say something to help his friend, but he was as much at a loss for words as everyone else. Several thoughts and an array of emotions assailed him at the same time, making it difficult to separate one from the another. He had only known Sandy Johnson a short while, but he was a likable, pleasant fellow, not much older than he was—and death, anyone's death, was not an easy thing to accept. Mathew was sick of death— his father, Giles, Captain Donal, and Zachariah Ward's. *How many more?* he thought as he stared down at the ring on his finger.

Teanna gave his arm a reassuring squeeze and smiled. Perhaps she was right, he thought. Perhaps they were two of a kind. But he felt very much alone at that moment.

Gawl solemnly picked up a handful of dirt and threw it

into the grave. Haynes and Quinn followed suit, then Teanna and Mathew.

"Being king isn't an easy thing," Gawl said quietly. "It's particularly hard when a fine young man like Sandford Johnson dies before his time. He was a good lad and a loyal soldier—loyal to his country, and loyal to his family. These are no small accomplishments."

He drew a deep breath and shut his eyes before continuing.

"Sandy leaves a mother, Lea, a father, Benjamin, and two brothers, Carl and Tilton, all of them good people. No one . . . no family should ever suffer such a loss. I'm sure if Siward Thomas were here he would say that the boy is in a better place now . . . a place free of pain and filled with love. Let us all pray this is so."

Mathew whispered a silent prayer for Sandy's soul. When he opened his eyes he and Gawl looked directly at each other before the king turned away and began walking in the direction of the mysterious buildings. The rest of them followed, each alone with their thoughts. He had had no idea that Gawl even knew Johnson's first name, let alone the names of his family. It impressed him more than he could say.

High up in the rocks Aldrich Kellner also heard the king's words, and they struck him to the core. He clasped his hands together and murmured a prayer for the soldier. The young man was not meant to die. It should never have happened. But his ability to control what the ring created was still new to him. It was an accident, he told himself, a horrible accident. God was truly mysterious in his ways. The only person who should have died was Lewin. He heard when Lewin yelled out a challenge to him and knew that he was trying to draw him into a direct confrontation. Alarice had foretold that was exactly what would happen and she was right. Father Kellner could feel that he was getting stronger each time he used the ring. And he knew he would defeat his foe in the end.

Soon . . . soon, he said to himself. God had picked him and he would not fail. It was only a matter of time, but that young man was so strong—incredibly strong. He had sensed it almost from the first time they made contact. Everything Alarice had promised was coming true exactly as she said it would. His prayers *were* being answered.

But no matter how hard Father Kellner prayed, his vows always came back to haunt him. Priests saved lives, they didn't take them. He had asked God for guidance. He had asked God to give him the resolve to do what must be done. In answer, Alarice appeared to him three nights earlier, and instructed him how to create both the storm and the dragon—things he never could have done on his own. But had failed to kill Lewin. Tears came to the priest's eyes. The soldier was such a young man . . . and the family. . . . It was so sad; so terribly sad. Aldrich Kellner knew he must not fail again. The hopes . . . no, the very survival of his people, depended on his ability to defeat the enemy. Evil had to be stamped out, no matter what the cost.

32

The Second Cavern

LARA PALMER WAS LOCKED IN AGAIN. AFTER FATHER Kellner had left, she tried the door a number of times without success. It was made of metal, and even if she had tools available, which she didn't, she doubted if she could make a dent in it. When she heard explosions in the outer cavern, she knew Mathew was out there. Lara had no doubt that the priest had set a trap of some kind. He really believed Mathew was evil and wanted him dead, though how such a ridiculous idea got into his head she had no idea.

Father Kellner was a strange man. His hands tended to shake when he spoke. He was an intense individual, intense in his beliefs and in everything he did, but for all that he could not look her in the eye for more than a few seconds. In the brief conversation they had, she was amazed to find he thought Mathew responsible for a variety of ills that had descended on Sennia, some real, and most imagined. No matter how many times she told him that he was mistaken, the priest refused to believe her. The most frightening thing was that he had convinced himself that he was right. It wasn't an act, and the rose-gold ring on his left hand terrified her.

Lara knew just how powerful Mathew was. She had been there when he blasted the Orlocks out of existence—along with a good portion of Ceta Woodall's stable. She was also there when he fought Karas Duren, and

had watched him bring a mountain down on the
Zargothans in the pass outside the town of Tremont.
Whatever Father Kellner was capable of, she very much
doubted that he was Mathew's equal. The whole thing
was so stupid it made her want to scream. Unfortunately,
screaming wasn't going to do her much good at the moment. Her immediate problem was how to get out of
where she was.

One large window ran the length of the room, a solid
pane of glass that extended from floor to ceiling. The
street was at least four stories below, and unlike the first
place Kellner had held her, there was absolutely nothing
in the room to break it with. Lara could see a narrow
ledge that ran along the building, just below her. She
might reach it, she thought, if she could find some way to
break the glass and crawl out on to it.

Exasperated, she leaned her forehead against the glass
and looked out at the plaza. A small clinking sound
caused her to glance down when her necklace bumped
against the glass pane. It was the one Mathew had given
her for her birthday several months ago. Except for saying that it was an antique, he had acted very smug and
mysterious at the time, refusing to tell her where he'd
gotten it. She was too polite, in her view at least, to press
the issue, though the gift did please her immensely. It was
the first piece of jewelry she'd ever received from him.
Collin and Father Thomas weren't much help either, having both been sworn to secrecy by Mathew. Since that
time she had worn it constantly. It consisted of a flat wo-
ven gold braid with a rectangular medallion in the middle. The medallion was a large purple stone with raised
facets and a small diamond set in the center.

An idea began to form in Lara's mind. Out of curiosity,
she took the necklace off and ran the large stone across
the glass. To her surprise it produced a sharp white
scratch. Lara tried again, pressing harder, and the scratch
deepened. A proverb Father Thomas once told her came

to mind—something about a journey of a thousand miles beginning with the first step, or beneath one's feet, or something like that.

She raised her eyebrows and took a deep breath. It was a very large window.

Mathew and company passed through the opening previously guarded by two statues. Now one remained—a scowling stone Orlock with hands on its hips. Mathew glanced up at the face, then looked away, because he got the feeling it was watching him. He told himself he was jumping at shadows, but after the episode in Gawl's garden, he reasoned, a little extra caution wouldn't be such a bad idea.

To everyone's surprise, there were not two buildings in the second cavern but an entire cluster of them situated around a plaza. Gawl said he thought they were almost directly under the Argenton ruins. It was the strangest place Mathew had ever seen. The architecture of the buildings was on a grand scale, with wide steps and columned entranceways. An ornate fountain stood in the center of the complex.

Mathew's mind was an extremely ordered one, particularly where figures and numbers were concerned, and without consciously going through the math, he noted that each of the buildings contained the same number of steps and columns—thirteen, although what that meant, he had no idea. The fountain had a pair of swans at the bottom and was made of black cast-iron, now empty of water. Brick walkways crisscrossed the plaza, running from the fountain to each of the buildings.

He had little question that Father Kellner was somewhere in the vicinity, no doubt waiting for his next chance to kill him. It seemed equally reasonable that both Lara and Collin might also be nearby. That they might be injured or hurt just because they were his friends made his blood boil. For hundredth time he tried to imagine what was driving Kellner. And for the hundredth time nothing presented itself. He supposed he would eventually ask him about it.

The party came to a halt in front of the fountain and looked around the plaza. There was no sign of life anywhere—only an eerie stillness.

"If the priest is hiding here," said Gawl, "we should begin by searching these buildings one at a time."

"If we split up, we could cover more ground," Quinn suggested. "Mathew could go with one group and Teanna could go with the other."

Everyone agreed it was a good idea so Gawl, Colonel Haynes, and Teanna headed for the closest building, leaving Mathew and Quinn to explore the white building on the opposite side of the plaza.

Lara stepped back from the window and looked at the square that was almost etched on the glass. She took a moment to sit down on the floor and give herself a brief rest because her hand had begun to cramp under the strain.

Just a little bit more, she thought.

Aldrich Kellner watched the party separate from his hiding place in a doorway on the ground floor of a building farther down the street, he saw that Mathew and Quinn were approaching. The priest moved back from the doorway, almost gleeful, and closed his eyes. God had answered his prayer. Lewin was coming. It was unfortunate that he was with the Elgarian constable. Kellner decided that he would do everything possible to keep the man from harm. His heart was racing so fast he had to take several deep breaths to calm himself. The priest clenched his hands into fists and got ready.

A strange group of people the king has brought with him, he thought. Colonel Haynes, he expected of course. Lewin was there, just as he knew he would be. But of Siward Thomas, there was no sign. He prayed that his fellow priest had seen the light and separated himself from the young devil. Thomas was said to be an intelligent man. What Kellner couldn't understand was why a woman was with them. He was too far away to see her face clearly, but something about her looked familiar. Unfortunately he had no time to dwell on it—his timing would have to be critical.

No sooner had she turned her attention back to the window than Lara caught a glimpse of movement near the fountain. Five people were dispersing in different directions. In the second she had she wasn't able to get a good look at them, but the figure of Gawl was unmistakable. She muttered a very unladylike curse under her breath, courtesy of Captain Oliver Donal, and attacked the window again with renewed vigor. Four minutes later, she decided the cut was deep enough to try knocking the glass out.

Lara steadied herself, leaned back slightly, and kicked. The heel of her boot struck the glass with a thud, but nothing happened. Not even a crack. Lara kicked again. On the fourth try she thought she heard a grinding sound and peered closely at one of the lines she'd scored. It was definitely whiter than it was a moment ago. A fine powder was now visible where the glass met the floor.

Lara backed away from the glass again, turned sideways, putting most of the weight on her left side. She drew her right knee up, and using her upper body for counterbalance, lashed out with all of the strength of her right leg.

It was hard to say who was more surprised when a four foot section of glass shattered on the street—Lara or Father Kellner, who was hiding behind a column of an adjacent building. The resounding crash caused the priest to spin around in shock. It might even have been Mathew and Jeram Quinn, who were just about entering the white building down the block.

Lara crawled through the opening, eased her way onto the ledge, and sat on it. She began sliding toward the archway over the building's entrance in the hope that she could find a way to climb down. She'd always been a good climber.

Father Kellner recovered from his shock and sent out a thought collapsing the base of the building Mathew and Quinn were standing under. His heart leaped with joy. It was turning out exactly the way Alarice had predicted. One by one the columns began to crumple.

Lara was fifty yards away and saw it begin to happen.

"Mathew!" she screamed.

When the priest heard her shout, he was unable to control his own emotions and lashed out in anger. The ledge Lara was on shuddered as if hit by a violent blow and it began to fall apart. Large chunks of stone crashed to the ground, shattering the silence of the cavern.

Lara was five feet from the archway when the structure fell in, carrying her with it.

The second Mathew heard her voice and saw the columns beginning to fall, he shoved Jeram Quinn out of the way. A section of a fluted stone came crashing down where the constable had stood only seconds before. Mathew dove to his left and narrowly missed being crushed to death himself.

He was just getting to his knees when he saw Lara fall.

Gawl also heard the crash and spun around. The king drew his sword and began running. Teanna and Haynes, who were already in the building, stopped in their tracks. Gawl was halfway across the plaza when he saw the center section of the building Quinn and Mathew had gone into explode upward in a thousand directions.

The concussion was so violent, it knocked him down sixty yards away. When the smoke and dust began to clear, he saw a single figure standing where a building had been and knew that it was Mathew. Even at his distance, the look Gawl saw on his young friend's face shocked him, just as it did Jeram Quinn, who was at the bottom of the steps.

For a moment everything seemed frozen in time then Mathew's head began to move from side to side, as if to deny what he had just seen. His face was filled with a pain and anguish so palpable Gawl could almost feel it. The scream that burst forth from Mathew's lungs echoed off the cavern walls, torn from his very soul.

"Lara!"

Aldrich Kellner felt the power surge. It was stronger than anything he could have imagined. Every window on the ground floor of the building where he was hiding exploded. He ducked, out of reflex as bits of glass stung him terribly. Seconds later the ground began to tremble. Large sections of masonry broke away from the building crashing into the street. The whole structure was literally falling apart around him. At the end of the block, the priest saw Mathew Lewin step across the rubble and slowly begin walking down the steps toward him. Panic seized him; Kellner ran out into the street. The boy was coming.

Aldrich Kellner drew on his resolve and steeled himself for the attack.

"Die!" he screamed at Mathew—but nothing happened. Over and over he formed thoughts of Mathew's death in his mind. He saw the young man's body bent and broken, but nothing changed.

Mathew was fifty yards away now.

In desperation Kellner looked at a column lying in the street, lifted it up, and hurled it directly at Mathew. It exploded into powder thirty yards in front of the boy. Kellner launched one piece after another, some weighing tons, but each one either veered away or blew up just as the first one had.

Father Kellner's heart was beating so wildly he could barely catch his breath. Step by step he backed away.

Everything he had done to destroy the demon had failed. Then it came to him. A wall of black fire sprang up in front of the priest with heat so intense, he was forced to lean away to avoid being singed himself. The fire consolidated into a thick battering ram and began rushing down the block toward Mathew Lewin.

Mathew was aware someone was screaming his name, but the man who had killed Lara was standing in front of him; the same man who had murdered his fellow priests and poor Sandy Johnson—the same man who was trying to kill him now. All he could think was that he was looking at an aberration—a disease that killed for no reason. The medical books he had read said one way to deal with a disease was to cut it out.

An answering wall of blue flame appeared directly in front of Mathew and rushed forward to meet black fire. Both met in a tremendous collision that shook the cavern. Seconds ticked by. Gradually the black fire began to give ground as Mathew drew more and more power into himself.

Gawl, Quinn, and Haynes reached his side and were yelling at him to break off the attack. Teanna was close behind them. As yet the Nyngary princess had said nothing, nor did she participate in the battle that was going on. Her eyes were glued to Mathew, watching him.

Father Kellner sank to his knees, spent, staring numbly as the blue wall of flames slowly devoured his black one. Still he fought back with the last remnants of his strength, knowing then that he was no match for Mathew.

"You must stop," Gawl shouted grabbing for Mathew's arm. "He's defeated. Can't you see that?"

Gawl's fingers never reached their objective. An unseen force slammed the giant off his feet and threw him backward.

Jeram Quinn looked at Gawl and Mathew in turn.

"Listen to me, Mathew," he said, speaking urgently.

"Gawl is right. Break off your attack. The man is finished. Let justice deal with him now."

Mathew didn't respond, but the blue flames suddenly flared and pushed forward again.

"Mathew," Quinn pleaded. "You told me that you're not a murderer. Will this be any different from what happened in Devondale? If the priest is guilty, it's the law that must deal with him, not you. I beg you—*Stop what you are doing!* No man can set themselves as both judge and executioner. If you are not a murderer, prove it to me."

Gawl had just gotten to his feet when he saw the wall of blue flames vanish. Father Kellner was on his knees, rocking back and forth, his head bowed, both his hands pressed against his temples. Mathew appeared pale and shaken, and if Jeram Quinn hadn't been there to grab the young man, he surely would have fallen.

Gawl made eye contact with Colonel Haynes and jerked his head in the priest's direction. Kellner's expression was dazed, and he looked around only half-comprehending what was going on . . . until his eyes came to rest on Teanna.

Tears began to roll down his face and he reached out to her.

"M-my lady," he stammered, starting to rise. "I tried, but—"

A sudden explosion and a flash of light nearly blinded everyone there. Colonel Haynes, who had started toward the priest, was thrown violently to the side and knocked unconscious. Dust and debris were everywhere, making it impossible to see. When things cleared there was no sign of Aldrich Kellner.

Mathew spun around and stared at Teanna, his mouth open.

"He was about to kill you and everyone else, Mathew," she explained. "I felt the power buildup and only had a

second to react. I'm sorry I didn't have time to warn
you."

Mathew turned to look at the depression in the ground
where Aldrich Kellner had been as Quinn ran over to help
Colonel Haynes.

"What in God's name happened?" Gawl demanded,
his face ashen.

"The princess just saved you the trouble of a trial,"
Quinn replied, over his shoulder, helping Haynes to his
feet.

"He's dead?" asked Gawl. "I don't understand . . . the
man was finished. We needed to—"

"I had no choice," Teanna calmly explained. "It was
him or us."

Mathew opened his mouth to say something, but
closed it again. The vision of Lara falling from the arch
snapped back into his mind with such appalling clarity, it
pushed everything else aside. He forced his feet to move.
Taking one step then another he stumbled down the
street.

The familiar pain behind his eyes returned and his temples were throbbing as they always did when he drew
heavily on the ring. Mathew continued to weave his way
toward the collapsed building, a hand of ice gripping his
heart. Somehow he forced his legs to move faster and
broke into a ragged trot. Pieces of masonry that made up
the arch Lara was on when she fell lay in the street. Sticking out from behind part of the ledge was a woman's leg.

Oh, God, Mathew thought, his stomach turning over.
He began to sprint.

When he saw her leg move, his heart leaped. Mathew
scrambled over the blocks of stone and reached her in
seconds. He could hear Gawl's heavy tread pounding
down the street behind him.

Lara saw him and smiled.

"It took you long enough," she said, her voice little
more than a whisper.

Dear God.

Her left arm was pinned under a large piece of stone and another was resting partially across her chest. Mathew got down on one knee and gently brushed the hair away from her eyes.

"Don't move. I'll get you out."

He started to push on the block, but then stopped and stepped away from it with a frown. "What are you doing, Mat?" said Gawl. "Let's get her out of there."

"Everything's interconnected," Mathew replied slowly, studying the rubble. "It's like that game with sticks we used to play when we were children. If we move this piece, that large one is going to fall."

Gawl examined the stones for a moment and said, "Wonderful. Can't you do something with your ring—make them disappear or whatever?"

With the headache it was hard for Mathew to concentrate. He shut his eyes and tried to reach for the power. He could still feel it there, but until his strength returned he knew it would be too dangerous to make the attempt.

"I need a little time before I can try again," he explained.

"Teanna, then," said Gawl.

Mathew looked back to see her coming down the street along with Quinn and Colonel Haynes, who appeared to have recovered well enough to walk on his own.

"We need to get these stones off her," Gawl called out.

Quinn and Haynes immediately started to run. Teanna, however, continued walking at the same pace.

"How is she?" asked Quinn, as soon as he arrived.

"I'm fine," Lara replied. "But I would appreciate it if you would hurry. This is not as comfortable as it looks."

"Mistress Palmer," said Quinn, with a small bow. "Give us a moment and we'll figure a way out of your predicament."

"Oh, dear," Teanna said, seeing Lara lying there under the stone. "Let me see if I can help."

Her eyes darted briefly to Mathew, then back at Lara.

"We can't move the stone pinning her without the others dropping," Mathew explained.

Teanna nodded. "That won't be a problem. If everyone will just step back a little, please. Gawl, when I lift the pieces, you'll have to be ready to pull her out. I'm a little weak, but I think I can manage. Mathew, will you be able to help if I need you?"

"Only physically," he answered, looking down at Lara, the worry plain on his face. "Maybe if we wait a few minutes until my strength returns . . ."

A small movement in the rubble pile about fifteen feet from where they were standing coupled with a groan from Lara answered the question for them.

"It's too unstable," Gawl said. "We have to do it now."

Teanna closed her eyes. Her brows came together and the muscles in her jaw clenched. There was a pause and Lara gasped as the stone on top of her began to lift. The ones on the side followed suit, first six inches . . . then a foot . . . then three feet.

"Hurry," gasped Teanna.

Mathew and Gawl rushed to pull Lara out. Gawl held her under her arms while Mathew and Jeram Quinn supported her head and back. They managed to free her just as the blocks of masonry crashed back to the ground.

Lara passed out.

One arm was clearly broken, and through a tear in her skirt Mathew could see a large purple bruise on her thigh and on the side of her knee. She had numerous other cuts and scrapes, but they appeared to be minor. He bent down and straightened her skirt while Colonel Haynes took off his cloak and made a pillow of it for her head.

"Thank you," Mathew said to Teanna.

She responded with a cool smile.

"That . . . was harder than I thought," she said, taking a deep breath and letting it out.

"It might be a good idea if we set her arm while she's

still unconscious," suggested Haynes. "It doesn't look too good."

"Right," Gawl agreed. "Mat, why don't you and Teanna stay with her, while Jeram, Haynes, and I see if we can find something to use for a splint?"

"Thank you again," Mathew said to Teanna once they were alone.

"My pleasure," she replied, with a small curtsy. "So this is your little friend? How long have you known each other?"

"Since we were children," Mathew answered, looking at Lara.

"I see. I suppose that would account for your concern. You seemed very worried about her."

"Yes."

There was a pause before Mathew spoke again. "Teanna, I want to ask you something . . ."

"Go on."

"Was it really necessary to kill Father Kellner?"

"I think so."

"I didn't feel any kind of power buildup. In fact, I didn't feel anything at all."

Teanna looked at him and raised one eyebrow slightly. "You really are much too soft, Mathew. I can't imagine how you managed to kill my uncle. What are we going to do with you?" she said, shaking her head.

She moved closer and put her arms around his neck.

"Don't you understand? The rings are a danger to us. When I came here I was prepared to hate you. I really was. I had this picture of you and a plan all laid out, but you're a very disturbing fellow. Did you know that? Do you remember what we talked about the first time we met?"

Mathew slowly removed Teanna's arms and took a half-step backward.

"You mean about power and ruling."

"Mm-hmm," Teanna nodded.

"I told you how I felt then. I have enough trouble running my own life without trying to run other people's. You didn't have to kill him."

Teanna made a small clicking sound with her tongue behind her teeth and shook her head sadly. She took a step toward Mathew again, but he put his arms on her shoulders and held her away.

"You're such a typical man," she laughed. "Sometimes it takes the right woman to point you in the proper direction. Don't you know that there isn't an army in the world that could stand against you or me—let alone the two of us together. Think of what we could create. Think of what we could accomplish. We could make the world a paradise."

She touched Mathew's face gently with her fingertips. "Derrydale is no place for you."

"Devondale. It's called Devondale," Mathew said, moving her hand away. "The sad thing is that you're probably right. I've been fooling myself into thinking I can simply go home again and things will be the same. But they won't—not ever. I realized that some time ago, but it doesn't mean I want to be anybody's king.

"These rings destroyed the world and the people who made them. I don't know why or how, but that's just what they did. With all their technology, the Ancients weren't able to stop what was happening. What makes you think you or I can?"

"So what will you do? Marry this little baggage?" Teanna asked, glancing at Lara. "Go live on a farm somewhere and have lots of babies? Darling, we're unique. You know that as well as I do. Come back to Nyngary with me."

Mathew looked at Teanna and shook his head slowly.

"You're a beautiful girl and I'm flattered. It's a tempting offer, but I don't want to be anyone's ruler. Killing the priest was wrong."

"Was it?"

"Yes. It was."

"Think about it, Mathew. There's one less ring in the world now . . . one less ring that can be used against us."

"Before he died, Kellner looked directly at you. There was something about you he recognized, didn't he?"

A coquettish smile appeared on Teanna's face.

"I can be many things to many people, Mathew. Teanna d'Elso, Princess of Nyngary, a simple farm girl if you like, or even Alarice, patron saint of the church. It's not particularly difficult."

Mathew watched in amazement as Teanna's appearance began to change before his very eyes. One second she was dressed in black leather pants and a vest and the next she was standing in front of him as a princess in the full regalia of her court. In the blink of an eye she became a blond, buxom country girl then changed once more, rising up three feet above the ground with a pair of white wings, short brunette hair, and a nimbus of light around her. Just as suddenly she became Teanna again.

"You manipulated the priest didn't you?"

Teanna smiled again but didn't reply.

"I thought it was too much of a coincidence for him to just stumble onto one of the rings and have it start working."

"Mathew . . . when I came here I was going to kill you. I had every intention of it—I really did. But then I saw how magnificent you were fighting the dragon and . . . I don't know. Armand is going to be furious with me."

"Armand?"

"My cousin, the present king of Alor Satar."

"The *present* king?"

"Do you remember what I told you once . . . a man who's not afraid of his destiny can hold the world in the palm of his hands?"

"Yes . . . I remember," he said.

"With my help you could be a king. No one could stop you . . . us. Not the Zargothans, the Mirdites, Bajan . . . any of them. Alor Satar and Nyngary were always meant to be one empire."

"Teanna—"

"*Listen* to me, Mathew," she said, the excitement shining in her eyes. "All of the other rings are gone. Only these are the two left now. Our power would be absolute. We could—"

"*Stop it,*" he said sharply. "First of all, we don't know that. Second, the Ancients created eight rings, so there are two more out there somewhere. They also spent their last hours trying to destroy them. Have you ever thought of why? I don't want to rule anyone. I've told you that."

"And is that what you want?" she asked, pointing at Lara.

Mathew nodded his head slowly. "If she'll have me . . . yes."

"I see."

"No, I don't think you do. You're beautiful, funny, intelligent. Anyone in his right mind would snap up your offer up in a minute. I'm flattered . . . truly I am, but—"

Mathew never got a chance to finish his sentence. A searing pain hit every part of his body at the same time. His muscles and skin suddenly felt like they were on fire. At the same time a terrible pressure began to build in his chest, crushing the air out of his lungs. From somewhere in the back of his mind, he heard a strangled sound and realized it was coming from him.

Teanna stood there and watched him collapse to his knees, her eyes ablaze with hatred as she walked toward him.

Mathew tried to fight back reaching for the power, but there was nothing there, only emptiness, a black void. His breath was coming in ragged gasps and bright points of light as floating stars began to appear in his field of vision. He fought with all his strength to remain conscious, but it was no use. He was dying and he knew it.

Teanna stood above him, her upper lip curled back in contempt.

"Stupid little man. I offer you the world and you're too ignorant and frightened to accept it. I don't know what I was thinking. *You* a fit companion—*an equal*," she laughed. "I suppose father was right after all. You can't spin gold out of straw. Pity."

Teanna almost spit the last words out.

Mathew could barely hear her; the words seemed to be coming from far away. He was dimly aware of it when she took his hand and twisted the ring off his finger.

"Goodbye, Mathew. Your little companion will be joining you in hell in just a moment. It's too bad, really—"

A shriek from Teanna abruptly split the air and her body arched backward, an expression of shock and rage contorting her beautiful features.

Through a red mist, Mathew looked up and saw that she had a knife sticking out of her back. A brilliant white light shot from her hands, accompanied by a loud bang. Then a second light seemed to envelop her. The crushing pain on Mathew's chest lessened, and as it did, the horrible burning sensation also left his body. The light around Teanna formed itself into a column then moved inward, becoming a slender line which compressed itself into a ball about the size of a fist and winked out of existence. Somewhere in the cavern the forlorn sound of a distant chime faded away.

Mathew's vision slowly began to return to normal. Indistinct shapes coalesced into familiar objects. Jeram Quinn lay on the ground about twenty feet away, a large charred spot on of his chest.

Mathew pushed himself up onto his knees and with an effort got to his feet. He half-walked, half-stumbled toward Quinn. The constable was up on one elbow, looking down at his chest when Gawl and Haynes came running up.

"Are you all right?" Mathew croaked. The sound of his own voice surprised him.

"I need a vacation," Quinn said. "I feel like I was hit by a bolt of lightning."

"Are you injured?"

Quinn tentatively felt his chest with the tips of his fingers and said, "No, I don't think so. Just give me a moment—I'm not as young as I used to be."

"What the hell happened now?" Gawl demanded.

"It seems the princess took a dislike to Mathew and tried to kill him," Quinn answered, getting to his feet. "Me too," he added, glancing down at the burn marks on his clothes.

"What? Where is she?"

"Gone," Quinn said with a shrug.

"Gone? What do you mean gone?" Gawl asked, looking around. "She didn't just disappear."

"I'm afraid that's exactly what she did," Quinn told him.

Gawl and Haynes turned to Mathew who nodded in agreement.

"I don't understand," said the colonel. "Why would she . . ."

Quinn took a deep breath and rubbed his neck. "It was Teanna's plan from the beginning to gain our trust, and when the time was right . . ." He shrugged again.

"How did you know?" asked Mathew.

"It's my job to know when people are lying," the constable replied. "I was never fully convinced that her sudden transformation was genuine. However strange her family might be, common sense says one does not simply forget the deaths of a mother and an uncle, even if they were Karas Duren and Marsa d'Elso. On top of that, there was the incident at the palace."

"Explain?" Gawl said.

"I confess I don't know a great deal about these rings.

I am a man who deals in cold facts. At the palace two men were killed in the attempt on Mathew's life. From all outward appearances, it appeared to be it was a case of self-defense," he said, nodding in Mathew's direction. "Nevertheless, something struck me as unusual about the scene. When I stooped down to examine the balcony railing, I saw that it wasn't broken and it hadn't pulled away from the foundation. The metal was melted . . . not bent or sawed through, or even rusted, but *melted*.

"Unless Mathew had suddenly developed a death wish, such a feat left only one other person with the ability to do so—Teanna d'Elso. Of course, I didn't know until later that another ring existed."

Gawl stood there digesting the information. He gave a short bark of a laugh and shook his head, but before he could comment a groan from Lara turned all heads toward her.

"Oh," she said, wincing in pain as Mathew helped her sit up.

"Slowly now."

Gawl squatted down next to her and smiled. Even down on his haunches, he was as tall as most men would be standing.

"How do you feel?" he asked softly.

"Like a building fell on me," she replied. Lara gasped the moment she tried to move her arm.

Gawl gently put a hand on her shoulder to restrain her. "Your arm is broken, Lara," he said. "We have to set it."

Lara looked at her arm, nodded, and leaned her head back against Mathew's chest.

"All right," she said.

"Brave girl. Haynes, do you have those pieces of metal we found?"

"Right here, your Majesty," the colonel replied, handing Gawl two pieces of metal. Each was badly bent and measured about three feet in length. Gawl examined them with a critical eye, then placed one of the pieces on a fallen block of masonry. He picked up a sizable chunk of rock and proceeded to hammer it straight, then repeated the process with the other piece. When he was finished he looked at them and gave a nod of satisfaction.

"They're still too long," Quinn observed.

"Hmm," said Gawl. He folded his arms across his chest and looked around at the rubble before spotting what he wanted. A few feet away lay a large piece of white stone. In two strides Gawl stepped over, picked it up, and set it on top of the first piece of masonry, effectively clamping the metal strips together. Mathew and Quinn opened their eyes a little wider—the stone probably weighed at least two hundred pounds. Gawl lifted his broadsword and with one swing cut both pieces neatly in half. He looked up at the three men who were watching him and displayed his teeth in what might have been a grin.

"We're going to need something to bind these with," he said, looking down at Lara.

"You can cut some strips from the bottom of my dress," she suggested.

"Do you understand what we have to do?" he asked quietly, then stooped down and sliced the material away with his dagger.

Lara looked into Gawl's warm brown eyes and saw that they were filled with concern and sympathy. Several seconds passed before she nodded to him.

He took hold of her wrist and braced her shoulder with his other hand. Mathew turned away, unable to watch. With a sudden snap Gawl pulled backward. The click made everyone wince.

Lara screamed and took several rapid breaths before she regained control of herself, though by what effort Mathew couldn't imagine. A vivid recollection of falling out of a tree and breaking his own arm when he was twelve flashed through his mind with such clarity it made his stomach feel funny. With a shudder he forced it away, knelt down beside her, and put an arm around her shoulders.

Lara's face was bathed in perspiration despite the coolness of the cavern air. Gawl positioned the splints and bound them together with deft fingers. All the while her large green eyes watched him, but she didn't make another sound. If the situation had been reversed, Mathew thought, he was certain he would have been yelling at the top of his lungs.

When it was over Gawl leaned forward and kissed her on the forehead.

"Good girl," he said.

Another piece of skirt was sacrificed for a sling after assuring the men her modesty wouldn't suffer too greatly. When it was done, Gawl examined the job and voiced his approval. He suggested they all take an hour's rest before trying to find a way out of the cavern. Nobody disagreed.

Mathew helped Lara to the ground and she laid her head in his lap. Gawl and Quinn stretched out next to them while Colonel Haynes insisted on remaining awake and taking the first watch. A few seconds after Lara closed her eyes, she opened them and whispered, "Gawl?"

The king rolled over and looked at her.

"Thank you."

For a moment it appeared that she was going say something else, but she changed her mind and put her head back on Mathew's lap. She was asleep in seconds.

33

The Second Cavern

MATHEW DID NOT SLEEP AT ALL. HE LEANED BACK against a section of a column and thought about the events that had just occurred. It was difficult keeping everything straight. There were a hundred questions he wanted to ask Lara before she fell asleep, though for the time being he kept them to himself. Not wanting to upset her he said nothing about Collin, though his friend was weighing heavily on his mind. It was possible Lara didn't even know he'd been hurt. No matter what he did, the image of Collin lying there bleeding simply wouldn't leave him.

He wanted to know the details about what happened and why Father Kellner had kidnapped her. He supposed it was to lure him into the cavern, but there was a lot that didn't make sense. It was clear now that Teanna had successfully played everyone from the beginning . . . Father Kellner and himself included. One ring was destroyed and his was gone—probably forever. The thought made him feel sick and hollow inside.

How could I have been so stupid?

He felt like a complete fool. He had let down his guard . . . and with Marsa d'Elso's daughter, of all people.

You've made a proper mess of things, he told himself. If Nyngary and Alor Satar decided to attack the West again, there would be no way to stop them, and that possibility made him even more sick at heart. For some reason his thoughts turned to his father. It had been almost a year since Bran was killed.

Has it really been that long? Mathew wondered. He wished that he could talk to Bran just one more time. Everything was such a jumble. His father was a practical, methodical man who never rushed into decisions without weighing the alternatives.

I should have turned out more like you, Father.

Mathew's fingers drummed absently against his thigh, careful not to wake Lara.

Bran often told him he had hands like his mother. From the small painting of her in their house, Mathew knew he favored her physically more than he did his father.

He tried pushing away the pain, but it came anyway. He glanced down at his hand and closed his eyes, wondering how much of Karas Duren lived on in his sons and in Teanna. How long before they turned toward Elgaria once more to crush it out of existence? Mathew didn't know the answer, and a sense of foreboding began to fill him. He stared at the third finger of his right hand, where his ring used to be, and a plan began to form in his mind, slowly at first and then with increasing clarity.

When he came out of his musings, Mathew looked down at Lara and with a small start realized that she was watching him.

"Did you just wake up?" he asked quietly.

"Um-hmm," she nodded.

"How are you feeling?" He kept his voice low so as not to disturb the others.

"I'm all right."

"Seriously."

"It hurts. Help me up, would you?"

"Maybe you should get a little more . . ."

The look he got put an end to the discussion. Mathew sighed and carefully placed a hand behind her head helping her into a sitting position. To his surprise she managed the rest of the way by herself.

"Stop looking at me like that; I'm not made of porcelain. The women in my family are all tougher than the men."

Mathew thought about it for a moment. He knew everyone in Lara's family, and decided she was probably right.

"Fine," he said, "but let's take it easy for a while, shall we?"

She surprised him by standing on tiptoe and kissing him on the lips.

"Walk with me," Lara said.

Colonel Haynes, who had been watching them, nodded as they crept quietly past Gawl and Quinn, trying not to make any noise. Gawl opened one eye, winked at them, then rolled over and went back to sleep, or at least gave the appearance of doing so. Mathew was not certain.

They strolled across the plaza toward the fountain, holding hands. Neither spoke. Mathew knew something was on her mind, and he also knew it would be best to wait until she was ready to talk.

The brick path led to the building Gawl and Haynes had originally started to investigate. At the top of the steps a pair of large bronze doors loomed. Each of the door panels, as well as the moldings surrounding it, contained miniature casts of scenes involving Orlocks and humans, something totally at odds with everything he knew about the strange creatures. Not only did Orlocks hate men, they were cannibals who killed without mercy. He stared at the door trying to make some sense out of it.

"I don't understand any of this," Lara said, breaking the silence.

Mathew slowly shook his head. "Neither do I. I guess at some point in the past we worked together with them, but it is hard to imagine."

"Let's go in," she suggested.

Once they had entered the building they found themselves standing at the back of a large auditorium. Frescoes lined the walls with scenes similar to the moldings around the door, but were so badly faded only hints of the original colors now remained.

Lara blinked and pointedly sniffed the air. "No one's been in here for ages," she said.

In front of them were at least thirty rows of seats arranged in a semicircle along three different aisles. The head of the room had a long marble podium with eight chairs behind it. In a niche off to one side was a statue of a blindfolded woman holding a set of scales. The opposite side of the room had a similar niche with an Orlock holding its arms out in what appeared to be a gesture of welcome. All around the walls of the auditorium were the names of countries Mathew had never heard of before. At least he thought they were countries: Gruneland, Talany, Vicoria, Bagani, Elgar Republic, Sentarian States. Though most were unknown to him, some, like the Elgar Republic, bore a striking resemblance to his own country of Elgaria.

"What is this place?" asked Lara.

"Some kind of court, I think."

"It doesn't look like any court I've ever seen."

"You haven't seen that many," Mathew pointed out. "It reminds me of the High Counsel Seat in Anderon. I was there once with my father when I was little."

Lara chose to ignore the first part of the sentence and said, "I don't understand what Orlocks and humans are doing in the same place."

Mathew was about to reply when he noticed an inscription carved on the wall over the doorway they had just entered. It read:

SEPARATUS T'EQUI

"What are you staring at?" she asked.

"That," he pointed.

"Those words?"

"It's the old language . . . 'separate but equal.' "

Lara considered the inscription for a minute and shook her head while Mathew walked around the room looking at a number of other inscriptions. She watched him and waited until he was through.

"This *was* a court," he said. "I'm not certain what all the words mean, but it definitely was a court. Those names up there must have been names of the original countries at one time. That third one . . . The Sentian States, probably became Sennia, and I imagine the Elgar Republic became Elgaria."

"So strange," Lara mused.

For the next ten minutes, they wandered around, poking their heads into different rooms. Most of them were empty, but a few still had pieces of strangely shaped furniture. On the side of the auditorium in an alcove, they found a list of names carved into a wall. Some of them were recognizable and some they couldn't even pronounce.

"Well, I don't see why we weren't told about this before," Lara said. "The Orlocks hate us, but it doesn't look like they always did. I wonder what happened."

"It's possible no one knows," Mathew suggested. "Most of the records were lost in wars."

Lara thought about it for a minute and started walking again. Once more she became quiet and preoccupied. She looked at the things Mathew pointed out, answering his questions with a simple yes or mm-hmm.

On the second floor Mathew stopped to examine a crystal chandelier hanging in one of the side boxes that overlooked the auditorium. He had seen chandeliers before, but this one was different. There was no place for any candles. In fact, where candles should have been were the same small oblong globes that Father Kellner had shown Lara in the ruins. He could see little wires in-

side them and got up on one of the balestrades on tiptoe
to get a closer look.

"Mathew?"

"Hmm?"

"Rowena is a traitor."

"What?" Mathew suddenly wheeled around to face her.

"Rowena is a traitor. So are Jared and her father."

Of all the things Mathew had been expecting to hear,
that was not one of them. He jumped down off the
balestrade and asked, "How do you know?"

"Her invitation for us to visit Camden Keep was just a
ruse. I overheard Lord Guy, Bishop Willis, Jared, and Father Kellner talking in their chapel about Sennia having a
new king. There was another man there, too. Guy called
him Lord Duren, but I'm almost positive it was his son,
Eric. They were using us to lure you here, so Father Kellner could kill you and Gawl. Collin and I tried to escape,
but I got caught again, and . . ."

"Oh, my God," she said, putting a hand up to her
mouth. "Collin! I haven't seen him since we tried to get
away. He insisted I take Cloud and make a run for it. I
was so worried about you with all this happening, I forgot. Oh, Mathew—"

"Shh," he said, taking her by the shoulders and pulling
her closer. "Collin's been hurt. I don't know how badly. It
was something Father Kellner did—an explosion of some
kind. I don't know where he is at the moment, but as soon
as we get out of this hole, I promise you, we're going to
find him."

Tears began to roll down Lara's face and she put her
head on Mathew's chest.

"I feel horrible. I should have said something sooner. I
started to before, but I didn't want to hurt Gawl. He's so
kind and gentle, and he loves Rowena. I know he does. I
just couldn't bear it . . . and then I fell asleep. Mathew,
we need to get the others and leave—right away."

"All right . . . all right," Mathew said, stroking her

hair. "You've been injured. Anyone can understand that. C'mon."

The news about Rowena and her father hit Mathew like a blow. *What kind of people are these?* he asked himself as they walked down the steps.

"Mathew, I don't know how I'm going to tell Gawl about this. This is going to—"

Lara's voice trailed away the moment they rounded the corner and almost collided with Gawl.

"Tell me what?" Gawl asked, rubbing the toes Mathew had just stepped on.

Lara opened her mouth to speak, but her voice seemed to have deserted her. Gawl's bushy eyebrows came together and he looked at Mathew.

"Tell me what?" he repeated.

Lara reached out and took Gawl's hand. "It's about Rowena . . . and her father," she began, searching for the right words. "Jared's involved too."

For the next minute or two Lara recounted what she had overheard in the chapel. She also told him about what happened at the ruins. Gawl listened without interrupting, his normally expressive face gradually turning to stone. Twice, he glanced at Mathew who had no idea what to do or say at that moment.

When Lara was finished, she said, "Oh, Gawl . . . I'm so sorry."

A small twitch appeared under the king's right eye and his chest rose and fell. He looked at each of them, then turned on his heel and left.

Mathew hurt for his friend. He wanted desperately to say something that would make him feel better. It was all so terribly wrong. No one deserved treachery and betrayal, particularly from the people they loved. Then his thoughts turned briefly to Teanna, and he berated himself once more for his own stupidity. He stood there watching Gawl walk away, his shoulders stiff and rigid. Lara slipped her arm around his waist and they stood there, together in silence for a time, before starting back across the plaza.

When they returned Colonel Haynes and Gawl were off to one side talking quietly. Quinn was busy trying to brush some of the black char from his jacket, where Teanna's blast had hit.

"Assuming everyone feels up to it, I suppose we'd better get a move on," Gawl said. "What about you, Lara?"

"I'm fine," she replied, even though Mathew suspected she really wasn't. On the way back she had stumbled on a brick in the path and the sudden movement caused her to gasp, her face going momentarily white. Mathew started to ask if she was all right, but she shook her head in annoyance and kept walking.

"I think the best thing to do is to try and find a way back up to the ledge, then see if we can locate one of the doors to the beehive room," Gawl said.

"What's a beehive room?" asked Lara.

"It's just what we're calling it for lack of a better description," Quinn explained. "It was probably the last room you passed through before you got to the ledge above the lake—the one with all the doors."

Lara frowned and thought for a second.

"We didn't see anything like that. There was the cave . . . then that long twisting passageway . . . then we just came down the steps underneath that strange house."

"What house?" everyone asked at the same time.

"At the end of the lake," said Lara. "Honestly, I don't see how you could have missed it."

"Which way did you come in?" asked Mathew.

"There," Lara said, pointing in the exact opposite direction from the way they had come.

"Perhaps you'd better show us," said Gawl.

Lara led them back to the main cavern and around to the far end of the lake.

"There's the house," she said.

"I don't see any house," Colonel Haynes replied.

"Look up."

"I still don't . . . oh, *good lord!*"

Mathew, Gawl and Quinn craned their necks back and saw what Haynes was looking at. Over a hundred feet up, set into a fissure, was a small house that appeared to be made of the same type of rock as the cavern wall itself.

"Incredible," said Quinn.

"Why in God's name would anybody even think of putting a house up there in the first place?" asked Haynes.

"Maybe they didn't like company," Quinn suggested, staring up at it. "It would certainly cut down on the number of callers."

"The stairs are over there by that big boulder," Lara said. "They come out in a long narrow room with a door at the end of it that leads to the tunnel."

"Where does that take you?" asked Gawl.

"It comes out on a hill above Argenton," she said.

Before they left the cavern Mathew stopped for a moment and turned around. In shifting light it was difficult to fix specific details clearly, but he tried picking out Sandy Johnson's grave. His eyes met with Colonel Haynes and he wondered whether they were both thinking the same thing. He had no idea if Haynes and Johnson had been close, or even how they felt about one another, but it was gratifying when the colonel saluted in Johnson's direction before following the rest of the party out.

Despite Lara's prediction, the way back proved to be a far longer journey than they anticipated. At some point during the trip it became apparent they had taken a wrong turn and they spent nearly an hour backtracking before they found the place they had originally started from. No argued with Jeram Quinn when he suggested they take a brief rest.

When they started again, Gawl took the extra precaution of marking their progress by placing three parallel lines on the cave walls every hundred yards or so. Judging from the grim expression on Colonel Haynes's face, Mathew guessed Gawl had already told him the news. Lord Guy's betrayal was bad enough, but to find the woman he loved was also a part of the conspiracy must have been a terrible blow. Mathew wanted to do something to ease Gawl's pain, but couldn't think of anything to say that would make a difference, so he walked along in silence with the rest of the party.

Lara's solution to the problem was uniquely her own. She separated from Mathew, caught up with Gawl, and slipped her arm through his. They walked the rest of the way together, her head resting against him. They talked for quite a long time. Mathew couldn't hear what they were saying, but he was more than grateful to see Gawl's face relax, if only a little. The king smiled at her, bent down, and kissed the top of her head. It was a gentle smile, though a sad one. Nevertheless, it was a step in the right direction.

In a little over four hours, after two more false starts, they emerged in the basement of a building. No one was in favor of backtracking again, so they began searching to locate a way out. It took five minutes to do so. One glance was enough to tell them they had somehow come out in the ruins. Night had already fallen and the sky was filled with stars. The temperature had also dropped considerably, accompanied by a sharp wind. Mathew took off his cloak and put it around Lara's shoulders. The climb had nearly drained her and she accepted it without argument. None of them had eaten in hours, and despite the brave front she was putting up, Mathew knew what the effects of the fall and her broken arm were having on her. The first thing he wanted was to get her someplace where she could rest and get the proper medical attention.

Colonel Haynes and Gawl moved to opposite sides of the street and took the lead. They were followed by Mathew, who kept a protective arm around Lara's shoulders, while Jeram Quinn brought up the rear. Mathew peered down a darkened alley as they walked, his free hand resting lightly on the hilt of his sword. Outside of crickets and the occasional cry of a night bird, the ruins appeared to be deserted. His assumption proved incorrect almost immediately.

A noise from the building on their left caused Gawl to turn and draw his broadsword. Stepping in front of Lara, Mathew did the same.

A slender figure separated itself from the shadows and said, "It took you long enough."

Mathew recognized the voice immediately—*Father Thomas!*

"My apologies, Siward," Gawl rumbled, crossing the street to embrace his friend.

Father Thomas was as tall as Mathew, but he disappeared from view when Gawl threw his arms around him. The moment the priest saw Lara, he extricated himself from the bear hug and came directly over.

"What happened, my child?" he asked.

"I'm all right," Lara mumbled, returning his kiss on the cheek.

Father Thomas looked at Mathew for an explanation.

"She broke her arm when—"

"Mathew knocked me off a building," she said.

Mathew opened his mouth to protest, realized he was being teased, and shut it again.

"And Kellner?" Father Kellner asked.

"Dead by Teanna's hand," Gawl replied, behind him.

The priest nodded and looked around, noticing for the first time that Teanna d'Elso was not with those who had returned.

"Was Teanna . . ."

"It's a long story, Siward," Gawl said. "We can talk about it while we walk. Where are the others?"

Father Thomas's hesitation caused Gawl to look at him closely.

"I'm afraid I have bad news, my friend," Father Thomas said, placing a hand on Gawl's forearm. "We were attacked by Edward Guy's soldiers shortly after we entered this place. Two men were killed—a corporal named Jones and young fellow whose name was Bill Baxter, I believe. The rest of the men are farther up the street. I sent one back to the palace for reinforcements."

"Reinforcements?"

"More of Guy's men began to arrive about an hour ago," Father Thomas explained. "Whoever their commander is, he's a cautious man. They sent a scout ahead to see if their ambush was successful. When he didn't return, they elected to make camp rather than launch a full-scale assault. That situation is going to last only until the morning. It's a bet whether the garrison from the palace will arrive in time."

"Treason," Haynes spat, when Father Thomas was finished. "Black, bloody treason."

Gawl listened, then told Father Thomas what happened in the cavern. The news about Teanna and the death of Aldrich Kellner only confirmed what the priest already knew. There was a rebellion in progress.

"Do you have any idea how many men they have, Father?" Colonel Haynes asked.

"I would say, at least two hundred. I took the liberty of going up into one of the taller buildings with Lieutenant Blake—an excellent officer, by the way. It's amazing how much one can see from up there."

"Two hundred," said Gawl. "That puts us in a proper fix. Guy's obviously thought the whole thing through. We're trapped and the only way out of here is back through the town or along the river."

"What about the mountains?" asked Quinn.

"Too much snow," Gawl muttered. "There's not all that much down here, but at the higher elevations . . ." The king shook his head.

"We need to look for Collin first," Mathew said. "He

may be here in the ruins someplace. Father Kellner told Lara they had him in the same building where they were holding her."

"All right, let's see if we can find him, then," Gawl said. "Which building was it?"

"It's on the next street—the second one on the left," Lara said pointing.

"Do you have any idea where in the building they were keeping him?" Haynes asked.

"Provided Father Kellner was telling the truth, it could be someplace on the seventh floor, but he may be injured," she added quietly.

Gawl turned to Colonel Haynes and said, "We'll try and find the boy. Get the rest of the men and meet us back here in ten minutes."

When they approached the building, they saw it was pitch dark inside.

"We're going to need torches," Mathew said.

"Give me a minute," said Father Thomas. He trotted down the street and returned with two blood-stained cloaks. A nearby tree and a few swings of Gawl's broadsword provided the branches to wrap them around. When they were through, Jeram Quinn retrieved a match from the pocket of his vest and was about to light the torches when Father Thomas stopped him.

"Wait until we get inside, Jeram. We don't want our friends to see what we're about."

Quinn did as instructed and handed one of them to Mathew. Once lit, the torches filled the lobby with orange light. It took Lara a moment to orient herself and locate the staircase. They decided to start with the same floor Lara had originally escaped from and then try the others if that turned up blank.

"Which one?" asked Jeram Quinn, looking at the rooms along the corridor once they got there.

Lara frowned and shook her head. "I'm not sure."

"All right let's check them all," said Gawl. "Siward and I will go this way. You, Mathew, and Lara take the others."

For the next five minutes they searched the rooms on the floor one by one, and with each door they opened the sinking feeling in Mathew's stomach continued to grow.

What if he's dead? he thought, as he closed yet another door.

Finally only one room remained at the very end of a long hallway. In the flickering torchlight their shadows floated along the walls at their heels. On the opposite side of the floor Mathew could hear other doors opening and shutting as Father Thomas and Gawl went through the last of the rooms. Though Lara was making a brave effort to keep up, Mathew noticed she was beginning to drag her feet.

The closer they drew to the final door, the more his trepidation increased. He prayed that they would find Collin there, alive and well, but it didn't seem likely. A second later his prediction proved correct. The room was empty. A number of footprints could be seen on the dusty floor and a trail led away from the door indicating something, or someone, had been dragged across it recently. Quinn poked his head into the room and looked around.

"No one here I'm afraid," he said.

"But there was," said Mathew, pointing down at the marks.

"So I see."

Mathew held his torch higher and walked to the window. The moon was already out. He was high enough up to see the town of Argenton in the distance and the road back to Camden Keep. He could also see the campfires of Lord Guy's men dotting the landscape behind the main gate. The ruins stretched out in the darkness, monolithic shapes from a dead past. Gradually he became aware that the city was not laid out on a square grid as so many of the places he had visited were. This one reminded him of Bexley's wagon-wheel shape. One street ran completely around its perimeter and in the center was a fountain with a number of other streets extending off it in different directions. He was about to mention the odd configuration to the others when he glanced down and noticed something on the floor. Mixed in with the dust were several dark brown smears that could have only been dried blood. He stared at them for a moment, then used the side of his boot to cover them up, hoping Lara wouldn't notice.

"We'd better find the others," Jeram Quinn said, turning to leave.

Mathew started to follow when Lara suddenly exclaimed, "Look!"

He and Quinn both turned to see what she was pointing to.

By the side of the door someone had written the words "Camden Keep" in the dust. Underneath was the letter "C." Mathew didn't have to guess who the author was. There was little question in his mind that his friend was injured, but there was a good chance he was alive or they probably would have left his body in the room. It felt like a weight had been lifted off his chest.

Gawl and Father Thomas met them into the hallway. While Quinn filled them in on what they found, Mathew stayed a little apart from the group. Something was bothering him. Try as he might he was unable to put his finger on it because of the concern over his friend. After a minute he gave up. Collin Miller was his first priority and everything else would just have to wait. It was obvious, they were holding him prisoner at Camden Keep. The problem now was how to get him out. He was still thinking about what to do when they reached the street. Rodney Blake and Colonel Haynes were waiting for them along with the other two men. Everyone looked badly in need of sleep.

"They're camped for the night, my Lord," said the colonel. "There are sentries posted every hundred feet and at least twenty men are guarding the road."

"Any chance of our circling around and reaching the river?" Gawl asked.

"None, your highness," Blake answered. "I sent one of the men to scout the area. Any attempt would be doomed."

"I think there is a way," Mathew said. Everyone turned to look at him.

"We entered the cave on the other side of Argenton and came out here in the town after we got lost. So we know there are at least two ways out. My guess is there are more. If we can find the original tunnel again, we could probably use it to get around the soldiers."

"And what if we can't find it?" asked Quinn. "The place is a maze."

"Some chance is better than none at all, Jeram," said Father Thomas. "If the garrison doesn't return in time, they won't have a king to rescue. Guy's men aren't going to wait beyond first light."

"Not many options," Gawl agreed.

"I don't see that we have another choice your majesty," said Colonel Haynes. "Our first concern is getting you to safety. Father Thomas is right; we can't stay here any longer."

"What makes you think we can find the original tunnel again?" Quinn asked Mathew. "If we get lost we could be down there forever."

"It's just a hunch, but I think it makes sense," said Mathew. "In fact, I'm not even sure the original tunnel is necessary. The cavern is big enough to hold a lot of people; so are the buildings. I can't believe that whoever built them didn't provide a more efficient means of getting in and out. There are probably any number of exits."

Colonel Haynes stuck his lower lip out. "I think we should try it," he said, nodding.

Gawl stared at the colonel and then at Father Thomas

for several seconds before turning on his heel and heading down the street in the direction they came from.

"I'll need a man at the point and another to bring up the rear," Colonel Haynes told Rodney Blake.

The lieutenant nodded and pointed to Hudson.

34

The Cavern

THE DESCENT DOWN THE STEPS WAS FAR LESS EXHAUST-
ing than the climb up had been. Prior to their entering the
building that led to the tunnel, Father Thomas asked
everyone to wait while he and Rodney Blake disappeared
for a few minutes. They returned carrying a sizeable
bunch of dark berries wrapped in Blake's cloak.

Mathew tentatively tasted one and found that they
were surprisingly sweet—not at all what he expected. His
first bite reminded him how hungry he was and he gob-
bled down his share in a few bites.

"They grow wild all around here in the winter," Blake
said, between bites." They can save your life if you're
lost. Travelers have been known to go for days on them."

The prospect of eating berries for days didn't appeal to
Mathew, but at the moment he was glad to have them and
even more gratified to see Lara perk up a little after trying
a few. With their meager meal completed and some of
their energy restored, the group, now larger by a priest
and two soldiers, made their way into the cavern.

Once they located the marks Gawl had left, it took less
than an hour before the last member of the party emerged
on the ledge to find themselves overlooking the cavern
lake. In the distance Mathew could see the statues; and
through the opening in the rock wall, the streets and plaza
of the second cavern.

The others began to clamber down the steps to the

lake's base, but Mathew remained where he was, staring at it. There was something about the plaza's layout that seemed familiar, and he stood there trying to pin down what it was.

"C'mon, Mat," Gawl yelled.

Still Mathew didn't move. After a few seconds he began tracing lines in the air with his forefinger as if he was drawing.

"Mathew," Lara prompted.

Then it hit him. The shape of the plaza, the streets, all reminded him of a . . . wagon wheel!

"That's it," he said aloud.

"What is?" Father Thomas called up to him.

"That," Mathew said excitedly, pointing. "I think I know how to get to the original passage."

Gawl turned and bounded up the steps three at a time and looked in the direction Mathew was pointing. He stared out across the lake at the plaza, his hands on his hips. Almost twenty seconds passed before he said, "Well done," and clapped Mathew on the shoulder, nearly buckling his knees in the process.

"A mirror image of the ruins," Jeram Quinn remarked. "I didn't recognize it from up there. Excellent work, young man . . . excellent."

"If it is, that street at the far end will continue around and eventually intersect with the tunnel," said Colonel Haynes. "That was brilliant, my boy."

Mathew accepted the compliments with a grin, then changed the subject.

The party skirted the lake, making their way to the second cavern. The brick paths that ran off the fountain all came to dead ends at different buildings. That didn't bother Mathew at all because he already knew they would continue on to the perimeter road that circled the complex. If he was correct, there would be a second, larger perimeter that would eventually link up to a surface passageway.

Without being asked, he took the lead. Rather than go through the building, Mathew went around it and found the street he was looking for at the rear. He followed it with his eyes and could see where it intersected the perimeter. The left side disappeared into the darkness. Mathew peered down it for a second, then thought about Collin and turned right heading for the original tunnel.

In time they reached the beehive room, though it was by an entirely different route. An almost audible sigh of relief could be heard from everyone there when they saw the passageway on the other side. They finally emerged from the cave on the hill above Argenton to a night alive with stars. From their vantage point they could see a few lights were still on in the town. Dawn was at least several hours away.

"The palace garrison will be coming from the southeast," the king said. "Assuming we can find enough horses, we'll ride across country and intercept our people before they get to Camden Keep."

"Your highness, I'm as much in favor of hanging every one of the traitorous dogs as you are," Haynes replied, "but we can't go charging into the Keep without knowing what we're up against. We also need to know who is involved."

Gawl looked like he was about to argue the point when he noticed Rodney Blake nodding in agreement and said, "Well?"

"I'm afraid the colonel is right, sire. We could very well find ourselves pinned between the walls of the castle and an attack force of indeterminate size. Intelligence is what we need at the moment. Considering the number of noble families that derive their income from wine production in this region, we need to know who is with us and who is against us."

When the lieutenant finished his speech he darted a quick glance at Father Thomas who gave him a smile.

"And I suppose you feel the same way?" Gawl asked, turning to the priest.

"I do. This might be confined to just one family, but I wouldn't be willing to risk your kingdom on a guess."

Mathew listened to the conversations, his concern mounting with each passing minute. He was torn between wanting to stay and help Gawl and the need to find Collin. He also had to get Lara to a place of safety.

Gawl's chest rose and fell as he considered what to do. "All right," he said to Colonel Haynes, "send one of your men down to have a look. I'll give you twenty minutes."

"I'll go," Blake volunteered.

While they were waiting for him to return Mathew walked over to a group of bushes, squatted down, and looked out at the sleeping town. Everything seemed quiet, but looks were often deceiving. Twice he caught glimpses of Rodney Blake moving from tree to tree down the hillside. A night mist still clung to the ground, and eventually it obscured Blake from view. Mathew was still trying to pick him out when a light footfall behind him caused him to turn away.

He and Lara exchanged smiles and she sat down beside him, resting her back against a boulder. She grimaced, and adjusted herself into a comfortable position, but made no complaint. Mathew moved away from the edge and sat down beside her.

"How are you feeling?" he asked.

"Well enough."

A silence ensued before she spoke again. "You're not going with Gawl are you?"

Mathew's surprise was obvious.

"You're probably a terrible card player," she said, resting her head on his shoulder. "Everything is written on your face."

"It is not," he said indignantly.

Lara didn't reply. She looked up at him for a second, then put her head back on his shoulder.

"All right, maybe it is," Mathew replied. "But I don't have a choice. Collin would do the same for me. So would you."

"So would I," Lara echoed quietly.

Mathew slid his arm around her shoulders and squeezed gently.

"Tell me about Camden Keep. I need to know how it's laid out."

Lara took a breath. "Basically it's a sprawl—a collection of different buildings that are all linked together. I think there are four of them. It takes a while just to find your way around."

"Is there a dungeon or jail where they would keep a prisoner?"

Lara made a little clicking noise with her tongue behind her teeth while she thought about the question.

"When I was there Jared and Rowena gave me a tour of the castle. It was probably just to keep me busy, but I remember that they had a tower. You can see it from the main road. He said that was where they kept King Behnam before he was executed . . . but that was more than three hundred years ago."

"The Sennians executed their king?" Mathew asked, shocked.

"That's what he told me."

"Well, I wouldn't believe anything that loudmouthed braggart says. They probably don't even have a tower and he was just trying to sound important."

"I saw it," Lara said wearily. "Lord Guy was regent before Gawl took the throne."

"Oh," said Mathew.

"You don't have your ring anymore," she said, changing the subject.

"No," Mathew answered, looking off into the distance. "How did—"

"I heard Jeram Quinn telling Father about what happened with Teanna d'Elso in the cavern."

"I see."

"Do you want to talk about it?"

"No. Not right now."

Lara shook her head slightly. "Mathew . . . I think you should wait for the palace garrison to arrive. I'm as worried about Collin as you are, but without your ring . . ."

"What chance do you think he'll have?" he said, recalling the bloodstains on the floor. "He's hurt and alone. And if I'm any judge of character, Jared won't hesitate to kill him the moment they see Gawl's soldiers at the gate."

"But—"

"I *have* to go, Lara. There's no other way."

A time passed before she said anything. She knew Mathew better than anyone in the world and admitted that she was in love with him. A lump began to form in her throat. More than anything she wanted to be gone from Sennia—to be back home in Devondale. *No more plots,* she thought. *No more intrigues. No more rings.* But at the moment home seemed very far away.

Mathew's decision to try and rescue Collin came as no surprise to her. She'd been expecting as much and initially considered trying to talk him out of it, but the set of his jaw told her arguing would be pointless. She knew the look.

"There's a door at the rear wall that leads into the castle," she told him quietly. "Rowena showed it to me when we went for a walk. You practically have to be standing in front of it to see it because it's almost completely covered by hedges. She told me that she and her older brother used it to sneak out when they were younger."

Lara didn't look up at Mathew as she spoke. She could feel him watching her, but she kept looking straight ahead.

"You saw it?" he asked.

"Um-hmm. We used it as a shortcut to the gardens the second day I was there."

"What's on the inside?"

"The kitchens and servants' quarters. There's a long tunnel with a door at the end and a staircase that goes up to the main dining room. It comes out behind a tapestry."

"Wonderful," Mathew said, "more stairs and another tunnel."

"Are you going by yourself?"

"If need be. Gawl has to get to his men. I doubt if he'll be able to spare any at the moment. From what they tell me, a direct assault on Camden Keep might take days or weeks, and we don't have that much time—at least Collin doesn't. I think one person will have a better chance of getting in and out unnoticed. An army can't do that."

"But there's not going to be one person on the way out," Lara said. "What if Collin can't walk?"

"I don't know. I just know I have to do something. I'll figure it out once I'm there."

"What about Father Thomas?"

"I can't ask him. And neither can you," said Mathew. "And, no, you can't come," he added, guessing her thoughts. "Not in your condition. We need to get you to a doctor."

Lara opened her mouth to speak, but Mathew cut her off when he touched her face with his fingertips.

"You know I'm right," he said. "It's got to be done. I'll leave once we get to the village."

Whatever other arguments Lara might have advanced were interrupted by the return of Rodney Blake.

"Everything looks clear," Blake said. "There are at least eight horses in the stables—more than we need. The stableman he told me Guy's men rode through late in the afternoon yesterday. He also told me that his lordship has announced you're dead, your majesty."

"Not quite," Gawl growled.

"He said that Guy's soldiers are stationed at the main road and, ah . . ." The lieutenant's words trailed away as he searched for the right words.

"What is it man?" Colonel Haynes snapped. "Out
with it."

"Anthony, that's the fellow I met, told me Baron
d'Jordin, Lord Alcote, and his brother, Lord Fenwick,
have sent soldiers to support Guy's takeover."

"All the major wine-producing families," said Colonel
Haynes, shaking his head.

"First we have to reach our people," said Gawl, "and
that won't be easy if they have the main road blocked.
They can probably raise at about two thousand men between them. How many do we have at the palace?"

"Fifteen hundred," Haynes answered. "But the southern army is only a day away at Stanhope."

"All right. We need to move and move fast. Send a
message with one of your men. It's a day there and a day
back. Hopefully, we can get them back here in time. If I
give up the throne, I'd like it to be my own idea, not
theirs."

"Gawl, I think it would be better if we sent two men to
make sure the message gets to General Ballenger," suggested Father Thomas.

"What if we encounter Guy's soldiers?" asked Haynes.

"Getting the message through is more important. If we
do run into one of Guy's patrols, two more bodies on our
side won't make much difference," Father Thomas replied.

"I agree," said Colonel Hayes.

The colonel thought for a moment, then turned to
Lieutenant Blake and said, "Pick whomever you think is
best, Rodney. Was there anything else?"

"Actually . . . yes," Blake replied. "Lord Guy's been
posting notices everywhere that he has assumed the regency again . . . with the blessing of the church."

He reached into his shirt and laid a folded piece of
parchment on the ground in front of Gawl. It read:

BY THE GRACE OF GOD, AND WITH THE BLESSING OF
THE HOLY CHURCH, IN ACCORDANCE WITH SENNIAN

LAW AND CUSTOM, EDWARD GUY, LORD OF CAMDEN
AND EARL OF STEWARD AND MACLAND PROVINCES,
HAS BEEN APPOINTED BY THE PRIVY COUNCIL TO
ASSUME THE REGENCY UNTIL SUCH TIME AS A NEW
KING SHALL BE CROWNED.

    THIS 6TH DAY OF TANRIL

                MARTIN CUMMINGS D'LEON, EARL
                LORD OF ALCOTE

"Well, you're just full of good news, aren't you?" said
Gawl.

"I'm sorry your majesty."

Gawl gave the young lieutenant a sour look and turned
to Father Thomas. "Any ideas, Siward?"

"Several. Let's start moving. Time is going to be of the
essence."

35

Argenton

DURING THE TRIP INTO TOWN MATHEW WAS DREADING what he had to say. When they reached the main street, he caught up with Gawl and Father Thomas, who were walking together and told them what he wanted to do. To his surprise, neither of them tried to talk him out of it.

"Siward and I were just discussing the problem," said Gawl. "We both agree that if Collin doesn't get out of there quickly, it's not likely he'll be seen again—alive anyway. There is a history of people going into the Keep and never coming out. On top of that—"

"He's too dangerous a witness," Father Thomas said, finishing the sentence for him. "At this point Guy doesn't know if his ambush has worked or not. If everything went as planned, Gawl is dead, and he's back in power. All they know now is that the soldiers at the ruins are missing."

"In all likelihood they'll send one of their men back to report," Gawl explained. "We're going to leave Mickens to see that whoever it is doesn't get through. That should buy you and Blake enough time to get Collin out."

"Blake?" said Mathew. "I don't understand."

"Rodney Blake and Jared Guy know each other. They're teammates," Gawl reminded him. "He's been in the Keep before, and you may need help if Collin is injured."

"Siward can fill you in on the rest. I need to speak to Haynes for a moment."

Gawl squeezed Mathew's shoulder and moved off to

the opposite side of the street where he and Colonel Haynes began talking. Father Thomas watched the giant for a moment and shook his head sadly.

"He's been very hurt by what happened. He and Rowena were going to announce their wedding plans at the conference later this week."

Mathew closed his eyes. The enormity of Rowena's betrayal was just beginning to sink in on him. It was amazing to him that his friend could still function at all. The fact that the whole thing was over wine profits made him ill. Mathew took a deep breath and looked at the priest.

In response to the unasked question, Father Thomas said, "I would come with you if I could, my son. But the present circumstances make it imperative for me to stay here and lend what help I can to Gawl. It appears Edward Guy has timed his actions extremely well. The southern army is two day's away, and the western units are at least a four-day ride. On top of that, Guy is claiming to have the church on his side, which makes matters much more difficult."

"I don't understand, Father. How can the church be on his side?"

Father Thomas shrugged. "They may be and they may not be; it's impossible to say without more information. The truth is that Gawl has not been on the best of terms with the church since he came to power. According to what Lara told us, Ferdinand Willis is with the traitors, and he's a member of the Upper Council."

"I don't believe the church would do that," said Mathew. "At least not without talking to him. It doesn't make sense."

"Neither do I. But to many people, appearances can be reality. I suspect this is what we're dealing with here. Sennia has always been a country where the king rules subject to the blessing of the church. If the people no longer believes Gawl has that blessing, they won't support him, and—"

"Neither will the army," Mathew said.

"Correct. So you understand why Gawl needs to have someone with sufficient military experience he can count on. I would go with you if I could, but at the moment the needs of the many outweigh the needs of the one."

"You think Collin's dead, don't you?" Mathew asked.

Father Thomas stopped walking and turned to him. "I don't know, Mathew," he said quietly. "They could have taken him for any number of reasons, none of them good. What I am clear on is that at the first sign of an direct assault, they'll make certain there are no witnesses left. Traditions are very important to the Sennians. They are likely to accept the removal of a king, if it's done according to law and custom, but they would never accept his murder."

The stableman Rodney Blake told them about was an elderly fellow named Anthony, who had a bad leg. He was waiting for them in the stables. Gawl frowned when he noticed the horses were already saddled. He turned to Rodney Blake.

"I thought your majesty would agree, so I took the liberty of seeing that things would be ready."

Gawl muttered something under his breath, then fished around in the pocket of his vest and pulled out his coin purse. He tossed it to Anthony, who caught it. The old stableman hefted the purse in his hand a couple of times then opened it and spilled the coins into his palm. He looked at the money and took out four crowns, then put the rest back in and handed it to Gawl.

"Fair is fair," he said. "There's a single track at the end of the town that will take you to the other side of the forest. The main road is about a half-mile to the southeast. You've been a good king so far; see you keep it that way."

"Thank you, my friend," said Gawl.

Anthony started for the door, but stopped when he saw Mathew and stared at him.

"You're the Lewin boy, aren't you?"

"Yes, sir."

"You really do all those things at Ardon Field that everyone's been talking about?"

"Well . . . uh . . ."

"Never mind. See you watch your back, son. The first thing Guy's soldiers did when they got here yesterday was to ask about you."

"Thanks for the advice," said Mathew.

"What advice?" Anthony replied, over his shoulder. "I haven't seen anybody since I went to bed last night."

Mathew watched the old man limp through the door and walk back to his house. The loss of his ring hit him again. In recent months it had become so much a part of him that it took all of his willpower not to spend every minute dwelling on it. Rescuing Collin was his first priority, ring or no ring. He'd deal with the rest later.

The track Anthony mentioned was only wide enough to allow them to proceed single file. In the crisp night air, the horses' hooves crunched noisily over the frozen ground. Given their circumstances it was impossible to risk using torches. Fortunately it was light enough to see by. The moon was far lower on the eastern horizon than when they came out of the cave, he thought. Sunrise couldn't be more than a couple of hours away. Ahead of him Mathew could make out Lara's silhouette in the dark as she rode along.

The thought of her filled him with love. She had risked her life to save him from Kellner's trap. It made him feel both good and bad at the same time, because it also reminded him of how he had flirted with Teanna. For some reason Lara chose just that moment to turn in her saddle and look back at him. He couldn't see her face very clearly and hoped she couldn't see his.

Maybe Daniel's right, he thought, and they *can* read

minds. Not wanting to test the theory, Mathew looked away.

When the trees began to thin, they changed their direction and headed southeast as Andrew had told them. A short distance ahead, twin ribbons of moonlight marked the road to Camden Keep and the way back to Barcora.

Colonel Haynes brought his horse alongside Sergeant Mickens and was saying something that Mathew couldn't quite catch. Mickens nodded as the colonel spoke, then spurred his horse forward and disappeared into the trees. The rest of the party continued to the fork where they stopped to wait for the advance scout. While they did Mathew and Lara dismounted and walked away from the others.

There were so many things he wanted to say. Twice he began to tell her how much she meant to him, but the words seemed to catch in his throat. He gave up and rested his forehead against hers. They stayed like that for only a short space of time before Lara pushed herself back, absently reached up, and brushed a single lock of hair away from his eyes.

"I love you, Mathew," she said. "Come back to me."

Mathew opened his mouth to reply, but she put her fingers over his lips.

"Come back to me," she whispered.

For a moment he felt as though his heart was going to break, and the pain was almost more than he could bear. In later years, when he thought about what she had said to him, and he did many times, he decided that perhaps she *had* read his mind, but they never spoke of it again.

36

Camden Keep

IT WAS COLD IN THE FOREST, A BITTER COLD THAT seemed to reach deep into the bones. Mathew Lewin pulled his cloak tighter and tried to keep his teeth from chattering. He was tired, sore, and damp. Rodney Blake sat with his back against a tree a few feet away. A hundred yards in front of them, the gray walls of Camden Keep loomed. Because the castle was situated on a promontory, they had been forced to leave their horses at the bottom of the hill and make the climb up on foot. Although the trip was slightly less than a mile, it was an exhausting one. Not only was the snow deeper in the trees than along the road, ice-coated rocks made their footing treacherous and frozen roots reached out threatening to snag their ankles. Despite the cold, Mathew was sweating by the time they reached the summit of the hill and was grateful when Blake suggested they take a short break to regain their breath. On the eastern horizon the sky was already showing signs of light.

"Lara said the door would be at the south end of the garden, between some cherry laurel hedges," Mathew said, keeping his voice down.

Blake nodded and squinted into the darkness. "We can use tree cover except for the last fifty yards or so."

"Have you ever been here before?" Mathew asked.

"A few times, but I don't remember much about the

layout. The castle is so large it's going to take us time to find out where they're keeping him."

"Lara thought the tower would be our best bet."

"I agree," Blake replied. "All we have to do is locate it. Unfortunately, we can't stop any of the servants and ask for directions."

Mathew smiled back at him and asked, "How are you feeling?"

"Like I could sleep for a week. You?"

"The same," Mathew said. "We'd better get moving."

Blake rose to a low crouch and began to thread his way through the trees with Mathew following close behind. Twice along the way they were forced to stop as the silhouette of a soldier walking guard duty appeared on the parapet above them. Fortunately, the man completed his rounds quickly and returned to the warmth of his guard hut. During the night the temperature had continued to drop, which was both good and bad. It kept people inside, but it also made it more difficult on Blake and Mathew.

"Still doing okay?" Blake asked when Mathew stopped again and leaned against a tree.

"Freezing," he replied, rubbing his upper forearms to restore some circulation.

"Me too. I think those are the hedges Lara was talking about," he said, pointing.

Mathew followed the line of the lieutenant's arm. "Right. Let's get our breath and make a run for it."

"If I've timed it correctly," Blake said, "the guards are walking rounds about every fifteen minutes, so we shouldn't cut it too close."

"Rodney, do you mind if I ask you a question?"

"What is it?" Blake said, turning to look at him.

"When we were in Barcora at the game, Jared said something about not wanting to sit with a bunch of Parbees. I was just wondering what he meant by it."

Blake's eyes searched Mathew's face for several seconds before he answered. "It's a derogatory term, Mat. Anyone who's not from here, Sennia that is, is a Parblood. Parbee is just an abbreviation; it means mixed blood. All kinds of people come to the stadium, but the tickets tend to go to native Sennians, despite what the Ashots say. Not everyone feels that way—in fact, most don't. It tends to be the northern sects, like Rowena and her bunch, but I'd be lying if I didn't say there's still a lot of prejudice around."

"I see. Wouldn't that make me a—"

"A Parbee. But like I said, not everyone feels that way. Old habits die hard. Until Gawl took power and began dropping restrictions on entering the country, we were pretty much a little community unto ourselves."

Mathew nodded, slowly digesting the concept. "What do you think Gawl is going to do with her?"

"Her?"

"Rowena."

"The king's a lot brighter than people give him credit for. He's not just some hulking giant who just happened to win the Olyiad. He's good with people, and he loves our country. I'm carrying a letter in my pocket that grants Rowena and her family amnesty."

Blake patted the breast pocket of his cloak for emphasis. "They'll be banished of course, but at least they'll have their heads. It's more than I would have done."

Rodney Blake's revelation surprised him. He had seen the look on Gawl's face when Lara told him the news about Rowena, and he knew firsthand how ferocious Gawl could be when angered. Not only had his friend been betrayed as a king, he'd been betrayed as a man, and by someone he was in love with. In one moment all of Gawl's hopes and dreams had been shattered, terribly so. Under the circumstances he wasn't sure he could do the same thing.

"I hope you don't plan on trying to deliver that letter in person," Mathew said.

Blake shook his head. "I'm just supposed to leave it in a conspicuous place, for all the good it will do."

"Do you think we'll find Collin alive, Rodney?"

"I don't know," Blake answered, putting a hand on Mathew's shoulder. "The taking of hostages is against our beliefs, but then so is treason. If Lord Guy were to kill someone he was holding, he'd have to deal with not only the church but the people too, and I can tell you that my countrymen won't take such a thing lightly. So there's a good chance—"

"Unless he makes it look like an accident," said Mathew.

"Unless he makes it look like an accident," Blake echoed.

"What I don't understand is why the church is going along with all this," Mathew said. "If they're so unhappy about what Gawl is doing, why didn't they just come and speak with him?"

"They probably did, Mat—more than once in all likelihood. Unfortunately, Gawl isn't the easiest person to talk to once he's made his mind up about something."

Mathew was about to ask another question when he heard a rustling noise in the bushes. He and Blake both turned to look at the same time.

At first he didn't believe what he was seeing and almost blurted out his surprise. Three pair of iridescent eyes gleaming in the dark stared back at them. It took Mathew a moment to realize exactly who they belonged to. His left hand slowly drifted to his dagger as three large gray wolves stepped out of the thicket about thirty feet from where they were. Rodney Blake muttered a curse under his breath and began easing his sword out of his scabbard. He slowly rose to his feet.

The largest of the three wolves let out a low growl and took a step forward, its teeth bared. Emboldened, its two companions followed.

"Mat, you'll have to take the one on the left," Blake whispered. "I'll go for the two on the right."

Mathew pushed himself upright, his eyes darting between the wolves, who had taken a few steps closer and stopped. They stood there glowering at Mathew and Blake, no less than twenty feet separating them. Mathew's hand moved to his right hip and he began to slide his sword free.

Whatever they were going to do, they would have to do it quickly and quietly. *The last thing we need right now is noise,* he thought. So far they'd seen only sentries walking the wall, but for all he knew Lord Guy could also have patrols in the forest as well.

Damn you, Mathew thought, looking at the wolves. *Go back where you came from.*

The wolf on the far left was advancing in a low crouch when suddenly it straightened up, let out a small whine, and loped off into the shadows. Its companions fled a second later, leaving a confused Mathew and Rodney Blake standing there. They turned and looked at each other.

"What the hell was that about?" whispered Blake.

"I don't know. I thought they were about to attack."

"I guess something scared them."

"Not as badly as they scared me," said Mathew, peering into the darkness. "Wolves don't behave that way."

"Well, they're gone now," said Blake. "I suggest we do the same before they change their minds."

Mathew returned his sword to its scabbard and began walking across the frozen ground toward the castle wall. In truth he was far more disturbed by what had just happened than he'd let on. Absently he touched the finger where his ring had been.

For a moment he considered telling Blake about the faint surge he felt a second before the wolves ran off, but it made no sense to him. He no longer had the ring, and without it he couldn't access either the crystals or the machine his ancestors had created. The only plausible explanation he could come up with was that his mind was playing tricks on him, but it felt so real. He'd used the ring enough times to recognize the feeling immediately, and it took him completely aback. It was like being touched by a dying echo. He dimly recalled reading something about the phenomena many months ago, but at the moment he couldn't remember exactly what the book had said. For several minutes he searched his brain, then gave up in frustration.

They were less than fifty yards from the row of hedges Lara had told him about. If she was right, they wouldn't see the door until they were practically on it. The problem now was getting across the field without being seen by the guards. After that, all they had to do was to locate Collin, and sneak him out again past the entire castle, and make their escape.

Simple, he thought ruefully.

Mathew felt a light touch on his shoulder.

"We only have about three minutes before they come back," Blake whispered. "You go first. I'll wait ten seconds and follow."

Mathew took one last glance up at the parapet then dashed across the field to the laurel bushes. He flattened himself against them and waited for Blake, who arrived right after him. The lieutenant put a finger to his lips and pointed up. Seventy-five feet above their heads, boots scraped against cold stones as a guard tramped along the catwalk. The sounds gradually receded and they heard a door slam, indicating the man had returned to the hut once again. They paused a few seconds just to be safe, then began moving along the hedges toward the opening. The sky was definitely lighter now and one or two birds were beginning to sing. In a little while the castle would stir.

The hedge itself was at least twenty feet high and more than six feet deep. Had it not been for Rodney Blake's sharp eyes, they would have walked right by the break, which turned out to be nothing more than a separation in the branches. The lieutenant indicated for Mathew to wait, slipped through, and was back again a few seconds later.

"This is it," he whispered. "The door is on the other side, but it's locked."

Mathew nodded and followed him through the opening. The door was badly weathered, but solid and reinforced with bands of iron at the top and bottom. Blake carefully inserted the point of his dagger into the lock and gently began probing. After a few seconds Mathew heard a click. Blake slowly turned the door handle and grinned at him.

"Evidence of a misspent youth," he whispered. "Didn't know I could still do that."

Mathew suppressed a smile and patted him on the back.

Cautiously, they opened the door an inch. A loud squeak followed, causing Mathew to suck in his breath. He glanced up at the catwalk, but the guard was still nowhere to be seen.

"All clear," Blake whispered, peering inside.

Once they were in they found themselves standing in a dimly lit corridor that ran at least seventy-five yards in both directions. At the far left end, a small square of yellow light from a lamp illuminated the stone floor. There were a number of doors along the corridor that Mathew guessed were the servants' quarters. He hoped they would remain in bed for another hour.

Mathew looked up and down the length of the hallway and said, "You've been here before, Rodney. Any idea which way to go?"

"It was over a year ago, but I think we'll need to get up to the main hall, cross it, and take the big staircase up to the second floor. If I'm remembering correctly, there'll be another stair that leads up to the tower."

"Don't these castles have dungeons or something where they would keep a prisoner?" Mathew asked, keeping his voice low.

"Lara thinks we should try the tower first. To be honest, I haven't been in that many castles. I was raised on a small farm about a hundred miles south of here."

"So was I," Mathew replied, pleased to think he and Rodney Blake had something in common.

Blake smiled back at him. "Let go. We don't have much time."

They came out in a vestibule covered by the large tapestry Lara had told them about. Mathew took the lead this time, moved it aside, and looked out into the great hall. Only a few night candles were still burning in the chandelier; the ones on a side table were already down to their holders. Directly across from them was a wide stone staircase leading up to a balcony that ringed the entire upper floor. On his right, through an archway, he could see a long dining room table and a fireplace.

Blake surveyed the scene as well. Apparently satisfied they were alone, he turned to Mathew and said, "So far, so good. Do you see that doorway up on the next floor in the corner?"

"Yes."

"It leads to an old hallway, stops at a stone wall, then turns right. I'm pretty sure that's where the staircase to the tower is. Jared gave us the grand tour when we visited, but I really wasn't paying much attention. If we're quick and Collin *is* being held there, we should be able to get him back down here in less than five minutes and . . . how are you doing?" Blake asked, noting the pale color of Mathew's face.

"Fine," he said, taking a deep breath to calm himself. "My stomach is a little queasy, that's all."

"Steady on. Mine's turning tricks too. Ready?"

"Ready."

The fact that Rodney Blake, a lieutenant in Gawl's per-

sonal bodyguard, was also nervous did more to calm
Mathew than anything else he could think of. Both men
looked at each other, pulled the tapestry aside, and ran for
the stairs. At the top of the landing they checked to make
sure they hadn't been seen and started down to the hallway. Mathew took an oil lamp off the wall to light the way.
At the end of the corridor they turned right and would
have started up the steps except for the fact that they almost collided with Rowena, who was coming down
carrying a tray with a plate and glass on it.

Their sudden appearance so surprised her, she let out a
gasp and stepped backward, dropping the tray. Mathew
lunged for the plate and managed to catch it, but he was
too late to reach the glass, which crashed to the floor and
shattered. The noise was so loud he was certain it would
rouse the entire castle.

Rowena recovered her composure before they did and
stared at the two intruders.

"Hello, Mathew . . . and Lieutenant Blake, isn't it?"

Neither of them replied.

"I suspect you're here to rescue your friend, am I right?
He was hurt, unfortunately, but the doctor says he'll be all
right in a few days. I'm dreadfully sorry it's had to come to
this, but Gawl left us no choice. His policy would have destroyed what's taken us centuries to build. Not being from
Sennia," she said, to Mathew, "I'm not sure you can appreciate the delicacies of the situation, but what we're doing is
for the benefit of the people. I hope you can understand."

"My lady, you and your family are traitors," Rodney
Blake calmly replied.

"Traitors?" she laughed. "Traitors? What do you know
of traitors? A thousand people rely on us for their jobs at
the wineries. Is it being a traitor to want to protect them
from going hungry? Because that is *exactly* what will
happen if Gawl succeeds. He's so stubborn he won't listen to me, or my father, or to *any* of the barons. Destroy
the industry and you destroy our economy."

"I call anyone a traitor who seeks to murder my king, Rowena," Blake said taking a step up toward her.

"Murder? What do you mean murder? No one's going to murder Gawl. That's ridiculous. My father would never stand for such a thing. He's only going to resume the regency for several months until the council—"

"Your father's soldiers set an ambush at the Argenton ruins. They killed two of my men. It was meant for Gawl."

"You lie!" Rowena said.

"Do I? I was *there,* my lady. Just as Mathew was there when your Father Kellner attempted to kill him only a short while ago. Fortunately, he was no more successful than your soldiers were."

Rowena's eyes darted to Mathew, who stared back at her, his face solemn. As the words sank in, her hand went to her throat and she began breathing more heavily. It was a marvel how she could maintain herself under the circumstances.

"I don't believe you," she said. "My father would never do such a thing."

"My lady, I have no time to banter words with you," Rodney Blake said, reaching into the breast pocket of his uniform. "I have been directed to hand this letter to you or the first member of your family I came upon if the circumstances warranted it."

Rowena started to reach for the letter, then stopped.

"Father Kellner is dead?" she asked.

Mathew nodded.

"You killed him?"

"Teanna d'Elso killed him, Rowena," Mathew said, speaking for the first time. "I don't know what Gawl has written to you, but Teanna's fled. After you've read it you'll have to come with us and give us your word not to raise the alarm until we're gone, then you can make whatever decision you have to."

Rowena stared at him for several seconds before she

nodded. She turned to go back up the stairs, but only took two steps before she stopped and faced him again.

"May I ask why you've both come alone? Surely you could have knocked the whole castle down with your magic."

Mathew was too tired to explain how his ring worked. He was about to tell her to keep moving when he noticed she was not looking at him, but at his hands. She darted a quick glance at the leather cord around his neck, now barren of the ring.

"Where is your famous ring, Master Lewin?"

When Mathew didn't answer right away, a smile spread across her face. Rowena folded her arms across her chest, took a deep breath, and opened her mouth to scream.

It was a scream that never came, for the second she did, Rodney Blake also did something he had never done in his life. He stepped forward and hit her on the side of her jaw. Rowena crumpled and Blake caught her under the arms. With a grunt, he hoisted her over his shoulder.

Mathew was so shocked by what had just happened he was rendered speechless. He stared at the lieutenant. Blake shrugged and raised his eyebrows.

"I didn't have any choice."

"Right," said Mathew. "Wait here for a second. I want to check and make sure they don't have a guard at the door."

"Fine, but hurry, will you? She's not exactly light."

Mathew edged past Blake and took the steps two at a time. The staircase was a circular one. When he reached the last turn, he could see a patch of sunlight on the stone wall ahead of him. He took out his belt dagger and holding it an angle, he looked closely at the reflection in the metal. It was difficult to see properly, but there was a landing at the top of the stairs with a table with a single chair, otherwise it was empty.

"All clear," he whispered back down.

A minute later, Rodney Blake came trudging slowly up the stairs carrying the unconscious body of Rowena Guy. The moment he reached the top landing the lieutenant set her down in a heap and used the back of his sleeve to wipe his face.

"Gawl's welcome to this one," he gasped, trying to catch his breath.

"I found the key," said Mathew, patting Blake on the back.

"Wonderful," Blake replied, straightening up. "I didn't fancy having to carry her back down the stairs again."

They opened the door and dragged Rowena into the room. Collin was asleep on a cot by the wall. The moment Mathew saw his friend's sandy-colored head poking out from under the blankets, a wave of relief swept over him. Camden Keep's main courtyard lay eighty feet below. An untouched plate of food was at the foot of the bed. There was one lone window there with iron bars on it. Mathew crossed the room and sat down on the edge of the cot.

"Collin, it's me," he said, gently touching his friend on the shoulder.

Collin started and looked up. One of his eyes was swollen almost entirely shut and there was a large purple bruise over his cheekbone. A smile slowly spread across his face as he recognized who was standing in front him.

"Took you enough time," he mumbled. "Who's that over there?"

"It's Rodney Blake," Mathew answered, his brows coming together. "Can't you see him?"

"Not very well. All I can see are shadows on this side," Collin said, indicating his swollen eye. "I can't see a damn thing out of the other."

Mathew was shocked, but his expression remained the same.

"Hello, Collin," Blake said, coming over to join them. "How are we doing?"

"Hullo, Rodney. Better than I was yesterday," Collin replied, pushing himself up onto one elbow and reaching out to shake Blake's hand. "I had the most god-awful headache after the explosion. Couldn't see a thing at first, which scared me to death, but little bits and pieces are coming back now. Imagine opening your eyes and the first thing you see is Mat's homely face."

"Truly frightening," Blake agreed.

"If you're both quite through," Mathew said, "the sun's up and I'd like to get out of here before the entire castle is awake. Can you walk?"

"I think so," said Collin. "Lara got out all right, then?"

"She did. We can exchange stories on the way down."

With Mathew and Blake helping him, Collin kicked off the covers, swung his feet over the edge of the cot, and stood up. He swayed slightly but then found his balance.

"Are you sure you can manage?" asked Blake.

"I'll be fine—unless you'd like to carry me, that is."

Same old Collin, Mathew thought shaking his head.

"My God, what happened to you?" Blake asked, noticing the back of Collin's shirt. It was covered with numerous little holes and tears and the lightest touch made him wince.

"Sorry," Blake added.

"It's all right," said Collin. "I got hit with stuff from the explosion."

While Mathew busied himself cutting the blanket into strips, Collin told them about what had happened at the ruins.

"You're lucky you're alive. What do we do about her?" Blake asked, indicating Rowena.

"Tie her up and leave her for the help," Mathew replied, cutting the blanket into strips.

"Agreed," Blake answered.

When they were through, they closed the door, locked it, and started down the staircase.

37

Camden Keep

BY THE TIME THEY REACHED THE TOP OF THE GRAND staircase Collin was steadier on his feet though clearly weak. They started down, but paused in the middle when Collin asked to rest for a moment. He told them that Jared had come to his cell on two different occasions trying to convince him to join their cause. While he recounted his story, the lieutenant's face continued to darken and his mood grew increasingly somber.

"I've never disobeyed an order in my life," said Blake, "but I'm just about an inch away from tearing this letter into little pieces."

"Huh?" Collin said, looking at Blake through his swollen eye.

"Rodney's carrying a letter from Gawl to the Guy family. It offers them clemency, provided they surrender and leave the country or something like that," Mathew explained.

"I see," Collin said. "How come you didn't leave it with Rowena, Rodney?"

"It must have slipped my mind," Blake replied dryly, "however, I suppose I should—"

Neither Mathew nor Collin ever had a chance to learn what Rodney Blake was going to say. His words were cut off in mid-sentence and replaced by a strangled gasp. Blake let go of Collin's arm and slowly fell forward, tum-

bling down the length of the stairs. A dagger was sticking
out of his back.

"I was never very good at being told what to do," Jared
Guy said, from behind them, "particularly from an over-
grown oaf like Gawl d'Atherny."

"What the hell . . ." Collin exclaimed, turning in the direction of Jared's voice.

Mathew spun around pulling Collin with him, in time
to avoid a second dagger that came whistling past his
head.

"Too bad, I was hoping to make this quick," Jared said.
He drew his sword and came down the steps toward
them.

"Hold on to the railing," Mathew said, placing Collin's
hand on it and moving away from him.

"This won't take long," Jared said to Collin. "I'll deal
with you when I've finished with your friend."

"Take him, Mat," Collin called out.

Mathew heard the words, but was too busy concentrating on the meaning behind them. The fact that Jared was
willing to fight, or even approach him, meant he knew he
didn't have the ring anymore. Mathew spared a quick
glance over his shoulder. Rodney Blake lay dead at the
bottom of the stairs. If he could deal with Jared quickly
and get Collin back to the horses, there was still a chance
they could make their escape. Unfortunately, he knew
Jared had no intention of letting them walk out the door.

"Don't be a fool," Mathew said, backing down the
steps. "You can't fight the entire Sennian army. Gawl
doesn't want to kill you. There's a letter in Blake's pocket
granting you and your family amnesty."

Jared threw back his head and laughed.

"First of all, Gawl is probably dead by now, and even if
he isn't it won't make any difference. By the time the
southern army arrives it will be too late. Oh, yes, we
know about that, too. We have better than seven thousand

fully armed men. The most he can field is fifteen hundred or so. Not very good odds."

Jared pulled a black leather glove from his belt and put it on, then walked casually down the rest of the stairs toward Mathew.

"I don't want to fight you," Mathew said.

"Oh, I'm sure about that," Jared chuckled. "Collin told me that you're quite the fencer. After I've killed you, do you suppose they'll start putting pictures of me in the shops? By the way, would you like a glove?"

"No," said Mathew, unbuckling his scabbard. He let it drop to the tile floor, and kicked it aside with his foot.

"Really? I always use one myself."

There didn't seem any point in replying so Mathew, who had now reached the bottom of the steps, held his tongue and watched Jared come. When he reached the last step, instead of attacking as Mathew expected him to do, Jared said, "If you'll excuse me for a moment." Then dropping to one knee, he closed his eyes in prayer. It was pure bravado, of course, and Mathew could have set upon him, then and there ending the matter, but such a thing would have been cowardly and he rejected the idea with no more than a passing thought.

Jared got to his feet and brushed the dust off his pants.

"I promised the bishop I'd be more diligent about my prayers," he said.

"Piety is an admirable quality," Mathew replied, taking a step backward.

"Isn't it? Pity about old Blake. Not terribly discriminating in his choices, but he was a decent enough keeper."

Jared spread his fingers and took his time pulling the glove on. When he was through, he faced Mathew, who responded by turning his body sideways to offer him the smallest possible target.

"Oh, very good, Lewin. Just the way they taught you in fencing class. Ever face a grown man with one of these before?"

Mathew didn't reply. He simply continued to move toward the center of the room, bringing his sword up into an on-guard position.

"Be careful, Mat, he's fast," Collin called out from the stairs.

"Your time's coming, little man," Jared snapped, without turning around.

Mathew glanced right and left, checking to see what was around him. A narrow rug ran across the hall to the dining room entrance. There were also several pieces of furniture by the wall next to the staircase, as well as a side table with a pair of silver candlesticks on them. Two high-backed carved wooden chairs flanked the ends of the table and there was another pair on the opposite wall.

Careful, Mathew thought, testing his footing on the rug.

Jared advanced, crossed blades, and made a probing thrust. It wasn't intended as a real attack, and Mathew flicked it aside with his wrist. Jared moved right and executed two quick beats on either side of Mathew's blade, still continuing to test his defenses.

For the next minute a game of cat and mouse played out. Jared continued to make a number of feints and false attacks while Mathew contented himself by merely deflecting them, making no move to attack himself. The purpose of Jared's forays quickly became obvious. He was deliberately keeping his low outside flank exposed, hoping to tempt Mathew into going for it.

Few things are truly free, so be cautious about accepting invitations from people you don't know, his father had once told him, just before the start of a fencing tournament.

Good advice then and good advice now, Mathew thought, parrying another half-hearted thrust at his chest. It suddenly dawned on him what the older man was trying to accomplish. He didn't need to kill him, he only had to delay him until the castle was up.

"Collin said you were fast. So far the only thing I've seen that moves quickly is your mouth."

The smile on Jared's face faded away and a second later he did attack, launching a powerful lunge to Mathew's stomach. Mathew swept the line from low to high, parrying the blade to his outside. But, instead of recovering backward as he expected him to do, Jared redoubled forward and attacked again closing the distance. The guards of their weapons came together with a loud clang. To his surprise Mathew found himself sprawled on his back after Jared rammed into him with his shoulder. Had he not rolled to his right, Jared's follow up would have cut him in two. Jared's stroke went wide and he immediately recovered, pressing the attack.

Still on his back, Mathew kicked out with the side of his foot and caught Jared squarely on the kneecap as he was stepping forward. The bigger man let out a yelp of pain as his left leg snapped closed. He cursed and backed away, glowering at Mathew, who scrambled to his feet.

"Very good farm boy," Jared sneered. "Is that what they teach you—"

Jared's words stopped abruptly as Mathew launched his own attack. The action caught Jared so much by surprise, he nearly tripped over himself trying to back away, yet at the very last moment he managed to make the parry and aimed a vicious blow at Mathew's head in return. Mathew ducked under it and lunged again. Both men closed and their blades became tangled. Jared, who was the larger and heavier of the two, landed a punch to the side of Mathew's head and followed it by driving his forehead into Mathew's face.

Mathew felt his legs go out from under him and he fell to the floor on all fours, losing his sword in the process. A blow from Jared's foot caught him in the ribs knocking the breath out of him. It was followed by another heavier blow, and then another. Each time Jared's foot landed, Mathew felt himself nearly lifted off the ground. In agony he rolled over onto his side. Another punch from Jared caught him in the back of his head and colored lights exploded before his eyes. Mathew's mind screamed at him to fight back. From what seemed like a long distance away he heard someone say, "I've had enough of this farm boy. I thought you'd at least give a better account of yourself—"

Collin knew that his friend was in trouble. One of his eyes was completely useless and he was only able to make out shapes through the other. He could see Jared and Mathew below him in the main hall, but they were no more than indistinct shadows. Cautiously, he felt his way down the marble staircase. When he reached the bottom and got close enough, he could tell the one on the ground was his friend. Jared was busy taunting Mathew and never heard Collin approach.

With a snarl, Collin lowered his shoulder and charged forward. He hit Jared squarely in the middle of the back. Jared grunted with surprise as the impact knocked them both to the ground.

Collin got to his feet and spread his arms wide trying to locate him.

If I'm going to die, he thought, *it'll be fighting.*

Had he been able to see properly, he would have seen Mathew slowly get to his knees again.

Behind him Jared pulled a third dagger from the side of his boot and drew it back.

"Generosity . . . that was my first mistake," said Jared. "Fun's over."

Mathew's scream *No!* registered with Jared Guy as did the sudden rush of hot air that seemed to come out of nowhere. He gasped in shock as the dagger in his hand winked out of existence.

Collin's desperate action had given Mathew the time he needed to recover. The first thing he saw was Collin standing in the middle of the hall with his arms wide, searching the air in front of him for Jared. The bigger man was stand-

ing behind him and to his left. At the same time he saw
Jared reach down and pull a dagger from the side of his
boot, which he flipped into the air and caught a few inches
down from the point. There was a cruel smile on his face.
The energy that had suddenly built up inside of Mathew
was the same as he had felt in the forest earlier. Instinctively, all of his attention centered on the dagger in Jared's
hand, which had promptly disappeared as though it had
never been there at all. Jared's look of shock replaced fear;
he stood frozen in place, staring at Mathew.

What Jared didn't know was that the feeble stream of
power that had caused the dagger to vanish dissipated as
quickly as it came.

"Pick up your sword," said Mathew.

Jared stared at him in disbelief. "But you don't have
your ring anymore."

"I won't need a ring for this," Mathew replied, in a
voice as cold as ice. "*Pick up* your sword."

Never taking his eyes off Mathew, Jared bent down and
grasped the handle of his weapon.

"Move to your right, Collin," Mathew said. "There's a
table and two chairs twenty feet from where you are."

Collin nodded and began to shuffle toward them, his
arms still extended out in front of him.

"You're serious?" Jared asked.

"Even farm boys don't murder helpless people where
I'm from."

Jared's arrogant smile slowly returned to his face.
"How noble of you, Lewin."

With all the strength and speed he could muster,
Mathew drove a lunge straight at Jared, making the feint
directly over his forearm.

His opponent responded by executing a circular
counter parry. He found nothing but the air as Mathew
disengaged smoothly around it. Another circular parry,
now in desperation, produced the same result. Mathew's
second disengage avoided the blade again and found its

target in Jared's stomach. The larger man's eyes opened wide in surprise and he looked down as though not quite comprehending what had just happened. A deep red stain began to spread across the front of his shirt. His eyes found Mathew's and held them for a moment before they glazed over and he collapsed to his knees. Jared Guy was dead before he hit the ground.

"Mat," Collin called out.

"I'm all right. Give me a second."

Mathew kicked the sword away from Jared's hand, stepped around him, and went to Rodney Blake. A wave of sadness sweep over him, and the strength that had sustained him in the heat of battle drained from his body. He retrieved the letter Rodney was carrying and gently closed the lieutenant's eyes. Mathew dropped it on the floor next to Jared's body as he walked by.

Whether Lord Guy, Rowena, and the rest of their relatives accepted Gawl's offer made no difference to him. He was beyond caring what happened to them. Betrayal and treason were not things one could look the other way about. The detachment with which he reached this point of view surprised him. A year ago, he would have been inclined to try and understand what drove them to take the actions they had, but now he simply didn't care, nor did he have the energy to waste. They deserved to hang.

That event and the sudden clarity of his convictions became frozen in time for Mathew Lewin, and they would remain sharply outlined in his mind for years to come. It was also a crossroad of sorts, some would say, and having reached it, the boy left his childhood behind forever.

Mathew turned and looked back at Rodney Blake, a variety of emotions assailing his mind. With an effort, he pushed them away and went to see about Collin.

The living were his main concern.

38

Cheatham Hill

IT TOOK THEM NEARLY A HALF HOUR TO REACH THE EDGE
of the forest. The going was painfully slow because
Mathew had to guide Collin along. The rising sun did little to warm them and a biting north wind only made matters worse. Both were chilled to the bone in a matter of
minutes. Slowly, laboriously, they picked their way
through the snow and over the frozen tree roots. Neither
of them spoke very much, the death of Rodney Blake still
weighing heavily on their minds.

Mathew's thoughts turned again to what had happened
with the wolves and in the castle. Though the reasons
weren't clear, he concluded that having worn the ring as
long as he did must have produced a kind of aftereffect.
Miraculously, a connection to the Ancient power source
still remained, though it was getting progressively
weaker and weaker. He tried recalling what the books
said once more, but couldn't. For the moment, it was
enough to know it existed, though how long it would last
was another question entirely. He might well wake up the
following morning to find that it was gone forever, and
that thought depressed him horribly.

It was obvious that Collin couldn't see well enough to
control his horse, so Mathew held the reins for him. During the trip, his friend recounted the rest of the story leading up to his injury. He gave Lara all the credit for
discovering Lord Guy's plan. In return, Mathew told him

what had happened in the cavern and about how Father
Kellner died, though when he got to the part about losing
his ring, he deliberately omitted mentioning anything
about his dealings with Teanna.

Three times along the way they were forced to leave
the road and hide in a thicket until a patrol of Lord Guy's
soldiers passed by. It was obvious that Lord Guy had
amassed a great deal of support, because Mathew
counted at least five different kinds of cloaks among the
soldiers. The situation was going from bad to worse. The
last time they were forced to hide he peered out from behind a bush and saw something he didn't expect at all—a
patrol dressed in Alor Satar's colors.

Memories of a sea of black and silver uniforms facing them across Ardon Field flashed into his mind as he
watched them pass. When they were gone he found that
he had been holding his breath. It wasn't just their un-
expected presence that caused the sinking feeling to
form in his stomach. Rodney Blake had told him that
they had sent a man back to get the palace garrison and
another to Stanhope, where the southern army was
camped. It would be two days before they arrived.
Mathew had no idea how many soldiers were stationed
at Tenley Palace, but if Jared's remark about his having
more than 7,000 men was true, Gawl was in trouble. He
had to get back and warn him as quickly as possible.
The question was how, since the road seemed to be
crawling with the enemy and he didn't know the countryside. In frustration Mathew cursed under his breath.

"What is it?" Collin whispered

"We've got a problem. Guy's got help—a lot of it. I
just saw a patrol of soldiers from Alor Satar."

"Makes sense," Collin agreed under his breath. "Lara
told me she saw Duren's son in the chapel at Camden
Keep. That's where she overheard them discussing their
plans. How far are we from the meeting place?"

"I'm not sure. My guess is about thirty miles. They're

somewhere west of here at a place called Cheatham Hill."

"Maybe it would be better if you left me. You could make better time alone."

Mathew turned and looked at his friend. "Not a chance," he said.

"But—"

"There are no 'buts' about it. Do you remember what you said to me several months ago near the Orlock cave?"

"No," Collin lied.

"Well, I do. We both stay . . . or we both go. That's it. There's no way I'm leaving you."

"Listen, Mat . . . I'm not trying to be noble, but we've got to let Gawl know what's going on, or he'll ride straight into them."

"I know," Mathew replied. "The sooner we start the better."

For the next four hours, he and Collin wove their way through the trees, keeping well clear of the road. Their progress was painfully slow, but they were able to avoid run-ins with Lord Guy's men. By the time they reached the town of Littleton, both of them were exhausted. Mathew stopped at a local tavern to ask for directions to Cheatham Hill. Because of Collin's condition they decided it would be best for him to remain outside, rather than risk attracting more attention. The innkeeper told Mathew the place they were looking for was no more than a fifteen minute ride from the end of town—once they reached the crossroads the left-hand fork would lead them directly to it.

He also learned Cheatham Hill was actually a farm, and a large one at that. It was well over two hundred acres, and located at the base of the mountains. Mathew thanked the man and paid him for a jug of wine and half a roasted chicken, then went outside. The midday sun continued to rise higher, burning off most of the early morning haze as the sky turned to bright blue.

Their passage through town appeared to attract no particular attention from any of the locals, with the exception of one man. Unknown to Mathew, a merchant sitting in the corner of the inn recognized him as soon as he had came in. Two minutes after he left the man got up from his table, quietly slipped outside, and made his way to the livery stable. He took his time hitching his horse to his wagon then headed out of town back to Camden Keep.

Mathew and Collin encountered a squad of Gawl's soldiers just after the town limits. Their leader, a tough-looking sergeant, named Miles Freeman, leaned across his horse and shook Mathew's hand.

"Well met, Mat. Glad to see you made it. What news?"

Mathew told him about what had happened at Camden Keep and about seeing the Alor Sataran soldiers along the way. When he finished, the sergeant spat on the ground and turned to one of the men.

"Charley, ride back as quick as you can and let his majesty know about this."

Then turning back to Mathew, Miles explained, "Gawl's getting ready to launch an assault on the Keep. He needs to know what he's up against. What's the matter with your friend?"

"I got into a disagreement with Aldrich Kellner as I was leaving the ruins," Collin replied.

"Sorry," Miles said. "I guess I should have asked you direct."

"It's all right," Collin replied.

"So, Jared Guy is dead?" Miles Freeman said, looking at Mathew.

"He is."

"Can't say as I'll miss him much, except maybe at the Felcarin games. Can I ask you a question, Mat?"

Mathew looked at the sergeant and raised his eyebrows.

"You said you and him had a fight and you killed him, right?"

"Right."

"Was it a normal kind of fight?"

"Are you asking if I used my ring to kill him?"

"Well . . . yes," Miles replied. "I mean just about everybody knows about you and that ring of yours, and I was wondering—"

"It was a fair fight," Mathew said. "We used swords, not rings."

He was aware the other soldiers were listening, but doing their best not to be obvious about it. When he said the ring wasn't involved, they all seemed to relax.

The sergeant slowly nodded his head, satisfied no code of honor had been broken.

"That's good," he said to Mathew.

The other men didn't offer any comments, but Mathew got the distinct impression they were in agreement with both the result and the method used to accomplish it.

Strange people, these Sennians, he thought.

The road to the farmhouse passed through empty fields, all of the crops having been harvested months before. Despite the bright winter day it felt lonely and deserted. In sharp contrast to the austere surroundings, the farmhouse, a white wooden structure with a brown shingle roof, and a neat front yard, was a surprisingly pleasant place. The stables were also painted white and were located next to the house. According to Miles, Gawl had appropriated it for his command center.

The place was alive with activity. With no prompting from the king, Farmer Cheatham had sent word to the neighbors that Gawl needed help, and they had responded enthusiastically. The soldiers from Tenley Palace were soon joined by an additional force of some three hundred men and women carrying everything from swords and bows to pitchforks and hammers. It was an amazing sight.

As Mathew rode along, he stopped a man and inquired if a physician was available for Collin, but before he could answer, a female voice from behind him said, "There are two doctors at the small guesthouse on the left." Mathew turned to see who had spoken. "I'm Melinda Cheatham," she said, extending her hand to Mathew.

To his surprise, "Farmer Cheatham" turned out not to be a man but a handsome looking woman in her late forties, named Melinda. Both her father and mother had been killed in an accident years before, while she was still in her teens, and she had taken over running the farm. It was now one of the largest in the province.

Like many of the people in Sennia he'd met, Melinda Cheatham was tall, blond-haired, and possessed what he would later describe as a very healthy figure. She was dressed in men's brown breeches, a dark green shirt, and a tan vest. Her boots were more suited for work than show and came up to her calves.

"You're cuter than she said."

"Ma'am?"

"Your young lady friend, Lara. You'll find her over there," Melinda pointed. "The doctor examined her arm yesterday and she's doing fine. We're using the small house as a temporary field hospital."

"I see. I'd like to have the doctor take a look at my friend as soon as possible. I'm Mathew Lewin, by the way."

"I know who you are," she said, looking him up and down. "Lara's got good taste in men."

"If the two of you are through," Collin said, from atop his horse, "I could use a little help getting over there."

"I take it this is Collin Miller," Melinda said. "I thought there was supposed to be someone else with you."

"Rodney Blake," Mathew told her. "He didn't make it."

What happened next surprised both Mathew and Collin.

The mistress of Cheatham Hill let loose with a string of oaths, (some of which they'd never heard before), all but turning the air blue. If Mathew's face was red before it was mild in contrast to the reaction Melinda's invective produced. Even Collin, who could curse better than most men, was taken aback. Neither of them had much experience with strong language coming from a woman.

"For God's sake, Melinda," a deep voice rumbled, "hold it down will you?"

Mathew didn't have to look to see who it belonged to.

Gawl was just coming out of the barn along with Father Thomas, Colonel Haynes, and two other men he didn't know. Melinda Cheatham looked at the king pointedly and spat on the ground.

"Gawl, you'd damn well better do something about that slime-eating, back-stabbing son of a bitch," she said, her eyes ablaze. "Treason's not enough, but now he's murdered one of your soldiers. Rodney Blake was a damn good man."

"I know, I know," Gawl said, holding up his hands. "They just told me about it. I'll send word to his family. Glad to see you're back, Mat." Then turning to Collin he asked, "And how are you, boy?"

"Fine," Collin said, looking in the direction of Gawl's voice, "apart from being hungry, frozen, and half blind."

Gawl laughed to himself and Father Thomas walked over to put a hand on Collin's knee.

"Come, let me help you down, my son. I'll take you to the doctor."

"I'll take him," Melinda said. "You *men* need to stop wasting time and get yourselves ready."

"Yes, Melinda," Gawl replied patiently.

Father Thomas's eyebrows arched, but he stepped aside and allowed Melinda to assist Collin down from his horse.

"I'll tell your young lady you're back," she called, over her shoulder.

Collin waved in their general direction and went with her. Before she left however, Mathew noticed an odd look pass between the king and Melinda that bespoke something other than just a casual acquaintance.

When she was out of earshot, Gawl explained, "We've known each other since we were children. She has a tendency to be a trifle abrupt at times."

Abrupt? Mathew thought. But rather than comment, he held his tongue and said, "I'm sorry about Rodney. There was nothing I could do."

He proceeded to recount once more what had happened at Camden Keep while Gawl and the others listened. Father Thomas and Colonel Haynes nodded occasionally, but neither spoke until he was finished. From the expressions on their faces he could tell the news about Alor Satar had come as a shock. The full extent of Lord Guy's support was still unknown, but it was now obvious that they were facing an invasion as well as a rebellion.

Colonel Haynes asked a few questions about what the other soldiers were wearing. And Mathew recounted them as accurately as he could. When he finished the colonel shook his head and said to Gawl, "It sounds like half the northern families have thrown in with them."

"Assuming Jared was telling the truth about their having 7,000 men, any attack on Camden Keep will have to wait until the reinforcements arrive," the soldier on Colonel Haynes' right said.

He was a slender, intelligent-looking man, in his late twenties or early thirties, and was wearing a uniform that marked him as an officer.

"Forgive me Mathew, this is Major William Wright," Haynes said. "William's normally attached to the southern army, but he was visiting the palace when the news arrived."

"Bill . . . to my friends," the man said, offering his hand to Mathew. "Pleased to finally meet you, Master Lewin."

"Mat," Mathew said, shaking his hand.

"And this is Captain Geoffrey Phelps," Colonel Haynes added, finishing the introductions.

The captain was older than Wright by at least twenty years. Mathew guessed him to be around fifty. He was a blunt-looking man with a broad, deeply lined face and large hands.

"Glad to make your acquaintance, young fellow," he said. "Heard a lot about you."

Mathew smiled and shook his hand.

"It might be best if we go some place where we can talk," suggested Father Thomas.

"We can use the main house," said Gawl.

"Captain, I think it would be a good idea to double the patrols along the road, particularly those leading into Littleton," said Father Thomas. "I don't want to be caught by surprise."

"Yes, sir," the captain replied, with a salute. "I'll see to it at once. Good to meet you, Mat. I can't wait to see the expressions on the enemy's face when they do too."

Phelps gave Mathew a private wink then turned and bowed to Gawl, who responded by giving him a friendly push to get him going.

"Be careful, Geof," Gawl said.

That was when Mathew realized that Phelps was under the impression that he still had his ring. *Oh, this just gets better and better.*

The inside of Melinda Cheatham's house was a contradiction to its owner. Lace curtains hung on the windows. The walls were all painted a pale yellow. An inviting fire was burning in a rock fireplace. Mathew walked over to it and wasted no time warming himself, while Gawl, who was apparently familiar with the home, retrieved a bottle of brandy and some glasses from a cupboard and poured drinks for everybody.

"Here, this will help," he said, handing Mathew a glass.

"But, I thought—"

"Melinda's even worse about religion than I am," Gawl explained. He flopped down into an oversized chair and stretching his legs out on a footstool.

Father Thomas suppressed a smile and sat down across from the king.

"You understand Mathew's information changes everything," the priest said.

"I know," Gawl replied. "Do you think we can we hold out here until Ballenger arrives?"

Father Thomas thought about it before answering. "With the additional help that Melinda has brought us, we have slightly less than two thousand troops. A portion of them are farmers who have little or no experience in battle. Not only will we be facing professional soldiers, we'll have the mountains at our back. No . . . I would much prefer to pick another venue if possible. We're much too confined here."

Without commenting Gawl turned to Colonel Haynes and Major Wright. "I take it, from your expressions, that you both agree with Siward?"

"In fact, I do your majesty," Colonel Haynes replied.

Major Wright nodded and said, "I was too young for the Sibuyan war, but General Thomas's reputation as a tactician is well known. His victories at Veshy and Jeremy Crossing are still studied to this day by our junior officers. If he thinks we need to leave . . . I'd like to start packing now."

"What about Melinda and her people?" asked Gawl. "What do you think is going to happen to them if we pull up stakes and run?"

"It's not a matter of running, and you know that," Father Thomas said quietly. "This place is not defensible."

Gawl opened his mouth to reply, but closed it again as Melinda appeared in the doorway. She was carrying a bow and a quiver of arrows that she deposited on the kitchen table.

"Oh . . . hello, Melinda," he said. "We've just been discussing our options."

"And?" she asked.

"Uh . . . we think it may be best if we move our people to a different location, one that can be more easily defended until Ballenger and his soldiers arrive," Gawl said.

Melinda walked over and gently tapped the soles of Gawl's boots with her foot. He promptly took his feet off the footstool and she sat down on it.

"Is this your idea?" she asked.

"No, it's Siward's. Haynes and Wright both agree."

"I see," she said slowly. "What about you?' "

The question was directed to Mathew, sitting in a chair by the window.

"Me?" he asked, surprised that his opinion was being solicited.

"You're the one with the ring, aren't you? By the way, I told Lara you're here. She'll be up in a few minutes, once she gets your friend settled. If half the stories I've heard about you are true, couldn't you just destroy Guy's men with a wave of your hand?"

Mathew took a deep breath before answering. "I don't have the ring anymore. It was taken by Teanna d'Elso—Eric Duren's cousin. They won't be able to use it, but, then . . ."

"Neither will you," said Melinda. "Well, that's too bad. I was planning on asking you for a pot of gold and some new dresses when this is over."

Everyone in the room chuckled at the joke except for Mathew, who said seriously, "I would have been more than happy to do it, Melinda, but the ring doesn't work that way."

"Oh, well," she said, with a sigh, "I guess I'll just have to earn it the old-fashioned way." She put one hand on Gawl's knee and pushed herself up. "I'm sure everyone has already eaten, but you must be hungry. Would you like something?"

"Collin and I bought a chicken and a loaf of bread on the way in, but I'll take a hot drink if you have one."

"Give me a moment," Melinda said, and started for the kitchen. "Would anyone else like something?"

Gawl opened his mouth and started to raise his hand, but didn't get the chance. Melinda cut him off and added, "*To drink*. You've already had your breakfast. Besides," she said, looking pointedly at his stomach, "I noticed you've put on a few pounds."

The king folded his arms across his chest and he sat back in the chair giving her a flat look. "Thank you, Melinda."

He swallowed the rest of his brandy in one gulp, put down the glass, and made a low noise in his throat that sounded very much like a growl to Mathew.

"Hmph," Melinda said, with a small shrug, and left for the kitchen.

Father Thomas had his hand over his mouth and was trying his best to contain himself, but with limited success. Colonel Haynes and Major Wright had apparently both decided there was something interesting outside the window, because they were looking out there rather intently.

"One word," warned Gawl, glowering at everyone in the room. "Just say one word."

Fortunately, there was a knock at the door and Lara came in. She immediately went to Mathew and gave him a hug. He put his arms around her waist and kissed her on the forehead. The sling she had been wearing along with the impromptu splints and bandages had been replaced by the doctor in favor of newer, cleaner ones.

"Did I interrupt anything?" she asked.

"Nothing terribly weighty," Father Thomas replied in a bland tone.

His comment proved too much for Major Wright, who nearly slipped off his seat. The major excused himself, got up, and left the room still chuckling.

"Very funny, Siward," Gawl grumbled, fixing a baleful eye on Father Thomas.

Lara looked from the priest to the king, then at Mathew for an explanation.

"Later," he said, out of the corner of his mouth.

Melinda returned a moment later with a steaming cup of tea, which Mathew gratefully accepted. He sat back and listened to Father Thomas, Gawl, and Colonel Haynes as they discussed the military options open to them. Melinda also joined in, expressing her opinion freely. After a few minutes, it became apparent that she knew quite as much about fighting and strategy as she did about farming. Much later, Mathew was to learn that she had fought in the Sibuyan war when she was still in her late teens, and was one of the few women ever to command a regiment.

"Well, I don't intend to simply walk away and hand over my farm to Edward Guy or any of his friends from Alor Satar," she said.

"Melinda," Gawl said, "no one's asking you to walk away, but as much as I hate to say it, Siward is right. Personally I'd love nothing better than to ride into Camden Keep and put Guy's head on a pike. The problem is we're outnumbered better than three to one. We've got to buy ourselves time until the southern army can arrive. Then we'll see who carries the day. In fact—"

A commotion outside stopped Gawl in the middle of his sentence and he turned to the window. Colonel Haynes got up and looked out.

"Here comes Geoffrey Phelps, and if I'm not mistaken that's Paul Teller with him."

"Paul Teller?" Father Thomas repeated, getting to his feet.

"Um-hmm," Haynes said. "It looks like there's been trouble."

Without another word, the colonel headed for the door with everyone in the room following him.

As soon as Mathew got there he could see Haynes was

right. Paul Teller had a large bruise on his cheekbone and the side of Phelps's left leg was stained red with blood. The two soldiers behind him were helping a third man down from his horse. He had a bolt from a crossbow sticking out of his shoulder.

"What happened, Geoff?" Colonel Haynes asked, running up.

"We ran into one of Guy's patrols. They'd just arrested the abbot and were taking him to Camden Keep. There was a fight."

"Did any of them get away?" Father Thomas asked.

"Two."

Father Thomas nodded and turned to Paul Teller.

"Glad to see you're all right, Paul. What brings you here?"

"This," the abbot said, drawing a paper from the pocket of his cloak.

Father Thomas, Gawl, and Haynes glanced at what Paul Teller was holding. It was the same announcement that Rodney Blake had shown them earlier, supposedly appointing Edward Guy regent of the country.

"I take it there's no truth in this," Gawl asked, looking at the paper.

"None whatsoever, your majesty. That's why I came. The church has definitely *not* given their blessing. These *things* are being posted all over Sennia. This particular one found its way to the abbey. I immediately questioned the man who brought it, and he said he was directed to do so by Ferdinand Willis. Either the bishop has completely lost his mind or he's being forced to endorse this trash. I can't understand what he's doing."

"Two members of the church council happened to be visiting the abbey at the time and we decided to let the people know that it's a lie."

"Well, it's refreshing to know the church isn't mad at me," said Gawl.

"Oh, the council's still mad at you," the abbot replied with a smile, "but not mad enough to engage in treason. We would much prefer to *talk* out our differences."

Gawl stared down at the abbot for a moment and began to chuckle.

"Then we should definitely talk as soon as the opportunity presents itself," he said, placing a hand on Teller's shoulder. "Assuming I'm still king, of course."

"I'm sorry to interrupt," said Father Thomas, "but we need to conclude our plans for evacuating this place at once. If the soldier who got away reaches Lord Guy with news that we're located here, the matter will become academic."

Paul Teller listened to Father Thomas and turned questioningly toward Mathew.

"I don't have the ring anymore," he said quietly. "Father Kellner is dead; his ring is gone as well."

The abbot was plainly shocked at the news. He looked from Father Thomas to Gawl, who both nodded in confirmation.

"I'll fill you in on the rest of the news later, Paul," said Father Thomas. "Right now we have to break camp."

"What can I do to help?" Teller asked.

"There are a lot of people here who aren't soldiers. They came because Melinda Cheatham asked them and because they're loyal to the crown. My guess is they've heard a lot of things being said lately. It would be nice if a member of the church could let them know the truth," Father Thomas told him.

"Leave it to me. Show me where to go, my son," the abbot said to Major Wright. Together they hurried off to where the farmers' tents were pitched.

"I'll get the orders out to the rest of the company," said Colonel Haynes.

"Go," said Gawl.

In minutes the activity level at Cheatham Hill increased dramatically. Mathew and Lara watched people dispersing in different directions and walked to the side of the main house so they could get out of the way. Father Thomas and Gawl headed toward the barn to retrieve the documents they were studying earlier. Neither voiced the slightest objection when Melinda went with them. Five minutes later Colonel Haynes and Major Wright returned and also entered the barn. Mathew watched what was going on around him with a mounting concern. It wasn't just that they were abandoning the camp. That made sense. Their location might be a poor one to defend, but the greater problem was that they were badly outnumbered. There was a sense of urgency in the air. Duty and his own sense of honor compelled him to lend what help he could, ring or no ring. When he looked at Lara, he had a very good idea of the thoughts going on inside her head. Pulled in two directions at the same time he started to speak, but she stopped him.

"I already know what you're going to say, so you don't have to say it. What's more, I'm not going to argue. With a broken arm, I'll be more help with the wounded than on a battlefield, but don't you think I like it one bit, Mathew Lewin."

"I know," he said gently.

"You could help too," she said, hopefully, looking up at him. "You read all those medical books, and . . ."

"That would be nice," he replied, "but—"

"You can't, I know," she said, disappointed.

Mathew smiled at her and pulled her close. "I love you . . . more than anything."

"I love you too, darling."

He was surprised when Lara used the word "darling" because she had never done so before. It made him feel good inside in a way that he couldn't quite articulate. Mathew hugged her and moments passed while they clung to each other, oblivious to everything else around them.

"Mathew?" Lara asked, resting her head against his chest.

"Hmm."

"Were you serious when you said you wanted to talk to Father Thomas about us getting married?"

He separated and held her at arm's length looking into her eyes. *She has such beautiful eyes,* he thought. They were a bottle-green color with brown flecks that seemed never to be completely at rest.

"Yes," he said quietly.

"Let's talk about it later, when things have calmed down."

"All right."

The two of them held hands and walked back to the front of the house.

In truth, Mathew was caught off guard by her sudden change in attitude, and wasn't sure what to make of it. Several days earlier when he had brought the subject up, she had rejected the idea, saying they were both too young. *Maybe Collin has a point,* he thought. *Women are definitely strange.* But at the moment he didn't care.

He was spared further reflection on the subject because of Melinda Cheatham's reappearance from the barn. The moment she saw them, she came directly over, her attitude all business.

"Siward Thomas would like to see you when you have a moment," she said, addressing Mathew. Then she turned to Lara and cast a critical eye over her.

"I understand you're as good with a sword as most men, but since your fencing arm is injured, it might be better—"

"We were just discussing that it would be better if I helped the doctors," said Lara.

Melinda laughed. "Siward said you'd give me an argument."

"I probably would have if I could hold a blade, but I can't and there's no use in fooling myself."

"I'd better go see what he wants," Mathew said. "If you'll excuse me." He gave Lara a quick kiss on the cheek and started for the barn.

"Mathew, can I ask you a question?" Melinda said.

"Sure," he said, turning around.

"Whcn I was taking your friend Collin to see the doctor, he said you hit Rowena Guy and knocked her out."

"Uh . . . well, actually that wasn't me. It was Rodney Blake," Mathew answered. His voice was distracted because he was watching a rider coming up the road toward them at a full gallop. The man skidded his horse to a halt, jumped off, and dashed into the barn.

"I'm sorry," he said, turning back to Melinda, "what was it you were saying?"

"Oh . . . nothing," she replied, a strange smile appearing on her face. "I always liked Blake, that's all.

"We'd better go," she added, slipping her arm through Lara's.

39

The Trip to Fanshaw Castle

MATHEW SHOOK HIS HEAD AND STOOD THERE FOR A moment, watching them walk arm in arm toward the guesthouse.

No question, he thought. *They're all strange.*

His musings were interrupted by Father Thomas calling his name from the doorway. Mathew turned and trotted over to the priest, but had to jump sideways to avoid being knocked down by a soldier coming out of the barn at the same time. It was Sergeant Mickens.

Uh-oh. Something's happened, he thought.

The moment he was within earshot, Father Thomas said, "inside," without any preliminaries. His tone left no room for questions.

A large table had been set up in the center of the barn. It was covered by a map of the surrounding countryside. Another map hung from a post on one of the stalls, depicting eastern Sennia's coastline and the Great Southern Sea that separated it from lower Elgaria. Gawl was bent over the map on the table while Colonel Haynes and Major Wright were studying the one on the post.

"Guy's army is about three hours from our present position," Father Thomas explained. "He and the other families are being supported by Eric Duren and a force of about five thousand men, which is consistent with what you told us earlier. If everything goes as planned, we will be ready to move within twenty minutes. I want you to stay close to me."

Mathew met the priest's eyes. "I may not have the ring, Father, but I have this," he said, touching the hilt of his sword. "I'd like to help."

"Mathew, I made a promise to your father. I—"

"It's my decision."

Father Thomas stared at him for a moment, then looked at Gawl, who shrugged. A look passed between the two men.

"Very well," he said. "I suppose you're right. You are a man now and it is your decision. Nevertheless, I still want you near me. The word about your ring hasn't spread yet, and a lot of people will be looking to you for inspiration, just as they will to Gawl. Since your face is known throughout the country, the enemy will think twice before deciding to attack. Come here for a moment."

Father Thomas strode over to the table and waited for Mathew to join him.

"This is where we are," he said, pointing to a spot on the map. "And this is Littleton. Guy's men are here, and Eric Duren's soldiers are moving up from the coast to join them. I'm told there's an old place called Fanshaw Castle, a little over an hour to the southeast. It sits on a hill and is supposed to be in passable condition. Assuming it can be defended, our best chance will be to get our people there."

"It can," Major Wright said, from across the room.

Father Thomas nodded and continued. "If we can reach the castle, it should buy us the time we need until the southern army arrives."

Mathew frowned. "We're cutting things very close, wouldn't you say?"

"Unfortunately, we have little choice in the matter, my son. The two men who got away are going to bring Edward Guy and his soldiers straight back here. I've sent out advance scouts to keep us informed of the enemy's movements, but we must leave, and leave *now*."

A knock at the door by Melinda Cheatham turned everyone's head.

"We'll be ready in thirty minutes," she announced.

"Make it fifteen," Father Thomas replied.

She muttered something under her breath and left, taking her bow and quiver with her.

Father Thomas watched her retreating back through the doorway for a moment and turned back to Mathew. Gawl came over to join them.

"Melinda will take command of one battalion," he explained. "Colonel Haynes, Major Wright, and Jeram Quinn will divide the regiment into three parts with each assuming command of a battalion."

"Quinn?" Mathew said, surprised. "My father told me they served in the war together, but—"

"He's quite competent," Father Thomas assured him, still concentrating on the map. "During the war he held the rank of major in the cavalry. For all our constable's proper manners, he'll be a good man to have on our side. At the moment, our chief problem is that we lack senior officers with sufficient experience to lead, so any help he can give will be more than welcome."

"I see."

"I intend to hold his cavalry in reserve. Depending on how things are going, they may need to shore up different areas at different times, and besides," Father Thomas smiled, "I don't believe in showing all my cards at once."

"You think there will be a fight, then?" Mathew asked.

"I would say there's very little question on that point. I'm going to assign you to the cavalry. You're a strong rider and that's where you'll be the most help. Is that clear?"

"Yes."

Mathew was about to suggest that the regiment might be a better place for him, because he was only an indifferent rider at best, at least in his judgment, however, there was something in Father Thomas's tone that stopped him. Before his eyes the priest had begun to slip back into a role he had played years before. Mathew had always known about Siward Thomas's military background. But what he hadn't known until quite recently was that the tall, soft-spoken man standing next to him had been a general in the Elgarian army.

Bits and pieces of information about Father Thomas's background had drifted to him during the past year, not only from Gawl and Teanna d'Elso but from others as well. He had discussed it with Collin and Lara on several occasions, but out of respect for the priest's privacy none of them ever raised the subject to him. Father Thomas's life was his own. When Mathew learned, quite by accident, that his friend was considered to have one of the most brilliant military minds in Elgaria, he decided there was very little that could surprise him after that. The man had more sides than he could count. The strategy he employed in defeating the Orlocks at Tremont was nothing short of genius. Mathew knew that now. Given the forces arrayed against them, a niggling voice in the back of his mind told him they were going to need every bit of the priest's experience just to survive.

The trip to Fanshaw Castle was troubling to Mathew for several reasons. Even with a heavy wool shirt and his winter cloak, he was numb from the cold in a matter of minutes. Winter was definitely not his favorite time of year. Considering the haste with which they departed and the urgency of their situation, he was confused by Father Thomas's decision not to push everyone harder than he was doing. Certainly the conditions were hard, but he was positive they could make better speed. And from the looks on Colonel Haynes's and Major Wright's faces, he was positive they were thinking the same thing.

Twice during the trip a rider came galloping up from

the rear of the column and spoke briefly with Father Thomas. The priest nodded, said a few words to Gawl, and sent the man back down the line. If the king was aware of the strange tactic being employed, he gave no indication of it.

After an hour of trudging through mud and slush, they broke clear of the surrounding forest and found themselves atop a bowl-shaped rise. Ahead of them the road separated. One part angled sharply across a barren plain, and the other continued westward into the mountains. Nearby a small stream splashed noisily over the rocks and descended into a valley. In the distance against a gray horizon, Fanshaw Castle finally came into sight. Father Thomas called a halt and prudently sent three riders ahead as advance scouts to check that it was clear. It was the first thing he had done that made sense to Mathew, considering the pursuit that was surely following them.

Mathew twisted one way in his saddle then the other, stretching his back muscles. The treeless plain gave the impression that someone had taken a giant scythe to the land. It was as dreary and bleak as the leaden sky above. Mathew squinted against the light and shaded his eyes, trying to follow the progress of the scouts. Once or twice, he fancied he could see them climbing up the hill toward the castle, that stood silently waiting for them.

Gawl told him that it was once the ancestral home of a man named Gibon Fanshaw, the last Earl of Meriweather Province. Never married, Gibon had been killed in battle during the second Orlock war, nearly a hundred and thirty years earlier. He died leaving no heirs, and the castle eventually fell into ruin.

Several minutes passed, yet Father Thomas gave no signal for the column to proceed, which struck Mathew as not only odd but downright foolish. Instead of following the scouts as he thought the priest would, he told everyone to dismount, rest, and water their horses.

A half hour passed and still they waited.

Mathew leaned against a tree and waited with the rest of them. The temperature had finally stabilized, and though it was bitterly cold, he was thankful the conditions weren't getting any worse. Mathew cupped both hands to his mouth and blew some warm air into them. He looked out over the plain again. Distances had always been easy for him and he guessed the castle was about ten miles from their present position. He performed some rapid calculations in his head and estimated that it would be at least another twenty minutes before the scouts returned.

At least we'll be able to get out of this wind and build a fire, he thought.

When Father Thomas finally gave the signal for everyone to remount, Mathew was more than ready. Gawl and the priest resumed their same positions at the head of the column with Colonel Haynes close behind them. Regardless of his other duties, the staunch colonel had insisted on remaining near the king, whose safety he was sworn to protect. Though Mathew admired the man's loyalty, he'd seen Gawl in battle before and decided the enemy would probably need the protection more than his friend.

As they started down the slope toward the plain, his first meeting with Gawl d'Atherny came back to him. The recollection caused him to smile. He imagined his reaction at coming face-to-face with a seven-foot-tall giant was probably about the same as everyone else's—shock. Whatever else could be said of him, Gawl had proven a good friend, and he was also a good king. It was clear from the first time they spoke, that Gawl loved his people and wanted the best for them. The political games that were being played out made Mathew sick. The sad thing, he thought, was that greed and money were at the bottom of it, not love of country.

Mathew rode in silence, alone with his thoughts. He mulled over several scenarios regarding his future, but they vanished as quickly as they came, replaced by feelings of loss over his ring. Whatever else he tried turning his concentration to, it all came back to the same thing.

I've got to find a way to get it back.

Emptiness began to flood in on him anew, and he tried, with little success, to force it away. The ring was a part of him and that part had been torn away.

Rather my left arm, he thought. *Rather my left arm . . .*

Mathew would have gone on thinking like that until they reached the castle, but a sudden blaring of trumpets pulled him back to the present. He turned in his saddle in time to see the green cloaks of Lord Guy's men emerging from the woods behind them. His heart sank even further when he saw there were soldiers from Alor Satar with them.

The moment Father Thomas heard the trumpets he pulled up sharply on the reins of his horse and began giving orders.

"Haynes . . . send a man down the line and tell Melinda to spread her people out ten rows deep in a semi-circle as we discussed. They will be the first to meet the attack. Quinn and his regiment are to report to me immediately. Major Wright and his troops will take up position behind Melinda Cheatham. They are to arrange themselves in exactly the same manner as she does. Do you understand me?"

"I do, but—"

"Under no circumstances is Wright to attack. Do I make myself clear?"

"But, sir, I don't—"

Father Thomas went on, cutting the colonel's protest off.

"You and your battalion will take up the last position. What we are seeing is their advance guard. The rest will be here in less than a half hour, so you had better move. That is all."

But Colonel Haynes did not move. Instead he sat there for a moment and appeared to be searching for his words.

"Father, I'm aware that you were once in the military. I

mean no insult, but Melinda Cheatham and her people are our weakest line of defense. They are not even professional soldiers. Wright's battalion is stronger than hers, but not as capable as my own. May I suggest that we reverse the order and—"

"Thank you, colonel, you have your orders," replied Father Thomas.

Haynes opened his mouth to argue further, but closed it again when Gawl shook his head slightly. It was clear the king was going to support whatever Father Thomas had in mind. Disbelief and shock were written on Haynes's face, but it was only a second before the soldier in him took over. He snapped a salute, wheeled his horse around, and galloped down the line to relay Father Thomas's orders.

"He's not happy, Siward," said Gawl.

"I'm not trying to win his approval. I'm trying to win this battle *and* keep your kingdom in one piece at the same time."

Both men looked at each other for a few seconds before Gawl said, "Explain."

"It takes considerable effort to ride as hard as they have, and more effort still to engage in a fight. My guess is that they haven't stopped to rest, nor have they taken any food or drink. They simply came charging after us the moment they learned where we were. We will not hold that castle against a full-scale assault unless we even the odds."

Mathew listened carefully to Father Thomas's words, his own mind working rapidly to understand what the priest had in mind. When it came to him he blinked in surprise. Father Thomas intended to draw the enemy into an attack. At first they would meet with only weak opposition; however, instead of the path becoming easier, it would grow progressively harder the deeper they pushed. The semicircle formation could mean only one thing— Father Thomas intended to collapse the flanks inward as the center gave way. The concept was brilliant, provided it worked. They were terribly outnumbered and the Alor Satar soldiers, who comprised the bulk of Lord Guy's forces, were seasoned veterans.

"And you think it's wise to make our stand here?" Gawl asked.

"I do," Father Thomas replied. "I would sooner not have to make a stand at all, but under the circumstances I would prefer to choose where and when we fight. Once inside the castle, food and water, or the lack of them, will become a problem."

Gawl reached forward, patted his horse on the neck and took a deep breath. When he looked up the familiar feral smile was back.

"All right, Siward, let's see if you have another miracle left in you."

There was suddenly movement from the very end of the line as Melinda Cheatham's troops spread out and took up their positions. A moment later, Mathew saw two flatbed wagons coming toward them; Lara was driving one with Collin seated next to her. The other was driven by a man dressed in a black coat and breeches, one of the doctors he assumed. It was carrying several passengers who were seated on a stack of tree trunks that Melinda had planned to use as barricades if the need arose. Collin's voice carried to him as the wagon drew near.

"Lara, I'm telling you stop the goddamn wagon. I can see good enough to fight."

She and Mathew saw each other at the same time, but she just shook her head as they drove by.

Typical, he thought.

The middle of the column was commanded by Major Wright. As ordered, his troops had taken up their positions behind Melinda Cheatham, arraying themselves in the same semicircle pattern she had used. Mathew watched it happening with a kind of morbid fascination. Moments later Colonel Haynes and his troops followed suit. From someplace near the center of the formation, approximately two hundred soldiers on horseback, led by Jeram Quinn, broke away from the main group and headed for what was now the rear of the line. When they got there, Father Thomas gave his last-second instructions, then he and Gawl rode off toward Melinda's people. Mathew could see them moving up and down the ranks, speaking words of encouragement to the troops. Several times he saw the priest point back at him. Whenever he did, a small cheer went up from the men and a number of heads turned in his direction. He responded by raising his arm in acknowledgment, which only brought more cheers.

It's all for show, Mathew thought. *They don't know the ring is gone.*

"We'll need to move to the edge of that rise on the right," Quinn told him. "Siward Thomas wants us to hold back until the signal is given. Do you understand?"

"Yes," Mathew replied.

He had just been thinking about what would happen if Teanna d'Elso decided to show up. There was still enough of the echo left from his ring to tell him that she wasn't dead—and if her ring functioned the way his did, her wounds would heal rapidly, and she'd be back on her feet in no time.

The cavalry unit quickly moved into position. After a few minutes observing him, Mathew concluded that Jeram Quinn was a very competent officer indeed. The quiet-spoken constable from Anderon, who had followed him across an ocean and two countries, issued his orders to the men in a clear, confident manner, and without any hesitation in his voice.

"Gentlemen, I'm honored to serve with you today. As a detachment of the Sennian Second Cavalry you comprise some of the finest soldiers in the world. Today, we fight not only to preserve a country . . . your country, from a vile usurper, we fight to preserve our very existence. Edward Guy seeks to overthrow the king and install himself as regent once more. He has sold the people of Sennia to the killers of Alor Satar, the same murderers who invaded Elgaria. The men who killed hundreds of women and children without a second thought.

"I say this to you . . . there is no room in this country for such as they," Quinn said, allowing his voice to rise. "There is no room in the civilized world for killers of children.

"The crimes I speak of may have taken place in Tyraine, but it was a blow aimed at the very foundations of what we believe. It was a blow to freedom. Many of you lost friends and family at Ardon Field. I tell you their sacrifice must not be in vain.

"Remember the children. Remember who you are and whose land this is. When the signal is given, we ride for Gawl d'Atherny and Sennia. Are you with me?"

Almost as one, the soldiers shouted, *"Yes!"*

"Are you with me?" Quinn roared again, raising his sword in the air.

"Yes!" two hundred voices shouted back in unison, Mathew's as loud as any of them.

He felt carried away by the emotion of the moment; blood rushed in his ears and his face was red despite the cold.

"We will divide into two groups," announced Quinn. "The first will proceed along this ridge and strike Guy's flank. If I should fall, Captain Charles will take my place. The second unit will wait in reserve to support us, or hit where it may be necessary. That group will be under the command of Lieutenant Walters."

Lieutenant Walters was a man Mathew had met several times during his stay at Tenley Palace, a rotund, indecisive fellow who looked incredibly uncomfortable on a horse. How he had gotten into the cavalry was a complete mystery. In fact, when he thought about it, he was astonished anyone of Walters's limited intellect could have risen to the rank of an officer. One glance at the miserable expression on the lieutenant's face only increased his concerns.

"Our signal to attack will be a green fire arrow, so keep your eyes sharp," Quinn told the men. "The second unit will watch and wait until the time is right for them to move. God be with all of you."

At the far end of the field the trumpets blared again as more soldiers in green cloaks poured out of the woods. They were clearly massing for an attack. On the plain, almost two thousand men and women waited to meet them.

Mathew studied the details of their position and the surrounding landscape. The ridge they were on ran almost completely around three sides of the plain, forming a U-shape. The result of it was that Lord Guy's soldiers would have to ride up an incline if they wanted to reach them.

Mathew turned in his saddle and looked over his shoulder at the wagon carrying the logs. Each was the length of a small tree and all had been coated black with pitch to prevent moisture from getting in and swelling the wood. *Pitch,* he repeated to himself . . . *pitch.*

He pulled his horse around and nudged it forward next to Jeram Quinn's.

"Jeram, I have an idea. Do you see that opening there?" he asked, pointing. "If we can get the wagon and those logs into position quickly enough, we can set fire to them and send them down the hill into Guy's men when they charge. There's enough tree cover so that they won't see us until the last moment."

Quinn stared at him for a second, then turned to look at the wagon. Mathew could almost hear him thinking.

"How much time will you need?" he asked.

"Maybe five minutes, but I'll need someone with me."

"You," Quinn said, pointing at one of the soldiers nearest to them. "Go with Master Lewin and lend whatever help he requires."

Mathew and the soldier introduced themselves as they rode. His name was James Fletcher, a corporal, who had been assigned to the palace cavalry earlier that week. Two minutes later they were threading their way through the trees on a wagon loaded with six twenty-foot-long logs. By the time they reached the clearing, the sounds drifting up from below told them the battle was joined. Mathew pulled up on the reins and jumped to the ground. Cautiously he made his way to the edge and peered over it. Seeing farmers and townspeople facing them with only pitchforks, pikes, and axes, Lord Guy's men and the soldiers from Alor Satar, began driving straight for the center of the line exactly as Father Thomas predicted they would. Melinda's archers, positioned at either end of the semicircle, released flight after flight of arrows at the enemy. For the moment their formation seemed to be holding.

"We'll need another fifty feet," Mathew said to James. "Let's bring the wagon up."

"Right. I'll get it."

Despite his pale face, the soldier managed a tight grin and dashed back and tethered their horses to a small tree. He climbed into the wagon seat and flicked the reins twice. Mathew took a roll of bandages he had brought out of the pocket of his cloak and wadded up three different handfuls. As soon as James was in position, he climbed into the back of the wagon and stuffed the cloth between the logs. He had barely finished getting the last piece into place when the wagon suddenly lurched and one of the wheels dipped over the crest of the ridge. He steadied himself and looked down the hill at the battle. A few faces looked up at him, but no one in the enemy camp was reacting to their appearance yet.

"A little farther," Mathew said.

James nodded and flicked the reins again, nudging the horse forward.

"That's it," Mathew said.

James jumped off, ran around to the opposite side of the wagon, and reached under the harness to release the horse.

While he was doing that Mathew fished around in the pocket of his breeches and found his tin of matches.

"Ready?"

"Better hurry, Mat, they know we're here," James called up.

Mathew looked over the logs. Several Alor Satar soldiers were pointing at them and yelling to their companions. With his mouth as dry as dust, he dropped to one knee and struck the match. It flared immediately. He lit the first cloth, then the second, and finally the third. As soon as they caught, he scrambled over the top of the wagon to where James was waiting and put his shoulder to the side and said, "Now!"

They threw their weight against the wagon and began to push. Twice Mathew nearly lost his footing on the frozen ground. Directly above their heads flames leapt up and quickly spread to the pitch-coated logs. In moments the wagon was ablaze, but try as they might, they were unable to lift the wheels off the ground.

"Once more," Mathew gasped, turning his face away from the heat.

"I don't think we can do it. It's too heavy."

"We have to. Let's try again. On my count . . . one . . . two—"

"If you'll excuse me," a deep voice said.

"Gawl!" Mathew exclaimed, spinning around.

"Your majesty," James sputtered.

"Both right," said Gawl. He stepped past them and put his hands on the underside of the wagon bed. "Siward thought you might need a little help."

Mathew opened his mouth to reply, but the words died in his throat as the massive muscles in Gawl's shoulder and back knotted. He saw the king's legs flex, and with one mighty heave, the entire wagon lifted off the ground.

Gawl lifted again, pushing the wagon higher and higher, driving with his legs. Ever so slowly the wagon began to topple over, spilling the burning logs out. They careened down the hill leaving a trail of smoke and sparks in the air. The Alor Satar soldiers who were making their way up saw it happen; and scattered. Most of them managed to get out of the way except for two men who were slower to react than their fellows. The flaming logs rolled over them. Gathering momentum with every second, they smashed into their companions at the bottom of the hill.

Pandemonium broke out. Other Alor Satar soldiers who weren't crushed to death made it to the top of the ridge only to be cut nearly in two by Gawl's broadsword. Mathew landed a kick to another man's jaw, snapping his head backward, and sending him down the hill in an unconscious heap. On his left, James parried a pike leveled at his chest and countered catching the man across the neck with the edge of his sword. For one horrible moment the soldier stood there swaying, his head partially severed from his body, before he crumpled to the ground. Buzzing sounds started filling the air as Lord Guy's archers fixed on their position.

"Back to the horses," yelled Gawl, ducking as an arrow missed his head by inches.

All of them started running and reached the safety of the trees in a matter of seconds. When they were mounted, Gawl raised a hand to his face and lightly felt his forehead.

"I believe that fire singed my eyebrows," he said.

"It's an improvement," Mathew replied, pulling up on the reins of his horse.

Gawl scowled at him and looked at James Fletcher, who returned a weak smile to the king.

From his vantage point on the ridge, Jeram Quinn, constable of Anderon for the last fifteen years, watched the battle unfold below him. When Siward Thomas had

asked for his help, his first inclination was to decline. The
internal affairs of Sennia, however unfortunate, were
none of his concern. He had come to Barcora to arrest
Mathew Lewin for the murder of Berke Ramsey. It was
true Ramsey probably deserved his fate, but no man was
above the law, and no one had the right to take it into their
own hands. From all appearances, young Lewin's crime
was understandable. Ramsey had murdered Bran Lewin
and the son took revenge; a crime of passion, surely. But
what if a jury concluded Ramsey's act was the result of
negligence—an accident? Quinn had wrestled with that
question many times over the last months. He liked
Mathew Lewin, genuinely so. He was a good lad with a
kind heart, and there was little doubt he had saved Elgaria
from destruction. But to look the other way would have
placed him on the same level as the person he had come
to arrest. *No,* Quinn thought, *the law is the law. Bend it
once, or look the other way, and we head down the road
to anarchy from which there is no return.* It was not a task
he relished, but he had sworn an oath, and his duty came
first.

When Mathew returned their eyes met briefly and an
unspoken communication passed between them. *He un-
derstands,* thought Quinn. *If we survive this battle, I'll
keep my word and we'll go back together.*

"The signal," someone called out.

Quinn jerked his thoughts to the present and looked up
in time to see a green fire arrow flash across the sky. A
quick glance at the battlefield told him all he needed to
know. As Siward Thomas had guessed, the center of the
Sennian line was collapsing, giving way to the more experienced soldiers of Lord Guy and Alor Satar. The
crossfire of the archers on the flanks was also doing its
job. The field was littered with green cloaks and a great
deal of black and silver ones too. Melinda Cheatham's
people were falling back. Instead of finding their path
easier, the enemy was gradually meeting tougher opposi-

tion from Major Wright's troops, who were not giving ground quite so readily. Whoever was in command of the first wave on the enemy side must have perceived the stratagem, because a large contingent of soldiers was now advancing on the nearest archery flank. That was what he had to stop.

Without hesitation, Quinn turned in his saddle and shouted, "The Sennian Second Cavalry will advance. We will proceed along the ridge and begin our charge at one hundred yards—triple column formation. Listen for the trumpeter's signal. After we have turned the enemy's flank we will proceed across the field to the opposite side and circle around back here—*Forward!*"

Mathew watched the first unit move out, splitting itself into three separate columns. He closed his eyes for a moment and said a silent prayer to deliver them intact. When the trumpeter finally blew the signal for the charge, he found that he was holding his breath and squeezing the reins so tightly his hands hurt. With an effort, he forced himself to relax and put on what he hoped was a calm expression. A glance to his left told him that Gawl had now rejoined Father Thomas, the huge form of the king obvious even across a battlefield. A steady stream of soldiers on horseback came and went from their position, relaying the priest's orders to the troops below.

Trumpets blared, and down the side of the hill the three columns of Sennian cavalry streamed directly at the enemy. Mathew tore his eyes away from the sight only for a second to look at Father Thomas. The priest was standing up in his saddle, watching the progress.

On the opposite side of the field, Edward Guy and Eric Duren, dressed in his usual green and black silks, finally left the shelter of the woods, surrounded by their officers. Duren blinked in surprise as he surveyed the scene. The field was littered with his soldiers.

"Their commander is a sorcerer," he said. "He arranges his troops inviting us to attack, yet he does not respond.

The farther we penetrate, the worse the fighting gets. We have more dead at seventy yards than at thirty."

"The man's name is Siward Thomas," Lord Guy told him.

Eric Duren's brows came together. "Thomas? I know that name, but I cannot think from where."

"He was a general during the Sibuyan war before he decided to become a priest."

"A priest? Well, judging from the tactics he's employing, it appears that he has an excellent memory. Priests in my country don't have nearly such colorful backgrounds."

"Their cavalry is charging," Lord Guy said, pointing.

"As expected," Duren responded. "We'll wait a few seconds before we order the counter charge. Either way it won't affect the outcome."

"It would have been a big help if the princess were here. A lot of my men are expecting Lewin to suddenly appear and blow them out of existence."

"That would be exceedingly difficult without his ring, my lord," Eric Duren remarked over his shoulder. Without turning around he made eye contact with an officer who was waiting nearby and nodded his head. The man saluted, spun his horse around, and dashed off to where the Alor Satar cavalry was waiting in the trees.

"Unfortunately, my cousin was injured in the cavern as I told you. I suppose we'll just have to do things the old-fashioned way."

"I suppose," Lord Guy said.

When the riders burst out of the trees, a smile slowly spread across Edward Guy's face.

"I suppose," he repeated to himself.

Mathew saw the Alor Satar cavalry suddenly appear and immediately knew something was wrong. Quinn's plan was to stall the momentum of the enemy's attack on the Sennian right flank, but the opposing cavalry was going to get to the middle first, and cut them off. A great roar went up from Lord Guy's forces as more and more men poured out of the forest and into the plain. Quinn and his men were doomed.

Mathew looked to Lieutenant Walters seated next to him. His face was bathed in sweat despite the cold.

"We have to counterattack," he snapped.

"What? Oh . . . uh . . . there's been no signal yet. We really should wait for the signal, you know."

"There's no time, man. Don't you see what's happening? Order the countercharge."

"Well, I don't know as that's the right thing to—"

"You," Mathew said to the trumpeter, "blow the signal and prepare for a charge."

The soldier visibly flinched when he addressed him, but he made no move to comply. Instead, he looked at his lieutenant for confirmation. Jack Walters was wringing his hands and watching the carnage going on down in the field. Out of the corner of his vision, Mathew saw a lone rider break away from the command post and begin heading in their direction at a full gallop.

Without hesitation he rose up in his stirrups and put what he thought was the wildest, most insane expression possible on his face, and pointed at the trumpeter. "If you don't blow the charge this second," he snarled, "I'll turn you into a snake."

The man's eyes went wide and a second later he put the trumpet to his lips and started to blow.

Mathew desperately searched his mind. Except for Quinn's attack a few moments earlier, he had only seen one other cavalry charge in his life and that was at Ardon Field.

If it worked then, it should work now, he thought.

"Lances at the ready," he bellowed. "Form the wedge."

He wasn't sure what would happen when he said it, but another set of notes issued forth from the trumpeter. Being tone-deaf, all Mathew could tell was that they were different, and it came as something of a surprise when the remaining hundred soldiers actually closed their ranks into an attack wedge formation, which left him at its very point.

Damn, he thought. *Now what?*

The only thing that occurred to him was to repeat Jeram Quinn's words.

"The second cavalry will advance. We will begin the charge at the bottom of the hill on my command—*Forward!*"

When Father Thomas saw the Alor Satar counterattack begin, he knew Jeram Quinn would be trapped and cut to ribbons in a matter of minutes. He immediately looked to the near ridge where the remainder of the cavalry was being held in reserve. Incredibly, whoever was in charge was hesitating. Impelled by the urgency of the moment, he tugged sharply on his reins and began riding toward them, leaving Gawl in mid-sentence. The king was asking if he thought his eyebrows had been singed.

Those men must move now or the battle is lost, Thomas's brain screamed.

Still more than two hundred yards away, he could barely believe his eyes when the remainder of the regiment abruptly formed into an attack wedge with what looked like . . . *Mathew at its head.*

The priest spat out a curse and whipped the horse's flanks, bending low over its neck, urging every ounce of speed out of the animal that he could.

Dear God, they're going to charge straight in.

Somewhere behind Father Thomas the trumpets blared. Miraculously, the troops on the plain heard the signal and obediently split to either side of the field, leaving Mathew a clear path to the enemy.

Thank you Gawl, Father Thomas whispered. His horse plunged down the incline in pursuit of the charging regiment.

A similar thought had occurred to Mathew only seconds before as his horse reached the bottom of the hill with a hundred lancers behind him. The end of the Sennian line was fifty yards away and he'd forgotten to tell the trumpeter to signal them. Worse, he didn't even know the right terminology that would get them to move.

Uh ... would you excuse me please? didn't sound right. *Fool!*

When the trumpets rang out from atop the hill and the ranks began to open, his heart started beating again. Apparently someone realized what was happening and had given the order.

Whoever it was, I'll thank them later.

Mathew dug his heels into his horse's side and accelerated to a canter.

I just hope the rest of them are following, he muttered to himself. A backward glance assured that they were.

Confused by the sudden change in tactics, the bulk of enemy forces were still arrayed in the middle of the field, in front of the charging regiment. Mathew could see Jeram Quinn and his men fighting desperately with the Alor Satar cavalry as Lord Guy's forces closed around them. Mathew drew his sword, looked over his shoulder at the trumpeter and bellowed, *"Charge!"*

A hundred lances came down in unison and the second unit of the Sennian cavalry thundered forward.

"Onward, men," Mathew yelled, pointing the way with his sword.

They hit the enemy dead on, splitting them in both directions. People were dying everywhere. To his left, James Fletcher lowered the point of his lance and drove it into the chest of a soldier who stood there transfixed, seemingly frozen in place. A second later James was pulled from his horse and stabbed to death. In the back of his mind, Mathew was aware the trumpets were blowing again. He had no idea what that signal meant, nor did he see the ranks of his own troops closing behind him once his cavalry had passed. Thirty yards ahead, Jeram Quinn and a small group were fighting with sabers from horseback, struggling to hold off a squad of green cloaks surrounding them.

The impetus of his charge carried Mathew and his troops forward. From his side vision he saw an Alor Satar soldier draw his bow, then felt a distinct thwack when an arrow imbedded in the saddle near his right leg. A second later the man was dead, beheaded by a soldier insane with the heat of battle, who galloped past Mathew wielding his sword like a scythe. The body of the headless soldier swayed for a second then fell back like a toppled tree. It was a gruesome sight that nearly caused Mathew's stomach to revolt, but he had scant time to think about it. Right in front of him an enemy soldier picked up a lance from one of his fallen comrades and thrust it at his chest.

Mathew swung his sword around, parrying the point over his shoulder, then dug his heels into the horse's flank and rode the man down. Blood was everywhere, soaking the earth. He had never seen so much blood. Men were screaming and dying. He never knew how the second cavalry unit succeeded in reaching Jeram Quinn, but they did. Mathew's charge had managed to throw the enemy into confusion and they were falling back. Out of nowhere Father Thomas appeared, staying the blow of a soldier running toward him with an axe by launching his own sword through the air and catching the man in the chest with it. The man's eyes widened in shock and he fell forward clutching the sword as he died. A Sennian soldier reached down and grabbed a sword from one of his dead companions, tossed it to the priest.

A cheer went up from the men and in seconds, it was taken up by the rest of Gawl's troops. The enemy was running. Father Thomas stared at their retreating backs for a moment, then slowly looked up at the hill where Lord Guy and Eric Duren sat on horseback surveying the scene.

"Blow the retreat," he said to the trumpeter. "We fall back to the castle."

40

Fanshaw Castle

MATHEW LOOKED AT THE COAT OF ARMS OVER THE ENtrance to Fanshaw Castle, a fierce-looking stone eagle, its wings spread wide and beak open in a scream. One claw held a spear; the other was holding four arrows. At some point in the past one of the eagle's wings had broken off, giving it an odd, unbalanced appearance. Like everything else there it was badly weathered. The only positive thing Mathew could see about the place was it was set high atop a hill and afforded an excellent view of the surrounding countryside. The walls were easily four feet thick and looked strong enough to stand up to anything. On the inside of the castle was a wide cobblestone courtyard surrounded by stables and the main house. Two circular watchtowers at either end of the complex were connected by battlements that ran atop the walls.

Mathew walked into the house, looked around, and found that Father Thomas, Gawl, Colonel Haynes, and Jeram Quinn were there already. Whatever furniture it once held had been removed many years before, leaving it barren and empty. It was a drafty, dark place, that gave no clue about the people who once lived there.

Melinda Cheatham and two of the physicians had set up a hospital in the stables for the wounded, of which there were many. Though Father Thomas's strategy worked incredibly well, there were still many casualties. Major Wright was among the dead, as was Jack Walters, the lieutenant Mathew had wrested command from. Despite the fact that Wright had fallen, his men held together and did their job admirably. The result was that more than a third of the enemy had been slain. The Sennians' odds were improving.

Before they went in Father Thomas watched Mathew giving orders to his troops who were obeying them without question. If they were aware he had not yet reached his twentieth birthday, no one said so. The priest had seen men come of age before and it always moved him. He had seen it during the war. The change was a fundamental one, as opposed to a loss of virginity, and so it was now with Mathew. Siward Thomas watched him interact with men twice his age, many of them hardened veterans, and listened to the tone of voice Mathew was using. The rose-gold ring might be gone, but it didn't matter. This was magic of another kind.

Across the courtyard, Lara was helping Melinda Cheatham get the wounded into the stables. She looked up, saw Mathew and waved, but he didn't wave back. Lara stared at him for a moment before going inside.

Strange, thought Father Thomas.

When their cavalry charge had failed and his men began to run, Edward Guy turned to Eric Duren. He expected the prince to be watching the battle and was surprised to find that he wasn't. Instead, the younger Duren's gaze seemed unfocused and he was staring off toward the horizon, and nodding his head as though he were having a conversation with someone.

"We need to counterattack before they reach Fanshaw Castle," Lord Guy said. "If they succeed in getting in there we'll—"

Duren held up a hand, cutting him short; he continued staring for a few more seconds. Then he turned back to Guy and said, "I'm sorry, what were you saying?"

"I *said* we need to attack immediately. If they reach the castle, it will be days before we can get them out."

"Days? Oh, I don't think it will be that long," Eric Duren replied. "Let's have the men make camp and rest for a bit. I don't know about you, but I could do with a good fire and something to eat. Your weather here is absolutely abominable."

Lord Guy stared at him as if he had just lost his mind. "Don't you see what's happening?" he said pointing. "They're getting away."

"Not really," Duren responded

In the main hall Mathew was gratified to see that someone had the good sense to light a fire. He walked over to the fireplace and stood there letting the warmth roll up his back. Now that the excitement had subsided, he felt very tired. He closed his eyes and stood there listening, and not listening, to the conversations around him until they blended together into a din.

"That was a brave thing you did earlier," a voice by his shoulder said.

Mathew didn't turn around.

"Thank you," he replied, still facing the flames.

"The next time you decide to lead a cavalry charge, it might be a good idea to let the troops in front of you know what you're doing," Father Thomas said, putting his hands on Mathew's shoulders. "I'm proud of you, Mat . . . very proud. Your father would have been proud as well. That was no easy thing you did today."

Mathew looked back at the priest and smiled, then turned back to the fire again.

"Good advice," he said quietly.

Unlike his companions he gave himself no credit for leading the remarkable charge. In truth, he didn't know what had impelled him to act. Had he delayed, even for another minute, Jeram Quinn might well have been killed and the problem of his going back to stand trial resolved.

Whether it was contempt for his own cowardice at having had such a thought, or fear of what people would say about him if he had actually done so, he didn't know. Perhaps a little of both, he concluded. The priest's words however did little to comfort him, they only made him feel like a hypocrite for accepting the praise. Such was the way he viewed himself.

On the way to the castle, Jeram Quinn had pulled his horse alongside Mathew as they rode. Neither of them spoke for a time. Eventually the constable held out his hand and said, "I'd like to thank you for what you did back there, Mathew."

Both of them shook hands. Quinn gave him a curt nod, pulled up on the reins of his horse, and dropped back to be with his men. Those were the only words they had spoken.

A general celebration was going on in the courtyard and the mood throughout the castle was buoyant. But for the past hour a cold fear had been growing in the pit of Mathew's stomach. Gawl's kingdom stood on the edge of a knife. Even with their improbable victory, the losses they sustained were heavy, and if the southern army did arrive, it might only be in time to bury them. *I could have prevented this if I hadn't been such a fool,* he thought. He wanted to talk to Father Thomas, but his own reticence wouldn't allow it. Mathew continued to stare into the fire.

Father Thomas glanced over his shoulder at Gawl, who was watching them. The king shook his head and looked away. Earlier, Gawl watched the men congratulate Mathew, pounding him on the back and vigorously shaking his hand. A cheer went up from the assembled troops when Mathew returned, but it did nothing to raise the boy's spirits. Gawl acknowledged it sadly and quickly averted his eyes,

Shortly after Mathew had entered the castle he found Lara. They moved off, away from the others, holding hands as they walked. They talked quietly for a several minutes. Father Thomas saw it from a distance as they strolled farther. He sensed that Mathew would be able to relax. This relieved Father Thomas. But whatever effect Lara's words had had on him, it must have been transitory because when Mathew returned to Father Thomas's side, he had retreated back into his usual reserve. Father Thomas was about to ask him a question when he felt Mathew's shoulders suddenly stiffen and without a word, he turned and walked outside toward the main gate. Both the priest and Gawl exchanged glances; confused by his actions, they followed him. Once he reached the gate, Mathew stood there staring at the distant enemy campfires dotting the hills.

"What is it?" asked Father Thomas, coming up behind him.

Mathew didn't respond.

"Mat?" said Gawl.

After a few seconds Mathew's head dropped and he whispered, "Teanna."

"Teanna?" Gawl said. "Where?"

"Out there," Mathew replied, rubbing his temples.

Gawl and Father Thomas squinted into the darkness for a few moments before they turned back to him.

"Are you certain, my son? I understood she was injured. It doesn't seem likely she could return so soon after the wound Jeram inflicted."

"She's there. The same thing happened to me after I was stabbed in Elberton and again in the pass above Tremont. The rings do it somehow. I don't know why or how, but the body recovers faster when you're wearing them, faster than anyone would believe."

Father Thomas's eyes grew distant as he recalled the ambush that nearly took their lives shortly before they arrived at the town of Tremont many months earlier. By all rights, Mathew should have been dead. The arrow he had taken was just above his heart. He had seen wounds before and that one was bad enough to have killed most men. Yet a day later Mathew was back on his feet and strong enough to fight both Karas Duren and his sister.

"It seems we have a problem, then," the priest said. "But something puzzles me—"

"I know she's there, Father. She's weak . . . definitely weak, but there's no question in my mind it's her."

"Marvelous," said Gawl.

"I was about to ask how you know these things," Father Thomas continued, "since you don't have your ring any longer."

Gawl apparently realized what Father Thomas was saying because he looked sharply at Mathew. As quickly as he could, Mathew told them about the echo. He had no explanation for it like so many other things connected with the ring. He only knew that it was there . . . weaker, but there.

"Can you fight her?" asked Gawl.

Mathew shook his head.

"I see," said the king. "Can you tell if she has your ring with her? Perhaps it might be possible for us to sneak into their camp and—"

"It's not there. It's someplace very far from here . . ." Matthew said. His voice trailed away and he looked toward the eastern horizon and didn't speak again for several seconds. "I knew it was her immediately, and I also know she doesn't have my ring. The feelings are completely different."

"I don't understand any of this," Gawl said, throwing up his hands. "But I'll see those bastards rot in hell before I turn my country over to them, Teanna or no Teanna. The only thing they care about is how much profit they can squeeze out of a barrel of wine."

Gawl continued to rant as Mathew's eyes found Father Thomas's. He was aware the priest had been watching and the two stared at each other without speaking. When Father Thomas finally spoke there was a urgency in his voice.

"Mathew, I want you to listen to me carefully and do not interrupt. What I'm going to say will be difficult, but I want you to follow my instructions exactly. You *must* trust me in this. I don't know how much time we have, but we cannot win this battle. Take what you need and leave immediately; get as far away from this place as possible. You will have to change both your name and your appearance, because half the countryside already knows what you look like. Do whatever is necessary; lie, cheat, steal, kill if you have to, but you must find a way to recover your ring. I cannot tell you what will become of us, but you are our last, best hope. In this you must not fail. We are all doomed if you do."

Gawl turned to look at Father Thomas.

"Siward, if you think I have any intention of giving up without a fight, you can get that notion out of your head right now. You can stay out here and talk till you're blue in the face. I'm going back to get the men ready," announced Gawl.

What happened next occurred so fast Mathew barely had time to react. A sudden roar came out of nowhere, and an orange fireball streaked across the sky, directly over their heads. It struck partway up the castle wall near the entrance, smashing a hole fifteen feet wide. Pieces of stone and earth flew up into the air causing them all to flinch. It was followed by another fireball that hit the opposite side of the gate.

Gawl started walking. Father Thomas hesitated only for a second, then drew his sword. Using the hilt, he clubbed Gawl at the base of his skull with all his might. The king staggered forward. Father Thomas hit him again twice more and caught his friend's body as he fell, gently lowering him to the ground.

He looked up at Mathew and said, "He would have fought until he was dead. They can't execute a king without a trial or the whole country would rise up against them. Edward Guy needs the blessing of the church to make his plan work. At least this way he'll have a chance."

Mathew opened his mouth to speak, but Father Thomas held a hand.

"You have very little time now, Mathew. You must go at once. He's not going to be in a good mood once he wakes."

"Father, I can't," Mathew said. "I've given Jeram Quinn my word."

"Can't what?"

They both turned to see the figure of Jeram Quinn silhouetted against the light of the courtyard. All three of them ducked again as another fireball roared overhead. The top of the watchtower exploded and Mathew could hear people shouting inside the gates.

Father Thomas quickly explained his plan to Quinn, who folded his arms across his chest and listened in silence. When he was finished Quinn puffed out a long breath and raised his eyebrows. He looked from Father Thomas to Mathew and finally to Gawl's prostrate form. Another orange fireball smashed into the trees a hundred yards to their left, sending a plume of sparks into the night. Quinn turned back to the priest.

"On my way out I asked one of the sentries what was happening. He said he thought the king and Mathew had just been killed. A long time ago I took an oath to uphold the law, so I cannot willingly allow a prisoner to escape. Unfortunately, since I don't know if Mathew Lewin is alive or dead, I can only guess as to his fate. Should you see him again, Father, I would appreciate if you would remind him of this. Rumors tend to be notoriously unreliable."

Quinn's eyes passed over Mathew, hesitating on him only for a second before he turned and walked back into the castle.

Father Thomas and Mathew stood there for a moment before the priest grabbed him in a fierce embrace. He put both hands on the side of Mathew's face, and kissed him on the forehead.

"Father, will you—"

"I'll explain to Lara, my son. You must go *now*," he said. *"Run."*

Father Thomas looked at the line of torches that was coming up the hill toward them. He took Mathew by the shoulders and gave him a push.

"If you should see Ceta before I do . . . would you give her a message for me? Tell her I love her and that I'm sorry."

Mathew took one halting step and then another. Without looking back he began to run, never seeing the tears that filled the priest's eyes.

though she appeared to be recovering at a remarkable pace according to her physicians.

On a misty spring morning, a Felizian merchant ship bound for Vargoth lifted its anchor and slowly pulled away from the docks in Barcora letting the wind take her. On the port side of its deck, the captain and his first officer kept a careful watch on the crew, many of whom were recent additions to the ship's complement. At the prow of the ship, keeping a weather eye out for a reef line that ran about three hundred yards off shore, was a tall black-haired man with startling blue eyes who had recently signed on as the ship's navigator. The captain initially thought that he was too young for the job, but he had presented himself with good credentials, having recently served onboard the clipper ship *Wave Dancer* as the assistant navigator. The man's name was Thaddeus Lane.

During the fitting-out process, it became clear to the captain as well as his first officer, the young man had a good way with the men, so all parties were satisfied. He was given the position of navigator and second in command of the ship.

The new officer looked up at the receding cliffs above the city, squinting through the mist. In the distance the gray outline of Tenley Palace was barely visible above the harbor. He stared at it for a several seconds before turning away toward a watery horizon.

SO ENDS THE SECOND BOOK OF THE FIFTH RING

EPILOGUE

IN THE WEEKS THAT PASSED FOLLOWING THE BATTLE AT
Fanshaw Castle rumors abounded about Mathew Lewin.
Some maintained that he had been killed during the at-
tack, and others said that he had run away, afraid to face
Teanna d'Elso.

Gawl d'Atherny, Sennia's first king in three hundred
years, was tried by a court of barons appointed by the
country's new regent, Lord Edward Guy. An ecclesiasti-
cal tribunal headed by Bishop Ferdinand Willis reviewed
the proceedings and gave its blessing. The king was sen-
tenced to twenty-years in prison along with his co-
conspirators, a Colonel Shelby Haynes, and a priest
named Siward Thomas.

Jeram Quinn, who was present in the country at the request of the Elgarian government for the purpose of ex-
traditing Mathew Lewin, was allowed to return home,
along with Lara Palmer and Collin Miller, in the spring,
when the passes cleared. Quinn told the authorities that
he believed Mathew had been killed in the initial attack
on the castle. He also proved instrumental in helping
them identify the badly charred remains of his body.

Eric Duren, who commanded the Alor Satar force was
skeptical, but eventually had no choice other than to accept the explanation before returning home with his ail-
ing cousin, Teanna. The princess, it seemed, had recently
sustained a knife wound and was still extremely weak,

GLOSSARY

d'Atherny, Baegawl Alon	A sculptor by choice. Also known as Gawl, King of Sennia
Alexander	Chief of staff at Tenley Palace
Alor Satar	Duren's country located to the northeast of Elgaria
Argenton	A town to the north of Barcora in Sennia. Home of extensive archeological ruins
Ashots	A religious sect whose priests don't marry. They celebrate the Lord's Day on the seventh day of the week
Barcora	Capital of Sennia and home of the famous religious sanctuary
Bajan	Country to the East of Elgaria
Blake, Rodney	Captain of Barcora's Felcarin team. Soldier attached to Gawl's personal bodyguard
Barton, Robert	Proprietor of the Drunken Duck Inn of Bexley
Batroc	Implement used in Felcarin
Baxter, Bill	Soldier, killed in the ambush at the Argenton ruins
Bexley	A town visited by Mathew, Father Thomas, and Ceta Woodall
Camden Keep	Ancestral home of Lord Edward Guy. Formerly housed Sennia's

administrative offices. Located in Hope Province.

Cheatham, Melinda — Childhood friend of Gawl. Formerly commanded a regiment in the Sibuyan war

Cincar — Country located to the northeast of Elgaria; ally of Karas Duren

Coribar — Large island nation to the south of Elgaria

d'Elso, Marsa Duren — Karas Duren's sister. Queen of Nyngary

Donal, Oliver — Captain of the *Wave Dancer* the ship that transported Mathew.

Drunken Duck — Name of the tavern Mathew, Father Thomas, and Ceta Woodall visit

Duren, Karas — King of Alor Satar. Killed by Mathew Lewin.

Guy, Edward — Former regent of Sennia; father to Rowena and Jared Guy

Guy, Jared — Champion Felcarin player

Guy, Rowena — Gawl's mistress

Elgaria — Mathew's country

Fanshaw Castle — Located in northwest Sennia. Where Father Thomas led Gawl's defenders in the final battle

Farsighter — Name of Daniel's invention

Felcarin — A popular game in Sennia played on a field with two teams consisting of seven players

Fletcher, James — Young soldier who helps Mathew at the battle of Fanshaw Castle

Francis — A soldier with Father Thomas at the Argenton ruins

Gawl — See d'Atherny, Baegawl Alon, above

Gravenhage — A nearby town to Devondale; participated in a fencing meet. A full day's ride away located to the N.W. of Devondale

Haynes, Shelby	Colonel in Gawl's personal bodyguard.
Hudson	Member of the patrol ambushed at the Argenton ruins
Johnson, Sandford	Member of Barcora's Felcarin team. Soldier attached to Gawl's personal bodyguard
Jones	A soldier with Father Thomas at the Argenton ruins
Kellner, Aldrich	A priest in Sennia
Lewin, Bran	Mathew's father
Lewin, Janel	Mathew's mother
Lewin, Mathew	Devondale resident
Layton, Thad	Devondale Farmer whose son was killed. Believed to have been murdered by the Orlocks.
Levad	A religious sect to which Father Thomas belongs. They celebrate the Lord's Day on the Sixth Day of the week; allowed to marry
Lindstrom, Fred	Member of Barcora's Felcarin team
Malach, Delain	King of Elgaria
Mastrich	A town Mathew once visited
Mechlen	A nearby town to Devondale; participated in a fencing meet.
Melfort	A town in Elgaria
Mickens, Sergeant	Member of the patrol ambushed in ruins
Miller, Collin	Devondale resident.
Mirdan	A country to the northeast of Elgaria. Capital is Toland.
Nobody's Inn	Name of the Inn located in Elberton. See also Ceta Woodall.
Nyngary	Country situated east of Elgaria. See also Marsa d'Elso
Orlocks	Records indicate they appeared after the Ancient War. Questionable eating habits.
Quinn, Jeram	Constable from Anderon.

Palmer, Lara	Devondale resident. Also known by alias as Lina Palmeri Batul Asad
Ramsey, Berke	Gravenhage resident. Killed by Mathew Lewin following his murder of Mathew's father
Roeselar	The longest river in Elgaria
Rocoi	Capital of Alor Satar
Rockingham	A town nearby Devondale.
Senecal	Peninsula at southern end of Sennia. Mentioned by Father Thomas on-board the *Wave Dancer*
Sennia	A country to the southwest of Elgaria.
Sibuyan	A people who fought the western nations along with Orlocks in a war twenty years before Mathew's birth.
Sommerlin, Marcus	Historian at the Abbey of Barcora
Stermark	A city in Northern Elgaria, Queen's Province attacked by Duren
Sturga	A large trading town on the Galwin River. Visited by Harol Longworth
Tate, Jack	Member of Barcora's Felcarin team. Soldier attached to Gawl's personal bodyguard
Teller, Paul	Head of the Abbey of Barcora
Thomas, Siward	Devondale resident and priest. Also goes by the names Miles Vernon and Tarif Ja'far Bruhier
Toland	Northernmost city in Elgaria
Tyraine	Port City in Elgaria. Their first stop after Elberton.
Vargoth	Country to the southeast of Elgaria; hires its soldiers out as mercenaries. See also King Seth
Walters, Jack	Lieutenant in Gawl's palace regiment who Mathew wrested command from during battle of Fanshaw Castle

Wave Dancer	Name of the ship Mathew sailed on from Elberton to Tyraine. See also Oliver Donal
White, Daniel	Devondale resident. Mathew's friend. Inventor
Willis, Ferdinand	Bishop of the Sennian Church
Werth Province	The province where Devondale is located.
Woodall, Ceta	Innkeeper of the Nobody's Inn in Elberton.